Judith Rossner

A NOVEL

SUMMIT BOOKS

HIS
LITTLE
WOMEN

New York   London   Toronto   Sydney   Tokyo   Singapore

Summit Books
Simon & Schuster Building
Rockefeller Center
1230 Avenue of the Americas
New York, New York 10020

SUMMIT BOOKS and colophon are trademarks
of Simon & Schuster Inc.

Designed by Elizabeth Woll
Manufactured in the United States of America

10 9 8 7 6 5 4 3 2 1

Library of Congress Cataloging in Publication Data

Rossner, Judith.
   His little women / Judith Rossner.
      p. cm.
   I. Title.
  PS3568.0848H5   1990
  813'.54—dc20   89-26128
                                                     CIP

ISBN 0-671-64858-6

For SBF

"... I know they will remember all I said to them, that they will be loving children to you, will do their duty faithfully, fight their bosom enemies bravely, and conquer themselves so beautifully that when I come back to them I may be fonder and prouder than ever of my little women."

Papa March in a letter home to
Mrs. March and his four daughters
—Louisa May Alcott, *Little Women*

BOOK

I GREW UP in Beverly Hills where beauty was particularly esteemed while its old partner, truth, was held in about the same esteem as anyone's old partner was held. If I set out now to tell the truth about our family and the libel suit that made us famous, it's not because I'm foolish enough to believe the truth will set me free. What I do hope is to find new ground to stand on.

My name is Nell Berman. I am an attorney with a strong interest in libel, dating from the suit brought against my half sister, the novelist Louisa Abrahms, as well as her publisher and the studio that made the film of her book. The court proceedings were so widely detailed and exploited that it seems almost unnecessary to review my family's background or remind people that my father, Sam Pearlstein, was the studio's president when the film rights were bought. On the other hand, the "facts" varied widely with their reporter, and I am better suited than most to the work of sorting out the impossible from the improbable, the reasonable-but-false from the ludicrous-but-true.

The fiction writer always seems to be breaking some contract with reality her friends and relations were sure she'd signed.

This is one of Louisa's clever lines; I find it equally true that the fiction writer is often startled to find people living as though they owned their lives rather than as though they'd been put on this earth to provide her with material.

It is startling to me as I read those words to realize how much hostility toward my half sister they reflect. It was not always thus. Louisa and I didn't even know each other while we were growing up. She was twenty-seven and I was a high-school senior in 1965, when she entered my life. I was intrigued, often captivated, by her endless stories and lively manner. And she was sufficiently interested in being my friend to pretend that her anger at our father did not extend to me.

He had left her and her mother on the East Coast when Louisa was very young. I was not even told of their existence until I was almost fourteen and he was preparing, with that extraordinary unconcern he showed for people from whom he'd disengaged, to do to my mother and me precisely what he had done to them.

His daughters by his third wife were three and six when I met them as well as Louisa, and that was under peculiar circumstances. It is difficult to see how the circumstances might have been other than peculiar.

All over Southern California God made rocky ledges just wide enough to drop a swimming pool into, and I was born, or driven home, to a house with a pool on one of those ledges in the year 1948. My mother was the movie star Violet Vann. Perhaps you know her history. Brought to this country from her native Holland at the age of sixteen and adopted by Abe Starr, the head of Starr-Flexner Studios, and his wife, Sylvia, Violet was supposed to become the new Garbo, and indeed she looked more like Mata Hari, her only starring role, than Garbo ever had. That is to say, Violet's blue-black hair, olive skin and huge, dark eyes gave her a much

12

closer resemblance than Garbo's to the Dutch girl who called herself Mata Hari, and apparently she threw herself into the role.

Or perhaps it would be more accurate to say that she allowed the role to absorb her, for it is difficult to associate a verb as strong as throw with my mother, who was languid to the point of inertia. Never have I known anyone more comfortable with being done to and for without feeling the slightest compulsion to do anything in return. On the other hand, she was harmless. I was raised by maids—housekeepers, as we called them, thus suggesting that some stranger brought in from an agency and paid a salary was capable not only of feeding us and vacuuming the rugs but of holding together our very lives.

Well, perhaps they did just that, for my childhood memories are as much of them as of her. There was Anamae, who picked up a hot skillet full of frying onions without using a pot holder, dropped the skillet on the floor, splattering her legs, arms and even her face with hot fat, and then ran screaming out into the Beverly Hills, never to be heard from again. And there was Blessed Marvelous, who had been brought out from the East Coast by a family who decided upon arrival that life in the Hills required a white European maid. The agency sent Blessed for an interview, and Violet, finding her at the door with a suitcase, asked her to make a tall, cool drink. Blessed lasted, if memory serves me well, for a couple of years. Then there was a girl named Irene who wanted to be an actress. She was more than reasonably competent, but Violet had no tolerance for another pretty face around the house, and Irene was fired before my father returned from his next business trip. There were others who stayed only a little longer.

Finally there was Estella, the stolid Mexican woman who remained with us until my father left, and who taught me as much Spanish before I began high school as I would learn after. As everyone who has followed us through the media knows, Estella was extremely important to Sonny, the older of my father's daughters with his third wife, Lynn Pearlstein.

Neither Estella nor any of the other women who cared for us had much importance in my mind. My father was the sole light of my life. If the world was involved with my mother's looks, with comparing her to Garbo and finding neither wanting, it was my father I found beautiful. What warmth there was in our household radiated from him, and the very space around me felt different when he was away. Cooler. Gray. It was lovely to be taken out for a hamburger and a movie, heaven to accompany him to New York

13

on one of his frequent trips that fit in with a school holiday. (In New York, away from Violet, I was a different person. Prettier, for one thing. It was generally agreed that my cute, freckled face with its frame of reddish blond hair the color of my father's would never compete with Violet's, but in Hollywood this was a sort of death knell, while in New York I was found to be a pleasant and attractive child.)

My sense of the movie business revolved around the financial figures that were my father's perpetual concern. When he and his associates talked about people's abilities and whether they could be trusted, they were walking on turf whose texture I could not gauge. The conversations I enjoyed and sometimes could follow were about money. A moment I relived happily for years occurred at a New York conference during which I'd been permitted to sit next to him at the long table. The financing of a particularly expensive epic was being discussed, and in looking at the sheet of figures in front of my father, I found a serious arithmetic error. When I put a note to this effect in front of him, I was rewarded with a great roar of laughter, a hug and a kiss and the announcement that the new treasurer had found an error in the budget.

Back home, the most fun I had was attending discussions with the man my father called Toot Suiteberg, Vice President of Stuff and Nonsense. Toot was in charge of the physical aspects of production. He arranged for horses and tomahawks for the Westerns; ice for the skating stories; sunshine and lights for park musicals; cars for car chases; lions for safari scenes; pennants and grandstands for football games. I gloried in the lists and calculations that Toot presented to my father; mathematics was a language Violet could not pretend to speak even in front of a camera.

My father was a very large man with curly, reddish blond hair, soft hazel eyes and a manner at once lively and sympathetic. He had been raised by his Lithuanian parents on a poultry-and-egg farm in Vineland, New Jersey, then sent as a teen-ager to live with Brooklyn relatives so he could take advantage of the free university system in New York. He had expected to practice law, but after finishing Brooklyn College he was unable, or so went the legend, to hurdle the barriers to Jews then set up by the law schools. He had a gift for mathematics and quickly became an accountant of such brilliance and ingenuity as to do for many of his accounts in effect what he would have been doing formally as a corporate lawyer. (Shortly after arriving in New York in the sixties, I met

14

someone who had attended Brooklyn College's law school, the existence of which my father had not seen fit to mention, and realized that this aspect of his life, like many others, was somewhat more complex than the tale he'd told me.)

In any event, it was while he was an accountant that my father met and made an impression upon Abe Starr. And it was in his capacity as the (rapidly promoted) chief accountant of Starr-Flexner that he met and fell madly in love with Violet Van Leeuw or, as she had become known during her brief movie career, Violet Vann. Violet was fond of relating the Romance of her Meeting with the Dashing Young Executive. (Being in love, after all, makes for those rare periods when life's intensity meets our childish expectations.) I was never certain how much she knew of what he seems to have considered another life.

He had left Louisa and her mother, Esther, in New York when he entered the Navy after Pearl Harbor, and while he had never returned to them, he hadn't legally abandoned them, either. He'd been mustered out on the West Coast and, after making desultory efforts to convince Esther to move there, found a job in the accounting office of the *Los Angeles Times* and proceeded to lead a bachelor's life in Los Angeles. There is no reason to believe he had been thinking of a wife when my grandfather introduced him to Violet.

I understand how my father once adored Violet, needed to please her, and so on. But my memories of our years together oppose that understanding. What I remember is that when she wasn't on the set, she was ill, or at least supine, and that when he was home, he and I were alone together—talking, playing golf or tennis when the time and the weather were right, chess or checkers, pinochle or poker when it was dark or raining. When he left us, my tennis game went to hell just as surely as though I'd been nothing but his puppet on the court, a frightening happenstance to which I reacted by spending the next decade or so looking for someone else to pull my strings.

It was several years since Violet had made a movie. The style in film stars had changed during the war years, when the women looked as though they could manage perfectly well on their own and just happened to be too adorable not to end up with Cary Grant. Lolling around the house, doing little but asking the maid for drinks and reading confession magazines (she hated movie magazines, which were full of photographs of beautiful women), Violet

15

had gained enough weight to hide her cheekbones and give her the hint of a double chin, neither of which was in her contract with Sam Pearlstein, not to speak of the one with Starr-Flexner.

Aside from the limitations of his marriage, my father was being affected by changes occurring within the studios. This was the period when many stars were ending what they'd come to see as indenture to the studio bosses and striking out on their own. Starr-Flexner, with its cowboys and dumb-blonde bathing beauties, had paid less and exploited more and was among the first to lose its (three) most important stars. In another era the studio might have lofted new ones with relative ease. But there were other things happening that made it difficult to know how to proceed.

For many years, a movie's being shown in a theater had guaranteed it would have paying customers. And virtually all movies were shown because the studios that made them owned the theaters. But in 1952, as automatic attendance was waning because people had grown accustomed to the magic of films, the studios were forced by the Department of Justice to sell off their theaters. During the remainder of the fifties the widespread sale of TV sets had encouraged people to stay home for their moving pictures.

In 1951 my grandfather, having made my father president of Starr-Flexner and given him half of his shares, proceeded to sell his remaining shares to PiCorp, a company with interests ranging from condoms to crude oil. PiCorp was happy with my father until 1957, when he made the mistake that led to the power struggle that eventually cost him his job.

Within Starr-Flexner he had been prime advocate of the notion that TV, with its tiny figures that failed to envelop you and make you believe in them, and with its nearly as important failure to get the housewife and her husband out for the evening, was a passing phase. As a result of this assumption he had made the deadly error of selling off Starr-Flexner's extensive film library for television at a price that seemed increasingly ridiculous as time went on. He not only refused to be defensive or apologetic, he went to war with the new owners. On a Sunday morning in the fall of 1960 they put new locks on his office doors and had someone phone to tell him he was out.

He did not explain to me but packed a suitcase and left for what he said was New York, giving me no hint that it wasn't just another one of his trips. There weren't the usual phone calls nor, when I tried to find him, was he registered at any of the usual hotels. I don't remember when and how I finally allowed myself to understand that he would not be back.

It would be difficult to exaggerate how disastrous the loss of my father was for me. He had been the one person in the house who did not have to rely on others for his very existence, and it often seemed that with his departure I had lost not only my model but my very self. Surely I did not know who that self was, if only because I had not yet become her. A mass of reaction and desire, I knew I was female in relation to him and to those few males of my acquaintance who were old enough to talk about interesting matters, most particularly the business of movies. Girls my age talked about boys and clothes. What it meant to be an older female I could not have fathomed, with Violet and a series of maids as my models.

In addition to maids, stars and starlets had passed through our home. I remember in particular a fifteen-year-old named Kiki Rhodes and her thirty-year-old manager-momma, Dustee, bleached-blond twins who years later would sell their story to *FRemale* magazine, a story of exploitation and abuse at the hands of a series of slave drivers. What I remember best about Kiki and Dustee is the breathtakingly professional way they worked our living room. I don't know how many conversations I heard in which, at the very moment that Kiki the Younger was being pressed by some half-interested assistant director to specify her age, Kiki the Older would drift into the conversation with a resumé or a business card. Until I came to New York I never understood that people occasionally enjoyed themselves at parties. Oh, yes. The other thing I remember about Kiki, the Kikis, is that they blinked if anyone talked about New York as though it were a real place. Born and raised in Hollywood and never having left it or known there was reason to leave, they both thought of Manhattan as a set someone had built for *On the Town*.

Males, even before consideration of their genitalia, were something else. Although few were as smart or as interesting as my father, they mostly did some work that wasn't putting on makeup or shopping for clothes, and they had, therefore, something to talk about. (The male starlets were an exception, of course, but there were fewer of the purely ornamental ones around in those days, and my father limited their participation at his parties to those who were doing work for him at the moment.) My father teased me because at any party he gave I would head for the nearest group of business types and listen attentively to their conversation. Later I questioned him about details he found it astonishing that I should recall. We developed a routine in which he would lead the conversation around to the profits and losses on various movies and then ask me for figures, which I would proceed to reel off as casually as though he'd asked what I'd eaten for breakfast.

In those days I had little doubt that I would grow up to be an accountant. It was clear that one needed something to do with one's time, and even if I had been able to imagine wanting a marriage and children when I was older, nothing I saw around me suggested that either occupied anyone's time but the maid's. Then again, I did not have an interest in them and assumed I never would. Though I liked many of the men who dealt with my father in business, and even an occasional boy from school, while I still had my father it never occurred to me that the others were good for more than casual conversation.

Remarkable. I write that phrase, *while I still had my father*, and tears come to my eyes as though the loss were yesterday's. As though nothing that has happened between then and now matters. As though he hadn't disappeared without reasonable warning and failed to contact me. But even then, as our home was sold, our servants dismissed and our belongings moved to a more modest if still pleasant house on the wrong side of the tracks in Beverly Hills, I was never angry with him.

It was clear to me that aside from Violet's being an unsatisfactory wife, he was terribly upset about the studio. Clearly he hadn't been able to bear to tell me what was happening and didn't want to make promises he wouldn't be able to keep. In my mind we had conversations in which I assured him that I understood why he'd had to do what he had done and told him not to send for me a moment sooner than it was comfortable for him to do so. (Then, and only then, would I need to decide whether Violet could manage without me.)

Actually, Violet was showing signs of managing, if only because she'd found someone new to take care of her. Tony Coletti, our neighbor at our new home on the wrong side of Wilshire, was a handsome, lively landscape gardener whose wife had died, whose children were grown, and who thought, even before he realized Violet had been in a few movies, that she was the loveliest creature he had ever seen. She was still very beautiful by reasonable standards, and she was not yet forty years old. Tony was fifty-six.

His love for Violet was beautiful to see, beginning with the day he introduced himself to us as we stood or, rather, as Violet sat on a kitchen chair and I stood in the middle of our overgrown garden, trying to tell a young Mexican who hadn't been in California for a week and had no English at all which weeds he should pull and which Real Plants he should leave alone.

"No, no," said this nice-looking man with a heavy Italian accent whom we hadn't noticed watching us from the other side of the hedge. That was philoxeria, or some such name. Then he smiled at Violet. He could never look anywhere but at her when she was around, and whenever he looked at her, he smiled. He tipped his straw hat.

"Madame," he said, "Tony Coletti at your service."

And indeed he was, then and forever, or at least until death did them part. First he took care of our garden, then he took care of our house, and then we moved in with him, and he rented out our house to provide an income for us beyond the basics provided in the tough agreement Violet's lawyers (who knew which of my two parents was more likely to employ them in the future) had negotiated, ostensibly on her behalf. Then, just before they were married, he made over the upstairs of his own home to accommodate us.

Everything Tony did for us, he did because he felt like it. Not because it occurred to him that there wasn't a long line of men waiting to give Violet whatever she wanted. While I appreciated him, I did not allow my appreciation to ripen into love. He was this nice man who had taken the responsibility for my mother off my hands. I never ceased to fantasize about the day when I would leave them both because I had received the summons from my father.

The summons did not come. In fact, it sometimes seemed he had disappeared from the face of the earth. In fact, he had arranged to do precisely that as he began a comfortable new life with a different cast of characters while holding on to and expanding the fortune from his old life.

As time wore on I began to live something resembling the life of a normal Beverly Hills teen-ager. The caste system at Beverly Hills High School is perhaps a little more rigid than that of your average suburban high school but there is, after all, something to be said for rigidity, particularly in ladders. Being a beauty was on about the same rung as being a star's or producer's (directors didn't count yet) daughter. Being a producer's divorced daughter could be almost as good if the producer was thought to have maintained a connection to you. This would have been enough to insure that I did not convey the extent of my father's desertion. More important, sharing the reality would have made it much harder to ignore.

In any event, I got good grades, had a few girlfriends and got along well enough with boys to have casual dates. This was the early sixties, when sex outside of the movie world had not yet become so readily available as to lose much of its interest to those poised hesitantly around its various borders. Certain boys made casual-to-earnest attempts to plumb the regions below my shoulders, but I wasn't remotely interested. When I finally lost my virginity, as we used to call it in those days, it was to an employee of my father's named Hugo Bernkastel, a married scriptwriter who had been dealing in the defloration of young girls since long before the time when people were willing to grant that such an activity might be an appropriate subject even for fiction.

I had accompanied my mother to a studio luncheon—one of those ceremonial events to which she was still occasionally invited when there was a need for someone of her description to fill a chair. (She wouldn't do anything alone except shop for clothes. Tony, who was at her service in all other matters, refused to attend studio events, since he didn't enjoy being treated as though he were a piece of baggage she'd dragged along. Further, he'd been heard to say that he worked in the daytime and thought social events should be held at night.)

Anyway, Violet was at one end of the table, and I was at the other, next to a man who was clearly neither a movie actor nor a studio executive. Tall, gangly and awkward in the manner of an adolescent boy, Hugo Bernkastel had small, bright eyes, a florid complexion, a shiny bald head, and a beard in an era when nobody had a beard except Raymond Massey as Abraham Lincoln.

At first he ignored me. There was a starlet seated to his left, and Hugo must have been perennially involved in a quest for someone who looked like Marilyn Monroe and would type his scripts for him. At a point late in the meal, when we'd all had a substantial amount of wine and he'd grown tired of pushing the conversational boulder uphill on his own, Hugo turned to me to explore my probably also-terribly-limited capacity to amuse him.

I asked if it was true that he cheated at cards.

He was surprised. Hurt. Turned on.

"Where on earth did you hear that?"

I'd overheard it said by the man sitting on my right side, but I wasn't about to throw away my advantage by telling him that.

"If it's true," I asked, "what difference does it make?"

"And will you believe me," he asked in his distinctive, soft, nasal, falsely humble manner, "if I tell you it's not true?"

20

"I might believe that *you* believe it," I said, thinking that I sounded rather jaunty, amazed and pleased with my ability to play with him, speculating that it might be the wine, because I certainly wasn't like this with the boys at school. "But that doesn't mean I'll think it's true."

The glaze was gone from his eyes. I had engaged him.

"I'm Hugo Bernkastel," he said.

"Hi." I looked into his small, pained eyes and sensed for the first time that pain had its own attractions. "I'm Nell Pearlstein."

"Pearlstein," he said thoughtfully. "You're not related to my friend Sam, are you?"

"Only by blood," I said, adding, when Hugo seemed disinclined to press me, "He's my father."

"No."

It was a yes. Long before the external stops began to come loose, Hugo had the operational advantage of not possessing internal ones.

"How is Sam doing?"

I said that he was doing just fine. I did not find it necessary to mention that I hadn't seen him in a while.

"And you are here accompanying your mother," Hugo said thoughtfully. "How is Violet? I've not had a chance to speak with her." He glanced down the table to the place where Violet was having a brief conversation with the woman sitting across from her, who happened, as I found out later, to be Hugo's wife. "How old are you, Nellie?" he asked.

"Well," I said, "we're talking statutory rape, but it goes on all the time."

He didn't even crack a smile.

"I have to admit . . ." The voice was even softer, incredibly seductive, and the mysterious process by which he was beginning to look better to me had been activated. ". . . I'm very pleased to have found you. These events are torture except on the rare occasion when one stumbles upon someone who can make conversation. And, of course, when she's a lovely young woman . . ."

It is nearly impossible to describe, or at least to do justice to, the promises Hugo's voice and manner conveyed to my fifteen-year-old ears. *This will go no further than the two of us. . . . Nothing will ever go further than the two of us. . . . I am a rabbit. A soft, white bunny rabbit who won't, who couldn't possibly, hurt you, but can be hurt all too easily himself.*

"How do you know my father?" I asked.

Well, he knew Sam because he'd worked for him on various

21

films. Then, of course, his acquaintance with various studio lawyers had made him prey to many studio issues—such as the one a few years earlier when there had been some question of Violet's needing outside representation in dealing with the studio, no matter whom she was married to, a question the mere posing of which had irritated Sam.

Hugo smiled tentatively, uncertain that I had the irony to appreciate this situation in the light of my father's subsequent abandonment of Violet. I nodded to maintain the sense of communication but I wouldn't smile; my father's dead body was the only one I wasn't ready to climb over with Hugo.

"When did you last see him?" I asked.

It had been at least two or three years ago. Sam and the woman he was living with had been at some dinner Hugo attended in New York. . . .

Of course he'd assumed that I knew where my father was and knew that he was, as always, with a woman. And of course I hadn't. But I concealed my dismay from myself by focusing on Hugo's reference to his own participation in that dinner as though it had been a solo. (Hugo always talked about himself as though he'd been alone and while he did attend functions alone, he often escorted various wives and girlfriends. Actually, Hugo's current wife, a high-ranking studio lawyer, was the reason Hugo had been invited to this particular luncheon, as I learned later from my mother.)

It is important to understand that Hugo did not consider the matter of whether I knew he had a wife or whether the existence of this person should affect his (or my) behavior in any way. The notion that a female of any age might require protection from him (and/or from herself) was foreign to him. Women were the desirable enemy, hated in proportion to his need, which he perceived as being great; great need birthed acceptable acts.

Hugo said he hadn't seen my father as much as he would have liked in recent years. Their schedules didn't seem to coincide. Or maybe (a grave smile) he himself wasn't as sociable as he'd once been.

"You seem pretty sociable," I said, feeling people nearby rise from the table, hoping Hugo would not do the same.

"Oh, I am, I am," he assured me. "But there are . . . I have a rather complicated life." He glanced down the table toward the woman I later learned was Polly Bernkastel. "Aside from having children I spend time with, I'm working on a book. A rather dry treatise, I'm afraid, that wouldn't be of any interest to most people, but it's a project I'm deeply devoted to."

22

Deeply devoted to a project! A book! How exciting! (Remember that these were the days when there were more people reading books than writing them.)

"Should I be jealous of this project?" I asked—seriously, because I was serious, if insane.

"On the contrary," Hugo said. Briefly he laid a hand upon my hand, which rested on the table. Then he rapidly withdrew it in a manner that made it clear that failed desire was not the issue. "I think it should be jealous of *you.*"

So there was a God, after all. And a heaven.

In the short time remaining, he told me that the book he was writing was about the man he'd been named after, Hugo Grotius, a Dutch scholar who a few hundred years earlier had written a book called *Mare Liberum*—"On the Freedom of the Seas." Grotius had argued that the Portuguese, who at that time controlled the Far Eastern spice trade, did not have the right to keep other Europeans—the Dutch, for example—from sharing in this trade. As Dutch power on the seas increased, however, Grotius's opinion in the matter of who should have the freedom of East Indian trade altered considerably. Hugo found it nearly intolerable that a great libertarian should have become so narrow in his nationalistic interests as to undercut his own magnificently stated position.

Be wary of the man with a professional interest in justice. Give money to his cause but not devotion to his person. It is the creepy right wing that crawls into bed with the same wife year after year; the left is more sinister. The right wing knows that everything it learned as a child was true; the left knows what was left out in all the talk of truth and beauty, justice and virtue.

Hugo called me the next day "just to make certain I have the right number and I can find you when I get back." He had been so pleased to meet me that the unpleasant fact of a research trip had been wiped out of his mind. He was at the airport; if he was compelled to be away for more than a couple of days, he would be in touch from the road. He had a meeting the following Monday in Los Angeles so he'd have to be back by then in any event.

On Monday he called to say that his meeting in Los Angeles had been postponed and he was going to take this unexpected opportunity to do some research where he was. When I asked where that was, he laughed and said that I wouldn't believe him if he was to tell me. I said, and of course meant it—a condition that would not obtain for much longer—that I had no reason at all not to believe him.

23

"Rome."

I giggled.

"You see?" he purred reproach. "I told you you wouldn't believe me."

"Of course I believe you," I said, my voice choking slightly. "I just think it's funny. You sound as though you're right around the corner. I guess it's a very good connection."

"No," he said, "or at least it's not the phone company's connection. It's that I *feel* as though I'm around the corner. Not even around the corner. I feel as though I'm in the room with you, looking at your wonderful, iridescent green eyes . . . perhaps touching one of your golden-red curls . . . or just holding two soft hands between mine . . ."

Oh, my God, Oh, my God! Stop! Don't stop! I love you! Take my hands, my curls . . . Take my eyes, if you really have use for them. Everything I have is yours. It's been yours all along, I just didn't know your name until now. Hugo. I love you, Hugo! Come home!

"I have to go now," Hugo said softly. (This was the Bernkastel gavotte, two steps forward and three steps back.) "But it's only the phone I'm leaving. Think of me, will you? Promise you won't forget me just because I'm so far away?"

Forget him? The clear and present danger was of forgetting everything else!

"When will you be back?" I choked out.

"I don't want to give you a date," he said. "Not because I'm afraid of disappointing you but because if I don't make it, I'll be horribly upset."

Hugo, come back to me! You are the light of my life—certainly of my imagination's life!

Until that week, not a day had gone by when I did not think frequently of my father, wonder how I might find him and convince him to bring me to live with him in New York, or wherever he was. Suddenly it was unthinkable that I might leave L.A., except to accompany Hugo on a trip to Rome. This, I promised myself, I would do, if invited, were it Finals Week or any other week of the year. After all, what had school ever done for me? What had *anyone* ever done for me that Hugo hadn't done better in two conversations?

He called from London the following week and from Hong Kong two days later. He said that he was hoping to be back within a week and that for all his traveling, he never ceased to think of me. He said that the red-blond color of my hair was more clear in

24

his mind than the color of his children's. I'd forgotten he had children, but that was silly of me. A man who was surely more than twenty-five years old. (He was forty-eight, actually.)

A couple of days later as I was riding down Wilshire Boulevard with my friend Jon, I saw a beat-up Volkswagen with a driver who looked remarkably like Hugo. I stared, craned my neck to see if it was he, tried to ascertain, I should say, that it was not, for he was wearing an old T-shirt and there was a woman in the car, and there was no way in the world this fellow had just gotten off an airplane.

I nearly asked Jon to follow when the Volks turned off Wilshire but then convinced myself this would be lunacy. It was entirely possible, after all, that I didn't remember the way Hugo looked. Possibly the blank cartridge in my mind had attached itself to the first distant profile bearing some resemblance to that of the man who'd sat next to me at lunch. It was, I hardly needed to remind myself, the *spirit* of that man that was so much with me, the *spirit* of the man that was in the pillow I hugged to my bosom when I turned out the light after doing my history homework (I had a sudden desire to excel in history) and storing up questions to ask my teacher the following day.

At dinner I asked Violet if she knew that guy, Hugo Bernkastel, or whatever his name was, who'd sat next to me at the luncheon. She giggled. Oh, yes. Sam had given Hugo some work for a while, but the two of them just didn't get along. And then of course there'd been the blacklist. If it weren't for Polly and a pseudonym, he probably wouldn't be getting any work at all. Polly had been sitting next to her at the luncheon. He had a couple of kids by Polly, and then, of course, there were all those other wives and children. It was astonishing, really, that someone who looked like Hugo Bernkastel could keep finding women to be crazy about him.

I went up to my room, locked the door and cried for about twenty minutes, during which time I managed to convince myself that if Hugo was still legally married, it was clearly a marriage in license only. Obviously, this woman did not make him *happy*. Perhaps he hadn't cared for any of his wives but had married to please the long line of women who'd fallen madly in love with him. It was clear, in any event, that his feelings about me were crucially different from those charitable sentiments that had led him to care for the others. Nobody could look at you the way he'd looked at me and care for another woman. (I'd just become one, although I hadn't thought of myself as a woman before, this being before the era when it was insulting to call a ten-year-old a girl.) For all my mother knew, Hugo and Polly Bernkastel didn't even share a home!

I looked in the phone book. Hugo Bernkastel was listed at a Westwood address. Polly Bernkastel was listed at the same address, with a separate number. Then there was a listing for the children's phone.

But the truth proved no match for the combination of Hugo's casual will to deceive and my own intense need to believe. He called a few days later, a Monday, exhausted from his "travels." He said he'd arrived home about ten minutes earlier but wanted to say hello before going to sleep for "at least twenty-four hours." Would I be free to have a drink, or a cup of coffee, or whatever, with him on Wednesday at about five? Of course I was. And how did I feel about the coffee shop of the Beverly Wilshire, which was mundane, not at all the sort of place he'd like to take me, but oh, so convenient? I felt just as good about the coffee shop of the Beverly Wilshire as I would have felt about any location on the face of the earth.

I moved through the next forty-eight hours on automatic pilot, being driven to school by Tony, sitting in my classes, riding home with my friends, who accused me of not telling them something. Once in my room, I stared in the mirror, reviewed my clothes, tried on my mother's makeup and made love to a couple of pillows named Hugo who had extraordinary praise for the looks and feel of my body. We treated our virginity in those days as though it were a person in its own right, and Hugo was finding it impossible to believe that this person had lived with me so recently.

On Wednesday, I dashed home, showered and spent half an hour trying on the three sets of clothing to which I'd narrowed down my possibilities, finally settling on a navy-and-green-striped jersey and a navy skirt that I thought were more sophisticated than the others. Makeup on, washed off, on again but less obvious. After all, I hadn't been wearing a lot of makeup on That Day and he had liked me then!

It was a ten-minute walk to the Beverly Wilshire. (I'd clocked it the previous day.) I walked on the street parallel to ours so that if Tony should happen to be driving home, he wouldn't see me in high heels and ask where I was going. If Hugo was going to want me around a lot of the time, I might have to make up some story about a part-time job, although then I'd have to cover about money. Furthermore, Tony didn't like the idea of my working. He said that my job was to do well in school and nothing should interfere unless it was absolutely necessary. Also, he didn't want people to get the idea that he couldn't provide adequately for me and my mother. I had no sympathy at all with either of these notions, nor did I distinguish between them. I had not yet allowed myself to enjoy the benefits of having a person like Tony to care for me but still thought of him as this sweet old fellow who'd taken my mother off my hands.

Hugo sat hunched over a cup of coffee at a small table near the window, looking like a big toe with an ingrown nail, all red and painful. He glanced up and saw me, then smiled; the pain didn't go away, but for a moment the pleasure seemed almost as powerful.

"Nellie!" he exclaimed, standing up, holding out his hands to clasp mine between them. "Now the sun can *really* shine!"

He was the first person since my father had named me to make the connection to the old song, and if he hadn't already owned me, he would have come into possession at that moment.

He beckoned me to the seat opposite his and told me he'd ordered a hamburger. What could he get for me? I said I'd have the same, although I had no appetite at all. (He ate my burger as well as his own while I sipped at the coffee that I needed about as much as I needed a shot of adrenaline.)

"Now, let me just look at you for a moment," he said in his soft, insinuating, sinus-whispery speech. "My, my, even lovelier than I remember." He took both my hands across the table and around his coffee. "I have to hear what you've been doing . . . and thinking about . . . while my thoughts have been only of you."

I stared at him. Mute. Helpless. God knows how long it took me to tell him that *I* wasn't the one who was doing interesting things and that *he* should tell *me* where he'd been and what he'd been doing there.

"Ah, yes," he sighed, "those of us who are not deeply interesting must find work we can talk about to those near and dear to us."

Those near and dear to him! I knew that *I* was in love, but now he was confirming my most hopeful impression!

Hugo said that even if a complicated life had forced him to be a movie-business prostitute, he was by nature an academic. To be left alone to finish his work on Grotius would have been true happiness. That and perhaps teaching a course or two in some cloistered grove of academe. But he supported a lot of people and he had to make enough money for all of them. Aside from having a reasonable gift for dialogue, he'd turned out to be good at scouting locations abroad and figuring out arrangements that worked well for producers. All this required, actually, was a reasonable grasp of what was going on in the real world of governments, economics, and so on, but of course that was precisely what few people in Hollywood possessed.

Clearly, this state of affairs (aside from the matter of the black-list, to which he never referred) caused him anguish, and as he spoke, I could only wish that we were someplace where I might comfort him. I wanted his massive—noble, as I was coming to think of it—head to rest in my lap so that I could stroke his "hair," and bend over to kiss his high (!) forehead.

The funny-awful thing about all this, Hugo said, was that here he was, a Marxist, trapped close to the very heart of the capitalist ideal.

So there was something to be said in favor of Marxism that my social-studies teacher had neglected to mention. I would have to read *Das Kapital*. Fast. I would have asked Hugo what else to read if I'd been willing to display my ignorance.

"It's not such a trap," I said, "if it allows you to travel to fascinating places all over the world."

He smiled sadly. "How did you become so wise at such an early age?"

It is perhaps unnecessary to mention that I did not ask what was so wise about my obvious remark. I simply basked in his approval while he finished our hamburgers and ordered a milk shake, which he drank down in one gulp. He then became restless in a way extraordinary to watch. It was as though the booth had become a cage with bars so strong that there was no point in testing them, the solution being to squirm, to take off one's jacket, cross and uncross the legs, and so on. I was afraid that if I asked whether he wanted to take a walk, I would be signaling the end of our time together, so I remained silent.

"Do you have to be home?" he finally asked. "Or can I persuade you to take a little drive with me?"

I smiled.

There is nothing you cannot persuade me to take with you.

He got the check and paid the cashier, dropping several bills of moderate denomination on the floor as he did so. I scooped them up and handed them to him.

He smiled guiltily. Guilefully.

"I don't want you to think I'm careless."

I smiled back radiantly.

"You seem to be full of care, actually."

He grabbed my hand and we walked out of the Beverly Wilshire swinging along like two teen-agers instead of one teen-ager and a man not quite old enough to be her grandfather. We walked a block and a half to the spot (illegal) where he had parked his car, a small, beat-up Volkswagen so closely resembling the one I had seen rolling down Wilshire that all the air would have escaped from the balloon that was my mind if it had been floating anywhere in the real world.

"Who drives your car besides you?"

"One of my kids, occasionally. But mostly they think it's not elegant enough. They take my wife's when it's free."

"Wife's." I echoed him without meaning to. So they were friendly enough to use each other's cars.

"Mmm. It's a station wagon and too large for their tastes, not to say, not, uh, hip enough. But this thing is an embarrassment to them." He rested his hand on the roof, patted it gently, smiled with infinite sadness. "To me it represents a way of pretending I haven't become just another high-priced sellout."

We got into the car and began driving toward Santa Monica. Hugo said he had a little shack near the beach where he retreated to work. Just to keep himself sane. From what I knew of his schedule thus far, there was little time for retreat, but he explained as he drove that this year had been unusually hectic for him. The only thing that kept him going was the knowledge that it wouldn't be like this for more than another couple of months. Then he was looking forward to settling down. Writing. Seeing me for long periods of time. Unless I had grown weary of him. He reached across the gearshift to take my hand. My heart leaped out of my chest into his palm at the moment that he had to drop my hand to shift gears.

My next question had something to do with whether he lived with his children. My adolescent-clever way of asking whether he considered himself married.

The answer, spoken with great sadness and punctuated by deep sighs, was that he and his wife were (I swear he used the phrase) married in name only and lived in a home large enough to guarantee their ability to lead separate lives. Only once in a while, when he met someone like me he could really talk to, was he forced to confront the barren quality of those lives. He was close to his son, less close, he admitted with pain, to his daughter, who had been turned against him early on by her mother. Going home to

29

the two of them was such a strange and unpleasant experience that he often found himself circling the area where he lived before heading into the driveway. Or calling his son to see if he'd like to meet for dinner. Hugo and his wife did not share a bedroom or very much of anything else. He was extraordinarily lonely for a man with a complicated life.

Tears filled my eyes. I clutched his hand. I promised myself that if I failed to cure Hugo's life, it would not be for want of trying. I would talk. I would listen. I would learn how to cook. I pictured a little room with a fireplace. (I'd seen fireplaces occasionally, though not with fires in them—except, of course, in the movies.) When life became difficult with the woman the world thought of as his wife, Hugo would come to our room. Our Cottage. The fire would be roaring. (It would be small, if the weather was warm.) A miraculous French dinner, or Italian dinner, or whatever he liked, would be waiting for him. He would talk. I would listen. We would Make Love.

I was going to tell my college adviser that she should stop showing me catalogues. There was no question of my going away to school. Go away? And leave Hugo with no one to care for him? Become just another in the long string of women who had disappointed him?

His little shack was just that and became a recommendation for its owner's truth in advertising. A large room with a Pullman kitchen in one corner, a tiny bedroom, a bath. All shabby but pleasant. (I'd never seen anything shabby but pleasant before.) There was a Moroccan rug on the floor and a madras throw on the studio bed, which also held large pillows covered with an assortment of frayed Oriental fabrics. Against one wall were bookshelves, a desk and file cabinets. An Olivetti, a half-typed page in its roller, sat among papers in the midst of the desk.

The perfect setup, in a world where some things never change, for a middle-aged man to get laid.

Hugo took a large bag of potato chips from the kitchen cabinet, tore it open and began eating chips as though he hadn't seen food in days. He looked at me, laughed at himself, offered me some chips. I shook my head. He sat down at his desk, swiveling to face me as I sat at the edge of the studio bed.

"So," he said, his manner suggesting that he had been pursuing me for months and had caught up only now, "at last I have you to myself!"

I smiled shyly. There was something pressing against my chest.

I could barely breathe. I became aware of my clothes. Office clothes. High heels! He probably thought I was some kind of idiot. Worse, a *bourgeoise!* A word whose modern connotation I had learned while studying the French Revolution at Beverly Hills High. (The teacher had later come under fire on various taste-related issues.) Why hadn't I worn my jeans, dammit?

"I got dressed as though I had a job interview," I said timorously. "I didn't know we'd be coming here."

"You look beautiful," Hugo said. "I would be happy to give you a job—or anything else you wanted."

Well, I knew what I wanted, all right. At least in its broad outline.

A self-conscious, teen-aged seductress, I kicked off my shoes, brought my feet up to the bed, rested sideways on my elbow. (If breathing had been possible, casual seductiveness would surely have been easier.)

Hugo gobbled a few more potato chips, dropped the bag and didn't so much move over as segue to the edge of the studio bed. He placed a large, strong, hairy hand on my foot and began slowly, rhythmically, to massage it. The extraordinary sexual feeling that had visited my body in waves during the days after I'd met him returned in full force, leaving my face flushed and my hands trembling. I twisted so that I was lying on my back, hands clasped under my head, which rested on one of the big, old pillows. He stared intently at my feet as he massaged them.

"You have beautiful feet."

Oh, my God!

I was trembling all over. He leaned over and kissed one big toe through my mother's nylon stocking.

Oh, my God. Oh, my God.

When Hugo had kissed each toe on that foot, he moved to the other one, all the while massaging their soles ... my soul ... altering forever the way that I would view the world and its possibilities. And when he had kissed each toe, he kissed—more slowly and suggestively, if that was possible—the inside of one ankle, then the outside. After which he moved slowly up my shin, pushing aside my skirt, feeling the nylon on my thighs as though it were skin. Now he was playing with one of my mother's flowery garters.

I moaned. "Aren't they awful?" *Capitalist toiles!*

"They're beautiful," he said, "because they're on you."

Resting on an elbow, he slowly rolled down one stocking-cum-garter, then the other, pulling them off my feet so gently as to suggest that they were velvet and my feet the crown jewels. Five years later I'd understand the kind of practice required for such dexterity, but I was a million miles away from such thoughts now. I could barely breathe and was focused on the matter of getting enough air to stay alive. Except I was just that, and if anything, more so than I could recall having been in the recent past. Now Hugo kissed my knees, then my thighs, and lifted my skirt to kiss my mother's lacy blue underpants and my own belly button. The rest of him followed so that he was lying on top of me and— But what was that big, hard thing between us?

Oh, my God, that was IT. The thing I'd heard about, seen in diagrams (but never in photographs, unless it was small and soft-looking) and giggled over with my friends. I looked up at Hugo's wonderful, kind face as it moved over mine to kiss me. It was all very peculiar, really—that soft countenance (well, maybe the nose offered a hint) coupled with this big, hard, insistent thing pressing against my pelvic bones, bruising, no doubt, the soft flesh that covered them.

He kissed me sweetly, softly, wetly, a dream much better than one I might have managed on my own before now, except that It was still there. I embraced him. Maybe I could shift my weight in some way so that It wasn't pressing down right in that spot. My belly, for example, had no bones in it that I knew of.

It was as he rested his weight on me in order to reach around with both hands to find the hook on my brassiere that I allowed myself to remember that this Massive Thing that was causing my outsides such discomfort was, unless everything I'd ever read or heard was a lie, about to penetrate my insides. Momentary disbelief as I remembered the size, the apparent size, of the available opening. And then terror. I kissed Hugo, hugging him tightly, nay, *clutched* at him as his free hand pulled up my sweater, pushed aside the brassiere and played with my breasts. He sucked one nipple, then the other.

Who could have known that those two things males made such a fuss over had as much pleasure to offer their possessors as their viewers? Why couldn't we just do this for a while? Why couldn't we just ... He was helping me out of my sweater now. And my brassiere. He reached around my back to find my skirt zipper, pulled it down without difficulty and then, with my help, got the skirt off, too.

Fear battled with excitement; both won.

Kissing my belly button, he played with the edge of my mother's silk underpants, finally sliding them down my legs. Not being able to breathe had caught up with me and I was truly suffocating now. I turned on my side; at least I could die gracefully.

Hugo stood up to take off his own clothes . . . and there *It* was— could I have hoped otherwise?—that massive tower of flesh, pointing at me like a machine gun in a war movie. Surely It would destroy me if It tried to force itself into that little hole between my legs!

Hugo lay down on his side, very close to me, facing me. He smiled reassuringly. Without having received any orders from me, my body moved itself right up against his, one leg raising itself to fit over the object of my concern. Waves of excitement crashed through me as Hugo played with my breasts and moved It back and forth between my legs. It didn't hurt. Maybe I'd misunderstood and this was all that was going to happen.

No. His fingers were groping between my legs, looking. Finding. A finger slipped into me with miraculous ease and felt remarkably good in there, causing me to moan with pleasure, making me reach out to see what I could do to make him feel half as good as . . . Uh-oh. His finger was still massaging me but I sensed that *It* was awaiting its moment.

I took a deep breath, one of the few that had been available to me since the beginning of this strange and complex process, and groped for It, finding It, as you might imagine, with ease, at first just holding It, rubbing a little, and finally stroking. It was quite a remarkable object, actually. Never could I recall touching anything that possessed such a combination of opposing qualities. It was at once the softest and the hardest thing imaginable. A sword in a velvet sheath. No, not a sword, which was too slender, or a bullet, which was too small. My mind began to range toward the larger forms of ammunition, but I stopped myself. I had to push all this stuff out of my mind and concentrate on what I was doing, simply stroking and rubbing the velvet over the extraordinary bone within.

What was remarkable was that excitement didn't leave me but existed with pain and fear in a kind of exquisite discord, the one perhaps even adding to the others as Hugo slowly, firmly, pushed his way into me, hurting me terribly at first but then, after he'd pushed and hurt me, pulling back, and as he did, letting me feel a little pleasure. Pushing and pulling back, good old Hugo, the Deflorationist Supreme, pushing and pulling until finally, *mirabile dictu!*, he was all the way inside. I was afraid even to moan lest

33

he become concerned about hurting me and withdraw, a fear which is amusing only in retrospect.

His load spent, Hugo withdrew from me with what it would take me years to be able to identify as inappropriate speed, turned his back to me, and went to sleep with all the concern of an eighteen-year-old initiate for his first practiced whore.

I remained, of course, wide-awake. I turned on my side, facing his back, and gingerly placed one arm around him in such a way as to avoid disturbing his sleep. I was all right. Orgasms hadn't hit the sports pages yet, and I didn't know that anything else was supposed to happen to me, much less whether it was supposed to happen the first time. If his withdrawal from me had not been so abrupt, I'd probably have felt fine. As it was, I needed a little something. With extreme caution, I kissed his back. He began to snore. Thank God I hadn't disturbed his sleep!

My body cooled. Carefully I pulled a little of the madras spread over myself. If I could move up against him and embrace him, I would be warm and happy and maybe I would even fall asleep. But the risk of disturbing him was too great, so I contented myself with looking at his broad, strong back, familiarizing myself with his moles, wondering whether he would make love to me again when he awakened and, if so, whether it would hurt as much as it had the first time.

I was served less than well, of course, by the fact that when he did awaken and make love to me again, he hurt me less than before at the beginning and not at all by the end. Thus did I learn about intense pleasure even as I was about to be deprived of it. Thus was I catapulted into that state of perpetual eagerness cum dread that was the residence of any female in emotional congress with Hugo Bernkastel.

Not that I wasn't begging for it. Hugo, after all, did not make masochistic mountains out of the molehills of adolescent turmoil but simply utilized whatever he found when he got there. No need to sit at home reading his early edition of the Marquis de Sade; he was in natural command of the means to cause suffering. Is this not true of most of us? And, if so, is it not fortunate that many of us lack the desire?

I never had to be home again, but Hugo did. As we dressed, he spoke of his hope that his life was about to become more reasonable. As we finished dressing, went to the car and drove back to Beverly Hills, he talked at length about his childhood. This was a time when, even in Hollywood, people meeting at parties were slower to present autobiographical calling cards . . . *Forgive me, my mother trained me always to ask people how much money they made without telling me that they'd all hate me for being nosy* . . . than they would be later on. If the fact of being in therapy had become conversational currency, nobody was heard to tell anything remotely resembling the truth about what had brought him or her into it. Furthermore, if people had begun to talk about that stuff at parties, I didn't know it because there hadn't been any parties since my father's departure. It seemed to me a sign of Hugo's attachment to me that he should be willing, even eager, during the drive home, to share with me the story of his dismal upbringing, surely one of the most pathetic chapters in the *Lost Boy's Book of Rejections.*

Hugo's mother was Kathy Kastle, originally Katya Schultz, the early feminist mogul who started the Kastle Kosmetics empire with money from Solomon Bernkastel, a bachelor and an academic whom she'd met at the home of friends and who'd fallen madly in love with her. Having consented to marry him as long as he understood she wanted to start her own business and would never have children, she'd become pregnant within weeks of the marriage and spent her pregnancy setting up the company with Solomon's help, interviewing chemists, exploring packaging and promotion, and so on. The brochures announcing the formation of the company had gone out with handwritten postscripts from Solomon informing their friends that a son had been born. Two weeks later, in April 1911, Kathy set out from their Chicago home in Solomon's Model T with a back seat full of cosmetics, a head full of commercial possibilities, and not so much as a backward glance at her husband, her bawling two-week-old son, or the Russian immigrant woman Solomon had hired to tend the baby.

Hugo remembered a lifetime of abuse and neglect in detail I found overwhelming at the time. After Hugo, any story of a man's life tended to terrify me.

We were together only once more, and that after elaborate promises that were broken and trembling protestations of love and concern and numerous phone calls, ostensibly placed from parts of the earth I hadn't known had telephones yet. When I finally saw him I was too mindful of the past and frightened of the future to take more than physical pleasure in his presence. I was, in fact, in a frenzy of love and hate, fear and mistrust, that should have outweighed any possible pleasure and caused me to erase him from my real life, if not from my fantasy one. It could not. I was a child.

I cried a lot and got too skinny. My mother thought I looked better, but Tony was worried. All his years in Hollywood hadn't convinced him that human bones looked good without flesh on them. He started cooking for me. Spaghetti, ravioli, lasagna—all the good, hearty food he'd always loved but seldom made because my mother, paranoid about her weight and not about to give up drinking, wouldn't touch them.

Tony had always been kind to me without actually approving of the way I was permitted to live. He continued to adore my mother and would never have thought of bringing her to task over my upbringing—my lack of upbringing, you might call it—so he had settled, from what I could overhear or divine, on blaming my father for lapses in my habits, taste and so on. He seemed, perhaps with my mother's help—though I doubt it, for in those days she didn't care enough about anything to lie—to have settled on a version of our previous lives that included an absentee husband and a wife who cared warmly for her child until that husband's desertion plunged her into a depression from which she never fully recovered.

Now, for the first time, I, too, was visibly sad, not to say skinny, and Tony moved to care for me. He even gave me driving lessons after school in the small, neat truck he used for delivering and picking up his men at the various gardens they tended. Evenings and weekends my lessons were in his white Cadillac. Afterward we would have a meal of spaghetti or lasagna while my mother nibbled at a piece of broiled fish or chicken.

Tony also learned me, as he put it, to appreciate opera. A man of no cultural pretensions, he loved vocal music of any kind except jazz, which he would have none of. Long before your average Beverly Hills home had a soundproofed room for movies and loud music, Tony had lined the walls of the small den near the kitchen with cork so he could listen to his music without disturbing my mother. Later he put an intercom between their bedroom and his den so her summonses were audible even if Verdi was making love to him at full volume.

I will never forget that first day when, passing the study door, which was slightly ajar, I was arrested by a beautiful tenor rendition of *Di quella pira* from *Il Trovatore*.

I poked in my head.

Tony sat in his red leather armchair, his eyes closed, his right hand directing the music. Sensing my presence, he opened his eyes and placed a finger on his lips; with the other hand, he beckoned me to join him. I tiptoed into the room, closing the door behind me, and moved to the second soft leather chair he had provided against the day when someone else might wish to listen. Relaxing into the chair, I watched him. I wanted to be part of what was going on between him and the music.

Di quella pira l'orrendo foco
tutte le fibre m'arse, avvampò!
Empi, spegnetela, o ch'io fra poco
col sangue vostro la spegnerò!

If Tony had kept his distance from me, it was not because of his nature, but because my mother's dazed permissiveness had created some sort of impenetrable barrier between us. If he had the opinion that some trip or project or friend of mine was no good for me, and I told him my mother hadn't objected, the issue was not joined because he wouldn't quarrel with my mother. If he found some object around the house that he held to be worthless, and if it turned out I had picked it up at my mother's request, no more was said about the matter. Permission he gave me to go someplace or do something was always followed by, "If it's all right with your mama." Or, I should say, "Ifa it'sa all right witha you mama," for he had the classic Italian accent to his English and never showed any desire at all to alter it.

Era già figlio prima d'amarti,
non può frenarmi il tuo martir.
Madre infelice, corro a salvarti
o teco almeno corro a morir!

Not until the side was finished did Tony open his eyes again.
"*Madre infelice*," I said. "What does that mean?"
He stood, stretched, turned off the record player.
"*Madre infelice*," he repeated, rubbing his eyes, yawning. "Just the way it sounds. Unfortunate mother. My unfortunate mother. She's more than unfortunate, she's . . ." He shook his head, sighed, sat down. "This is her son who sings to her. She's on the pyre. The stake. She will be burned for avenging her mama's death."
"Tell me," I begged. He was delighted to do so.

"Manrico has to save her. Her son. He tells Leonora, the woman who loves him, 'I was a son before I loved you. I cannot stay back when they do this to my mother. Even if I die at her side.' "

There were tears in my eyes. Tony was nodding. He had always suspected I possessed a soul.

"Could I hear it again?" I asked.

"Maybe we start from the beginning," he said. "I talk, we play."

That afternoon was one of the happiest of my life. My mother never summoned either of us, and we went through the entire opera, Tony talking, then playing the music, me asking questions, crying, listening, crying again.

The troubadour Manrico is in love with the Lady Leonora, who loves him in return. Count Luna is also in love with Leonora, who disdains him. The Count is determined to avenge his brother's fate at the hands of the gypsy Azucena—who is Manrico's mother! I could even cry for the evil Luna, who wasn't really evil but was under the burden of avenging his brother's death, as the Count sang:

> *Di geloso amor sprezzato*
> *Arde in me tremendo il fuoco!*

And then Azucena tells Manrico her dreadful secret—that in her agony and confusion she had thrown her own baby on the fire, so that Manrico is really the royal brother—only to take back what she's said because if Manrico knew the truth, he would be unwilling to destroy Luna!

I was pulled out of myself in a way that I hadn't been since my father was with me and I was safe and could allow myself to be immersed in fiction, in the unreal.

> *Ah sì, ben mio, coll'essere*
> *io tuo, tu mia consorte.*

Ah, yes, my love, when we belong to each other my courage will be greater than it is now, my arm stronger. But if it is written that I should die tomorrow, felled by the enemy's blade, then in my dying moments, my thoughts will move to you and I will remember that I am entering heaven before you. . . .

Ah, Manrico! Ah, Hugo!

When Leonora went to Manrico to tell him he was free, and Manrico, knowing she must have promised herself to the Count to gain his freedom but failing to realize she had already swallowed the fatal poison, furiously rejected her until she fell to the floor and he understood what she had done for him, I wept uncontrollably.

Tony came and sat down on the arm of my club chair and put his arm around me, gently patting my shoulder without trying to comfort me prematurely. He allowed the opera to end and me to cry for as long as I felt like crying. When I had finally finished, I felt better than I had in days. Weeks. *Years.*

I raised my head from the arm of the chair and smiled at Tony. I had just decided that I loved him like a father.

"I don't understand," I said, "how I could have heard it all these years without really hearing."

He shrugged. "Now you ready, now you hear."

Now I was ready, now I heard.

In the coming weeks we went through all of Verdi, then through Puccini, Rossini and Bellini. *La Bohème* was his great favorite, and he was puzzled by my indifference to it. In fact, hearing the music before I knew the plot, I had responded with pleasure, but then the story had irritated me. This perfectly wonderful man in love with a dying consumptive when surely there were terrific girls all over Paris who would have wanted him . . .

When Tony one Sunday overheard me refusing to go to a movie with my friends because he and I were scheduled to listen to a new record, he began to talk about taking me to the opera when it was in Los Angeles. He said he had relatives in New York who would put us up if we wanted to go to a few performances at the Met, a point from which he quickly retreated because there was no way he could get my mother to join us and no way he was going to leave her behind. Then he began telling me about the European opera houses, most particularly La Scala, where everything was so much better than it could be at any American performance. And was, of course, infinitely safer to daydream about.

I still could not think of Hugo without pain and confusion. His vanishing echoed some event in a not-quite-remembered time when bliss ended in a similarly abrupt and incomprehensible way. I couldn't simply wish for him to come back because to have him again would be to risk a similar experience. Yet I could not give up the elaborate fantasies in which I rejected him until he was able to prove to my satisfaction that he had been called to the other end of the world on a mission that did not allow for explanations.

For weeks I searched for a hypothetical version of my Hugo story—minus sex, of course, or a wife—to discuss with Tony. I had always placed a reasonable trust in him, but now I felt a filial reverence as well. If I could convey the quality of what had happened without getting bogged down in nasty details, Tony might give me advice that would be useful both now and in my future life.

"I want to ask your opinion about something," I told him one day when we had been listening to a medley of arias sung by Ezio Pinza. "It's about men."

He was dusting the Pinza record. He sat in his armchair, rested the record on his trousers and continued to wipe it with the chamois cloth, but in a more deliberate fashion.

"If you like a man, and he seems to be interested in you, and you have a sort of informal date with him . . . and you think he was very nice but you don't hear from him for a while, and then you see him again and you don't hear from him at all when you thought he liked you even more . . . What would you think if that happened?"

Tony turned over the record and began making his circular motions on the other side.

"Man?"

"Mmm."

"Man is too old for you. What you want is a boy."

"Tony!" I protested. "You don't know that. You don't even know how old he is!"

"All right. How old he is." It was flat. A challenge, not a question.

"Well, I don't know, exactly, but I don't see what difference it makes."

"From a man to a boy makes a big difference."

"Why?"

He paused, sighed, stood up, put away the record, returned the cloth to its place in the end-table drawer. Then he took a pencil and paper from the small desk in front of the window where he sat to pay the bills and, leaning on the end table, drew a picture, which he handed to me.

On a series of seesaws, two stick figures, a small one with long hair (girl) and a larger one without hair (man) remained in the same basic position: The large one held the ground on his seesaw seat while the small one, up high, waved her arms and legs but was unable to bring down her end.

"I don't understand," I lied.

"Sure you do." He took back the paper and drew some more. When he handed it back to me, there was another series, this time with figures of equal size, so that the seesaw moved, one side up in the air and then that side down, as the pictures progressed.

"Oh." I stood, dropped the picture in my chair. I was not so much angry with him as frustrated by his presentation of the truth in a form too simple to allow for argument.

I sat down again and began to cry.

"Uh-oh." He came over to me, sat on the edge of my chair, patted my head. "What's'a matter, baby? He's a married man you're talking about?"

Stunned, I stopped crying.

"Why did you say that?"

He shrugged. "They get to the age, they marry."

I was silent. If the world could be so easily codified, I was far from ready to learn the code.

"What happened to that nice-looking boy you went out with last term?" Tony asked.

I shrugged.

What happened, although surely I couldn't have said it, was that the playfulness Hugo had spurred, not to speak of the sexuality he had engaged, was absent when I went out with young boys, and they didn't ask me a second or third time.

My affection for Tony was tinged with a new and respectful wariness. He didn't mind. He'd raised two girls of his own and was accustomed to trying to safeguard the virginity of teen-agers over their own mixed feelings.

"So where is this guy?" he finally asked me. "The married one? He better not show his face around here."

I smiled sadly.

"He won't."

"He's gone?"

I nodded.

"That's'a good. I know you don't see it that way now, but I swear to you, sweetheart, it's a good thing."

It didn't *feel* good.

What puzzled me was that Tony hadn't been interested in any of the details. Older man. Well, now, practically everybody married men who were older, and it seemed tricky to decide at just what point an older man became an Older Man. Furthermore, it was clear to me, as it must be to Tony, that there was more than one kind of marriage. In fact, Hugo had told me he'd been determined to have a *real* marriage, and failing to accomplish this was his most bitter disappointment. He had been shocked and grievously upset when the mother of his children announced her intention to return to her law practice while the children were still young. Nor was she a wife-mother in other ways he might reasonably have expected. He hadn't had to tell me that he was remaining with her For the Sake of the Children. I understood and approved mightily of his doing this against what might be his own best interests!

There were times I could believe that all of the above was true and Hugo was staying away because the attraction to me was so great as to endanger his sense that he could remain in his marriage until the children were grown. Other times when I was certain something I'd said or done or, worse still, some very basic inadequacy of mine, had been directly responsible for his loss of interest.

It was clear, in any event, that I had best stay away from males altogether, a position that, however arrived at, served me in good stead during my remaining high school years. I went to classes, did all my homework and various papers for extra credit and, during my senior year, with Tony's encouragement, applied to UCLA as well as a couple of fancy Eastern colleges. Tony was proud of me.

On the third Sunday in December of 1965 I came downstairs at around eleven, thinking I would prepare my breakfast and bring it to Tony's room, where music was already playing. It was the meltingly beautiful *Ah! bello, a me ritorna* from *Norma*. I almost went in to give Tony a kiss on the top of his head before making my breakfast but decided to heat my coffee first. He had taught me to enjoy the rich Italian coffee that he made with hot milk, but then his doctor had ordered him off it because of a heart condition I'd never heard another word about. He had stopped drinking all but a single morning cup greatly diluted with milk. This was, he said, a condition of life he could not relinquish.

Recently I had noticed there was more coffee left for me than there'd once been. I was drinking that and more, sometimes making a new pot when the first one was finished. I think I enjoyed the ceremony as much as the coffee itself, though oddly, it was one of the few habits I'd ever acquired that Violet had noticed—and deplored. On the occasional Sunday when Tony persuaded her to join us for breakfast, she invariably expressed concern about coffee as an artificial stimulant that would prevent me from relaxing. On this particular Sunday morning she was nowhere to be seen.

In the kitchen I took the strainer basket out of the percolator (Tony had failed to do it, which was unusual), turned on the light and added sugar and milk to the pot. In recent weeks he'd seemed to have lost interest in the music, and I was happy to hear it playing again. I took a cruller, filled the big white mug with his name on it, a Christmas present from me to him that I used more often than he did, and with the mug in one hand and the napkin-wrapped cruller in the other, made my way to the den.

The record was finished, but Tony hadn't turned it over. I could see the top of his head over the back of his armchair and thought he must have fallen asleep. I kissed his bald spot, set my cup and cruller on the little table next to my chair and went to the phonograph to turn over the record. Then, as music filled the room, I sat down.

Tony's eyes were wide open, but he wasn't looking at me. His arms rested along the arms of the chair, palms down. His body was taut. Not a moment's uncertainty was granted me. It was clear beyond a shadow of a doubt that he was dead.

I sat back against the chair cushions and listened to the entire side from *Norma* with a mind that was, at first, remarkably clear of other thoughts. When the side was finished, I turned off the record player and sat down once again, drinking my coffee and watching Tony's face, which looked mildly surprised. It was only when the buzzer sounded—Violet summoning her faithful servant—that I began to cry.

What would happen to us now?

I thought of that day when I'd suddenly *heard* the music Tony was playing, and I thought of the day when we'd met, when he had distinguished the flowers from the weeds. I thought of how careful he had been not to act like my boss until the day he'd perceived that I was looking for one, and of how scrupulous he had been since that time not to conflict with Violet's wishes.

The buzzer sounded again. I went to the wall, pulled the intercom plug from the socket. I wondered how long it would take Violet to notice that no one was responding. Perhaps, when she did, she would come downstairs.

She had just better not touch him.

I was puzzled, not simply by the fierceness of the thought but by the fact that it had come at all. There had been little touching in our household since the early days of Violet and Tony's romance, and that not by Violet, who, if Tony patted her shoulders as he passed behind her chair to get the next course, reacted with the warmth of a porcelain figure toward the housemaid's cloth.

I walked over to Tony and closed his eyes by gently running the side of my hand down his face from the top of his forehead, one of the few acts I have ever performed that is no more difficult than it looks in the movies. Then I went to the window and stared out at the dead street.

After a while Violet drifted into the room.

"I've been ringing over and over," she complained.

I turned to watch her as she came around Tony's chair, looked at him for slightly longer than one might have expected her to, then looked back to me.

"I think he's really gone," I said.

"Oh, yes," she replied in that same, small, quavery–complainy voice. "He's been tired lately."

Then she drifted away and back up the stairs, leaving me wondering whether she understood or whether, indeed, she had just crossed the border from barely sane to quite mad.

Tony could not remain here like this.

I could not remain here, but that was another, slightly less urgent matter.

The phone rang in the kitchen. I ignored it. It ceased to ring.

There were jobs to be done, but I didn't know precisely what they were, or whom I should call to ask. I leaned over, kissed Tony's forehead and whispered, "Goodbye. I love you." Then, having deposited the cup and cruller in the kitchen, I picked up the phone to call the doctor and ask him what I should do. I decided to get the number from Information rather than search through the directory or go upstairs to deal with Violet.

But the line appeared to be dead.

I went upstairs. Violet lay in bed, her breakfast tray set aside, the usual magazines scattered around her. The receiver was off the cradle.

"Oh, there you are, dear," she said. "My tray's been ready for hours."

I didn't touch it. It was a symbolic refusal, petty but important to me, to go along for a moment with the notion that I, too, had been put on this earth to serve her. Her suggesting I should have taken care of it told me she had seen, if she hadn't precisely registered, Tony's death.

I asked her why the phone was off the hook.

"Oh, yes," she said. "There's a call for you."

I replaced the receiver.

The address book was kept on a cord next to the phone on her nightstand.

"Dear," she said in a voice that sounded closer to tears than her normal one, "will you just get the tray off my bed? I keep thinking it's going to fall off."

With an internal curse, I pulled the book and its cord from the phone, picked up the tray from the far side of the huge bed and brought both downstairs to the kitchen.

Dr. Summers was one of those wonderful old soap-style general practitioners to whom old-lady patients are always leaving their fortunes. He was tall and lanky with flowing white hair that hadn't ceded any volume to time and a smooth pink face held up by impressive gentile bones. I keep wanting to put him in a black cape and top hat—Raymond Massey as Lincoln, again—but aside from his mouth's being very different from Massey's, reflecting neither sensuality nor dissatisfaction, he was very much of his place, which was Hollywood, and wore tropical suits all year round while making the house calls he professed not to mind in his Lincoln Continental.

I dialed Summers's number and got one of his six silky secretary-nurses. I asked if I might speak with him, and there was a brief, incredulous silence.

"May I ask what the problem is?" the nurse inquired when she had recovered from the shock of my presumption.

"The problem is," I said—it's much easier to deal with bastards at times like this—"that there's a dead person in the house."

A pause. "Is this person a patient of The Doctor's and is there any doubt of his or her condition?"

"Yes, the person is a patient of the doctor's, and I don't have any doubt, but of course I'm not a doctor."

"Of course." She already knew that any medical school would have been crazy to admit me.

"His name is Anthony Coletti," I said.

She asked a few questions and told me she'd try to find the doctor, a not so easy task in those days, when there were no portable phones on the golf course. He, or someone, she said, would be there very soon.

I hung up and drank the small amount of coffee with milk that was left in my cup, then sat down at the table and began to go through my mother's address book. In a remarkably short time an ambulance with an emergency squad had arrived, and someone had examined Tony, asked me a few questions, given me something to bring Violet to sign and taken him away. I wanted to cry some more, but it was as though I'd been put on hold.

She'd just better leave me alone for a while. She'd better not get hungry or thirsty or need someone to tidy her room.

It was odd how few names there were in the phone book that it might have been reasonable to call. I thought of my Other Father, as I'd come to think of my real father in those rare recent times when I'd allowed myself to think of him at all. We hadn't spoken in a little over four years. To the best of my knowledge, my mother hadn't been in contact with him since the divorce. Still, if anyone was responsible for Violet, it was he. He was the one who'd been smitten by the beautiful young Dutch orphan who wasn't fit to be a mother and given her a baby who happened to be me.

Florist. Grocer. Hair. People were mostly arranged not by their names but by their function in her life. Tony had listed a few people alphabetically, including his two married daughters, Theresa Campbell, who lived in Alaska, and Patsy Biancardi, who was in the Valley north of L.A. (I wasn't prepared to think about telling them yet.) *Maids. Saks. Studio*, with the names and numbers of various personnel. There were Irma Valenstone, who contacted Violet with invitations, and Mindy Sabin, who had designed her costumes and still occasionally ran up something for her. I turned the next to the last page and my breath caught as though someone had clamped a pillow over my face. *Sam Pearlstein.*

It wasn't simply another listing. There were two facing pages covered with addresses and phone numbers for him. Some were crossed out and some were not, but there were ten or fifteen numbers in all—Beverly Hills, Palm Springs and New York. There was a number for someone called "Lynn P." and one for Peggy Cafferty, who'd been his secretary as far back as I could remember. Lawyers had a small section to themselves.

I sat looking at those pages for a long time. First of all, there was an order to them that was not visible in the rest of the book. Under *Hair,* for example, there were eight or nine names, but the old ones hadn't been crossed out when new ones were added. On the Pearlstein pages, there were cross-outs, dates and explanations. (I'm not sure I'd known before then that Violet had a perfect script.) It looked as though she'd known his whereabouts on any given day

46

during the four years since he had left us—or at least had had the comfort of believing she did. Among the numbers were a couple that just said "Messages," as though she'd been provided with a sense of contact even at times when she had no idea where he was.

I looked at the clock. It was two in the afternoon. Most of Sunday was left. Sunday was my day with Tony.

My friend Ingrid called and said she'd been trying to get me earlier, but Violet must've gotten lost on the way to telling me. She and Lana wanted to go to a movie. I told her I couldn't go with them.

"Why not?"

"I just can't," I said. "I think I might have to do something with Tony."

I hung up and dialed my father's Beverly Hills number, which my brain had folded in as the page came in contact with my eyes.

A little kid picked up the phone and said in a squeaky, high-pitched voice that sounded like a television commercial, "Hello? Who is it? This is Sonny."

I hung up again. Then I went upstairs and asked Violet if she wanted some lunch.

"Mm," Violet said. "I'd love a nice salad."

I tried to devise a strategy for dealing with her and finally settled on a question that still seems to me to have been brilliant.

"Is there anyone you want me to call about Tony?"

"Oh, dear," Violet said, "I don't . . . I suppose your father will want to know."

I hesitated, surprised in spite of myself. Was it possible she hadn't thought of herself as concealing something from me?

"I didn't know you were in touch with my father."

She looked up from the magazine in her lap for the first time.

"Of course I am," she said. "You know, if it hadn't been for your father, I probably never would have gone into the movies."

"Have you been talking to him all along?" I asked, having failed in my efforts to convince myself not to press the matter.

"Of course," she said. "Well, that is, since the divorce. At first it was simply too difficult, you know. But once he settled down . . ."

Okay, Nellie. Now turn around and leave before it gets worse.

"Do you ever talk about me?"

"What do you mean?" she asked.

"Nothing. I was just wondering." I turned to leave the room, looked back at her for a moment.

"Tony's gone."

"Oh, yes?" She didn't look up again. "Well, that's just as well."

Downstairs, I dialed my father's number again. This time he answered.

I said, "This is Nellie. Tony died." And then, in violation of all my own warnings and instructions, I burst into tears.

My father said, "I'll be right there," but I couldn't stop crying for long enough to respond.

I was still sobbing, my head down on the kitchen table, when he walked into the kitchen ten or fifteen minutes later, saying, as he placed a hand on my shoulder, "Listen to me, sweetheart. I want you to stop crying now so you can talk to me and we can do what needs to be done."

I stopped. Maybe I'd just been doing it for long enough. He handed me his handkerchief. I blew my runny nose, then looked up at him for the first time. I started violently and perhaps my face lost its color, for I was looking at an unfamiliar copy of my father.

His weight had always been erratic. Now he was thin and his face hadn't its sometime roundness; there were unfamiliar wrinkles and thin, deep lines etched into his tennis sunburn. The stubble on his chin was gray, although the hair that had remained on top of his head was still reddish blond. His eyes monitored me. I couldn't meet them, but I couldn't stop staring at him either. He pulled over one of the other chairs and sat facing me. Curly, reddish blond hairs poked through the open neck of his white polo shirt and covered the long, strongly muscular legs below his tennis shorts. He wore sneakers but no socks. He'd always refused to wear socks, and his sneakers had always smelled. I'd loved that smell, which I associated only with him; I'd forgotten about it for a long time and remembered it only now, as it reached me. In the old days he'd thrown away his sneakers after a few wears. He might still be doing that; these looked brand-new.

My throat was constricted, and I wanted to cry again, but I was afraid of annoying him. He took my hand in his, which he rested on his thigh. I found myself mesmerized by the feeling of his rough, hairy skin and the sight of my own pale and relatively small hand in his large, reddish tanned and sinewy one.

"Okay, sweetheart," he said. "Let's try to get business out of the way so we can talk."

I searched his face for a sign, any sign . . . of anxiety . . . or guilt . . . or humor. Some acknowledgment that something had happened between us in the past that was not entirely unrelated to what might happen in the future. An implied promise that life was real and continual. If neither his words nor his manner appeared to have a relation to reality as I had experienced it since his departure, I wanted there to be some explanation for this discrepancy that I simply wasn't in touch with as yet.

"Business?" I echoed. I was hooked into his hand, into the way it *felt*, and I couldn't think at all.

"I don't mean business, love. You know what I mean. What we have to take care of."

I almost echoed, "Take care of?" but caught myself. I had forgotten Tony. I said, "I love—loved—Tony." As much to remind myself as to inform him.

He nodded. "Sure you did. You're a sweetheart."

"How do you know?" I asked, without irony.

He laughed.

"The fact that your mother wanted me to leave you alone doesn't mean I haven't kept track of you."

This, of course, was more than I could manage to digest—or even, at that point, to question.

I stared at him.

"Listen to me, Sunshine."

There it was. The name I'd been waiting for in spite of warnings to myself not to do so.

He took my other hand and joined my two hands so that they were clasped between his.

"I have an idea. I think we should try to do everything that has to be done here, and then we'll make some arrangement for your mother, and you'll come back to the house with me, and we can talk. How does that sound? By the way, how *is* your mother?"

"I can't tell," I said matter-of-factly, as though I were accustomed to discussing her condition with him. "She might have gone over . . ." I didn't need to say where. He nodded.

"And where's . . . Whatsisname?"

"Tony," I said mechanically. "He's gone. I called his doctor. They took him."

My father nodded. "Good girl. Are his kids in L.A.? He *has* kids, doesn't he?"

"Two daughters." *Three, if you count me.* "One in Alaska and one in the Valley." Tony often visited the Biancardis in the Valley, where the Campbells stayed when they came to town because they couldn't stand to be around Violet. No one had ever told me this, of course, but they acted decent, if not warm, when she wasn't there.

"I don't suppose you've called them."

49

I shook my head.

He flashed a grin. "That would've been too good to be true."

I was improbably, unaccountably, ashamed of myself. As though I'd failed him.

"Well, we'll have to do that. They'll probably want to come back and take care of the funeral." He dropped my hand to look at his watch. "Unless they don't want a funeral, in which case our lives'll be much simpler."

"*I* want a funeral." My brain wasn't really working. I was glad that my mouth was.

A split second in which he tried to decide whether he would tolerate this assertiveness and made up his mind not only to tolerate but to enjoy it.

"Okay, Tootsie Pie." Had he always bequeathed me a different nickname with every new sentence? And had I once loved those names? Surely I remembered many of them. "You want a funeral, you got it! Unless *they* don't want it, of course. Which is unlikely. Guineas love that shit."

Each thing he said was wrong in a different way. Why, then, did I once again feel that he owned me?

He stood up and pushed back his chair, leaving it four feet from the table. He never put anything back where it had been. In the old days I'd found that carelessness to be one of his lovable traits and had taken pleasure in straightening up after him. Perhaps it had made him seem like a kid. Or perhaps, in the old days, all his traits had been lovable because they were his.

"Look," he said, "here's my idea of how we proceed. You can stop me"—an ironic, verbal bow to his recognition that my feelings had to be taken into account—"if I say something that doesn't work for you. I have to leave you here for a while." Two minutes earlier he'd been talking as though he were going to stay with me. Was it my mild defiance that had caused him to remember an errand? "I want you to do two things while I'm gone. Call the daughters . . ." He waited for me to protest, but I didn't know how. "And keep an eye on your mother." He hesitated, looked toward the stairs. "As a matter of fact, maybe I'd better look in on her before I go. What do you think?"

I shrugged. "Maybe. If you've been talking to her all along."

He laughed. "If I'd wanted to talk to her all along, I wouldn't have left her."

We looked at each other.

"What did she tell you?" he asked after a moment. "That I just disappeared?"

"She didn't tell me anything," I said. "You *did* disappear."

He laughed without amusement. "Okay, okay. I was under a lot of stress, and I disappeared. But as soon as things calmed down a little, I wanted to see you and she talked me out of it."

I couldn't tell if I *wanted* to believe him, much less whether I did.

"How?" I asked.

"She said you were used to not having me around and I'd just stir you up again. She also had Whatsisname by then, and she said he was like a second father to you."

I didn't want to cry, he'd only tell me to stop, but I couldn't tolerate the feelings that were being aroused in me. I was angry with him on Tony's behalf, anxious and guilty on my mother's, and terribly, terribly needy on my own. "I can't believe, or I can't understand, anyway, how she could've . . . you could've . . . I wasn't close to Tony till . . . I can't understand anything." The tears came and rapidly grew uncontrollable.

My father uttered a soft oath, pulled his chair over to me, sat down again, changed his mind, took me by the hand and helped me out of the chair, then led me into the living room where we sat down on the sofa. He put his arm around me, and I cried for a long time. At some point he said he realized he'd made a mistake, he hadn't understood that I was afraid of being left alone with my mother and he wouldn't suggest it again. He said it was also clear that he and I had a great deal to talk about in the days ahead. Not that he was certain talking ever cleared up matters the way people hoped it would. Indeed, it was possible that all we really needed was to be together for a while and get to know and trust each other again.

It is tempting in writing about the past to present it in a sort of emotional tandem with the present. I find myself wanting to claim now that sitting with my father's arm around me that day, I thought of Hugo. It would surely be fair to say that they were the only men who had ever aroused in me those simultaneous and extreme feelings of love and rage, distrust and need. As it would be fair to say that for much of my life I've steered clear of men who might again arouse feelings powerful enough to overwhelm me. But I don't think I thought of Hugo or of anyone else. I thought of my father and of the past, of the present and what might be the future. I thought of what was true and what was false and what part of each he might be telling me. I held back from him as much of my brain as I could, but I seem not to have had the option of holding back my self.

I had a self now—surely one had to have a self to love opera—but to acknowledge the possession of a self is to admit that one might need protection. If the past was not amenable to reason or susceptible to control, surely that self who existed so clearly as to love opera and Italian food while she was home, rock music and tortillas when she was with her friends, still needed some protection—assistance, if you will—in making her way through the world. And unfortunately the person most clearly capable of assisting her was also the person from whom she might most need protection.

I said I had a terrible headache. My father found me some aspirin in the powder-room cabinet. I said I didn't think I could call Tony's daughters. He called them. (He took me into the kitchen with him when he made the calls because I tended to clutch at him when he tried to move away.) He did it beautifully—gave them the warning, let the seconds lapse, then told them. Each said she would be there as soon as possible and asked if her sister knew.

I said I was afraid to be alone with Violet. He said he would bring over Estella to take care of her.

I stared at him.

"Estella?" Estella was supposed to have returned to her family in Mexico at the time of my parents' divorce.

My father smiled.

"The very same, sweetheart. And won't you be happy to see her."

"I thought she went back to Mexico."

"She did, but I went down after her and dragged her back."

"When?"

His smile hardened. I hadn't intended to be difficult, but the years since I'd seen him were coming between us in a tangible way. I found myself wondering how he'd managed without a studio job and why, if he was doing well, he hadn't insisted upon contacting me. It was ludicrous to think of his having been controlled by Violet.

"I'll tell you what," he said a trifle grimly. "Let's take care of everything we have to do today. Then some day, as soon as we have some time to spare, we'll dig out my old checkbooks and get the precise date of employment."

"I didn't mean—" I began to protest, but he interrupted me.

"I know, I know." He rumpled my hair and spoke gruffly, but he was making the transition. If his conscience had been as fully developed as the rest of him, he would have found it more difficult. "Look, we're bound to have some rough spots here and there, especially until we have time for some real conversation so you can at least know what was going on with me these few years. Without that, I'm just this son-of-a-bitch who left you for . . . Anyway, for now . . ."

He proceeded to deal effectively with the For Now.

First he arranged for a car to be sent for Estella. Then he talked to his wife, whom he called alternately Sweetheart, Lovechild and Lynn, to explain why she would have to part with Estella for a couple of days. He waited impatiently as she registered what were apparently strong objections to this scheme, and responded in a voice kinder than anyone who'd been watching him as she spoke might have anticipated. He told her that Violet was in crisis and if she were not properly cared for now, the burden on "everyone" might become greater (a marvelous threat, delivered in tones of loving concern). He reminded her, in a tone bordering on righteous indignation, that there were people in the world beside herself to whom he had some obligation. He told her that the cook would certainly help her with the children until such time as a good temporary maid could be arranged, but that she should know that until such time, perhaps a matter of a couple of hours [sic], she would not be alone in the house. On the contrary, he would be bringing with him a lovely young woman whom she did not yet know, but who was—a wink at me—one of his favorite daughters. Then he let her do whatever she was doing on the other end of the phone for what seemed like a long time before asking, in an exaggeratedly polite tone, if she was finished.

"We'll be there within an hour," he said. "Tell Estella to get ready to be picked up. Pronto."

And he hung up without waiting for a response.

"So. What next? Do we have to warn Violet?"

I shook my head. "As long as there's someone taking care of her, she doesn't care who it is."

A slightly grim smile. "Let's hope that continues. Because it's not going to be you."

Gratitude flooded me, making speech impossible. The tears in

53

my eyes were too respectful of him to fall out. My hands clasped each other in what would surely be permanent congratulation. My previous doubts felt like symptoms of ingratitude. I watched him and waited.

He stretched and yawned.

"Mmm. Hungry. What time is it, anyway?" He looked at his watch, whistled. "No wonder. What's to eat around here?"

I scrambled to my feet and went to look in the refrigerator. The first thing I saw was a jar of homemade marinara sauce. Tony put up bushels of tomatoes at the end of each summer which he used to make his two basic sauces, meat (with sweet sausage and chuck) and marinara. Even during these last weeks, when he'd done relatively little cooking, there'd always been sauce at hand.

Guilt returned. Where was Tony in all this?

My father saw my stricken expression and misinterpreted it as concern for him.

"Don't worry about it. We'll get a pizza. No, wait a minute. We're in L.A." He flashed one of his best smiles. "I've been spending too much time in New York. Half the time I don't know where I'm at. Tacos."

"We need to have some real food in the refrigerator, anyway," I pointed out. "If Violet . . . and Estella . . . are going to be staying here."

"Good thinking."

He picked up the phone, dialed Jurgensen's, where we'd always had an account (Tony was outraged by their prices and wouldn't shop there for the smallest item), and proceeded to dictate a list that included items like "a ton of vegetables and cottage cheese and some ripe fruit, and some not so ripe." It seemed clear from the speed with which he was able to proceed that they were accustomed to his style. This was interesting. I could not imagine the same would have been the case in the days when we were together, when he would take me to Nate and Al's for breakfast before he would think of buying bread to make toast at home.

Estella arrived, greeted me with a combination of familiarity and embarrassment and commented favorably on the way I was growing up. We let her make a trial run up to Violet's room to make sure there would be no difficulty. She came down to report that Miss Violet had asked her about dinner.

"Terrific," my father said. "If you do any ordering, make sure they get the address right."

Make sure they get the address right.

It hit me as he said it—the same groceries going to a different address—though I didn't understand why until later. Perhaps he'd been that way even before he came to California and The Business. His first married groceries, after all, had been delivered on the East Coast. But my father was always leading the same life with new personnel. He didn't mind if the old personnel turned up as long as we fit easily into the new picture.

On that day he brought me to the house where I had been raised, which Violet had told me had been sold to someone named Grey. (It had, but Grey was Lynn's name from her first marriage.) In that house was much of the furniture that I'd been told had been purchased by the people who bought the house. Also there were the cook and gardener who had been our cook and gardener when we were all married. In addition to servants and furniture, there was in the house a small but attractive family consisting of Lynn, who was blond instead of dark-haired but almost as beautiful as Violet—or so I would decide in consciously objective fashion when my brain could work again—and two beautiful little girls. These girls were, of course, my father's third and fourth daughters, Sonya, more often called Sonny, perhaps because it had been Lynn's conviction during pregnancy that she was carrying a boy, and Liane.

I think it's possible that if those two girls had not been a part of the picture, I might readily—*eagerly*—have allowed myself to ease right back into it. Lynn didn't really bother me. She did not deal with me directly. If she needed something done that I might be able to do for her, she would ask my father, in my presence, who he thought might be so good as to perform that task. Her way of dealing with other men was to let them look at her and wait for them to offer their services. Her way of dealing with Sonny and Liane was to ask them not to do something and ignore whether or not they obeyed, except that if some specific inconvenience arose, she would call, in order of preference: my father, Estella, the cook, me, anyone else who happened to be around.

This last, alone, made her *modus operandi* distinctly different from that of Violet, who never gave orders that did not pertain to her immediate physical comfort and probably wouldn't have noticed if I had chosen to play with matches, for example, unless she was afraid the room would become too warm. On the other hand, it bore a certain resemblance to my father's way of moving through life as though each new group of people had been sent by Central Casting and could be replaced at will without anguish—virtually

55

without difficulty of any kind. Of course, when difficulties did arise, the fact that people didn't exist made them much easier to handle.

I slept when my father wasn't home and followed him around the house when he was (I should say, when he was home and not locked in his study with the men with whom he was forming Egremont Studios). I was afraid of dreaming about Tony and waking up, frightened, in the middle of the night. Instead I dreamed about Violet and couldn't wake up in the morning. Well, not actually about Violet. I dreamed about Violet's doll.

Violet had been orphaned when her parents, fighters in the Dutch Resistance, were killed during the Nazi occupation of the Netherlands. Smuggled to cousins in London, she had later been shipped by those cousins to a family up north. Back in London at the end of the war, now sixteen years old, she had been discovered by the person I called my grandmother, Sylvia Starr, who was childless, and who had persuaded Abe to adopt Violet and bring her to Hollywood.

Violet had a doll she kept in a glass-fronted cabinet in her silver-and-lavender bedroom. The doll's name was Mooty, or at least that's the closest I can come to a phonetic spelling (the two o's are pronounced as they are in "book"). Mooty's porcelain face was cracked, her legs were gone and her arms had been resewn to her cloth body so often that the shoulders were now attached at the middle of her bedraggled cloth torso. She wore a beautiful black lace gown and a mantilla. My father had tried more than once, while he was still with us, to convince Violet to allow him to bring Mooty to a dollmaker who would restore her, but Violet was unwilling to let the doll out of her sight. They had been through the war together. A birthday present from Violet's parents, Mooty had slept with her in an Amsterdam basement; accompanied her (neither having any clothes but those on her back) to the north of England; been carried in a blanket back to London and traveled first class to America. In the period between my father's and Tony's occupancy, Mooty had slept next to Violet in the big bed. Violet was convinced that if anything happened to Mooty, her own life would end.

I hadn't thought much about the doll in recent years, but in those first nights back in my father's house, I dreamed of her all the time. Sometimes she had her own face, and sometimes she had Violet's, and there were still other times when she was surely some-one I knew, but I couldn't say whom. In one of the few dreams that

I remembered, Mooty wanted to come to Tony's funeral, and I grew increasingly frustrated trying to make her understand how inappropriate this would be. (Upon awakening, I became even more upset because I couldn't remember what my arguments had been.)

If Lynn and her children were not in my remembered dreams, their presence in the house that had been my home often seemed to resemble a dream more than it did real life. Lynn's manner toward me was gracious even as it managed to convey the distinct sense that we had no past together to quarrel about or future together to enjoy. (My adult view is that she thought about neither while she had sufficient household help.) Long ago my father had called girls who looked like Lynn *supergoyls* (I don't recall our Jewishness being expressed except in opposition to someone), but I had no idea of whether he would remember that now. Indeed, I couldn't be sure if he thought the same way about anything anymore, largely because I couldn't be sure he was the same person. I looked forward to the talk we were going to have as a way of learning how he really felt about Lynn, not to mention how I really felt about him. Things were too hectic just then, he'd made clear, for the kind of conversation we needed.

Lynn worked at the studio in some job the specifics of which were not clear to me—and indeed there might not have been any—except that she had an office. Some day she wanted to "do" a film. She was a little distraught my first days at the house because without "The Real Estella," Sonny, the older girl, was difficult for anyone but my father, who was away all day, to control. There was, as I've said, plenty of other help, but Sonny would have none of them. She kept demanding The Real Estella, which irritated Lynn hugely since another perfectly pleasant and reasonable Mexican woman, "another Estella," as she told the child, had been sent by the same agency. Sonny continued to throw one tantrum each morning as my father left and others at unpredictable times during the day. Three days later, when her own Estella returned, I was astonished to observe a radically different child in Sonny's body, a little girl who followed the woman around the house like a happy puppy on an invisible leash and readily obeyed any order or prohibition that rather solemn person issued.

Sonny was seven and, like the platinum-blond four-year-old Liane, she was a beautiful little girl. Her reddish blond curls were just beginning to deepen in color toward what would finally be a

57

reddish brown, and I recall her proudly telling me how some day her hair would be as dark as Estella's.

"Oh?" I asked, pleased that she'd deigned to speak to me at all. "Is that the way you want it to be?"

She nodded. "Black and all shiny. Like Estella's. I don't want it to be yukky"—I doubt that was the word she used, but it was the sixties' equivalent—"like Liane's."

We were in the lanai. She and I had been looking at magazines. Sonny lay on the rug while I sat in one of the rattan armchairs. Liane sat in another, doing absolutely nothing. She was the first person, not to say child, I had ever known who could do nothing for some time without appearing to be sleepy, depressed or contemplative.

Sonny giggled and went into one of her baby-word routines—on the order of "Yukky pishy ukky poo," the sort of thing she never did when Estella was around. Liane appeared not to hear her, but I was uneasy.

"Oh," I said, "I wouldn't call it—"

"Look!" Sonny exclaimed, scrambling to her feet with the magazine she'd been reading, which she thrust under my eyes. I was looking at a full-page color photograph of Elizabeth Taylor. "Look at Estella. I'm going to have hair like Estella when I grow up!"

My brain carried around, in a sort of weird tandem, old and new images of my father. When the rosy old image threatened to block out the later one, when I found myself following him out the door as he left the house because whether or not there was another Sunshine, *I* could rise and set only on him, I dragged back the older and more suspicious Nell as a sort of control. Watching his back as he walked toward the car, wishing only that if he couldn't stay, he would take me with him, I'd close my eyes to picture the same walk on a younger, heavier man who might, without warning, disappear for five years. For all I knew, he would not be home that night. After all, he was talking about controlling Egremont so the filmmaking couldn't be dominated by the New York money men, but in the old days, he had been fond of saying, when people tried talking film to him, that he didn't know from film, he was just a guy from New York who knew something about money.

I fought a perpetual battle with my sense of unreality by eating all the time. I ate more in my first two or three days at my father's house than I normally did in a week and hung around to help out in the kitchen, where no help was needed. I couldn't read or listen to music of any kind. Packing to leave my mother's house on the night of Tony's death, I had gone to his study and taken his favorite (Caruso) record of *Il Trovatore*, which I'd wrapped and placed in the bottom of the valise I was bringing to my father's. But I didn't play it when I got there nor, indeed, did I listen to opera again for many years.

Tony's daughters made the funeral arrangements, having ascertained that there would be no interference from Violet and me. By common consent my father's secretary Peggy Cafferty was the daughters' contact, while Patsy's husband, Leonard Biancardi, was ours. The name of Theresa's husband, Jack Campbell, is familiar to everyone who followed the lawsuit.

I had met both couples when Violet married Tony. Neither of the Campbells had made an impression strong enough to last during the interim years, when I'd seen the Biancardis perhaps once a year, but the Campbells not at all. Leonard was even-tempered, Patsy bossy and hostile. I was not surprised when the daughters failed to contact Violet or offer to share our common misery. On the contrary, they advised Peggy that anything Violet had to say should be said to their lawyer. And during one of my conversations with Peggy Cafferty she conveyed to me her distinct impression that Violet was not "expected" at the funeral.

Violet had nothing to say and nothing to ask about the funeral or anything else. I'd called her once or twice, more out of guilt than concern, and the conversations had centered, as always, around her anxiety about her physical comfort. In the context of Tony's death, that anxiety had come to seem like madness.

I had no desire to talk to any of my friends, although a couple of them tried to reach me. My father had offered to have a phone installed in my room (Beverly Hills was, of course, the birthplace of the teen-ager's separate listing), but I'd told him I had no need of one. (Later he would do it anyway.) I had always made friends easily, but I lacked the desire for that one closer-than-close pal who was of monumental importance in a girl's life. Girls were good to hang out with, accompany you to the movies, and so on. They tended to trust you if you didn't tell their secrets, and not only did I lack some critical desire to tell, but most of the time I found those secrets scarcely interesting enough to remember. If you got really close to another girl you would surely find a Mooty in her closet, some cracked and pathetic remnant of childhood need that told you more about her than you wanted to know, certainly more than you could learn from all the pajama parties and two-hour phone calls after school.

Actually, Ingrid and Lana had decided to attend the funeral without telling me. It's difficult to say whether they did this because I was hard to reach or because they knew I would tell them not to come and they were determined to take part in the festivities.

I haven't been in that part of Los Angeles in twenty years, but my memory is that the church was called St. Mary's and that it was somewhere around Ninth and Valencia. If I were told that neither the name nor the location was possible, I would believe it. My father had offered to send me in a studio car but instinct had made me tell him I wanted a cab.

If churches are good for anything, of course, it's funerals. They foster an appropriate solemnity while discouraging you—or me, at any rate—from a display of all those messy feelings you'd rather hold at bay. I had hoped my father would offer to accompany me, but he had two important meetings, one at the office of his lawyer, another at home with a director, and I'd not even asked. Tony's daughters and their solicitous husbands, greeting people just inside the entrance, nodded politely but did not invite me to stand with them as they received people or to sit with them inside. Thus I was relieved instead of annoyed to find Ingrid and Lana sitting midway down the chapel, the rows in front of them already full, the back rows still empty. It wasn't until the end of the ceremony that a couple of things happened to make me regret not only their presence but my own.

The coffin had been closed, and we stood as the pallbearers moved slowly down the aisle. The front doors of the church were open. I was looking around, thinking of how many friends and relatives Tony had had and understanding for the first time the extent of the life he had given up in marrying Violet.

The obituary, written by Patsy and Theresa, made no mention of Tony's second marriage, so we hadn't drawn the creepy would-be-feelies Violet's name would have attracted, and the ceremony had been appropriately sedate. Now, however, our luck came to an end. As we stood facing the aisle, there was a stir toward the back of the church. Heads turned. Violet walked in, leaning on my father's arm, looking like a cross between Scarlett O'Hara after Rhett tells her off and Victoria Regina after the death of Albert. She wore a black silk dress with an unsuitably low V-neck, a black pillbox with an elaborate veil, sheer black stockings, high-heeled patent-leather pumps and a pearl-and-diamond choker with matching earrings. She was carrying a lace-trimmed handkerchief, which was just as well, since a substantial number of tears were visiting her face for the occasion. The veil fell loosely enough to allow her to dab at those tears and was dense enough to conceal any damage they might do. Added to my embarrassment at being related to this person was a certain anger with my father over his consent to accompany her.

TV cameras were visible on the sidewalk. The cameramen had been too smart to try to follow the lovely couple into the church but had remained on the sidewalk outside the front door, doing what they generally described as just their job. If I'd had to put money on it then (or now) I would say it was Violet who had summoned them. But she was a trouper. When Jack Campbell, with an oath, made a dash around the two charming figures (my father wore a sports jacket and slacks but had forced himself to put on a tie) and pulled shut the two doors, Violet did not appear to notice but simply continued down the aisle. Tony's people, astonished, appalled and helpless but probably curious and here and there sympathetic as well, stared at her and at each other as she proceeded toward the coffin, which was moving slowly toward her. When they met, the pallbearers stopped and not only allowed Violet to reach up and touch the coffin but actually stooped to lower it so that she might kiss it as well.

I glanced at Patsy and Theresa. Both were frozen still, but Patsy was red with rage. I could feel Ingrid and Lana in back of me. One of them (I couldn't remember at the moment which one had been directly to my right) reached for my hand as though to squeeze it; resolutely I folded my arms across my chest. The procession, now headed by Violet and my father, moved through the once-again-open doors into the daylight.

Sounds of a fracas reached my ears although the people in front of me blocked my view of what was happening. The people in back of me wanted to see the action, too, and I could feel pressure to move into the aisle, but I was unwilling or unable to do so. Finally I turned so I was facing the front of the pew, and they were able to get past me. All of them, including Ingrid and Lana, which made it easier for me to know how to treat them in the future. I turned back.

Those people who were still inside were craning their necks to get a view of the action outside, except one young woman who remained standing in the very last pew. She appeared to have little interest in what was going on but rather to be staring at me. Even before my brain had any idea of who she might be, my body started in that way infants have that makes them seem to have just arrived from another dimension.

She was tall and had increased her height with high heels. She wore clothes that were black but still managed to be inappropriate for a funeral—a satin cowboy shirt with nailheads in the yoke and a straight, tight-fitting black skirt banded by a wide belt with a weird buckle in the shape of a coiled snake. It was apparent even from a distance that she wore a lot of makeup. Still more striking was a wavy, wildly disordered mane of hair exactly the same reddish blond color as my father's and mine.

Louisa—perhaps you've figured out even if I hadn't that she was my older half sister—smiled.

I want to describe Louisa's smile as I came to think of it, rather than in the way I might have seen it at the time. I came to think of it as her storyteller's smile—a small, slightly lopsided grimace promising that while life was not turning out as she'd wished, she would have her revenge in writing about it. (Or about something people would *believe* was it.) The smile did not reflect pleasure. I don't mean just at the funeral, when pleasure would have been inappropriate. I mean that I never saw Louisa purely happy, simply enjoying herself, unless she was drunk. When she was sober, she always had some agenda nobody else could follow.

Even before catching sight of her I had been less than eager to join the mob on the sidewalk. Now I could hear loud voices outside. A young priest glided across the empty vestibule and closed the big doors, nodding nervously toward us and then back to the doors, as though to assure us that we would be able to leave when we wished. Because I didn't know what else to do, I moved up the aisle. Because I felt I had no choice, I stopped at Louisa's row and waited.

She smiled that funny, pained smile and said hello. One of her eyes focused just slightly off center, which made her look as though her mind were elsewhere.

I nodded. My lips and throat were dry. I wondered if they had been that way all through the funeral and I just hadn't noticed.

"You know who I am?" she asked in her New York speech that I'd seldom heard outside of gangster movies.

I shook my head because I didn't, although I felt as though I were lying.

"Louisa Abrahms," she said in a manner suggesting that I

would find the name significant. She ran the fingers of one hand through her hair and waited for me to react.

"I'm sorry," I finally said. "I—"

She was both curious and disconcerted.

"You don't know who Louisa Abrahms is?"

Again I shook my head.

"How about Louisa Pearlstein? That's my maiden name."

I waited, speechless, although it had begun to get through.

"Do you know that you have another sister someplace? Or, I should say, half a sister?" She flashed a small, sardonic smile, another of her specialties. "A half sister?"

I nodded. I knew, if I didn't exactly *know* it. My father had told me just before he left us, but it was in the middle of a discussion about something else and it had refused to register in the file where my brain kept its accounts.

"Sure," I said. "I'm sorry. I knew, but I didn't know. I mean, I didn't know your name."

"Oh, terrific," she said. "That sounds just like him."

I think it struck me even then that while she was older than I, she sounded like a disgruntled kid.

She waited for me to respond, to encourage or at least to engage her, but loud noises outside the church door reminded me of the reason I was inside. If I didn't exactly *want* to find out what the noises were about, it seemed incumbent upon me to do so.

"I'm sorry," I said. "I'm . . . I think I have to go out and see what's happening."

She fixed me with that intent stare of hers, or, rather, with a stare that would have been intent had it not been sabotaged by the disobedient, wandering eye.

"Do you want me to just go away quietly?" she asked.

"No," I said, beginning to feel slightly desperate, "of course not. I mean, I don't know *what* I want. I just have to go out and see about Tony."

I didn't wait for a response but left her standing in the pew. I walked to the back and with some difficulty pushed open one of the big, heavy doors.

The sidewalk was chaos. The pallbearers had gotten the coffin into the hearse, but the hearse's back door was still down, and Violet stood to one side, both hands on the coffin, her head as close to it as could be managed, weeping. The cameras and cameramen had been pushed back into the street but they were still working. My father was shouting at Jack Campbell that he hadn't asked the cameras to come and hadn't the power to make them leave. Patsy was standing—or trying to stand—between the two of them, screaming that my father was a liar and they should get the hell out of there, this wasn't a movie star's funeral, it had nothing to do with the movies. My father said in his voice-of-reason voice that he gathered the young lady thought that because the widow had been in the movies, she had no right to mourn for her husband.

At this point, Patsy went for him with her fingernails, the cameraman turned his camera away from Violet and the procession and onto the two of them, and I went back into the church, closing the door behind me.

Louisa stood where I had left her. I didn't look at her but sat down in the corresponding pew on the other side of the aisle, resting my elbows on my knees and my face in my hands. I closed my eyes. My face tingled as though it had pins and needles, a phenomenon that was new to me.

Where are you, Tony?

It was as though I needed him there before I could mourn for him. Not only could I not cry, I couldn't get any sense at all of what I could or *should* do. My father had not warned me that Violet might decide to show up. (It hadn't occurred to him until he'd called her from the studio that morning to check on the new maid, and Violet had complained about having to read the *Los Angeles Times* to find out that there was a funeral. Probably she hadn't thought about Tony until she read the paper and was turned on by the prospect of an occasion for display.) My father had said that if Patsy and Theresa wanted me to go to the cemetery, they would find room for me in one of the cars. Now that seemed even less likely than it had before. (It had never been likely. A lack of sophistication prevented me, thank goodness, from understanding that Patsy, at least, resented me as much as she hated my mother.)

Finally I looked up. Louisa was still standing there, watching and waiting.

"Please sit down," I said.

She sat, but I felt as though she were still standing.

I could ask her to leave me alone, but I didn't actually want to be alone, and there was no one else around who seemed the least bit concerned about my welfare. Perhaps my father cared more about me than about Violet, but his concern was not visible at the moment, if only because the events that required his attention were occurring around *her*. Lana and Ingrid—was it a wonder I had never trusted them?—were out there also. Given the choice between keeping me company and participating in an event they could talk about in school, they hadn't hesitated for a moment.

"I hope you didn't like that guy a lot," Louisa said. "This is a hell of a funeral."

"He was like a real father to me," I said.

She laughed.

I looked at her again, really looked, for the first time since we'd met. She made me uneasy. The fact of her *existence* made me uneasy, but it wasn't just that. Maybe it was the outward-turning eye that made you think she was reserving judgment for sometime when she'd be in a position to cut off your head.

"Are you going to the cemetery?" I asked.

She shrugged. "Don't know."

I hesitated. "How come you're here?"

"Curiosity," she said. "I guess I was curious. About you, I mean. Not about him."

"Do you live in L.A.?"

She hesitated. "Not exactly." A rueful little smile. "I mean, I do now, I suppose. I moved here but I still don't exactly think of myself as *living* here."

I wanted to ask how old she was, but I was sure I was supposed to know and she'd question (or make fun of) my ignorance. If I'd had to guess, I'd have said she was twenty-seven, and since I'd never had to guess ages, and she was exactly twenty-seven, it's my assumption I remembered more of that conversation with my father than I knew I did. On the other hand, Louisa seemed to change from moment to moment in stance and attitude and, somehow, in age. At this moment, with her belligerence in remission, she seemed even younger than she had before.

"Does my f—our father—know you're here?"

She laughed. "Our Father." (The initial caps are hers.) "Yes. Our Father . . . your father, as I think of him, knows I'm here. When I moved here, I tried to get a job, get myself all set up without needing him so when I called he wouldn't think I . . . Anyway, it was no dice. I wasn't good-looking enough to be a secretary at a studio, or any place remotely interesting. Finally we took a meeting, as they say, and he got me a job. At *Honey* magazine, to be precise." She rolled her eyes in mock despair. "Although I don't trust everyone enough to tell them that."

I couldn't blame her. Long before the flowering of the Women's Movement, females of all ages and many descriptions were made uneasy by *Honey*'s odd mating of high-fidelity equipment and naked girls.

"Actually," she said, "the work's more ordinary than anyone

65

dreams. Only the frills are different. But you probably know all about it from your father."

"Why?" I asked. "What does *he* have to do with them?"

"Are you kidding?"

I shook my head.

"He half-owned the magazine," she said. "The owners, Teddy and Sal, they got most of their start-up money from him. They were army buddies, they and your father. You really didn't know that? Actually, I don't know why I'm surprised. The man didn't tell you he had another kid for years, why should he mention a lousy magazine?"

I grew uneasy and began to listen for sounds at the church door. Louisa was off on what I would later recognize as one of her interior monologues that just happened to be spoken aloud, and failed to notice my squirming.

"I'm not saying it's a lousy magazine. I mean, it is and it isn't. I'm just in a bad mood this week so you have to take a cross between what I say now and what I say next week when I love it. Teddy and Sal raised about five thousand apiece and then came to your father for the rest of it. They've earned it a thousand times over since then, as I've earned the job, whether he got it for me or not. I brought order out of chaos. From the time when they left the beach house . . . Never mind, I can see you don't know anything about it. Anyway, I once told Teddy they should call me House Mother instead of General Manager. Actually, I wish I'd never said it. I could swear there's been a change in the way he treats me since then. I think he's got a thing about Mother. Just the *word* bothers him. It gets edited out of articles and stuff. If he had his way, little girls would get their ovaries removed and just grow tits. He has a kid, actually. He was married for a couple of years. He *calls* it a couple of years, it was more like eight or nine. He air-brushed it after that. The marriage, I mean. Just like . . . The women he goes for—the little girls with big tits, I should say, that he goes for—they look as though someone did an airbrush job on their brains before they got to the centerfold and someone propped up their boobs. Anyway, here's the real question. Are we going to stay here until they've all left or are we going to brave it out? Get to the car? Go to the cemetery? A cup of coffee? Whatever?"

"Whatever," I repeated. She had moved so rapidly from one subject to the other that I felt helpless and confused, if still willing to do as she liked. It wasn't as though I had a plan of my own.

Beckoning to me to follow, she walked cautiously—it would

have been tiptoe if it hadn't been for her very high heels—to the back. Nothing could be heard through the heavy wooden doors. Slowly she pushed one open just a little. Then farther.

"You're not going to believe this," she said, stepping down so that she was half outside, "but there's nobody here."

"Nobody?" Perhaps I'd hoped until that moment that when I finally decided to venture outside, my father, with or without Violet, would be waiting for me.

"Come see for yourself."

Indeed, the sidewalk was empty, the TV trucks, the hearse and the limousines were gone from the street. Cars whizzed past in what felt, at the moment, like a denial of what had been happening earlier. Was it all over because the TV people had folded their gear, or vice versa? I let the door swing shut behind me and followed Louisa down the block to her car, a little black Volkswagen that reminded me of Hugo's. Where was Hugo now? I hadn't thought of him in ages. And where were we going anyway? It would be nice to sort of run across him accidentally and have one or two of those old sessions that had been such fun. I was more sophisticated now and could probably handle a little pleasure without all that non-sense of thinking I was in love.

"Are we going to the cemetery?" I asked Louisa.

She said it was up to me. She had directions and could probably find it if I wanted her to.

"Don't you care one way or the other?" I asked.

She shrugged. "If I want to see what a funeral's like, I can always find a funeral to go to."

This is a perfect example of Louisa's telling the truth in a way that made you want to argue. Her very manner of being in the world had to do, and still does, with weaving life's events into a narrative with a striking if crucially lopsided relation to reality, at once inaccurate and unanswerable because she never claimed to be reporting. Unless you referred to pure fiction, in which case she was likely to say there was no such thing—even a plane flying through the clouds had to have taken off from someplace.

She had wanted to meet me because she was curious, and she needed to meet people in general because she was lonely. But she'd choose villainy over being a creature of need, and in fact she's always done the same job on her characters as she does on herself. Men who are themselves confused and bedeviled (I'm not speaking here of my father who has always, in my mind as well as hers, occupied a class by himself) and who do some damage to others along the way end up as unconflicted and unquestioning villains when she writes about them. Events determined by a multiplicity of people and coincidences generate plots in which the women need to comfort each other while the man is, at the very least, hung on a crucifix of irony. Not that the women, in the long run, act a lot better than the men. But you tend to rationalize their acts, if only because you see events through their eyes and better understand their motives.

It is perhaps unnecessary to say these were not the thoughts that were running through my head on that day in 1965 when Louisa was twenty-seven years old and I was not quite seventeen and the most important adult in my life had just died and Louisa had decided to be my friend but needed first to wear me down to a point where she could tolerate me. Nor is it possible for me to know how I would have reacted to her had she not been my father's daughter. What I remember feeling from the beginning was a witches' brew of neediness, curiosity, pleasure and unease. I think I might have run from her like crazy had I not felt, briefly but keenly, that I needed her as a friend.

We got in the Volks and drove in silence for a while. I did not pay attention to our route. I assumed we were heading toward the cemetery, since Louisa hadn't told me that we were not. (She hadn't told me we were not because she assumed that we were, although she also knew that she had a tendency to get lost in Los Angeles.)

"Did you grow up in New York?" I asked after a long while. It wasn't the question that most interested me, but it seemed like a reasonable preamble.

She sighed. "Your father and my mother were teen-age sweet-hearts. When he came from Vineland so he could go to school in New York—you must know about that—he came to live with her and my grandparents."

I was silent. I had not yet heard of Vineland or much of anything else in my father's past. He always sounded as though his life had begun in California.

"I'm sorry," she said. "I know how that sounded. I was feeling defensive." Louisa was always sticking knives into people and then analyzing the composition of the blade. "I feel a little ridiculous. I've been following you, sort of knowing your life, chapter and verse, and then I walk in feeling as though I know you and . . ."

If she was waiting for me to finish her sentence or to assure her that everything was all right, she was going to be disappointed.

". . . and then it turns out you barely knew about me. Or if you did, you didn't care."

"I only found out there was another family when my father was leaving," I said after a while. Then I heard what I'd said. "I'm doing what you told me to do, calling him mine, but I don't know why. He's yours, too."

"Not really. I never really knew him. I was too little when he left. I wasn't even five."

I couldn't remember what I'd known when I was five. There was the time when I'd had my father and the time when he was gone. The time when Tony had made it possible for me to forget him, and now . . .

"Didn't your mother remarry?" I asked.

"Mmm," Louisa said, "but he was a real . . ."

"A real . . . ?" I prompted. I was genuinely interested.

"Oh, what difference does it make." The subject irritated her. "He was a real little shit. We got along for about two and a half minutes and then—it was war for the rest of the time I was home."

We were silent for a while, moving rapidly along the freeway (being in unfamiliar territory never stopped Louisa from driving at well above the speed limit). Occasionally I glanced at her without turning my head; I had the sense that she was struggling constantly with herself over things she wanted to say and thought she shouldn't. After a while she took an exit and began heading inland. After another few minutes, she told me that we were lost. She'd thought she remembered the directions, but she hadn't written them down, and at the moment she wasn't even sure we were traveling south, as we were supposed to be.

I told her that we had been moving south on the freeway but now we were heading east, that if she didn't have a feeling yet for California directions (I didn't know there were people who never acquired one) she should try to remember that most often when you were facing a wide range of mountains, you were heading east. Inland.

She said, "No shit," a phrase that fell more harshly on my ears in those days than it would later, being much less in general use. I remember thinking that if she was representative of the girls where she'd lived, perhaps I ought not to think of going East to college.

Her response to my silence was to tell me about her life.

I was accustomed to hearing Hollywood discussed as though it were the capital of the world and its doings more important than anything that might transpire in New York or Washington. (Kennedy's assassination was the first real-life event that had touched us as heavily as the failure of a movie, perhaps because of the movie form in which we received the news.) But I had never heard anyone talk about herself in the way Louisa did—somehow conveying the impression that if her body had left home, her mind was still there twenty-four hours a day, hashing over history in a way that made it feel more real than current events. Nor had I ever seen anyone so adept at using the world of the self (both her own and others') to fill conversational spaces and/or to pull the talk away from matters of what you might call, for purposes of identification, the real world. She loved to talk about her own self, but she was almost as happy to discuss other people's. She might find some anecdote that was, or appeared to be, at least peripherally related to the topic under discussion—the Kennedys, Op Art, the new Beatles movie—but she invariably used that anecdote to lead the listener away from the Kennedys, Op Art or the Beatles into her private world.

If I remember correctly, the first link in this particular conversational chain had to do with the mountains. Louisa said it was funny she'd made that particular error, since she'd wanted to drive into the mountains since the day she'd first seen them on the way from the airport; she had lacked only a proper driving companion. Now here she was with someone she'd been wanting to talk to anyway, driving toward some mountains that looked about as good as any of the others she'd seen. . . . This reminded her of the first time she'd seen the Smokies. The creep her mother had married loved taking these ghastly long driving vacations, and she had a choice, basically, of going to some lousy girls' camp or going on vacation with them. There was no way it would have been fun, any way you looked at it, but Reuben's idea of a vacation was driving through the Smokies with the car windows shut tight, looking for bears to be scared of.

"I'm not sure I ever would've left home if it hadn't been for Reuben," Louisa said. "My mother and I had a perfect setup, the two of us. She was depressed for a long time after your father copped out, but then she went back to school and became an accountant. Probably a better one than he ever was. Well, let's not get into that one. Anyway, she ended up being Reuben's boss, and he was such a creep he didn't mind. Speaking of minding—do you mind if we don't get to your pal's burial? I'm sorry. Your stepfather's. I know he was very important to you. I was just feeling . . . It was like when I had my eye operation, and they promised they'd be there when I woke up, no matter how long it took, and then of course they weren't."

I sat in a confused and increasingly resentful silence as she drove through neighborhoods I had never seen and told me stories I didn't want to hear. I began to think about Tony and to blame Louisa—unfairly, of course—for my not having been able to find consolation in the funeral. I *wanted* to think about Tony. It was bearably painful to think about Tony. While every time I remembered my father's escorting Violet in her Victoria Regina O'Hara outfit down the church aisle, I felt like screaming or jumping out of the moving car. *Why hadn't my father thought about my feelings?* Why hadn't he seen what it would do to me, the two of them walking in like that, even without the damned television cameras in back of them? And if he couldn't dissuade Violet from doing her little number, at least he could have found some way to warn me!

When I opened my eyes, with no memory of having closed them, we were parked in front of my home. That is to say, Tony's home.

"Found it!" Louisa announced triumphantly when she saw that my eyes were open.

I shook my head.

"No, what?"

"I've been living with my father since Tony died."

"You have?"

I heard it as an accusation. I started to explain that Violet was being taken care of but then became aware that Louisa wasn't listening to me but was watching something in the rearview mirror.

"Don't look now," she said, "but they're back already. Or someone is. There's a limo pulling to the curb in back of us. What do you say we just get out of here?"

"Mmm."

She started up the engine and drove into, then through, the center of Beverly Hills, heading up toward my father's house. By this time she had resumed the saga of her life.

She had left the Bronx after a couple of years of college, got married to Dave Abrahms, had a kid, Benjamin (my head whipped around at that one but she pretended not to notice), left the kid, Ben, with Dave, whom Ben liked much more than he liked her, and come out to Los Angeles, figuring she'd finish school out here if her job wasn't too absorbing but then finding that whatever else was true, the job at *Honey* was just that. Absorbing. She had to thank Sam, as she would call him, if I didn't mind, just to eliminate further confusion—it did get pretty confusing, didn't it? This big fish fertilizing eggs all over the ocean and swimming away so you never knew just where he was or what he was doing, you just knew he was supposed to be your daddy fish. . . . Anyway, she'd been too busy since then, too involved with the magazine's inhabitants (her word) to think about going back to school.

All this was delivered at almost the speed and with the lack of distinction between important and unimportant matters as I have related it here. And left me, of course, feeling confused, overwhelmed and in sore need of the nap from which I had just awakened. How could she have walked out on a child when she had a father who had done that very thing to her? (To *us*.) How had the father of her child allowed this to happen? Was there some connection between her leaving her child with his father and coming to look for her own? Then, had she really come to "Sam" because she needed work or had she daydreamed of doing it for years? She'd made it sound as though it had happened almost by chance, but after all, she'd talked the same way about his leaving—as though she'd barely have noticed if she hadn't detested his replacement.

I'm not sure these questions occurred to me at the time, at least in the form I've given them here. I do remember that what I wanted by the time Louisa had finished her quaint exposition was that she go away and leave me alone. I felt threatened by her very existence, by the places (the place, I should say) where her history paralleled mine and the places where they diverged. My brain balked at accepting the way she wove her life into a story, although I couldn't for the sake of my own life have explained why. I didn't dislike her. I *enjoyed* her. Or would, once I had recovered from what ailed me. It seemed clear that I needed a bosom buddy in a way that I hadn't before. I might have relished our coincidences, been diverted by our differences and reveled in her desire to understand and comfort me, had she not overwhelmed me with the force of her personality and with her determination to control events. Perhaps it was due to the absence of any such control over real life that Louisa became so involved in the fictions that happened to create havoc of one kind and another.

Apparently she had always told stories. If I cannot here examine the differences in impulse between a liar and a storyteller—beyond posing the obvious question of why the storyteller claims that she's not telling the truth and the liar claims that she is—it would surely be interesting to explore those differences, and the similarities as well. If the storyteller pretends to be lying and the liar pretends to be telling the truth, are they more similar than we

72

think they are, or even more different? In everyday life, Louisa told more of the truth than anyone wanted to hear, but she also made up little stories and embellished true ones in funny, harmless ways I'd barely have noticed if they had served any purpose. (She usually had some explanation as to how they did, and often I came away from her explanation with the sense that my query had become yet another chapter in her tale.)

For me, one of the most interesting aspects of the libel trial had to do with Louisa's exemplary behavior in court. She said nothing inappropriate that did not prove to be useful. She addressed every question with a specificity and a sense of the underlying issues that were breathtaking. It was as though the courtroom rather than the outside humdrum world were her natural home, the place where she belonged when she wasn't writing.

As we pulled into the driveway that first day, Peter Saltzman, who had been creative head of Starr-Flexner during my father's presidency, was getting out of the back of his limousine.

"Oh, my God," Louisa said, "what's that?"

Saltzman stretched and yawned. He was no more than five feet three inches tall and had a blond beard and moustache, chubby cheeks and a potentially rotund little body that he kept under check. He wore jeans, a tweed jacket and cowboy boots that seemed almost to make a point of having ultra-flat heels.

"His name is Peter Saltzman," I said, assuming the name would have no meaning to her.

"You're kidding," Louisa said. "I don't believe that's the guy. He looks like some little creep!"

"The guy who what?" I asked curiously. I didn't understand why she would know him. Saltzman and my father had made a perfect team, with Peter having no interest in economics or corporate management while my father had neither judgment nor feeling for selecting scripts, or matching them with directors and rewriters, or the myriad creative judgments involved in the actual moviemaking process. Peter's having been "stolen" by another studio had made it easier—although I knew none of this at the time— for my father's enemies to get rid of him. Now Saltzman had grown unhappy with the controls placed on him and wanted to come "home" to Egremont.

"The guy who made the movies your father got the credit for," Louisa said.

I looked at her. I was coming from Tony's funeral. My brain

was trying to find a path that would allow me to mourn him properly without being buried by grief, to contemplate the future without feeling disloyal, to know who I was without my reference points, good (Tony) or bad (Violet), around me. This path could not have on it someone who needed to mess with my already complicated feelings about my father.

"I'm doing it again," Louisa said with that uncanny sense that never prevented her from saying the wrong thing but told her instantly when she'd said it. "I'm sorry. It's just I've been hearing about this guy ever since I got to Hollywood, and I didn't . . . He's supposed to be a genius at spotting directors, working with writers and so on. There's no one out here I'd rather work for."

"Do you want to be a writer?" I asked.

She laughed. "I don't *want* to be. I *am*. I've never *not* been one."

"Well," I said, "why don't you come in with me? Maybe if he likes you . . . you know."

She smiled. "You're basically a good kid, aren't you. I guess it's worth a shot."

Neither of us moved to leave the car although Peter Saltzman had rung the bell at the front door. Louisa took out a makeup kit, tilted the car's rearview mirror and began what was still called repairing the face. Peter Saltzman hadn't so much as turned to see who was in the car that had come into the driveway just after his. Estella came to the door and admitted him. She glanced in our direction, but she was well trained, and when we made no move to get out of the car, she simply closed the door.

I waited. It was the first manifestation of a sometimes welcome peculiarity of my relationship with Louisa that she could get me more absorbed in whichever dilemma *she* was experiencing than I was in my own problem of the moment. Was she planning what she would say to impress Saltzman or simply trying to figure out how my father would react to her showing up with me and without calling? Come to think of it, what was my father's reaction to Louisa in general? It wasn't something I'd thought about until now, but knowing as I did his insistence on being the boss, could I imagine his getting along with this girl who hadn't even grown up in Hollywood yet refused to acknowledge reality's bossdom? Who had not stayed home simply because she had a child at home to care for?

Then there was the matter of Saltzman. As I waited for Louisa, I grew increasingly uneasy. I don't want to give my seventeen-year-old self undue credit for sensing that the wild little ball of energy that had just bounced into my father's home was the last person in the world who would want to deal with the tower of power that was my newfound sister. But I did cross my fingers and promise myself that it was too soon after Tony's funeral for my father to get mad at me.

Estella let us in but refused, or so it appeared to me, to look at Louisa. When Louisa asked if the Mahster was home, Estella glanced at me and then muttered, "I will see who is here."

"Oh, shit," Louisa said to me—loudly enough for Estella to hear as she retreated—"how long do you have to be here before you stop being treated like a visitor?"

As I tried carefully to frame an answer, she laughed. "Never mind, I just figured it out. Everyone's a visitor except Sam. Right?" She allowed me a moment to blush before saying, "Okay. So where's the visitors' waiting room?"

What was startling was how thoroughly she appeared to have forgotten Peter Saltzman, who had come to the door of the living room and was staring disapprovingly at her back, trying to figure out just who this loudmouthed, extremely tall visitor might be.

She saw me looking uneasy and turned to see who was there.

"Well, for heaven's sake," she said in a tense, babbly sort of way that made me ten times as uncomfortable as I'd been a moment before, "are you really Peter Saltzman or do you just look like him? I'm Sam's oldest daughter, Louisa Abrahms."

Saltzman nodded once but didn't bother to speak. He was unaccustomed to having to humor people, sane or crazy.

Lynn was coming down the steps to greet him. She nodded at Louisa and me but went directly to give Saltzman a kiss on the cheek and tell him that Sam had been held up at the studio but he'd be home in a few minutes. Peter should come into the study and make himself comfortable. There was a pile of manuscripts, if he was in the mood, and she would send Estella in to see if he wanted a bite. She was making all his favorite foods for dinner. She took his hand and led him through the foyer to the study.

Louisa yawned loudly and stretched. "How 'bout a swim?" she asked me.

"Swim?" I repeated wonderingly, unable to switch moods— or perhaps I should say modes—with her alacrity.

She laughed that tense, high-pitched laugh that I could already identify and made crawling motions with her arms.

"Yeah, you know, like, uh, moving around in the water? First one arm, then—"

"I know what swimming is," I said coldly. "I just—"

"All right. I'm sorry."

There she was again, robbing me of my reaction and then depriving me of my irritation at being robbed.

"I have a tendency . . . I'm afraid that little creep took my breath away . . . and then stomped on it. Anyway, I'm all hopped up, and I love to swim, and I always carry a suit in my bag, you know, out here you never know if even the funeral parlors have pools." A split second's pause. "I'm sorry. I keep forgetting you're in a different mood than I am. Maybe you just want to be alone. I have to keep remembering that the person who died is someone you really cared about."

I had a headache. I'd had more headaches since Tony's death than in my whole previous existence. (Louisa once said that kids never had headaches before TV had aspirin commercials.) I didn't know if I could manage a swim or not. All I knew was that whether or not I wanted her company, I did not wish to be *understood* by Louisa. It wasn't that I was ashamed of anything, at least nothing I could think of at the moment. But she was so damned casual about invading my brain that when she talked about me she sounded as though she were talking about herself, and whether she was right or wrong in what she was saying, it wasn't her, dammit, it was me!

I mumbled something about changing and meeting her out at the pool. Then, without waiting for a reply, I went up to my room.

It was only two o'clock in the afternoon. I stretched out on the bed, but thoughts of Tony threatened to overwhelm me, and after a few minutes, I got up and looked down at the lawn. Estella sat on one of the straight-backed wrought-iron chairs, mending a yellow garment, a big wicker sewing basket on the table beside her. Sonny sat on the grass at her feet, reading. At the edge of the patio, Liane was playing with a doll, alternately rocking it in a diminutive shiny white carriage and taking it out of the carriage to hold in her arms. The doll's hair, from a distance, appeared to be precisely the same soft, blond stuff as Liane's. (It was. I learned later that my father had had a wig made for the doll, a birthday present, from Liane's own hair.)

After a while, Louisa came out in a white bikini that showed to good advantage her full-breasted, small-waisted figure. She sauntered toward the pool and climbed the diving board, standing poised at the edge for some time in such a way as to make me wonder if she hoped that someone was watching. Finally she yawned, stretched, and executed a simple dive with such grace and apparent ease as to let anyone who was watching know that she could have done a much more complex one if she'd so chosen. She swam the length of the pool in a lovely crawl, head coming up twice during the eighty-foot length, and swam back the same way. Then she began doing what she would later call her own "special cockeyed version of laps," a sort of zigzag between the pool's sides. She hadn't taken a towel, so when she finally came out into the cool air, she made a beeline for the poolhouse.

Sonny put down her book for the first time.

I went back to bed. Moments later there was a knock at my door. I didn't answer.

"Nell?"

It was, of course, Louisa.

"Listen, if you don't want to talk to me, just tell me to go away, but don't not answer. It makes me crazy."

"I'm sorry. I'm half asleep."

"Okay. See you later."

Silence, but I felt she was still there. I closed my eyes, hoping that my father would be home by the time I had to see her again. Then I fell into a sleep that had as much to do with escape as with exhaustion.

I awakened because Liane and Sonny were playing–fighting in the hallway outside my room, and the sharp, lush smells of Mexican cooking were drifting out of the kitchen window and up into mine. It was after five-thirty. I dragged myself into the bathroom, feeling as though it were five-thirty in the morning. I washed my face, combed my hair and opened the bedroom door just in time to catch Sonny on all fours, giving Liane a piggyback ride and making sure Liane fell off her back.

Liane whimpered as she touched the floor but did not cry.

"You fell off on purpose," Sonny announced as she saw me.

I stepped around them into the hall just as my father entered the house. Louisa, fully dressed now, was standing in the entrance hall.

"Hi," she called down to him, "I was in the neighborhood— haha—and I thought I'd drop in."

I wondered if he'd noticed her at the funeral. She appeared to have no such concern.

He raised his left hand in an unjoyful salute that confirmed my suspicion that there would be problems between them.

"Who else is here?" he asked.

She shrugged. "Estella's cooking what smells like a wonderful dinner, hope I'm invited. Lynn's someplace around. Nellie, of course. And some little guy's locked away in the study."

My father turned away from her and walked toward the study. The two little girls, who had stopped fighting the moment they heard his voice, disentangled themselves from each other, scrambled to their feet and ran down the stairs. Near the bottom, Sonny tripped and fell, while Liane continued running until she reached my father and was scooped up in his arms. Sonny trailed after them into the study, where they all remained until a short while later, when Estella announced that dinner was served.

It wasn't one of those meals that melt together in memory with most of the other meals you've ever had.

I was still in the mildly paranoid mood of one who's awakened in the middle of a dream that might otherwise have had a reasonable resolution. I suppose I'd hoped my father would find some way to talk with me about Tony, perhaps ask a question or two that would give me cause to reminisce. But his mind was so much on Saltzman and the studio that the funeral might have been a year in the past—or the future. As we sat down to dinner, I asked whether Violet was all right, and he replied, with a grimace, that she seemed to be okay with the new housekeeper. "Or maybe I should say with the new Violet keeper." Then he turned back to Saltzman.

Estella was apparently Peter Saltzman's favorite cook in the whole world. She had been ordered to prepare all of his favorite Mexican dishes. Lynn was anxious because she knew how much my father needed Saltzman to want to make the films whose scripts he'd been given as part of his new studio deal, and she had not been able to get from Saltzman the tiniest hint of a first reaction.

The little girls had been allowed to remain in the dining room because Peter liked having them around. (I was told subsequently that while he had once liked girls until they were well into their teens, he'd recently become convinced that in their early teens, even as they developed hips and breasts, they went through alterations that destroyed their souls beyond any possibility of repair.) Sonny and Liane's two chairs, identical to the grownups' but smaller and with longer legs, flanked my father's at the round table in the lanai that had been set for dinner. My father ordered us to our places as we arrived: Liane sat to his right, followed by Peter, and then Lynn. Sonya was at his left, then came Louisa, and I was between her and Lynn.

"Have you met the big girls?" my father asked Peter brusquely. "Nellie and Louisa?"

Peter nodded but did not raise his eyes from the food Estella was piling onto his plate.

Beside me, Sonny began singing in a low, but not very low, voice a nonsense song on the order of "Big girls, bi–ig birls, have–you–met the bi–ig curls?" that appeared to enchant Peter sufficiently to draw a fraction of his attention from the food. Liane stage-whispered something about her seat to my father, who promptly plucked her out of her chair and set her on his lap, from where she began to pick at his food with her fingers.

"Big boys, bi–ig goys," Sonny continued, to the momentary amusement of everyone at the table but Saltzman, "have you met the big toys?"

"Okay," said my father, who certainly would have been amused had he been less intent. "Enough. Eat your enchilada."

"I need to be on a lap, too," Sonny said.

"Would mine do?" Peter asked humbly.

"I'll try it," Sonny said. "But I'm bigger'n Liane, and he's bigger'n you, so we prob'ly ought to switch."

"Oh, Jesus," my father said. "Maybe we'd better just get rid of them both."

"Don't be silly," Peter said. "You know only children can be counted on for the truth. Come, let's give it a whirl," he said to Sonya.

"A whirl, a birl, give it a girl," Sonya said, scrambling down from her seat and moving around to Peter's, where, not without difficulty, she settled in his less than ample lap.

My father made a brief stab at discussing with Peter some of the stock-option material in the changed contracts, but Peter was eating with a gusto that made you sure he'd readily exchange the whole contract for another enchilada. The little girls were eating from their respective lap-seats. Lynn picked at her food. My father was managing, but just barely, to eat and wait for Peter to deign to speak. It was the first time I had ever seen him in anything resembling a helpless position. As Estella moved toward the kitchen, he beckoned to her to come back and put more food on the director's plate. The tension was palpable. It would never in a million years have caused me—or anyone sane—to speak.

"And a hush," Louisa said, "fell over the small group."

My father looked irritated, but she didn't appear to notice.

"D'y'know," Louisa said to him, "that your friend Teddy has enchiladas every morning for breakfast? Enchiladas and industrial-strength coffee?"

"You don't say," my father responded, his manner so polite as to convey a dangerous hostility to anyone willing to notice.

"Mmm," Louisa said, "the coffee is all day, just to stay awake, but for breakfast it has to be enchiladas and coffee." My father was glowering at her, but she didn't appear to notice. "He said he never saw Mexican food until he came out of the army when he was . . . I guess he's almost the same age as you. Anyway, Sal can't stand anything Mexican because it reminds him of Italian. He's really the least Italian Italian I've ever known. Aside from his looks. The man's favorite snack is tea and toast, for Christ's sake." She was becoming nervous now, but she was too wound up to stop simply because it was the obvious thing to do. Liane was wandering around the dining room; Sonya, seeing my father's lap vacant, had abandoned Peter's for the bigger and better one. Louisa began a whole new riff on the subject of Teddy and Sal, but at some point in her monologue, my father, looking straight at her, said that he and Peter actually had some fairly important matters to discuss, and it might be best if they were left alone for a while. Louisa put down her fork and looked around as though she were waiting for him to tell the rest of us to leave as well. Instead, he said that, on second thought, he and Peter would move into the study with their meals.

Sonny said she wanted to go, too.

My father told her she and her sister were to get ready for bed. When they were ready, they could come back down for a goodnight kiss.

"Me, too?" Louisa asked with a strained grin.

He did not deign to respond.

Louisa picked up her fork and dug into her food again.

Saltzman was heading for the study, carrying his beer, but without his plate and silver, which he of course assumed someone would bring. (It was the sort of thing I'd never have thought about a week earlier, when I'd grown accustomed to living without servants.) Liane came over to Saltzman, who took her hand and proceeded with her toward the study. Lynn put down her fork and sat looking at her plate. Sonny began to whimper, saying that she wanted to go to the study, too, but then Estella came back into the dining room and told her she was not to cry. She was to sit on the bottom step, and when all the dishes had been moved to the study, the two of them would go upstairs for a bath. Sonny stopped whimpering, turned obediently and ran toward the staircase.

"Holy shit!" Louisa said. "What are we doing here, a remake of Jekyll and Hyde only with a six-year-old girl as . . . Actually, that's not such a terrible idea, when you come right down to it. Jacqueline and . . . mmm . . . Miss Hades? No. Not quite. But it's the beginning of something, no?"

I smiled. Lynn did not appear to be listening. She was eating slowly. As though under orders.

"Sonny's very attached to Estella," I said uneasily.

"Attached!" Louisa exclaimed. "It wouldn't be so noticeable if she were attached!"

I think I might have glanced at Lynn, if only to convey to Louisa that we might not want to have this conversation with the child's mother around. Louisa proceeded to stare at Lynn as well. Finally she put down her fork, finished her beer, wiped her mouth and stood, pushing back her chair about twice as far as it had to go.

"Listen, you'll have to excuse me," she said. "I just remembered a subsequent engagement. I'll be in touch."

And as I sat, struck silent by a mixture of discomfort and relief, she walked out of the house.

I have tried to remember another incident involving Estella that occurred in Louisa's presence and was more dramatic or suggestive than this one. I cannot. Nor, to get an even more important issue out of the way, can my mind locate a time when Louisa might have met or been in the vicinity of Jack Campbell, the plaintiff in our libel suit. In theory it's possible that she saw him before the funeral service began, when he was receiving people in the lobby along with the other family members. But Louisa has always insisted to me and to her lawyers that she had difficulty finding the church, which is in perfect accord with what I know of her, and that she slipped into the chapel *after* the service had begun. I believe her, not only because I haven't found her to be a liar under direct questioning but also because I'm convinced I would have noticed her if she'd been there before the service.

I remember as vividly as I do any moment during those years the one when I spied her standing in back of the chapel and noted her in a different way than I'd ever registered a stranger. I knew I hadn't met her, but I felt as though I knew her. No doubt it was partly the reddish blond hair. But I had seen, without particularly noticing, other people with the same hair color. Louisa bristled with an energy she took for granted but that struck other people in a variety of ways, most often as a vague threat to their well-being. Although she sometimes made me a little uncomfortable, I did not feel threatened. I felt, if anything, that she wanted to take care of me, and I would have the option of accepting her care. This was why I was so surprised when it appeared for some time that she'd chosen to disappear from my life.

But her disappearance would, years later, enable me to re-spond unequivocally on the witness stand to questions from Jack Campbell's lawyer aimed at proving Louisa had seen and/or had some contact with Campbell. I was able to testify that while I'd mentioned the Campbells and the Biancardis being at the reading of Tony's will, I was certain she had not met them. Nor was there any way in the world I would have described to her or anyone else that meeting in the lawyer's office.

Violet had asked my father to accompany us to the will reading. The one station that had shown the funeral on the six o'clock news had cut the brawl outside but shown the weeping widow on the arm of her first (important) husband, a scene that had encouraged her to continue playing the role. Even if my father had not been preoccupied with the final stages of the Egremont incorporation, it would have been complicated for him to attend, but he had sent with us his "Number 1 Assistant," a beautiful and competent young woman named Dagmar Saperstein, who would "take care of Vi-olet" for my sake as well as for Violet's.

If I say that I found Dagmar not only beautiful but intelligent, charming and civilized, I speak the truth. The Whole Truth, on the other hand, would have to include a suspicion about who she was and what she wanted that made me determined to keep my wits about me in her presence while warning myself not to make any assumptions about how well she knew my father.

The lawyer was a huge, expansive, cigar-smoking New Yorker named Charles Silver whom Tony had trusted and admired, with good reason. His manner of doing business was impeccable, and his feeling for the various participants might have been the crucial factor in keeping us out of legal difficulties at the time. To be specific, I think he had talked to Tony's daughters before the meet-ing to prepare them for Tony's having left Violet his house. I think he might have convinced them of Tony's deep concern for Violet and Tony's certainty that my father would not take care of her, advising them that attempts to get the house back would be expensive and, in all likelihood, futile.

Silver came out to the small reception room to greet us. He was courtly to Violet, pleasant to Dagmar and me. Having introduced himself, he led us into the larger, lighter room that was his office. Tony's daughters and their husbands stood talking in front of the bookcase wall, the effect somehow being of players huddling for the pregame signals. As we entered they froze. The difference between the two sisters was clear from the positions they froze in: Patsy looked ready to pounce while Theresa was simply waiting.

There was a strong physical resemblance between the two women. Neither was tall; each had brown hair and dark eyes set in a pleasant but not pretty, somewhat bony sort of face. There the resemblance came to an end; Patsy was wiry thin and dressed like a businesswoman rather than the housewife she was, while Theresa, soft and plump looking, wearing the black dress she'd worn to the funeral, seemed very much the housewife. Patsy was thirty-one at this time, Theresa twenty-eight.

Leonard Biancardi was a tall, angular, sorrowful dentist whose attitude toward the proceedings was probably close to what it was toward the rest of life; nothing good was likely to come of any of it.

Jack Campbell was another matter. Years later, when I first heard of the complaint he'd filed over Louisa's novel, *Joe Stalbin's Daughters,* I had a moment of guilt—as though the adolescent crush I'd developed on him that day had made its way into Louisa's writing brain.

Campbell's handsome features, grim expression and broad shoulders made him, during the trial, a familiar figure on the evening news as well as in the gossip magazines, where he was invariably described as hulking (he is a few inches *under* six feet), dark-complexioned (he had black hair then but was otherwise no darker than most of the people involved in the lawsuit) and a brooder (it would be difficult to find a central figure in a lawsuit who wasn't either brooding or crazy). That day he wore a dark blue suit, a white shirt and a tie, and if he had complaints about having to do this, I wasn't the one who heard them. But I'd grown up in a place where men tended to dress casually, and I'd still never seen a man who looked less correct or less comfortable in a business suit, the general effect being that of a tiger someone had sedated for just long enough to get it into clothes.

He was ill at ease but not hostile. He nodded but didn't speak

83

when Silver asked if we all knew each other and proceeded to introduce each of us by name, just in case. I don't remember seeing Jack Campbell smile, then or later. I do remember that he stared at Dagmar when he thought nobody was looking, and that I had the feeling both sisters were aware of this. As was I. If I was not yet in the grips of a severe teen-age crush, I was staring at him at all times when there was nothing to prevent me from doing so. By the end of the afternoon I was his slave.

Silver said he didn't have to remind us that Tony had loved us all. In figuring out how to divide his worldly goods, the issue had been not so much showing affection, as he always had, but giving what was needed where it was needed. There were provisions in the will, as we would see, to encourage everyone to exchange anything he'd left with someone else who had something he or she wanted. He then read the important provisions, in which Tony bequeathed the house to Violet (advising that she retain Silver to manage both his home and hers, which had been rented out when we moved into Tony's) and his substantial savings, as well as his landscaping business, to his daughters (suggesting that Leonard Biancardi be asked to oversee the management of the business, if he was willing, and if they chose to hold on to it rather than sell).

I looked at Violet; there were tears in her eyes again, and she was softly saying Tony's name, as though there might still be cameras around even if they weren't visible. Patsy and Theresa were silent. Stoical. Each reached for her husband's hand as the part about the house was read.

Then there was a bunch of smaller items: The jewelry that had belonged to his first wife, as well as her stored clothing and other possessions, was to be divided by his daughters; a couple of pieces of furniture were to go to cousins and nephews who'd admired them, unless Violet decided she liked them more than she once had; his radio and phonograph and his record collection were for his stepdaughter, Nellie.

I began to cry.

The others were quiet for a little while, but when I didn't stop, they grew restless. I could feel them looking at each other, making signals, but I couldn't cut off the tears. I had thought of myself as being in that office on Violet's account, and I was unprepared for the feelings a gift to me would arouse. If I'd been in a familiar place, I would have left the room and gone to another one. But I could barely think of where I was, much less of how I would get to somewhere else.

I felt rather than saw or heard someone walk over to me.

"You wanna take a walk? I'll go with you."

Grateful even before I was certain whose voice it was, I looked up. Jack Campbell stood over me. I nodded, glanced at Theresa and Patsy. They weren't displaying any reaction to the idea, so it must be all right. I thought Dagmar was looking at me in a concerned way, but I didn't look back because I didn't want to acknowledge her right to see me cry, much less have *her* offer to walk with me.

I followed Jack Campbell out of the office and down the flight of stairs to the street, where he slowed up enough so I could keep up with him but didn't talk or do any of the other things that would have taken the edge off my gratitude. I felt utterly comfortable with him. I'm sure that not having to make conversation was one of the reasons. But what I see only now as I write is that my brain, unwilling to revert to its prior reliance on my father, was ready to find a substitute in this man I'd met only once before in my life.

I think we must have walked two miles along Sunset Boulevard before guilt rather than desire made me suggest we go back. He asked if I was sure I wanted to, and I started crying again. He put one arm around me, gave me a strong hug, and we started walking back, but slowly. I thought of the provision in Tony's will about his landscaping business. My mind overlooked Tony's specified desire that Leonard Biancardi run his business. How nice it would be, I kept thinking, if the Campbells moved to Los Angeles, and Jack Campbell took Tony's place!

Patsy and Theresa and Leonard Biancardi were standing in front of the two-story building where the office was, looking slightly impatient. I was exhausted, but I wasn't crying anymore. I asked where Dagmar and Violet were, and Patsy said they'd gone. Violet was tired, and Dagmar had to get back to the studio. Theresa asked if I was all right, and I nodded. Then I thanked Jack, and I thanked Theresa, I suppose for having married him and brought him along that day, and walked away without having any idea of where I would go or what I would do when I got there. I didn't want to ask for a ride, but I was in an unfamiliar part of Los Angeles and didn't even know if I had a dime to call a cab.

"You want a lift home?" Jack called after me.

Feeling mildly ashamed of myself, I nodded, and we walked together to the car.

Everyone was silent for the first part of the drive. Then they began to talk among themselves, almost as though I were not there. (I sat in the back between Jack and Theresa.) I've had many occasions to try to remember their conversation—if only so I could deny repeating any of it to Louisa.

Leonard Biancardi was the peacemaker in the group, his wife and Campbell being the antagonists. Various practical issues were addressed. I managed to hear the conversation without being affected by it except at moments when I remembered that the "Papa" whose possessions they were talking about was Tony.

Jack Campbell apparently worked at a bar in Anchorage, and they'd promised his boss, as well as the friends who were taking care of their children, that they'd be home for the weekend. Patsy Biancardi pointed out in a manner both aggressive and aggrieved that crush or no, there was a great deal of work to be done in the sorting out of Papa's possessions. If Theresa didn't work with her, it would take weeks to do everything, and she happened to have two *very young* children at home whom she couldn't leave forever with Leonard's sick old mama. Patsy saw no choice but for her sister to stay and help.

Jack said something angry—something I remember as who the fuck was Patsy to tell anybody what there was no choice about. Leonard Biancardi responded gently, saying that of course they understood it would be difficult. For everyone. On the other hand, if they all pitched in, they could do it. There would be a lot of things to figure out. Not just who wanted what, but major questions like whether they were going to hold on to the landscaping business, and if so, who would be running it. The important thing to remember was that Tony had managed to leave them a rather nice amount of money (Patsy turned to give him a dirty look, as though he had divulged a state secret), when you considered that it was on top of their regular incomes. It wouldn't be so awful if one or the other, or even all of them, had to make some extra phone calls or do a little traveling.

After a while, Patsy asked which plane the Campbells were supposed to take back to Anchorage. Jack looked out the window but Theresa said it was eleven Monday morning. She and her sister could work together through the weekend. If it turned out there was more work to be done later, *she* would do it. As a matter of fact, she found herself thinking about Los Angeles and about the landscaping business, which she had to admit she hadn't given much thought while their father was alive.

Patsy asked me if there would be any problem with Violet's letting them into the house. I'd begun to wonder how I would spend my days until the time when it would be bearable to return to school. Her question made me remember the opera records that had set me off in the first place. My brain fumbled around in the dark for a moment before it could figure out what I wanted to say that it was all right to say.

"I don't think it'll be a problem," I finally said, "but why don't you let me talk to . . . there's a housekeeper there, taking care of her. She hasn't been in such hot shape. She sort of pulled herself together for the funeral. I know you don't . . . Anyway, she sort of fell apart when Tony died." (It was true, so why did I feel as though I were lying?) "Most of the time she just stays in her room. I don't think your mother's stuff, aside from the furniture . . . I mean, you know, all your mother's clothing, jewelry, things . . . I think they're all stored in the attic." Patsy glanced at Leonard as though I'd said they were out on the sidewalk. "I'll tell the housekeeper you're going to call, and then you can figure out the times with her. I don't think there'll be any problem."

I waited. Leonard said, "Thank you," and Patsy looked straight ahead, but Theresa reached over and patted one of my hands.

We pulled into the driveway of my father's house. Theresa took my phone number and gave me the one where she and her sister could be reached for the balance of their stay in Los Angeles. I thanked them all, thanked Jack once again for having walked with me, got out of the car and ran into the house.

A couple of hours later, Estella told me that a gentleman had left a record player and eight cartons of records and had said I would know what they were. I thanked her and asked if there was someplace they could be stored for the time being. It seemed likely I would never listen to music again. Certainly I wasn't going to play opera.

BOOK

2

IT WAS ONE of those rare Sunday mornings when Lynn was out and my father was home and not Otherwise Occupied. The servants were not in evidence because, my father said, there should be one day a week when a man could beat his wife without witnesses. He and I were supervising the little girls in the fenced-off area around the pool. The pool water was heated, but the air wasn't warm enough for anyone to feel moved to swim. My father was talking about the deal with which he had been able to lure Saltzman to Egremont—a series of three films involving time travel by a young girl of the nineteenth century into our present, the ancient past and the future. Saltzman's studio had insisted upon the right to back out after the first or second if one or both did poorly. Only my father had trusted Peter so thoroughly as to sign on the dotted line for all three. (The first was the studio success of two years later, *Lorna Talbot,* dubbed by some *Variety* wag "Lorna Doom," in which Lorna, a chaste and obedient nineteenth-century maiden, is transported to a future that is our own sixties.)

Earlier my father had been giving the little girls piggyback rides. Now Sonny was trying to recapture his attention by riding Liane on her own back. Each time she collapsed under her sister's weight, she would complain, and there would be a fight, but when Liane didn't want to remount, Sonny would push her to do it one more time. They'd been going on this way for a while, frequently calling him for mediation, which he performed without losing his own conversational line. He'd just begun to explain why he was willing to take the risk of committing himself to Saltzman, a serious gambler, aside from his taste for young girls, but someone he felt he was uniquely capable of controlling, when Louisa appeared on the terrace and walked toward us. It was the first time I'd seen her since the funeral.

She wore jeans and a cowboy shirt. I noticed a sort of macho swagger to her walk and wondered whether she'd moved that way the first time I saw her and it hadn't registered.

"Hi," she said. "I was in the neighborhood—haha—and I thought I'd say hello."

She dropped to the ground and waved to the little girls, who did not appear to notice.

"Actually," she said, "it strikes me now, this isn't a place you'd call a neighborhood, is it."

She looked directly at my father for the first time. He had not been engaged by the question and appeared to be paying somewhat closer attention to the little girls than he had been before her arrival.

"Hello," Louisa said. "New York calling."

He smiled grimly. "How've you been, Louisa? How're my pals?"

"Pals? Oh, your pals. They're okay. Same as ever, that is. As a matter of fact, I'm beginning to have the feeling that if someone asks me ten years from now, I'll be saying the same thing. Same as ever. They don't really change, do they."

He shrugged. "Who does?"

It was one of those times when the words being exchanged cannot account for the tension in the air.

"Plenty of people," Louisa said. "I've changed beyond belief. Just for starters."

He shrugged.

"You don't believe me?" she asked irritably. "You didn't know me five years ago."

"Fine, fine," he said, waving a hand as though at a fly. He stood up, suddenly restless, and ambled over to the spot on the lawn where the little girls were rolling a ball back and forth between them. There he fell on all fours and proceeded to give the two of them a piggyback ride, with Sonny trying to push Liane off so she could have the whole back to herself, and Liane not retaliating but managing to hold her place by clutching at the neck of the piggy's shirt.

The look of concentration on Louisa's face was so intense as to be frightening. After a moment she asked loudly if anyone would mind if she took a swim. Then, without waiting for an answer, she went into the poolhouse. A minute later she came out in the white bikini and proceeded to go through a series of dives and swimming strokes so close to the last performance, when she hadn't known I was watching, as to make me extremely uncomfortable.

My father lay with his hands under his head. Liane appeared to have fallen asleep on his chest. Sonny stood watching, a finger in her mouth, the other hand playing with the hem of her shorts. I sat still, barely able to breathe, so tense did the moment feel. My father resumed his account of the various gambling activities that had engaged Saltzman to the extent that he might have had to mortgage his future to someone much less inclined than he himself was to let Peter have his own head. (My father had no gaming instinct at all and had said more than once that if he put a quarter in a slot he expected to get something in return.)

Louisa came out of the pool. As she walked toward us, my father, without having appeared to notice, abruptly switched the subject to what we were having for dinner that night. Estella had, as usual, filled the refrigerator with dishes, fresh and leftover, but he found himself thinking along the lines of some grilled burgers, maybe his own favorite guacaburgers with avocado and white cheese, which the little girls also adored.

"Someone should do a thesis some day on Teddy and Sal's food stuff," Louisa said without missing a beat. "Aside from the enchiladas, I mean. You know, Nell, Teddy's a rabbi's son. His favorite sandwich in the world is chicken salad and bacon on one of those big *goyish* white rolls, which isn't terrible except he has it with a stack of fries with mayo, ketchup *and* mustard. If it's *goyish* it's got to be good. Romeo—Sal's—the opposite. The most genteel Goddamned Italian you ever saw. Aside from tea and toast, which is breakfast and his favorite snack, it's steak, salad, baked potato. No fish."

Out of the corner of my eye, I noted that Sonny was growing restive. After a moment she covered both ears with her hands.

"He hates fish almost as much as he hates tomato sauce. I guess I really think—"

Suddenly Sonny let out a shriek. My father barely responded, but Louisa, startled, asked what was wrong.

"You're hurting my eyes!" Sonny yelled at the top of her lungs. "You're hurting my eyes!"

On my father's chest, Liane had awakened and was rubbing her own eyes.

"Those are your ears, kiddo," Louisa responded while I sat in shock. "If you're going to be a fresh brat, at least learn your body parts."

Sonny began to run around the lawn, emitting a series of Indian war whoops.

I looked at my father, who stood up carefully, still holding the sleepy Liane. He was looking at Louisa as though she were an employee he didn't mind having to fire.

"It should be possible to bear in mind," he said with greater deliberation, not to mention more formal English, than I was accustomed to, "that she's a child. One doesn't have the same expectations of children as one does of adults."

"No kidding," Louisa said—again without pause for thought. "Well, I never learned about all that stuff because I grew up in a house with only one adult, and she was working all the time."

There was a moment of ghastly silence. On the other side of the azalea bushes, even Sonny had paused to view the drama, or so it seemed. I could feel Louisa looking to me for support. Even if she'd had greater justice on her side, I could not have given it to her.

"I think you should leave now," my father said.

Liane, fully awake, clung to him as though she were afraid he would order her out next. He hugged her, fondled her hair, did not look away from Louisa.

Now that it was too late, Louisa held back from speaking. Majestically she rose, raised a goodbye hand to me, turned and walked back to the poolhouse for her clothes. My father went to the house with Liane. Sonny began crying for Estella. When I reminded her that it was Estella's day off, she ordered me to hold her. When she'd been in my arms for a few seconds, she announced that I wasn't soft enough and returned to the lawn and the book she'd been reading.

Lynn came home a short while later. No one made any attempt to convey to her what had happened. We ate lunch in nearly total silence, after which my father told Lynn to take the girls upstairs for their naps. She did not come down again. My father paced the lanai for a while, then turned to me.

"How's your tennis, kid?"

I shook my head, ruefully confessed I hadn't been playing.

"Want some practice?"

"You'll just get annoyed. You won't even get a workout. I haven't been playing at all."

"All right," he said. "Then let's make believe we're in New York and take a walk."

I said I'd love it, and he told me with a grin that it was essential I put on some shoes. A couple of minutes later he called to Lynn that we were going out for a while and, without making certain she'd heard him, beckoned me to the front door. I can feel myself blushing anew when I remember how, joining him on the front walk, I reached for his hand as though I were a little girl again and we were going to cross a busy New York street or watch a parade. I withdrew my hand; my father responded by grabbing it back and squeezing it. I blushed and pulled free.

"What's'amolla?" he asked jocularly. "You're not my kid anymore?"

"I was feeling like a *little* kid," I told him.

"Mm," he said. "Well, it'll pass." He looked around at the deserted street. "Saltzman claims it's his ambition to make a movie in Beverly Hills that has thousands of people but no cars. He has a funny routine about how it could be done. Extras swarming all over the streets. Maybe they'd see a mirage—a car—and run toward it but it turns into another person." He glanced at me, saw I was smiling politely, put an arm around me without slowing his walk. "I'll tell you something. I don't know what I'm going to do about that sister of yours. She's a real pisser."

I looked up at him; he squeezed me.

"Got any suggestions, kid?"

"Uh-uh." We walked a little farther. "I was surprised . . . She told me about how you got her that job. She seemed to be grateful . . . I don't know. She always talks that way, sort of rambling, and one part leads to another, and you never know exactly how she got there, but you can tell the connections are there in her mind. I mean, I don't think you should get mad at that part. It's just the way she talks."

"Yeah, but mad is the way I react to the way she talks. Anyway, that's not what I got mad at."

I was silent, knowing precisely what he'd been mad at and what she'd been mad at as well.

"I was surprised about the magazine, too," I finally said. "About *Honey*. She said you gave them money when they were starting."

"Not just money. Labor. I set up their books, did their bills, figured expenses, anything that required a brain functioning in the real world, I did for them."

"When was all this?"

"After the war. When I was still on the L.A. *Times*. We were all there. We met in the army, and when we came out, I got the job on the *Times*, then I got Sal in there as a sports reporter, no, wait a minute, it was vice versa, he worked there first. Anyway, together we got Teddy hired as an editorial cartoonist. Teddy wasn't fit for that life, though. He didn't last long. It's a man's world, newspapers, and that's not what he really likes."

So I'd been young, and he, my father, was still home. Well, of course there was a large part of his life I'd never known about. If he'd had another "wife" who was pregnant and a little girl I didn't know about, why should I be surprised that he'd had pals who started a magazine?

"I never met any of them, did I?" I asked cautiously.

He laughed. "Having something to do with that magazine was like having an affair. You didn't talk about it when you got home." He glanced at me, ascertained that I was registering amusement, and readily launched into the story of Teddy Marx, Romeo Salivieri and *Honey* magazine. Which happened to include the story of his first marriage.

Esther was a cousin—third or fourth, he could never remember which—and, like the fact that she was a few years older than he, she'd never been eager to have it known outside the family. He gathered she'd never even mentioned it to Louisa. At a time when he was working during the day, going to school at night and finding it virtually impossible to meet girls, he and Esther had become lovers. Esther was, not to put too fine a point on it, madly in love with him, and he had to say that he'd been enormously fond of her, though he'd never for a moment been in love.

After some months Esther got pregnant. She told him that she would try to find an abortionist if he insisted, but if she did, she would not continue to be his lover. In fact, she would never speak to him again. They were married the week after Esther missed her second period, in May 1937. Louisa was born in January 1938. He dropped the notion of going to law school and devoted his time to Esther's family's fur business, studying accounting—which required much less work than law school would have—at night. He was a devoted husband and father, in case I was interested, and in case I'd heard anything different from Louisa. But the truth was that Louisa was a difficult kid, or had turned into a difficult kid somewhere during her second or third year, after the troubles with her eyes began.

"Listen, kiddo," he interrupted himself, "I assume I'm safe, talking to you like this. I assume you're not going to . . . Never mind. I know you're not. I could always trust you from the time you were a little kid. You were nothing like . . . Anyhow, she started grade school, Louisa did, that is, right around the time the war began. I was bored, I was restless, I was dying for some adventure. In those days nobody got divorced if they weren't rich. Oh, yeah, and I was *patriotic*. Nobody's patriotic anymore and it's hard to remember how it was, but for the Jews, especially, the war was a holy crusade, and I was dying to get into it and fight."

In the army he'd made two good buddies, Teddy and Sal. Ted Marx was not only the sole other Jew in the outfit, he was the son of a rabbi from Minneapolis, though he could have passed for not Jewish, with his Midwestern speech and dubious last name. He was a talented cartoonist and a photographer whose ambition was to work for *Life* magazine when he got out of the service. Sal, who'd been a sportswriter before the war, grew up in Hollywood, where his father was a gardener and his mother a cook on the estates of various movie stars. Sal was one of the few guys in the outfit who'd ever seen a Jew before. A lot of the men didn't even know from Italians. Sal had a wife and two kids and was a real family man. Just like himself.

They'd talked all the time about starting a magazine together after the war. It would be a magazine that gave male readers what they wanted and could not find in the other magazines that were published for them: good pictures of sexy, naked women and stories that were too realistic or too risqué to be published elsewhere. Responsibilities seemed to divide themselves rather neatly, he, himself, of course, handling all the financial matters. Otherwise known as the realities. Eventually it became clear that if the magazine was going to be more than a daydream, the three of them would have to settle in the same city after the war. It was almost as clear that by far the best city for such a magazine would be Los Angeles.

Esther's response, when he'd written to her about the idea of moving to L.A., was hysteria. She couldn't be persuaded even to consider the *possibilities*, such as meeting him on the West Coast when he was mustered out of the service and taking a look around. Maybe, he had finally written her, it would be just as well if he explored the Los Angeles area, the work prospects and so on, before they talked about moving the family. Esther wrote back that the family wasn't moving to California no matter what he found there.

Ted was the only one of the three men who, during the years after they got out of the service, remained dedicated on a daily basis to the idea of the magazine. He never found it within himself to go to New York and make a serious attempt at working for *Life*, but he earned a decent living free-lancing for various papers and agencies in Los Angeles, and in his spare time he drew cartoons and played with photos and layouts. Teddy had been convinced before he ever got there that L.A. was the wave of the future.

Sal lived in the Valley with his wife and two (soon to be three, then four) children, but my father and Ted signed a lease on the ugly old beach house in Santa Monica from which they began *Honey* and which Ted later bought. This was the house where Louisa was now living. He didn't know if I'd seen it or not, and he wasn't inquiring. He wanted me to feel free to be friendly with my sister whether he was speaking to her or not.

The Honeycomb now looked somewhat different than it had in those first days, when there was little in the way of furniture— a few secondhand beds, a couple of chests of drawers and hundreds of Teddy's photographs, not to speak of some wonderful cartoons. One of those cartoons had been used in the first issue of *Honey* and its original still hung at the beach house, unless it had been moved to Teddy's new place. It showed a large public fountain with a frieze composed of linked mermaids, the foremost mermaid being a voluptuous blonde whose enormous breasts, with their two spouting, faucetlike nipples, comprised the picture's riveting center. Levitating blissfully just below one breast and above a large desk that was made up with linen, like a bed, his eyes closed and his mouth wide open, was Teddy Marx, Publisher.

There were issues among the three men, but they seemed always to be able to resolve them and even to enjoy their differences.

Ted wanted *Honey,* once you got through the sexy stuff, to be a vehicle for crusading journalism, while Sal had a keen interest in sports and crime. Ted came from a relatively liberal Jewish family, but Sal had grown up in a community where people with dark skin came to work, had to be watched carefully and weren't visible after dark unless they were cleaning up. He hated and feared black people and Mexicans, while Ted and my father, typical Jews, held the position that what had been done to these groups had to be undone before anyone could judge them.

While in the service, Ted had drawn a cartoon showing two leering white men, one of them clearly Sal, the other a caricature of himself, both with bulging eyes and slobbering lips which they licked as they played with their own erect members. A gorgeous blonde was passing in front of them. From Sal's lips issued a monologue about how all the niggers ever thought about was fucking and how they could never, therefore, be trusted. It was a tribute to the men's friendship that Sal could laugh at this cartoon, acknowledging its critical truth even if he couldn't claim that it altered his feelings.

Sal often had to cover events in the city at night. At those times, rather than drive back to the Valley, he usually ended up at the beach house in Santa Monica with some girl he'd taken to the event. The men, of course, were in bachelor heaven there on the beach with a longer chain of girls than had been dreamed of in their previous existences. Teddy had actually made the mistake of thinking he was in love and getting married at one point. He and his wife had shared the beach house with my father until she became pregnant, when they, too, had moved to the Valley. When Ted's wife became pregnant again a while later—shortly, as a matter of fact, after *Honey* had been launched—he'd left the entire family and moved back to the beach.

My father said it might have been a sort of predictor of the future that of the three of them, he himself was the only one who'd been interested in a range of women of various types and ages, many of whom were reasonably intelligent in addition to being attractive.

Whatever the quality of the girls to whom he was drawn, Teddy had always become very much involved in their lives, wanting to hear about their previous boyfriends and sexual experiences, if any, as well as their plans for the future. (Invariably they expected to get married and have children after becoming movie stars; invariably Teddy expressed the opinion that motherhood was a woman's finest destiny and the hope that they would still be interested when he got ready to settle down again.) He advised them on clothes and took photographs of them in the nude, explaining that he wanted the photographs to help him remember them when they got tired of him and left. He would never use them in his magazine without both their written consent and their earnest assurances that to be so used was the fulfillment of a dream.

Rather more quickly than he would have expected to, my father had grown bored. If he continued to enjoy the good life, the thrill was not what it had been. There was insufficient challenge. One of his bosses at the newspaper gave parties at which there were always a large number of good-looking single women, and he grew accustomed to the fact that most of them would go to bed with the guy who delivered uniforms to a studio commissary if no one else "in the movies" proved to be available. In the minds of many of these females, newspapermen were the next best thing to the ones in the movies.

At one of these dinner parties my father met and got into a conversation with Abe Starr, a Russian immigrant already in his sixties who had worked his way up from being a cutter in a Manhattan fur factory to having his own highly successful fur salon. Through Mildred Flexner, one of his best customers, he had become successively an investor in Flexner Studios, an executive, a partner, and finally, when Marvin Flexner had an incapacitating stroke, the head of the studio that by this time bore both their names. Starr had been very taken with my father's description of inventory tricks, some well known but others not, that led to large tax savings in the fur business. Before the evening was out, he had offered my father a job. Within a year my father was head of Starr-Flexner's accounting department. Abe felt that he had found a man to whom he could hand over control of the studio someday. This feeling was surely enhanced by the fact that during that year, Sam had married Abe's adopted daughter, Violet.

My father hoped I understood that whatever else was true about his career, his marriage, or anything else I might have heard, he'd been madly in love with Violet from the moment he'd seen her and for a surprising length of time thereafter. If he was sensible of the advantages of being Abe's son-in-law, they felt secondary to his great good luck in winning Violet, who possessed some quality, perhaps you could call it mysteriousness, lacking in the wholesome blondes of Santa Monica and the more accomplished but no less mundane women he'd met at work and elsewhere. Abe hadn't told him, as he surely should have, of Violet's breakdown when she was brought to this country. On the other hand, he doubted that if he'd known, he would have behaved differently.

When Violet, with his active encouragement, became pregnant with me, he was delighted. When she was frightened of childbirth and motherhood, he promised her all the help and support she would need. When she'd given birth to me and remained in bed, breathing and drinking malteds but doing very little else for two years, he'd not only made certain that we were well cared for while he was at the studio, he had spent as much time as possible with us when he was free. Separately, more often than not, because Violet tended to panic or feel ill if he paid attention to me when she was around.

My father paused in his narrative for the first time. We had been walking steadily for perhaps an hour or more, heading in toward what was pleased to call itself the city rather than out in the direction of the beach.

"I can't tell," he said, "if you know any of this stuff. I only know you never heard it from me."

"I remember that you were the one who took care of me. You and the maids."

"Me and the maids." He reached over affectionately, messed up my hair. "I'm going to miss you if you go away to school. I finally find you, and now I'm going to lose you again. The only other redhead in my first two families." I could feel him waiting for a response, but once again he was arousing too many sentiments to allow me to address one. "Louisa's hair turned brown when she was three or four. I don't know when she began bleaching it to the same color as ours."

"I don't know if I'm supposed to know that."

"Me neither," he said. "We won't tell."

"You're not really banishing her, are you?" I asked. "I mean, I know you were angry, but . . ."

"Will I stay angry? I doubt it. But she'll say something else. Or do something. I've got a problem with Louisa. Or, I should say, she's got a problem with me. Whichever. It began almost the day she got here. I have to tell you—I could see right away she had a difficult streak a yard wide. When I sent her out to Teddy, I can't honestly say I thought it would work out, I just figured it was worth giving it a shot. He's softer than I am, though not necessarily more malleable. Anyway, I'm surprised, *delighted* she's still there, but I never counted on it. From the day she arrived, or pretty nearly, I had the feeling she'd come just to stick the past up my ass."

Even now, as I write the phrase, I marvel at its picturesqueness, its concision, the amount it reveals about his mental processes. At the time, it not only took away my breath but made me feel there was just one person I could go to for more. I hung on that person's every word, kept up with his steps so he wouldn't become impatient, and reached for his hand when we drew near the next curb as though I'd never crossed a street on my own.

We must have walked for another hour, or close to it, before he stopped at a bar-restaurant and called the studio for a car. (He never used cabs when his own driver wasn't around but would call for a studio car at any time of the day or night and tip the driver as lavishly as he did the maître d' at the Stork Club.) He ordered a martini for himself and a Coke for me, and as we waited for the car, he talked about Louisa's mother, who was, he said, as different from Violet as night was from day.

Esther was a dynamic, capable woman who would never have discovered her abilities if he hadn't left her on her own to do so. When they were young she'd been so set on marrying him, this great prize no one else wanted, that all her energies had been focused in his direction. It was possible that even if they'd remained together she would have developed her talent for business, not to say her appetite for bossing people around, but she certainly did it earlier this way. And, he might add, she'd finally found herself a fellow who was a much better match for her than he himself had been, a docile chap who probably never got a hard-on except when she pointed at it and ordered it to beg. (My father was no longer glancing at me as he made these remarks.) Violet was actually a much more appropriate mate for a bossy, high-energy type like himself, although she was so incredibly beautiful that he likely would have fallen in love with her even if that hadn't been true. Then there was Lynn, who, he supposed, fell somewhere between the two. There was a time when only women who were much smarter than they were beautiful had been ambitious, but perhaps that was ending now. In a world where men had greater freedom to come and go as they pleased, women were more likely to develop their own abilities.

He talked some more about Ted and Sal and how he'd grown bored with their version of the chase. If you'd listened without knowing about his life, you'd have thought him a sweet, temperate being who had long, stable relationships with women. (Reading this, he would say our only problem was in defining "long.")

When the car finally came, he dropped me off at the house, saying he was too hopped up to go home. He would do some work

100

at the studio. He'd see me later. I should tell Lynn there was a Saltzman crisis and he'd be back after he straightened it out. There was no air of embarrassment or complicity as he gave me these directions. That is to say, as far as I could see, he didn't feel as though he were lying.

There were two phone messages for me from Louisa. The first contained a couple of numbers where she could be reached. The second requested I call right away because she was preparing to leave California. Dismayed, feeling guilty over issues I could not have identified with any precision, I called instantly. When I said, "Hi, it's Nell," she told me she was giving notice the following day, Monday, and returning to New York as soon as someone was found to replace her.

"Why?" I asked. "Just because he—Da—Sam was a little mean to you?" (I had prepared the line without expecting to hear precisely what I'd heard.)

" 'A little mean,' " she said. "Very funny. Being thrown out of the house isn't exactly a little anything."

"I think he gets that way," I told her, "if you make him feel as though he has to defend himself."

"I didn't make the son of a bitch feel *anything!*" she squawked. "He's on the defensive all the time. Or *should* be."

I was trying to figure out, in my less than infinite seventeen-year-old wisdom, how to get her to understand that the defensive position was one my father could not be made to occupy, when she began crying into the phone. She cried for a long time, apologizing periodically that she simply couldn't stop. Once, she asked if I wanted to hang up. I said no, unless *she* wanted me to. She said she didn't. Finally I offered to drive over to Santa Monica and just sort of hang out for a while. (My father had given me my own car for my seventeenth birthday.) She said, sounding pathetically eager, that she'd love it. I got instructions on locating the original Honeycomb (Louisa thought I was kidding when I said I didn't know where it was; she hadn't yet shaken that small-town kid's awe of the Honeycomb legend) and hung up, regretting my offer while understanding that I'd not had a choice. I felt wise and weary. It is an odd fact that Louisa, for all her greater age and real talent, often had this effect on me.

The Honeycomb, the first home of *Honey* magazine, was a shack, but a reasonably large, Victorian-style shack on a corner plot directly facing the Santa Monica beach. The inside had been renovated as the magazine began to earn money. Still later, much of the operation had been moved to the place Marx named the I-land. The outside of the house in Santa Monica had been kept as it was, perhaps because if they'd modernized it, they would have disrupted the visual harmony of the block. The houses were gray, yellow or white, and while they varied greatly in size, they were then still uniformly shabby.

Two huge black dogs lounged at the bottom of a flight of steps that led to a porch with two rocking chairs and what I later heard Louisa call the "casting swing." The dogs eyed me sleepily as I got out of the car but did not seem disposed either to attack or to move so that I could pass. Until that moment I had been thinking more about what I would say to Louisa about what had happened with my father than about where I was going or what it would be like when I got there.

If I'd been surprised to learn of my father's connection to *Honey*, my surprise did not have the quality of awe that it might have had I grown up elsewhere. Teddy Marx had managed to turn the Honeycomb and later the I-land into attractions that pulled in an occasional male movie star or columnist in midlife crisis, in addition to scads of young girls eager to be discovered, but he'd never left the wrong side of the tracks as far as anyone who counted in the movie business was concerned. If the Beach Nuts and various other singing groups, not to speak of a few nightclub comedians, had gotten their first big break at one of his Honeycomb clubs, their bios rarely emphasized that fact, and Teddy Marx had yet to "discover" a star, or even have a notable association with one. So my mind did not link him to the movie business, and I had less of an idea than I might have had of what I would find in this house.

I smoothed my hair, glanced down at my jeans and green camp shirt and somewhat timidly called Louisa's name. No answer. I called again, a little louder. One of the dogs dragged itself to a nearly standing position that left no more room on its step than there'd been before. But then Louisa, holding a telephone to her ear, appeared at the screened porch door and beckoned me in, telling me not to be scared.

"I'm not scared," I said, "but I can't get past the dogs."

"Just come up," she called back. "When you get there, they'll move."

I walked up the first few steps so that I was just below the dogs, who did not move.

"Frankie!" she shrieked with such force that the dog who was still lying down bolted to a standing position. "Pablo! Get your lazy asses off those steps!"

Slowly the two beasts made their way to the bottom step, where they sniffed at my sneakers. Quickly I made my way up to the porch, where Louisa was holding the door open for me. Only then did she tell whoever was on the phone that she had to go, she had a visitor.

"Frankie and Pablo weren't fancy enough for the new joint," she said. "There they have Dobermans, not to speak of men with guns. Come on in."

I entered as casually as though I were entering a home—and had a bit of a shock. I hadn't noticed when I was outside that the windows were covered—the house was centrally air-conditioned—with louvered wood panels. I was in a room that took up most or all of the ground floor and whose walls and ceiling were painted with a gleaming enamel that could be described, according to one's mood, as Chinese- or blood-red. The most important piece of furniture was an extraordinary length of what looked like hot-pink jersey (collapsible) tubing but was, in fact, a sectional sofa that threaded its way around the four walls and could be used for, or I would say now, that *trumpeted* itself as being usable for, a variety of sexual purposes. Lamps in the shape of women's torsos, reminiscent of the figureheads on old-fashioned ships' prows, were spaced along the wall. There was no other furniture. The floors were covered with something that pretended to be a darkish sisal but was actually woven carpet.

In one corner of the endless pink tubing a man was sleeping. He was wearing jeans and was, as far as I could see, the caricature of the absent-minded professor. He had long, receding brown hair streaked with gray, a walrus moustache, and wire-rimmed glasses perched crookedly on his nose. He was snoring. Neatly laid out on the portion of sofa next to where he was sleeping were a dark suit, white shirt and patterned tie and a briefcase.

"One of Teddy's cousins from New York," Louisa said. "Blood relations aren't allowed on the I-land. Except for his mother and his kid."

I felt that she was waiting for some response from me, but I wasn't amused, and I felt at a loss for anything to say. I had come on what I'd thought of as an errand of mercy, but the person who was watching me, if she wanted mercy, wanted admiration—or stupefaction—more. I was bound to disappoint her. I'd grown up

103

with a poor sense of the ridiculous, if only because I was surrounded by it and had no idea of the alternatives. That September I would go East to college (my father urged me to try Barnard because I was "a little hick" and spending some time in New York would be good for me) and would make a large number of friends, in part because I took everybody seriously. I don't remember when I began to understand that people other than Charlie Chaplin and the Marx Brothers could be funny, but maybe I will as I go along.

"C'm'on," Louisa said, "I'll show you the rest of the house. It's not as bad as this. My room isn't, anyway. They let me fix it the way I wanted to, once I said I'd stay."

I followed her upstairs (same rug, same walls). She had the room at the top of the steps, partly, she explained, because she was sort of a caretaker. Someone up the block did the plumbing and other repairs, and an ex-girlfriend of Teddy's came in once a week to clean, but she, Louisa, was the guardian of the house and had to "notify the I-land" if she was going away. A considerable improvement over her childhood, she said, when once her stepfather moved in, all he and her mother wanted was for her to disappear for long periods, and they couldn't have cared less where she was.

Before I had to think of a response to that one, she threw open the door to her room.

I smiled. If I had little sense of humor, a sense of contrast was inescapable. Pierre Deux hadn't emigrated west yet, but this was a room designed by a rich 1950s sorority girl for her now teen-age daughter—a flowery boudoir with tiny purple pansies on the wall-paper, sheer, white curtains on the windows, and a fluffy violet rug on the floor.

"How pretty," I said, because it was clear that that was what I was supposed to say. In fact, I loathed the color violet (I'm always tempted to initial-cap the word) and virtually every other color in what I suppose one would have to call its family.

Louisa beamed. "Isn't it beautiful?" Then her expression grew dark. "If I'm delaying giving notice, it's only because I hate the thought of leaving this room. It makes me happy. It's the first ror ɹ I've ever had that was exactly the way I wanted it to be."

"Then I *especially* don't understand why you think you have to go," I said, as she closed the door.

"It's not that I *have* to, it's that I *want* to. Maybe it's not even that. Maybe it's that I think He wants me to."

"You mean Marx? Why should he—?"

"No, dodo. I don't mean Marx. I mean He with a capital H. Your father."

I shook my head in what I hoped looked like firm denial, even as I remembered his words to me earlier that day.

"I don't know where you get these ideas," I said.

"I don't either," she replied. "But they're never a hundred percent wrong. Anyway, I need something to drink. At the very least, I need coffee. How about you?"

I said that I'd love some coffee, and she led me back to the main floor, then down another flight of stairs to the basement.

Aside from an open kitchen and a closed shower-bathroom, the space was dominated by a huge swimming pool around which were scattered some chaise longues. There were two little windows that would have let in light and air had they not been covered. The man who'd been lying on the sofa upstairs was now lying on one of the chaises in swimming trunks, but he was still—or once again—fast asleep. Sitting at the edge of the pool, near the foot of his chaise, with her own feet diddling around in the pool water, was a very young, not bad but not terribly good-looking blonde in a black bikini. She appeared not to notice our entrance but to be carefully studying her toes, or perhaps it was her toenails, each time they came out of the water.

"Stay close," Louisa whispered in my ear. "This whole place is bugged, or at least it used to be, and it can be still. Teddy did it because he was turned on by some of what went on down here, he never came except to look or listen, I'm pretty sure he can't swim, but anyway . . . once or twice I know people've been hit with stuff they said down here, so just cool it."

She prepared coffee in an electric percolator which she then decided to bring upstairs so we wouldn't have to keep coming back for more. But when we got to the front porch, we found two young women, one quite pretty, both in tennis whites and holding rackets, sitting on the big porch swing, talking and giggling and waiting to be discovered.

"Oh, shit," Louisa said. "Look, girls, there're no men around and you're wasting your talents. If you want to get to where Teddy is, I'll give you the directions for the airport. The plane only leaves once a day, but there's a boat, if the captain's in the mood."

The less pretty girl stared at Louisa. The prettier one picked herself up out of the swing, bent over to help her friend up and led her toward the beach in a sassy walk that was clearly a response not only to the unpleasant information Louisa had conveyed but to the abrupt manner in which she'd conveyed it.

"Oh, shit," Louisa said again. "I'm hungry. I don't keep any food in the refrigerator here or I'd be eating all the time. Let's just take a walk and get something to eat. Or drink, for that matter. I'm not sure which I'd like more, but there really isn't any place close enough to walk to that has food you can stand to eat."

I must have been staring at her; she was still holding the tray with the percolator and other coffee fixings.

"You prob'ly think I'm nuts, don't you," she said, disconsolate but still hopped up. "I'll tell you what we'll do. I'll plug in the percolator up here, and we'll go to the grocery and get some lunch. Dinner. Whatever you want to call it. And bring it back here. Or would you rather get some Mexican food? Oh, goddamn, I don't know what's wrong with me, I swore off Mexican food for at least a week. Maybe I'm not even hungry, I just *think* I am. It seems more like a week than a couple of hours since I was, you know . . . at the palace."

I was getting a headache. Further, I craved some coffee. My eyes must have gone to the percolator. Louisa, ever the observer, used this as an occasion to launch into a fresh attack on herself, specifically on the matter of why she was in such a state that she couldn't even be reasonably hospitable and pour a goddamn cup of coffee for someone. All of which was accompanied by her doing just that and then, when the rest of the monologue was finished, sitting down and urging me to sit with her.

I sat and sipped. It tasted terrible.

"I know it's terrible," Louisa said. "I have to buy some fresh stuff. I've been going out for breakfast. I'm all alone in this big house that's supposed to be so full of people all the time and I wake up and . . . I've had one really terrific lay since I was here but the rest . . . Oh, shit. Maybe you'd just better go back to Beverly Hills and forget about me."

I remained silent.

"And I," she added after a moment, "I should go back to New York and forget about me, too."

I smiled and sipped at the dreadful coffee, neither without difficulty.

"You seem older than you are," Louisa said. "That's why I keep thinking I can talk to you. Of course, you're also my sister. Sort of. But that's a trickier one, isn't it?" She waited for a response, and when she didn't get one, said, "Or maybe you don't think it's tricky. Maybe I can talk to you about anything I feel like talking about."

"Sure," I said doubtfully.

Her need was too great to allow her to register the doubt.

"The biggest problem with this place—no, *my* biggest problem with this place—is that I came in on a roll. It ruined me for the rest. The first lay I had here was the great one, and I thought I was all set. He was even smart, but that wasn't what counted. He was the one I bought the car from. I met him at a party at your father's house when I first . . . he was . . . still is, I just talk about him in the past tense 'cause I wish he was dead. No, not dead. That's evil. Just chained to a rock somewhere having his gizzard pecked at by birds. He's a scriptwriter for the studio. Blacklisted so he can't even use his own name. Has to work like a dog because of alimony demands."

Louisa went on at some length on the subject of the son of a bitch who was Hugo Bernkastel. They'd fallen into conversation at Sam's house shortly after she'd arrived, and when she'd just landed the job with *Honey*. He'd driven her home in the Volks and when she'd said she was going to have to buy a car, he'd told her he was unloading this one and she could have it for half of what he'd planned to list it for in the Classified. They'd made the deal and he'd disappeared from her life. She hadn't seen him again until he'd shown up once or twice at the I-land.

As it became apparent that Louisa was talking about Hugo, I had started and then withdrawn. Now my body was in the frozen mode of an animal not wanting the hunter to detect her, but my brain was racing backward to my own brief encounter with him, forward to whether I would run into him simply because I was spending time at *Honey*, and sideways toward the matter of composing myself in such a way as to avoid detection. There was no way I was going to share my own Hugo misfortune with Louisa.

Fortunately, she required only a sympathetic listener as she went through the list of what sounded more like her conquests than like men she thought of as having conquered *her*.

"Oh, well," she said finally with a sigh, "enough. Talk to me. Tell me something. Or ask me."

"How come this house is so empty?" I asked. "I thought there were people coming and going all the time."

"There used to be," she said, "but they cut back the budget. The I-land costs a small fortune, not a small fortune, a *large* fortune, to keep afloat, and Teddy's accountants have been after him to sell this place. Not that it costs anything compared to the I-land, but it's still plenty. Anyway, he's not selling it but he's not putting any money into it either. No drinks at the bar, food, the amenities. The whole *feeling's* changed, so nobody comes anymore except his cousins from Minneapolis or an occasional teen-age pussycunt."

In spite of myself, I flinched at the phrase. She noticed without understanding my reaction and apologized for being on such a downer.

"I'd offer to take you to see it," she said, "but you're not legal, and they're in one of their phases where they're checking I.D. That doesn't mean they don't smuggle over an occasional thirteen-year-old on the plane, but it has to be one of the pimps who does it, not Teddy. I'm sorry. I can tell the way I talk is too much for you sometimes, but I like you, you seem like a pretty good kid to me, and as soon as I like someone, I just sort of relax, and the truth comes tumbling out, whatever the truth is, and I don't really know anyone out here to talk to, just, you know, two-hour phone calls, all that stuff you're supposed to have outgrown at my age. Oh, shit. I'd be better off at home with my . . . No, I wouldn't. I'm better off here, if I can stand it, at least while I'm writing."

"I forgot you were a writer."

"Mmm. I don't talk about it. I mean, any asshole in the world can say he's a writer, you know? When I get a book published, then people'll know."

"Out here, it's not so much that everyone's a writer as everyone's going to get into the movies." I felt shy as I said it. There'd been some radical change in her demeanor; someone new had slipped into her body. For the first time, she was the adult to my teen-ager.

"Mmm," she said. "A good point. The prevailing fantasy changes."

The sun was hidden now, but there were plenty of people on the beach. Some played ball, others walked, a few surfers were in the water. Every once in a while a walker on the street stopped to pat the dogs, or crossed the street with his or her own dog to avoid them.

"What's the prevailing fantasy in New York?" I finally asked.

"Oh, I dunno," she said. "Anyway, I didn't live in New York. I lived in the Bronx, and when I got married I lived in a suburb. I don't know if you know what a suburb is because out here there's hardly anything *but*. Even the so-called City here feels like . . . I shouldn't really talk about it because I haven't spent time there to speak of. But it's like . . . the black ghetto's a suburb and the City of Los Angeles . . . what they're pleased to call a city . . . is just a few office buildings. Anyway, the fantasy's changed in the past couple of years. It used to be two point five children and a house in the suburbs was going to make everyone happy. It's just beginning to occur to some of them that maybe they missed out on something. They just don't know what it is yet. Nobody in the town where I lived ever heard of dope or sex until the past year or two. I'm not kidding. They're just beginning to try to figure out why they're not happy."

"Is that why you came here?"

She grinned, shrugged her shoulders.

"Sure. I'm just a typical suburban housewife."

"When did you begin to feel it? I mean, curious. Or whatever." I was aware of the likelihood that she was joking, or at least half-joking, but I couldn't think of a way to incorporate the notion into our conversation.

"Ohhh . . ." She stood up, yawned, and with her hands in her jeans pockets began pacing the porch, "I never *didn't* feel it, really. I mean, I married a nice, superstraight fellow—the first super-straight fellow who asked, if the truth must be told—an engineer who had about as much imagination as . . . doesn't matter. Didn't matter. At least I thought it wouldn't. I figured I had enough imag-ination for both of us. I figured I'd live a nice life, kids would fill up whatever spaces there were, and I'd make all the recipes in the ladies' magazines and use the best detergent and I'd be as happy as everyone else. Didn't work out that way. Or at least if that's as happy as anyone is, I'm not ready to know it."

I waited. If she mentioned her son, I might have a better idea of what I wanted to ask. But she'd fallen silent.

"How old is your son?" I finally asked, not without trepidation.

"Five," she said calmly. "Almost six. He was five when I left."

Do you miss him? Do you talk to him on the phone? How could you do it? I can see that you're not easy to get along with, but you're not a monster, either. How could you? It's just what was done to you and you've never forgiven him!

She stopped pacing.

"What do you want to know? How I could do it? He'll barely know the difference. He adores his father. When he was younger he didn't know the difference between when his father was there and when he was at the office, and in those days I was with him all the time. Now he waits for the jerk at night as though he's not going to survive until the train pulls in at the Scarsdale station. What do you think of *that* for the name of a place to live, by the way? Scarsdale. I used to think that'd be the name of my first book, except I'm afraid I'd get nauseous every time I looked at the cover. Anyway, at the time I left, the kid's whole life was waiting to go to the station at night for Papa. Or it was someone else's turn to do the pickup so suddenly the front door opens, and there He is. Daddy! The Man! Anyone who cooked and cleaned could do what I was doing for him. Services. I was a hired hand. Anyway, even if I hadn't been, who the fuck is Benjamin Abrahms to have two parents? I didn't at his age, and I grew up. Not happy, but I grew up, and who grows up happy anyhow? Who says a kid has two parents and then he's happy? Anyone who says it'll have to prove it to me."

I was, of course, silent. I tend to believe that ten years later I'd have reacted with the same dismay, if not the same puzzlement, to such an outburst, but at the beginning of that summer of 1966, the so-called Summer of Love, which turned out to be almost as short-lived as any ordinary summer, I'd never heard the likes of it. There is a tendency among outsiders to think of Hollywood as the cradle of hip, if not its birthplace, but the cradle of discontent is a more accurate description, the place to discover that even when all your dreams come true—*You're a Movie Star, Baby!*—you don't feel the way you thought you'd feel if it happened, or understand how to make life work as you'd once assumed it might.

I suppose movie people surrendered to the domination of sex much earlier than the population at large, its pleasures and intensities being even more than normally welcome in a place where people need constantly to convince themselves that they're real. If dope was already used by the hippest group at my school, the dissatisfaction mothered by dope (the bomb being, I suppose, the father) was not yet pervasive or even visible. It had been possible for me, while Tony lived, to proceed under the influence of his benign authority, steering clear of the sexual-pharmaceutical possibilities that presented themselves to me. Even now, a member of the second hippest group, which was still into politics rather than sensual surrender, I presumed that real life had an order to it. If I thought of myself as not having grown up within that order, I hoped it could be found when I began to look. More particularly, when I began to look away from home. Most particularly, I thought it might be found on the East Coast. Even in places with names like Scarsdale.

Louisa said, "Let's go get something to eat."

I said, "I think I'd better get back."

"I'm sorry. I'm doing it again," she groaned. "I wouldn't have said it if you hadn't asked."

I nodded.

"It's because you're so calm, I keep forgetting. I've been lonely out here, and I . . . . Oh, shit." She sat down next to me on the porch swing, which had been swaying ever so slightly with just me in it. She planted her feet firmly on the ground so that it was still. "Makes me seasick," she said. "You don't mind, do you?"

I shook my head but I couldn't look at her.

"Let me take you to lunch," she said. "Dinner. Whatever it is. Seriously. You don't have to eat if you're not hungry. I just need a real drink."

I was silent.

She stood, walked over to the door, reached inside, came out with one of those huge, pouch-style leather pocketbooks. She sat down next to me, rummaged around in her bag, brought forth a wallet, and from the wallet extracted a plastic picture holder, which she held out to me.

"Here," she said. "You wanna see him? Ben? My kid? Here he is."

It was a color snapshot of the kind taken in schools at the end of the semester or blown up from a group photo. Ben had reddish blond hair precisely the color of my father's, Sonny's and mine (and, of course, now the same as Louisa's), dark eyes and a schoolboy's official-picture grin.

"That's the end of nursery school," she said. "If you turn over the holder"—I did so—"you'll see him with his father a month ago. They send me snapshots every month or two. Does he look different? Less happy? Less healthy?"

The photo showed a very tall, skinny, boyish looking man pitching a ball to Ben, who was waiting with the bat.

"We all have the same color hair," I murmured. "Except Liane."

"And me," she said flatly. "I bleach it. Not because I want to be like everyone else. My hair's a shit-color. I just look better this way."

"Your son's adorable," I said.

"Mmm," she said. "They all are."

After a moment of silence, she stood and stretched. "So. Have I shown my credentials? Do I like my kid just enough so you can have a drink with me? Or should I say, so you can watch while I have a drink? Who knows?" she went on when I hesitated, "Maybe if I get drunk I'll see the error of my ways and run home to the poor thing. Whaddya say, Sunshine?"

Had she heard my father call me that, or had she made it up on her own?

111

"Better yet, maybe you'd like to go to the I-land. I can get drunk for free, and you can have some fun looking around. I can get you past the guard."

I was tempted. I wasn't peaceful enough just to read in my room in Beverly Hills, nor did I have any idea of whether my father would be back yet. Certainly I had no desire to deal with Lynn and/or the girls if he was not.

"Is it that you really want to go and you're afraid to tell me?" Louisa asked. "Because you don't have to be afraid, and you don't have to have a good reason. You can be just plain curious. Don't worry about it," she said. "I'll cover for you. I'll tell them it's an errand of mercy. I really need to go and get drunk, and I don't have any money and I don't feel like going by myself."

A half hour later we were on a large motorboat, heading for the I-land, that mythic 3.7 square miles of land several miles off the California coast bought by Teddy Marx, as some wag once remarked, when *Honey* grew too big for its beaches.

The novel Louisa was eventually sued over was called *Joe Stalbin's Daughters*. Its dictatorial Hollywood producer Joseph Stalbin has a family not entirely unevocative of my own. But Joe Stalbin's vacation palace was not like any of my father's luxurious yet ordinary places. It was Teddy Marx's fantasy-brought-to-life I-land that constantly came to my mind as I read Louisa's book.

We were the only passengers, aside from the Doberman that sat at the skipper's feet and remained on the boat when we left it. The skipper was a huge and hugely fat man named Richie with platinum-blond hair and bright pink cheeks, the sort of person who would have been the symbol of good health in a country where everyone was starving, and indeed appeared to embody strength, if not health, even in this one. His outline was jovial, but his thin lips never exactly smiled, and he wore a gun in a shoulder holster over his black cotton turtleneck, while the outline of a knife was clearly visible through the back pocket of his jeans. Louisa had not stopped talking during the drive to the dock, and she continued her monologue during the boat ride.

"It's not that I really want to leave, yet," she said. "I mean, there's no place I want to go. But I just . . . I'm all right when I can separate Sam from the rest of the *Honey* crowd and not feel as though I'm working for *him*."

"But he's separated from them already, isn't he?"

"Yes and no. I mean, they don't work together, or see each

other much, but Sam's still got money in it, not to speak of . . . Where do you think Dagmar came from?"

"Dagmar?" I was playing for time. It was one of many occasions when I felt that Louisa was drawing a net around my head, if not my entire life.

"He's had her almost as long as he's had Lynn. She went to the Honeycomb to do an exposé. She met your father, and that was that. They've been together ever since."

I felt ill. Every time I thought I'd gotten used to the notion that my father was just who he was, I reacted to some new bit of information in a way that forced me to acknowledge that getting used to him was not one of the possibilities. (I persist, incidentally, in viewing Louisa's method of disclosure as an aggressive act. She pretends to think you already know something so she can talk about it without qualms.)

"Dagmar was the first person I met when I came out here looking for a job. She'd gone from the Honeycomb to the studio in twenty-four hours or less. I have a feeling Teddy's never forgiven Sam. As a matter of fact, my theory is that he bought the I-land to make up to himself for the loss of one of the few people who, you know, he could tell the difference when she left. Also, she's one of the few women . . . When I first came out, I stayed at the house, Sam's house, for a few days, and there was a party. The same party where I met Hugo. The bastard I told you about. I overheard a conversation, Sam telling Lynn that Dagmar would be at the party, and Lynn, I mean, it's not just that she displayed emotion for the first time I'd ever seen, I mean, she had a *shit fit*. And I have to tell you, I don't think she was wrong. To feel threatened, I mean. Dagmar isn't just beautiful, she's smart, decent, altogether wonderful in every way. I'm crazy about her. If I could work for her at this . . . Whoops! Not supposed to talk about it yet. Well, it's not really a secret, anyway. Once five or six people know something, there's no way it's a secret from the rest of the world. Maybe once two people know. Anyway"—a short pause—"I still remember the difference in the way I felt about Sam and the way I felt about Dagmar from the first moment I met them. I mean, she was there the first time I went to the studio. His high-powered assistant, so-called, except she was so *gorgeous* and so *nice* that even if she was smart, she never offended all the people high-powered assistants usually offend. She never throws her weight around, tells you she's the boss's girlfriend, she's starting a magazine, whatever it is. She has none of that need to . . ."

113

The panegyric to Dagmar continued for some time, making me uneasy for reasons I could not have explained, except, perhaps, to say that it was too much. Having exalted the woman at length, Louisa turned to the specifics of her perfection and the places where it spent or intended to spend itself.

Dagmar felt that there was no really decent magazine around for the emancipated female, and if most women had said this to Louisa, she'd have said, so what? That's because most women don't want to be emancipated. But when Dagmar said it, she had to think. Dagmar wanted to do a woman's magazine that would cure the situation, that would be a vehicle for and an incentive to the liberation of the women who *did* want it. When she'd first come to L.A., as much as she'd adored Dagmar, Louisa had found the idea somewhat off base. Now, watching what went on with Sam Pearlstein and with Teddy and Romeo, she had to say . . . "But maybe I don't. Maybe I should just let you see for yourself. I'm going to be interested in your reactions. Welcome to the I-land."

We were standing on the front deck, draped in hooded, khaki-colored rubber ponchos supplied by Richie that protected us from the cold salt spray. We had been riding for ten or fifteen minutes, able to see nothing ahead of us in the dense fog. But now, while there was still no land visible, hundreds of bright lights that had to be in a building—a palace—twinkled at us through the mist. If my judgment was suspended, my heart hadn't been told about it, and I felt as though it were beating wildly to be let out.

I glanced at Louisa. "Do they always keep the whole place lit up that way?"

"I think Teddy's scared of the dark," she said. "But also, most of the lights stay on all the time because there's so much fog out here that even when it's sunny on the mainland, it's darkish here. Someone told me he was depressed for months when he first moved out here because it reminds him of Minneapolis. Where he grew up. It was foggy on the mainland the day he came and saw the place, and he was wild about it, and he put down a huge deposit right away because the agent convinced him some corporation was interested. He never realized till after he moved that it was this way all the time."

The engine was cut. The boat drifted toward what I could just begin to make out as a large dock with a moored yacht and a few small boats tied to its posts.

"Well, here we go," Louisa said. "Just remember, whatever

you see, a lot of good stuff comes out of here. Respectable fiction. Hard-hitting articles. Actually, it's an interesting thing about the arti—"

The boat bumped against the dock. She fell silent. The captain lassoed one of the posts and climbed over the deck rail to finish the job with an agility that was astonishing in someone of his size. A couple of minutes later, he helped us onto the dock.

We stepped from the dock onto a huge, asphalt-paved area where a small plane, a helicopter, one limousine and a couple of pickup trucks were waiting. It occurred to me that I should have called home to say I wouldn't be there for dinner.

"Most of the cars are kept up at the house," Louisa said. "But Teddy doesn't like to keep trucks there because they make people think of work."

Richie went to the driver's seat while Louisa and I climbed into the back of the car. I hadn't yet heard him speak, so that when Louisa asked if he knew where "the master" was, and he answered in a thick New York (it was Brooklyn, actually) accent, the likes of which I'd never heard until I met Louisa, that Mr. Marx was probably in the usual place, I glanced at her in spite of myself.

"He sounds like Sam, only worse, right?" she said with a grin. (A classic example of the difference in our perceptions; to me, her own speech sounded closer to Richie's than Sam's did.)

The smooth, paved road led up a winding hill, and within a minute or two we were in the circular drive in front of the huge mansion, which I could now feel, if not precisely see. A man in a uniform that looked like a real policeman's, holding a Doberman on a leash, came out of the little gatehouse off the circle, checked to see that Richie was driving the car, and handed us a ledger so that we could enter our names, addresses and phone numbers. As Louisa handed him back the ledger, he reached for a phone.

"I'll have to call home and say I won't be there for dinner," I told Louisa.

"Mmm," she said. "But you'll do better if you don't tell him where you are. Unless you don't care if you stay."

I was silent. I had no idea, yet, of whether I'd want to stay or whether I'd be prepared to lie in order to do so.

There was yet another guard with dog at the front door to the mansion, although Louisa was able to get me past this one simply by saying she knew me. A small entrance hallway had stone floors and wallpaper showing various fish one might find in the Caribbean. It opened into a wider hall that, in turn, led through arches to huge rooms on either side. The floors were stone throughout the halls, which is worth mentioning primarily because at this moment two cherub-faced blondes came wandering in our direction, each with one arm around the other, each wearing blue jean shorts but nothing at all on top, or on her feet. (At the moment, the no-shoes seemed a much more radical act.) One had a flower and the word LOVE tattooed above her left nipple. They were talking and giggling and appeared to be oblivious to the cold, to us and to anything else that was going on.

I asked Louisa if they weren't freezing and she said that they all convinced themselves that they weren't because if they covered their breasts or their feet, Teddy wouldn't look at them.

In the room on the right, a huge den with mahogany furniture and Oriental carpets, a large group of people stood or sat around a roulette table presided over by yet another young blonde, this one in a sort of bikini made of sheer stretch fabric that turned itself into a tutu-like short skirt. Everyone attended actively to what was happening at the table, but little noise issued from the room.

The room on the left was the library. Dark wood built-in bookcases held thousands of books and magazines as well as a stunning array of pornography; the upper shelves could be reached by using one of the lovely curved ladder-stools parked at either side. One long wall was entirely covered by a built-in aquarium in which hundreds—or perhaps thousands—of tropical fish swam. Comfortable chairs and sofas were scattered around the room and there were telephones next to each of them. The phones there and throughout the house rested on elegant little filing cabinets in keeping with the decor of their respective rooms. Louisa pointed out to me that each of these pieces had a wide mailbox-style slot in the top and had actually been designed to take garbage. Teddy couldn't bear to throw anything away, and one of his more trusted assistants went through the trash before it was ground up in a machine in the basement and used as landfill on the I-land.

I called home and told Lynn I wouldn't be there for dinner.

"Well," Louisa said when I'd hung up, "whaddya say we look for the Big Stinger?"

I was dumb with wonder and discomfort and could barely shrug my shoulders to indicate that I was willing to be led. Louisa led me.

First downstairs, to what must have once been a monstrous basement and was now a more luxurious version of the basement in Santa Monica, complete with monstrous indoor pool, stone grotto, dense foliage and tropical-bird cages so large as to leave the impression the birds were not in captivity at all. Back up to the main floor and around the quarters sacred to Marx and his intimate (the women that week, the male business associates for many years) crew. Then through the adjoining maze, where women, as I thought of them then, young girls as I would call them now, were reading movie magazines, giggling, giving each other massages; through a steam room, an exercise chamber and a sauna where men in various stages of undress that revealed as much paunch as muscle were lifting weights, pedaling stationary bicycles or just sweating profusely, while young girls in diaperish bikini bottoms waited to provide them with lotions, towels or other amenities. Louisa explained that the girls were free to use the equipment until two in the afternoon, by which time the men were beginning to arrive or wake up.

We returned to the main foyer and moved up the winding crimson-carpeted staircase that led to the second floor.

"You want to sit down for a minute?" she asked as we reached the top. "I was thinking about fucking Hugo, that's Fuckin' Hugo, the adjective, not the verb, because this was the only place I ever saw him after . . . anyway, with his hand on some sixteen-year-old tit . . . one of the few who ever managed to get it up in a place where everything's encouraging them to do it, like you used to be supposed to drink your milk 'cause it was good for you. Do you think all great lays are bastards? Running through women the way women run through stockings? Never mind. Don't answer that. Sorry I asked." She plopped down on the top step and beckoned to me to sit beside her, which I did. "I'm sorry I keep harping on the son of a bitch, but it's hard for me to forget him. Especially here. When Hugo turns off, he does it all the way. None of this drippy-faucet stuff; when he's finished with you, he barely recognizes your face. So then what do you do? Go crying to your daddy? 'Daddy, this guy who worked for you fucked me!' 'Yes, dear, and what is your complaint, that he didn't fuck you well?' 'No, Daddy, that he stopped.' Oh, shit, I'm doing it to you again, aren't I, Miss Nellie. Well, you've survived me this long, I suppose I'm not going to ruin you now." She paused, glanced at me. "Am I?"

I smiled, not without difficulty. I shook my head. In fact it was impossible for me to tell how much of my numb wonder was brought on by Louisa, how much by my surroundings. I think her idea of me as a child of the movie colony prevented my half sister from perceiving my naiveté. Just as my idea of the movie business was framed by considerations of business, my picture of filmmaking itself was a realistic one that included bored and sweating actors and actresses, hot lights, and hard work so repetitive as to be numbing. No one but actors and actresses in the middle of love scenes could ever have confused what they were doing with pleasure. While here, in a place that felt less real than any set I'd ever been on, people seemed to be working almost as hard to convince themselves they were alive and having a good time.

We were in a long, wide hallway with smaller hallways that branched off it. The feeling was impersonal, like that of a chain hotel; the doors *looked* locked. A Mexican woman in a maid's uniform scurried by with a cart of linens and cleaning stuff.

"Most of the doors don't lock," Louisa said. "We were having some trouble—*they* were having some trouble with dopers locking themselves in. There were a couple of fires. And then someone we found out was a cop visited and scared Teddy out of his mind. The cop just wanted to get laid, but it was like a warning, and Teddy listened. Now there are special rooms where you can, you know, do your thing. . . ." She laughed. "No, you don't know. And it's *their* thing, isn't it. Not yours. Anyway, there's not that much that goes on here anymore. I mean, there's more dope than sex these days. They say Teddy still likes it but has a harder time, or I suppose I should say a less hard time, getting it up. The sex is mostly between the women. Whatever that is. You can try some of the doors if you feel like it. If they're not supposed to open, they won't."

I shook my head. I couldn't imagine what I might find and lacked the desire to know.

We'd reached a place in the hallway where a smaller hall branched off to each side of us and a staircase was visible at each end. A blond girl in a sheer pink negligee and high-heeled pink mules was mincing down the left staircase, yawning. She was followed by a tall, Mexican man in a Kung Fu uniform.

"Teddy's suite's at that end," Louisa said. "Don't ask me what they were doing there. The only thing that really freaks me out here is . . . Never mind. What did we miss?"

"The other staircase, I guess."

"Ah, yes. The other staircase. I'll tell you what we'll do. We'll go down to the bar in the basement, I have to talk to Teddy anyway, if he's around, and I'll tell you about the other staircase."

I hesitated. I don't know why. Maybe it was just her sudden eagerness to get me out of there. But I was also tired.

She laughed.

"Okay, you wait here, and I'll go get a drink and bring it back. I don't see any of the porters around and *I'm dying for a drink!* Sit on the steps. But wait for me, okay? There're a couple of places you probably shouldn't go."

She went down the stairs. I sat on the top step for some time, waiting for her to return, thinking about Louisa and Hugo in bed together someplace, trying to figure out what feelings more specific than a mild nausea this aroused in me. Two blond girls in bikini bottoms, carrying towels, came out of a room and headed down the stairs. Still no Louisa. I was growing uneasy. Maybe she'd been swallowed up in some dark cavern under the mansion and I'd have to find my own way home.

Cautiously I stood, stretched, walked down the hall toward the second staircase in a manner so casual that it was possible to fool even me into thinking I had no destination. At the bottom of those steps I paused and, hearing nothing, walked slowly up them. The first two doors were closed but the ones on either side of the hall just beyond them were open. I could hear a child's voice and the answering murmur of what sounded like an old woman. I half walked, half tiptoed toward the open door through which the voices were coming.

It was a huge, well-lighted room with floral-papered walls and sheer organdy curtains. There were neatly made twin beds, each with a white-painted rattan headboard and a pretty white organdy spread. White night tables with delicate glass lamps on them stood next to the beds. The wall at the end of the room was covered by a series of low white tables and bureaus above which were mounted shelves that ran the wall's length. The table in the center was a vanity which, instead of being full of makeup and perfume, held a milliner's wooden head with a veiled red hat on it. Scattered over the rest of the vanity's surface as well as on the carpet nearby were ribbons, veils, velour crowns—the gadgets and materials of a milliner's salon.

The woman who sat at the vanity, looking into the three-sided mirror and holding a fourth in one hand, was tiny and quite old, with silvery hair on which rested a lovely little green pillbox (I'd not heard of such a hat at the time, and when I first heard the name, I laughed). She wore a pink velour bathrobe. Standing on a stool behind her and in almost direct profile to me was a boy who looked about Sonya's age, but who, I learned later, was ten. He was a nice-looking boy with curly black hair and bright pink cheeks, wearing what was essentially a one-piece ankle-length pale blue leotard. He was quite absorbed in the matter of correctly pinning a delicate green veil to the pillbox, so that I was surprised and discomfited when he asked, in a rather dignified tone and with speech that had a strong lisp to it, whether I was looking for someone or he might help me in some other way.

I started.

He looked up, eyed me in a not unfriendly way and said, "I'm Theodore Markth, Jr., and thith ith my grandma, Jethie Markth."

"How do you do," I said, managing politeness in spite of my astonishment. "My name is Nell. Nell Pearlstein."

"Pearlthtein, Pearlthtein," he said, coy and thoughtful. "That'th a familiar name."

"My father is Sam Pearlstein." Out of the corner of my eye, I could see Louisa coming down the hallway toward me. "Louisa's my half sister."

He nodded amiably, said something that sounded like "Half thitherth better'n whole," then added, "I'd like you to meet my grandma."

I raised my hand in salutation just as Louisa came up beside me, carrying a drink the color of whiskey and looking as though she might already have had a few.

"So," she said, "you have deprived me of the pleasure of introducing you to Ted's family."

"Oh, can it, Louithe," Teddy said with gentle irritation. "We're perfectly capable of introduthing ourthelves. Grandma, thay hello to Nell."

The old lady swiveled solemnly so that she was facing me, and without lowering the mirror in one hand, raised her other in the manner of an Indian chief.

"How," she said.

"Not so much How, but Why?" Louisa muttered near my ear.

The old lady swiveled back.

"I think we'd better be going," Louisa said.

"Let me know if there'th anything I can do for you, Nell," the boy said, making a neat little farewell gesture that was somewhere between a curtsy and a bow.

I thanked him and followed Louisa through the hall, then down the steps to the ground floor, where she turned to me with a grin.

"I suppose you know we weren't supposed to be there. I mean, Teddy tries not to make a big thing of it, if anything, he just talks about Junior's need to not be invaded constantly by strangers, but the kid absolutely adores being invaded by strangers, and I think it's just about Teddy's image. With a capital I."

I was too dazed to respond.

"Do you want something to drink?" she asked. "Or eat? The food in the cafeteria's terrific, everyone's favorites of what isn't Mexican. Peanut butter and jelly sandwiches, Roquefort cheese, tomato and avocado on pumpernickel, that's Teddy, Jr.'s favorite." She finished her drink, set down the glass at the side of the top step, under the railing.

I told her I wasn't really hungry.

"All right," she said after a moment's hesitation. "I'll tell you what we'll do. Or, at least, what *I* think we should do. I think *you* should ramble around the library and the gambling rooms for a while. Look at the fish. Whatever. Just sit and relax for a few minutes. *I'm* going to get another drink"—again I had that unpleasant sensation that she'd been inside my head, that she was only mentioning the drink because she'd picked up my noticing it—"and check to see if Big Ted's in the bedroom, his office, as he calls it, and if so, what kind of a mood he's in, whether he wants to meet you, and so on. Then, depending, we'll either have dinner here or we'll get Richie to take us back to the mainland. Okay? You don't have to worry about my drinking, by the way. I have what's known in the trade as a hollow leg."

I nodded mutely. She hadn't questioned whether I wanted to meet the boss but only whether he would want to meet me, so there was nothing I had to think about.

She waved jauntily and headed toward some back hallway I hadn't noticed yet. I remained where I was for a few moments, dazed, certainly incapable of figuring out what to do or where to go. The gambling rooms weren't appealing, and there was no way I could relax enough to sit and wait in the empty library. I might have enjoyed looking at the fish if Louisa hadn't suggested it.

The hallway was extremely wide and ran from the front entrance clear to the glass French doors in the back, with doors and open arches lining it on both sides. Near the glass doors, a very large, that is to say, very tall, and big without being fat-looking, female with a tough face and wavy platinum hair sat straddling a bench, playing solitaire and, it appeared, guarding the doors. She wore a long-sleeved, elasticized black tube top, white shorts and knee-high black-leather boots over a dancer's black-mesh stockings.

I hesitated, remembering the outdoor pool Louisa had mentioned before we came to the island. I could be a good girl and wait and ask her to see it. Or I could be independent and find it without waiting. There was a certain appeal to breaking rank again; no single one of the castle's phenomena had thrown me, but collectively they'd given me the sense of being in a dream that couldn't even be labeled good or bad. Outside, sitting in cool darkness, I might be able to collect myself enough to tell which it was, if not precisely what I felt about it.

I walked back to the glass doors, nodded politely to the woman, who looked me over and asked if I wanted to go out.

"Please," I said.

She shrugged. "So go."

I would have laughed except she didn't seem to think she was being funny. I twisted the handles of both doors and started to push them outward, but they swung open in a way that made it clear they were electronically controlled. I walked out onto a flagstone path. The doors closed behind me.

I was in a garden so large that I couldn't see its boundaries. It was lighted but dimly, rosily. The time was close to six by now, and the sky had more darkness than that lent by the fog. The trees I could see were evergreens, the plants cacti and semisucculents whose thick leaves, swollen with their own juices, could resist a desert's dryness or the sea's salty spray. There was upholstered outdoor furniture scattered around. Here and there a couple sat on one of the settees, speaking earnestly or even, in one instance, arguing softly.

Following the lighted path, I found myself at a huge, beautiful pool with a dark bottom and curvy, irregular fieldstone edges. There were no lights on around the sides, but the water was lighted by pink lights within the pool, and it was very beautiful. My breath caught because at the shallow, dimly lighted end farthest from me, there was a series of deep, broad steps, and on one of them a man was making love to a woman whose head rested on one of his arms. Her long blond hair trailed in the water. They were both naked. The man half looked up, as though he'd sensed an intrusion without actually seeing me. After a moment he returned to his lovemaking. I'd seen only part of his profile and that fleetingly. But I thought—even at that moment I was far from certain because he was fifty or sixty feet away from me and the light was dim—that he was Jack Campbell.

I ran back to the house, where I knocked lightly on the glass doors and was admitted by the guard blonde. Inside, I sat on the bench near the glass doors and hoped she wouldn't ask why I was trembling.

So what? You know men do things like that, so what's the big deal even if it was Campbell?

122

But it didn't work. He had been so sweet, so good, the first man I'd allowed myself fantasies about since Hugo! Was there no safety even in fantasy because anything could turn out to be true? I reminded myself of how unlikely it was that Jack Campbell would be on the I-land, assured myself that it was only because I'd been thinking about him that I thought I'd seen him. But I couldn't make myself believe me.

When Louisa came up a couple of minutes later, she took one look at my face and asked what had happened. I told her nothing had happened, and she said I shouldn't lie to her, that if I didn't feel like telling her about it, I didn't have to, although that was leaving her uncovered, in a sense. In any event, she didn't like being lied to.

I hung my head.

"Was she in the garden?" Louisa asked the guard blonde.

The guard blonde nodded.

"The pool?" Louisa pressed.

The guard blonde didn't answer, but my head must have bobbed, or hung even heavier.

"Oh, shit," Louisa said. "That's the only place here where anything ever . . . Look, we can talk about it later. Teddy's down there and he wants to meet Sam's other daughter."

I looked at her. There was no way I could even respond, much less stand up and follow her.

"I should've prepared you. There's not much sex going on here but when it goes on . . ."

"I want to go home," I said, and then, thinking that I sounded like a little kid on the first day of kindergarten, I added, "I mean, I think I ought to get back."

I was sure that sounded better, but Louisa, with those antennae that worked so well when they weren't being blocked by some static of her own, was staring at me.

"Did something else happen? Nobody bothered you, did they? You didn't see something bad?"

I shook my head, but I couldn't look at her.

"Oh, Jesus. We'd better . . . Look, come downstairs for a few minutes, we'll—"

Again I shook my head.

"Look," she said with a sigh, "if you really can't, you can't. But if it's humanly possible . . . He gets very cranky when you promise him something and you don't deliver. I'm not saying he'll fire me if you don't decide to stay, but . . ." Dolefully, she let her words trail off.

I couldn't speak, but clearly I couldn't refuse to go with her, either. I nodded. She thanked me, turned, and led me through a maze of corridors I would have guessed, if I hadn't known where we were going, led to the servants' quarters. The ceilings were lower, the halls narrower, and where there was decoration it was a photograph of a park or a variety-store oil painting of a sailboat.

"I tried to get him not to be too outrageous," Louisa said, "but just don't act surprised about anything."

Louisa knocked at a door and opened it without waiting.

"Hi," she said. "Here we are, Pearlstein's daughters."

I'd been in too much of a daze to have expectations, but now I was thoroughly diverted. Here were the pink walls of the old Honeycomb, along with plush red carpeting and a ceiling draped in red velvet. Along that wall where the throne might have been if this were a throne room was a platform with a series of extremely comfortable-looking easy chairs lined up to face the room's center. Along both of the longer walls were large photographs of naked women, their immediately remarkable quality being the greater variation in the size and shape of their breasts than in their blond hair and parochial-schoolgirl faces. The room had no windows. Below and in front of the photographs on one wall was a series of swings and jungle gyms of the sort found in school playgrounds. On another was a series of flat and tilted surfaces on which were spread out photos and illustrations that might have been under consideration for the magazine. Over these was a display of riding whips, old guns and knives.

Louisa moved aside so I could follow her in, then she closed the door.

In the middle of the room, which measured at least sixty feet square, was a sunken pit about eight feet across and entirely upholstered in the same red velvet as the ceiling drapes. Resting comfortably along the pit wall facing us was a diminutive figure in a one-piece black outfit reminiscent of the drop-seat pajamas we used to call Doctor Dentons. His arms rested along the edge of the pit back. On his right side a blond girl in a black satin bikini whose bra had a right cup but not a left one held a Coke can with a straw against her breast in the place where the left cup would have been. Teddy Marx nodded at me in a friendly way and leaned toward the girl for a sip of the Coke. On his left side another blond girl, wearing high heels, black net stockings and a black satin garter belt, was wrapped in a beautiful embroidered shawl of the sort I would later see in the Ukrainian stores on Second Avenue in New

York. She was massaging in a professional manner the fingers of his left hand. Like the other woman, she appeared to be substantially larger than he was.

"Well," Louisa said with an uncomfortable chuckle, "here she is, my favorite sister. Nell, meet the big boss, Teddy."

Teddy said in a perfectly normal male voice, "Hi, Nell. It's nice to meet you."

I nodded, but I was incapable of speech.

"Why don't you come down here so we can talk?"

"She's a little overwhelmed by the whole place," Louisa said. "And she promised she'd be home for dinner. Maybe next time. She just didn't want to not say hello at all."

Teddy shrugged and turned his attention to the hand that was being massaged. Louisa said we'd better be on our way, she'd already summoned Richie. Then she waved, and we left.

Within half an hour she'd found Richie, and he'd driven us to the boat. Within another few minutes, he'd given us our ponchos, and we were motoring across the bay. Louisa and I were sitting on an open bench only a few feet from Richie, who appeared to have no interest in us or in anything we were saying.

Louisa thanked me for having done what I didn't feel like doing. I said it was okay. She then said she wasn't trying to tell me what to say to my father but she thought if I could find it in myself not to mention the trip, life would probably be easier for everyone. I told her truthfully that I couldn't imagine circumstances in which I would want to tell him. She said that in that case I might all the more like to get off my chest whatever it was that had happened at the pool. But she didn't press me.

I wish she had because the likely effect of her urging would have been to silence me, and maybe some trouble would have been saved, although the truth is, I doubt it. Whatever her reasons, she didn't urge but appeared to fold into herself in a way I might have welcomed in other circumstances.

What I finally said, I am quite certain, was that I thought I'd seen one of Tony's sons-in-law in the pool.

Louisa laughed and said something like "You're kidding. The Italian one?"

And I *might* have said, there are times, that is, when I think I did and other times when I'm certain I *thought* it but simply shook my head, "Uh-uh. The one from Alaska."

She drove me home. I was relieved, as I later told the Campbells' lawyer, that she didn't ask me any more questions. No questions at all on any subject. Most particularly not about Jack Campbell, or about whether a woman was with him in the pool, or about Alaska. This I remember most distinctly. I remember, too, that she began whistling and that she was startlingly good at it. Unfortunately, the song I can hear her whistling, just as clearly as I can hear her saying, "You're kidding," when I told her about Jack Campbell, was, "You can get anything you want at Alice's Restaurant." Which, it was pointed out at the trial, had not yet been written.

We were already in Santa Monica when she told me again that she wasn't sure how long she'd be around or just where she'd be, whether she'd go back to New York or what, but that she would try to stay in touch. I was startled. I had been thinking about Jack Campbell, wondering if it had been a mistake to let her know what it was that had upset me. On the other hand, she'd behaved well once I told her, and I suppose I was feeling that I'd rather have her near me than far away. I said I didn't understand, I thought she'd forgotten the notion of quitting.

"Mmm," she said. "Hardly. I think of it every day. It's just a question of how serious I am about it each time. There's a lot I haven't told you that makes it complicated for me to stay. I had a little thing, a one-timer, with the boss when I arrived. The Teddy boss, not the Sal boss. The Sal boss, nobody talks about this around the place, I don't even know if your father knows it, Sal went back to school a couple of years ago. Medical school. He wants to be a gynecologist and find out all those terrible things about women's bodies he always suspected anyway. I'll tell you something about the Sal boss you probably don't know, probably don't care about either, but anyway, I don't know anyone on the whole island or in Santa Monica who knows for sure that he's ever stuck it into a female in the right place. Except, of course, three times to his wife.

"The same is not true, or certainly never used to be, about Teddy. One might question his taste in females or his technique or the tricks he needs these days, but he appears to like it, especially with these dopey . . . Sometimes I wish I was one of them. I mean, here I am, legally separated, sexy as hell, and living in a place where the only good fuck around is saved for eighteen-year-old blond *shiksas* who don't even like it.

"Anyway, I need to get out of here, look around, do some writing. There's no real future for me in this place. Women don't advance vertically. I mean, they don't advance horizontally, either, but it's possible not to notice that for a while. I guess the truth is,

I think I'll be better off as far as the writing's concerned if I don't have a job that interests me too much. Not that this one's fascinating the way it was supposed to be. When I came here, I mean . . . *Honey* magazine . . ." This magazine that was anathema to most of the idiots she grew up with, a forerunner in the advocacy of sexual freedom when that was exactly what was on her mind after a classic fifties first marriage with no real sex to speak of. It published a lot of respectable stuff as well as the dopey sex advice and stuff. She hadn't thought twice, then, about the *Honey* girls' retouched tits and glossy pink asses. She hadn't been bothered by the notion of hundreds of truck drivers jerking off in centerfolds in motels across the country, happy as pigs in shit because for the first time the quality of the paper was such that they didn't even have to worry about washing the ink off their dicks.

"Whoops. Sorry. I'm forgetting again. Anyway, we're almost at the house. You're welcome to come in, but if I guess right, you're going to head for home, pronto. Listen, kid, I wish you well, in case I don't see you for a while. And I wish . . . Look, if you can stand it, stick with your resolve, you know, not saying anything to your father. If he knows I took you out there, he might get Teddy to can me before I make up my mind to leave."

The car pulled to a stop. I stared at her, at an absolute loss for words. She pointed to her cheek and said that I could kiss her goodbye if the urge was overwhelming. Like an idiot, I thanked her and then sat struggling with myself because I didn't feel like doing it. It wasn't just Louisa. I never kissed females, couldn't understand why some of my friends did. In any event, at some point during my struggles, Louisa glanced toward the house's well-lighted porch and said, "Oh, oh. Someone's waiting for me. Shit. Oh, well, I'm not going to get any work done, anyway. You can come up if you want to. Maybe you want to go to the bathroom or something."

Indeed. I followed her up the steps to the porch. The dogs that had been so vigilant earlier were invisible and inaudible now. The woman on the swing was huddled into herself as though it were freezing, although she wore a black leather jacket over her clothes and the temperature must have been around sixty. She was a peroxide blonde whose dark roots hadn't been worked on for a while. Only when we had reached the top and Louisa had walked over to her did she look up. Her makeup was so badly smeared, presumably from crying, that I couldn't really see her face.

"Hi," Louisa said. "What can I do for you?"

The woman said, "I need a place to hide."

"From whom?" Louisa asked, her manner so cool and collected as to suggest she'd had this conversation many times.

"My husband," the woman said, bursting into tears. "He's threatening to kill me if I leave him, and I . . ." The words became incoherent as the tears took over.

"Look," Louisa said after a moment, "I don't know if we can help, but we'll try. Come on in for a while, and we'll make some coffee, and—wait a minute. He doesn't know you're here, does he?"

The woman shook her head. "He's in Venice. At the place where we work. Worked. I'm not going back there. I hitched over here after he said he would—"

"All right, all right. Hold it. Come on inside."

The woman rose from the porch swing as though she were aching all over and any movement was an effort. Louisa held out an arm to support her. Gratefully the woman took it, and they moved inside, with me trailing as Louisa unlocked the front door and turned on the inside lights. The woman did not appear to be daunted or even mildly distracted by the decor. Louisa led her to the big pink tube and directed her to sit down while she brought in the coffeepot with the coffee she'd begun making in the afternoon and plugged it in. The woman and I sat in silence during the process.

"I'm Louisa, and this is Nellie. What's *your* name?"

"Alice," the woman said. She wasn't crying anymore, but her voice still shook. "Alice Donaldson."

"And your husband's name is—"

"Mitch."

Louisa grinned, glanced at me. "They come from Michigan and they sell—"

"We *don't* come from Michigan," the woman said, clearly upset. "We come, *I* come, from Iowa."

"Sure," Louisa said. "I'm sorry. I wasn't saying . . . There's a ball game we used to play when we were kids. A, my name is Alice, and so on. I . . . Anyway, I'm sorry I interrupted your story."

"I don't have a story," the woman said. "I just . . . I married the first s—guy who promised he'd take me away from it, from the boredom and the . . . I knew he had a record, but he told me he went straight and if I married him, he'd stay straight for life. Instead . . ." She was silent for a while. "I can't stand it anymore, but he threatened to kill me if I tried to get out. I was eighteen

128

years old when I met him. I didn't know anything. I don't know what I'm going to do now!"

"All right," Louisa said. "We hear what you're saying. Nobody's going to make you go back there, so don't get hysterical." She poured coffee into two cups, handed one to Alice, said with a grin that she assumed I didn't want any. She stood up and with her coffee cup in one hand, proceeded to pace around the room.

"Did you bring any of your clothes with you?" she asked Alice.

"Only what I could stuff into my bag," Alice said. "I couldn't look as if I was leaving."

"Mmm. Well, we'll have to figure out a way to get you some stuff. Without some decent clothes, you won't be able to get a job, and without a job . . ."

Louisa proceeded in a breathtakingly organized and managerial manner to figure out how Alice—how *they*, really—were to proceed. She asked questions about Mitch's resources for finding Alice (he had done it before; Alice never knew how), about the place in Venice where he was bartending (it was called, in that incarnation, Shoals; by the time I was taken there by my father on college vacation, it had become the ultra-fashionable Prawn Shop, with its emblematic red-and-white prawn crawling over three brass balls outside), and finally whether she was interested in pursuing the matter with the police. Alice said she had tried it in other cities, and it never worked except to make more trouble for her when the police didn't keep track and Mitch found her again.

Louisa nodded sympathetically. She understood about trying to get protection from the cops. This was incomprehensible to me since I had never known the police to be anything but helpful and protective. They patrolled Beverly Hills as though they were keeping an eye out for their favorite relatives.

I missed some of the conversation when I went to the bathroom. When I returned, Louisa was winding up a little riff about changing Alice's looks so she couldn't be so easily identified.

"Oh, thank you," Alice said, reaching out a hand to Louisa, who was halfway across the room. "Thank you." Again she began to cry.

I was very much the extra person. I didn't sit down again but moved toward the door in what I hoped was a casual manner so Louisa wouldn't think there was anything to *know* about my leaving.

"Listen," I said, "I really have to get home. I'm very tired. Please call me if . . . you know . . . if there's anything . . ."

129

I wasn't certain I wanted to do anything for Alice Donaldson, but I was impressed by the way Louisa had swung into action, and I wanted to show goodwill in this new Alice project. Or in *some* way.

Louisa barely looked at me but waved and said she'd be in touch. I left and was all the way down the stairs and halfway to my car before I realized I'd left my pocketbook behind. I went back up and walked in without knocking. Louisa, who'd been asking about Alice's skills as I left, was sounding like the other woman's best friend, saying that for now Alice would have to take what she could get, but a friend of hers was starting a magazine for real women, not the kind of doughnut-heads who read the ladies' magazines or slobbered over Teddy Marx's pinups, and if they got this magazine going, there'd be plenty of work for both of them. Meantime . . .

I picked up my bag and tiptoed out of the house.

I threw myself into the business of school, which, in my senior year, included college applications. In the first days after returning to my father's home it had been impossible to contemplate going East to school as Tony and I had agreed I probably should. ("I don't like you to go so far," Tony had said to me. "But if you don't go now, later you'll feel you missed something.") Now it began to seem that aside from the East Coast's other lures, I might see *more* of my father if I was there.

He was making frequent trips to New York on studio matters. These were surely important, although their importance didn't necessarily explain why Dagmar always accompanied him. Dagmar was the person he'd appointed to be what he teasingly called my baby-sitter. Problems about money, dentist appointments or needing a physics tutor were to be referred to her. I was more likely to want to talk to Dagmar when my father wasn't around but quickly discovered that when he was out of town, she was as well.

Nor did I see much of Louisa during my remaining months in Los Angeles. Alice moved in with her, and the two of them were as close as the Bobbsey Twins, a name Louisa herself gave them at one point. It turned out that Alice was strong in all those areas— most particularly math and practical matters, everything from fixing toasters to figuring out what was wrong with the plumbing— where Louisa was weak. Louisa was able to get her on the *Honey* payroll as a bookkeeper, it being Alice's job to bring order to the economic records of *Honey*'s first years of existence, before the magazine had been moved to the I-land. The IRS was making audit noises, and Alice was trying to substantiate deductions the examiners might question.

On the rare occasion when Louisa did show up at our house, she evinced no particular interest in the little girls or in Estella. Anyone trying to figure out the subject of the novel she was writing in her spare time might have concluded it had something to do with Lynn or with me. She was particularly interested in the matter of where I was going to college, her attempts to influence my decision being peculiarly inconsistent. Once she would urge me to remain "Western and unspoiled," another time she'd list the reasons I had to try New York, then say she was urging me East on the theory I would decide to stay in Los Angeles just to shut her up. The notion of her having weight on either side was foreign to me.

Her questions and comments about Lynn were pointed and frequently hostile. More than once she tried to draw me into speculation about what our father's fourth (and/or fifth, sixth and seventh) wife would be like. She asked whether I thought he would ever marry Dagmar, and if so, how long it would last. These were the sort of questions I fought off, on the occasion when my own mind came up against them, with daydreams about going to New York and meeting a man just like the man I'd once assumed Jack Campbell was.

Oblivious to Louisa, if not to all of us, Lynn moved around the house as though she were acting in a detergent commercial that could be halted at any moment. There was no sign, even as I look back with a more sophisticated eye, that she minded what she must have known—that my father's sexual as well as mental energies were directed elsewhere. I don't know what she was like at the studio, but at home she was pleasant, competent within the narrow limits she set for herself, unflappable.

Earlier in 1965 there had occurred the Watts riots, about which Lynn eventually tried to make a film. But during that year she, not to speak of everyone else I knew, had no concern with the Watts riots or any other riots, or with the plight of black people. It was as though the events had occurred thousands of miles away rather than at a relatively small distance from Beverly Hills. I recall distinctly my father's coming home from a New York trip and laughing over the fact that someone there had asked him whether there was "continuing fallout in L.A., since the climate never changes." So while it's possible Lynn was already involved with events in Watts and elsewhere in the real world, I am inclined to doubt it. I lived in the same house as she did for a period of eight months and never heard her say a word about them. What I am sure of is that after the day when Louisa expressed astonishment at the change in Sonny's behavior when Estella was present, I never observed her paying particular attention to Sonny *or* Estella.

In 1970 Grove Press brought out *A Servant's Diary* by Elena Martinez, a book that was not reviewed in any New York publication and attracted little attention then or for some time thereafter. I picked up the *Diary* years later in my father's library on a visit from New York, where I was living and attending law school. I remember the casual curiosity I felt as I opened it, the near-hypnosis in which I continued to turn the pages.

I thought S.S. was gone from the house.

I stood behind V., brushing her shiny, platinum-white hair as she sat at her dressing table, looking into the mirror. In the time that I had come to be with her, her hair had grown down to below her waist. It felt like silk, and I loved to rub it against my lips. She wore a pale blue satin kimono she had not troubled to belt. It fell away to show her perfect round breasts. Her eyes met mine in the mirror.

"I have never nursed my children, Elena," she said, "because I wanted to be perfect when I met you."

The room became brighter. The wallpaper's red roses grew more brilliant. The sun reflected more powerfully off the paper's white background. I felt that I might grow blind but I wasn't frightened. It was more as though my eyes had seen everything I had ever dreamed they might see and I would not need them any more.

V. swiveled around on the little stool. I sank to my knees and buried my face between her breasts, which my hands pressed into my cheeks. I rubbed her nipples between my fingers and she moaned. They grew hard and bumpy. I bent my head to—

Behind me a door opened. There were heavy steps on the polished wood floor, then soft ones as he approached us on the carpet.

"Don't stop," V. moaned to me softly. "Don't stop now."

What follows is a sort of *orgie à trois* that is extremely sexy without being heterosexual, a phenomenon still unfamiliar to most of us at the time of the book's publication. I don't mean the book is homosexual in feeling. Rather, it seems to go to some place where it barely matters which part of which sex's body is involved. Where often one can't tell whether the sucking of the master's penis or one of the mistress's breasts is being described.

Nor is it only sexual parts that are difficult to distinguish. The house where the action occurs feels crucially sealed off from reality. More than once as I read the *Diary* I remembered how when I was younger my father, seeing a set or some prop he didn't like, would say, "That ain't a set [or whatever], that's a flying lox box!" The house is a flying lox box, not locatable in time or space. The bedroom where the action occurs is a child's fantasy in fur and blue satin; the physical objects are described with the same sensual attention as the skin, hair and other physical properties of the three protagonists.

Well, that's not quite accurate; we don't really see the male of the triangle, S.S., except in terms of his effect. We know that he is big and strong, a sexual cyclone, because of the acts he performs and the effect they have on the women, not because his features are ever delineated. The females are another matter.

V. is a slender reed of a woman with tiny, beautifully round breasts and buttocks, long platinum hair and eyes that reflect her surroundings like a clear pond. Elena never describes herself, but V. and S.S. find her incredibly beautiful, talking to her and to each other about her shiny pitch-black hair, her generous breasts and her skin, so soft as to put the bed's satin coverlet to shame.

S.S., V. and Elena are the only characters in the book, which never leaves V.'s bedroom. But we are aware of a *presence* just outside the room and clamoring to join the magical trio. There is the distinct sense that this presence is a child who wants Elena's attention. Elena is aware of the child's desire and occasionally leaves the room to tend to her. The two "adults" can barely wait for her to return.

The cover of *A Servant's Diary* is a photograph so fuzzy that it's difficult to make out the buttons on a maid's uniform being opened by a strongly masculine pair of hands. The author's biography in the back of the book reads as follows:

Elena Martinez was born and raised in a cottage in Delicias, Province of Chihuahua, Mexico, the oldest of four sisters and five brothers in an impoverished family. She married and had a child, but the poverty of her parents' family as well as her own forced her to leave the baby with her parents and seek employment in Los Angeles. She found a job with the Hollywood director she calls S.S. and stayed with the family for years because the excellent wages S.S. paid enabled her to support her entire family in Delicias. At some point, however, the situation became more than she could tolerate, and she arranged to fly home with the friend of a son of S.S. who had his own plane. Shortly before their scheduled departure, she became convinced that because of what she'd been through with S.S. and V., she could never face her family again. She persuaded the young pilot to take her to British Columbia. He left his family a note saying that in case of an accident, he wanted them to understand it had been Elena's choice, not his own, to conceal their destination.

It ends with a description of the wreckage of the small plane in which Elena's and the pilot's bodies were found.

I'll detail later the way I became aware that *A Servant's Diary* had been written by Louisa. For now let me just say that when *Scarsdale*, published a few years later, was called her first novel, I had no reason to question its being just that.

I went East to Barnard College, arriving in New York the summer of 1966. I did some dope; went to rock concerts at the Fillmore; walked the Lower East Side, then at its apex as a hippie-rock-drug center; and shopped for old clothes in rich ladies' charity shops, it still being possible to believe that issues other than style were involved. This was the Summer of Love but in fact I did not find love until my sophomore year, 1967–68, when I met Saul Berman, whom I dated, then lived with and, upon our graduation from law school, married.

The school year ending in June of 1968 was also, as many will recall, the year of the Columbia student uprisings. Had I not met Saul or someone like him, a certain lack of imagination might have allowed me to remain fully engaged by legitimate schoolwork and a casually committed social life as the sixties were taking hold of many of America's children. But Saul's Jewish scholarship and Southern charm made him excitingly, lovably radical to me.

A person who had never left the South before coming north to college, he knew that a job in his father's law firm awaited him upon graduation, and he had always assumed he would take it. At Columbia he'd become a member of SDS. While he hadn't allowed political activity to eclipse his studies, he was, or so it seemed, deeply involved with the group and its ideals. As a Southerner he felt a stronger-than-average need to prove to himself and others that he was not a racist, and he was even more interested in the domestic issues SDS was fighting—Columbia's using part of Morningside Heights' community park for a gym with separate entrances for the school (westerly) and black (easterly) communities—than in issues like the Pentagon's funding of the Institute for Defense Analysis.

The period after the January Tet offensive, when SDS entered its strongest and best-publicized period, was also the time when my sexual friendship with Saul was turning into a love affair. To this day it is difficult for me to sort out the pleasures of that first true love from the air of excitement at school and the heady feeling that we had a role to play in fixing a grown-up world gone wrong.

We were part of the group that followed Mark Rudd to Hamilton Hall to present our demands to the dean. And we—most particularly Saul, for I was not recognizable—showed up in one of the photographs that accompanied the Associated Press account of the rally, a photograph used by the *Atlanta Courier*, among others, in its coverage of the event.

We were making love, both of us mildly stoned, when the phone rang the following night. Without breaking his rhythm, Saul picked it up and said hello.

"Sweetheart, are you all right?" asked his mother in her soft, anxious voice, almost as close to my ear as to Saul's.

"Of course I'm all right," said Saul, who didn't know about the photo, much less that it had appeared in Atlanta. He stopped moving and rested his full weight on me.

"Thank goodness," said the trembling voice, which was then replaced by the deeper and steadier one of his father.

"What are you up to down there, young man?" asked Saul's father, who in the years that I knew him steadfastly refused to acknowledge that geographically we were *up here*, and *he* was down there.

"Mmm," Saul said. "Well, there's a lot happening, but I don't know just what you're asking me about."

He wasn't being evasive. It didn't occur to him that his parents had learned of the rally and were concerned for his immortal soul, or at least for the portion of it that would require admission to law school.

I'm not sure I ever fully believed Saul's version of what happened after that call, not even in those days when I wanted to but not believing him couldn't affect the way I felt about him because love was too new. Be that as it may, it is a matter of my brain's record that following this phone conversation, in which his father told Saul that youthful radicalism was one thing and having to

135

live and work in a community for the rest of your life was quite another, Saul, gradually enough so he could later claim it had nothing to do with parental pressure but only with the increasingly wild radicalism of the group, withdrew from SDS, bringing me with him. He pointed out that the steep incline of Morningside Park was such that two entrances were the only practical way to handle access for both the black community, at the bottom of the park hill, and the Columbia community, at the top, and claimed that SDS was becoming absorbed in symbols to the exclusion of reality. The real problems, he said, were too complex to allow us to fight for abstractions. The organization was taking a path we could not follow.

It was much later before I could admit that his very lack of true rebelliousness, his unwillingness to displease or discomfit his family, were part of Saul's attraction for me. The lure of the straight and solid, as opposed, I guess, to the filmed and filming, were considerable. Now that enduring, romantic love has become so scarce as to be an object of interest—books talk about achieving love the way they used to talk about reaching orgasm—I can appraise that first love and find it to have been not only true, but full of magical elements that could not be replaced by real life once they diminished or disappeared.

I'd gone home to California for my freshman Christmas, but in December of my sophomore year my father had called to say that he would be in New York for most of the holiday, and he'd love it if I would remain. I'd been delighted with the idea. But nothing had prepared me for the loneliness of spending that unique and most American of holidays in a dormitory from which every one of my friends and just about anyone else was gone.

I had a standing invitation to stay at the apartment with my father and Dagmar, but I didn't want to. I was uncomfortable and would remain so with the notion of sleeping in a place where the two of them were together in bed. It was the only sign that I was not comfortable with the fact of their endless affair.

The boy I'd been dating most often was spending his holiday in the New York suburb where his parents lived—I think it was Pleasantville, although time may have tricked me into giving it that perfect name. I had promised to join him there for New Year's weekend, when my father would have returned to California.

It was a night or two after Christmas. My father and Dagmar had been invited to someone's house for dinner, and I was very much on my own. At first I felt only mildly disgruntled. Then it began to snow. Snow is, of course, even more magical to those who have grown up without it. Added to its natural wondrous qualities was the way I'd seen it for the first time.

I was five or younger. My father had taken me to a Sonja Henie movie. Enjoying my endless excited questions about the ice and snow, neither of which I'd ever seen in real life, he had promised to take me to New York that winter when there was snow. One evening some weeks later he called from New York to say that a snowstorm was predicted for the following afternoon and he had instructed Peg Cafferty to bring me to New York fast enough to beat the storm.

There was no school holiday. Nor were there, I might remind myself as well as the reader, jet passenger planes. The trip took ten or twelve hours. Peg Cafferty and I were on the plane, I with an emergency winter wardrobe culled from the studio's costume supply, at seven that evening.

Excitement kept me awake for several hours but finally I slept, so I was unaware of the snow, or of anything else, when the storm began. In the airport, Peg carried me, still asleep, out of the plane and into the terminal, where I was transferred, by then only half-asleep, to the arms of my father, who stood waiting for me. Peg said it hadn't been necessary for him to get up so early, she could have gotten me safely to his place, and he responded that he wouldn't for anything have missed watching me see snow for the first time.

It is stories like this I remember when people question why my father's behavior did not deter me from loving him.

In any event, we walked out of the airport into the night, my face against his sweater. (I don't recall ever seeing my father in a topcoat.) His sense of drama was stronger than mine, if only because he knew already about snow. As the glass doors opened (I can't remember whether they were mechanical, then) we moved through them.

He stepped down from the curb, took several steps, gave me a kiss and whispered, "Hey, Sunshine, look up at the sky."

I did, and my breath caught. Suddenly I was fully awake and aware of the magical cold flakes falling on my warm face.

On this December night, twelve or thirteen years later, I finally put down the book I'd been trying to read, got on my boots and parka and walked downstairs and out to Riverside Drive.

There were fewer people than usual on the Drive, which added to my sense of abandonment. It crossed my mind that I could find

137

out where my father was having dinner, call him there and tell him that I needed him to come out in the snow. I laughed at myself, but then I grew angry—whether with me for being an idiot or with him for neglecting me, I'm not sure.

I began walking downtown. A light snow-frost was already covering the dirt edging the park walk. I told myself that it was too cold to snow, but then the very thought of having to make myself such promises moved me from anger to sadness and brought tears of self-pity to my eyes.

I became aware that a couple walking in back of me were having an argument. His tones were low, so low as to remind me of the way my father bellowed when he was angry, and his speech, though I couldn't precisely make out the words, seemed mellow. Her voice was high-pitched and a little shrill. I heard her say she didn't understand why he was being like this, they'd spent only one day, Christmas Day, with her parents, and this was just one night and not a very late one. I glanced at them as they moved up abreast of me; they were both tall and dressed as for an occasion, she in high heeled boots, he in a topcoat. I couldn't be sure, but I thought that as they pulled ahead of me, he was counting aloud the hours he had already spent with her parents and her sisters. A moment or so later and several feet in front of me she stopped walking, faced him and announced in a voice loud enough so that I couldn't have missed the words if I were trying that *she* was going to Mary's house, and he could come or not, as he liked. He did not respond but stood silent, facing her. As she flounced off, he became aware that he was blocking the narrow path next to the stone wall where we'd all been walking.

"Well," he said, "I don't know whether to be embarrassed that we had a witness or pleased that I might have some company."

Doubtless I would have been charmed by the readiness of the nice words even if they hadn't been couched in a sweet Southern accent riding on a beautiful baritone voice.

I smiled, but I was uneasy at the idea of being too readily seduced and made as though to walk around him.

"Don't go," he said. "I'm safe. I've seen you around Columbia. I'm a student."

Now I waited more than willingly.

"You at Barnard?"

I nodded.

"My name's Saul Berman," he said.

"Nell," I told him, unwilling to go all the way to my second name on such short and off-beat acquaintance.

"If only it had snowed a little earlier," Saul Berman said, "then I wouldn't have minded going to her sister's because I could've gone sledding with the kids."

So. There we were. I confessed that I had just been thinking about snow, and he told me that he had never seen snow until the year before, when he came North for the first time to go to Columbia. I told him that I was from California and hadn't seen it until I was five or six years old and had flown to New York in a snowstorm. By this time we were walking again, and by a few hours later we were in bed with a bottle of Chianti he'd stolen from his roommate's trunk, telling me he would replace it before the guy returned.

Saul was amused to hear that I hadn't assumed he was Jewish, hadn't, in fact, thought once about it, and *extremely* amused by my astonishment upon learning that he'd known, without being told, that I was Jewish, too. He made some joke about his first time in bed with a girl who didn't have to have circumcision explained to her and, when I looked at him uncomprehendingly, said that he'd used his first year and a half away from home to become seriously (sexually) acquainted (solely) with gentile virgins. I must have continued to look blank.

"You do know that I'm Jewish," he said, still jesting.

"I guess," I said doubtfully. "I mean, I haven't thought about it, but . . ."

"But you sort of took it for granted."

"I don't know." I shrugged. I was lying on my back and he was leaning on one elbow, half next to me and half over me. "I don't think so. Unless I take it for granted that *everyone's* Jewish."

"Oh, Jesus," he said, smacking his forehead with the hand that had been playing with the nipple of my left breast, exciting my body as my mind attempted to concentrate. "You must be a New Yorker, they're the only ones who think the whole world is Jewish. No. You said California. Los Angeles. What does your father do for a living?"

"He's a businessman." I had developed this answer the year before because people in New York got too excited if I said he was a producer. Usually, "businessman" ended the questions.

"What business?"

"The movie business," I said, after debating with myself for a moment about whether there was good enough reason to lie.

He laughed, began to play with my nipple again, leaned over to suck it and from the sucking position, raised his head just enough to ask if it was true Steve McQueen was Jewish. When I said with-

139

out laughing that I had no idea, he dropped the matter. In fact, he appeared, during our lovemaking, to have forgotten it altogether. Except that when we were finished, and he had taken a brief nap in my body—I'd made love with a couple of other boys in my year and a half away from home, but no one had been at once as skilled and as cozy as Saul—he rolled back onto the mattress and began to recite a list of every actor and actress in Hollywood who was known or suspected to be Jewish. I remember that the list began with Edward G. Robinson and ended with King Kong, and he kept telling me to correct him if he was mistaken, and I assured him more than once that I probably wouldn't know the difference.

He groaned, smacked his forehead once again.

"Jesus Christ, I finally find a Jewish girl I like and she doesn't even know she's Jewish. They'll never believe you're Jewish."

"*Who'll* never believe it?" I asked. It did not occur to me then or later to question his frequent invocation of Jesus Christ, their lord.

"See that?" Saul said. "I knew you were a fraud. Any Jewish girl knows *They* is your parents."

If the bedrock of the movie industry was overwhelmingly Jewish, it was in analyzing the composition of that bedrock that one had problems. I knew just as well as Saul did that I was a Jew, but to me a Jew was someone who didn't have school on certain holidays. (Business was conducted as usual on those holidays; if my father had stayed home I might have thought they were special.) Now, I would add to my definition that a Jew is someone whose habit of mind tends to the dual sense of events. But this wouldn't have occurred to me at the time. The extent to which one obeyed the Jewish laws or called one's parents They had never, in my mind, been related to these matters. In fact, I lacked any sense, until I went South with Saul for the first time, that being a Jew might actually affect the way one lived in the country of my birth.

In any event, from that night on, we were a pair. Liberal in our sympathies, briefly radical in our actions. Doing just enough dope to be hip and have friends, talking a good enough game so that all but the most committed of the radical students could trust us. If Saul occasionally made cracks about my "quasi-Semitism," like pretending to take a bite out of one of my buttocks, then announcing that now I was *really* a half-assed Jew, it seemed clear that he felt lucky to have found someone with a Jewish name who required nothing of him in the way of ceremony, who presented no inconveniences like being kosher or requiring that he accompany her to temple. I was just Jewish enough to please a young man who'd had bacon with his eggs for the first time less than one year before.

Saul spoke little of his home life or about strict Jewish observance but taught me your basic Yankee's Yiddish and introduced me to a friend who would instruct me in the making of *latkes*. (The instruction didn't take; I was and still am hopeless as a cook.) When he finally met my father, Saul professed to find him a fascinating human being. My father flatly refused to express any opinion of Saul.

Three days after I'd met him, Saul left for a long New Year's weekend in Atlanta, and he went home without me for Thanksgiving and each of the serious Jewish holidays during our remaining two and a half years of college. He accompanied me to Los Angeles often enough that his parents knew he had an away-from-home girlfriend. But until we took an apartment together in our first year of law school, they seem to have thought of me as the repository, or perhaps I should say the granary, of Saul's wild oats. That he might not come home to marry the rabbi's daughter who had been his high school sweetheart was not, apparently, a possibility in their minds.

So I would be lying if I claimed to have had no sense of the problem I might present to Saul's parents. What I did not comprehend, until our plane ride to Atlanta, was the degree to which his sympathies were with them. The man might adore bacon and eggs, but the boy craved matzoh balls and the Friday night ceremony that was among his earliest memories of a week's proper ending. In fact, it was only with Saul's family that ceremony and some sense of obligation to the past entered my own life. I was briefly able to fool myself into thinking I had missed them.

We'd been on the plane only a short while, I would guess we were over Pennsylvania, when Saul mentioned that the presents we had brought with us were for Chanukah, not Christmas. He hoped the cards and tags didn't say anything about Christmas. I nodded, rather absently. Then he said something on the order of "Being Jewish is different down here, you know."

I swear I do not exaggerate when I say that at first I failed to understand what he meant by "down here." I smiled, leaned over, kissed the part of his neck just above the shirt collar.

"Oh, yes?" I asked lightly. "Is that why you're wearing a suit?"

"Damn right," he said.

I was put off by a certain righteous tone as much as by the words themselves.

"What's going on?" I asked. "I'm confused."

"What's going on," he said, "is that I'm trying to explain something to you."

"Not for the first time," I said, attempting to maintain a lightness of tone. "But usually, if you want to explain something, you just explain it. I don't get a whole song and dance about—"

"It's not a song and dance," he interrupted irritably. "I'm trying to tell you something, and you don't want to hear it."

"Oh?" Already I felt hurt in some way that was new to our long friendship. He was angry with *me*, as opposed to with something I had said or done.

"I'm trying to tell you that you're going to a place where Jews are really Jews, not just . . . some . . ."

"Some?" I prompted.

"Some sort of imitation, no, not imitation, some sort of *remnant*, mmm, actually, that's what I mean, remnant. The whole cloth of being a Jew is gone, but there are these little bits and pieces left lying around. A couple of Yiddish words and bagels and lox on Sunday."

I nodded, understanding what he'd said, if failing to comprehend why it should be making him angry with me.

"What I don't understand," I said, "is what's going on with you right now."

"What's going on," he replied, "is that I'm bringing home a *shiksa* for the holidays."

So. The fact that I was going to meet his parents had changed our relationship, at least for the time being.

"Is there anything I should offer to do about it?" I asked. "It's a little late for me to go home."

He did not order me to stop being ridiculous, a sign in itself. For a couple of minutes he just gazed out of the airplane window as though the clouds might provide an answer to his dilemma. I remember thinking, when he began to speak, still without looking directly at me, that it was as if there were a third person present, monitoring his words.

"We were both born after the war, and we don't really know what it was like. I mean, even I, being raised by real Jews who were still in touch with people in Europe, who had parents and aunts and uncles who were observant Jews, kosher and so on, and

142

with a strong sense of what their relatives went through, even I couldn't imagine, without the *Life* photographs and the stories and everything, what it meant to be a Jew. A Jew in Germany. A European Jew. But where *you* come from, I mean, when I'm out there in Hollywood, in Beverly Hills I guess I should say, but it's all Hollywood—I keep thinking, these people really believe the war was fought by Dana Andrews and Adolphe Menjou!"

In spite of himself, Saul turned to see if I had appreciated his joke. I hadn't. He turned away so that I was looking at his profile again.

"My people, my *family*, I mean, live with a sense of Jewishness that's going to be very hard for you to understand. It's partly just being in the South. I mean, it must be, because it's very different where we are. At school, for starters, where from the first day you know you have to be at the top of the class because you're upholding the honor of the whole . . . of the whole. Maybe there are other places where it's just as big a part of life as it is where I live, where I come from, but I don't know about them. It's not all bad, either, if that's what you're thinking. It's a very liberal tradition, in many ways more so than in the North. They understand better than a lot of Northerners what the blacks have been through because they've been subjected to a lot of the same shit in a way that's absolutely foreign to a Northerner like you."

I didn't ask when I'd become a Northerner. I was thinking of other conversations we'd had over the years, when he'd told me that the liberalism of the Southern Jews was a genteel fraud, like other aspects of their lives, that the fact that the Jews understood what it was like to be despised didn't mean they knew what it was like to be black and unable to escape the shit by going to New York or Chicago; that if anything the older Southern Jews' fear of the blacks and black sexuality was greater than that of the gentiles because they'd had their sexuality smothered earlier and better, as part of their survival training. And so on. It was supposed to go without saying that young people like himself were immune to such feeling.

Perhaps Saul, too, was remembering some of those conversations, because abruptly he changed the subject, or at least altered its focus.

"What they have is a sort of dual sense of who they are. The rituals are a kind of constant reinforcement of history. Of being Jewish. For some of them, my father, for example, who goes off to his law firm and handles a lot of matters that don't have anything

143

to do with being Jewish, it's like coming home in some daily way that goes beyond just walking in and out of the door. He comes home to his *history*. He *loves* to go to temple. He loves the chants and the rituals. And if he's ever broken the kosher laws, I guess I should say, *when* he's broken the kosher laws, because he eats out most lunches . . . Anyway, what I'm saying is, he'd never dream of breaking them at home. My mother keeps it perfect. The home, I mean. The maid's been trained, we've had the same maid since I was little, and she knows kosher better than I do, and she respects it, too. As a matter of fact, she buys her food in the Jewish markets, kosher meat and all, because she knows they're cleaner. What I'm trying to tell you is, it's a way of life, and it's going to be a shock to you, and I wish . . . I just wish . . ."

It was the first time I'd seen him rendered inarticulate by his wishes. He fumbled around for a way to finish the sentence, but he couldn't do it, and finally, in a mood as angry and confused as it was mischievous, I asked if he was telling me I shouldn't give his parents the Virginia ham I'd bought them for Christmas.

He forced a wry smile, but he wasn't any more amused than I was and we spoke very little during the remainder of the flight. By the time we reached the airport in Atlanta, he appeared to be his normal, friendly self.

It seems to me now that if there was one day when that dual sense of the world that is crucial to humor, or at least to irony, came under my brain's full light, it was that one. Or maybe it wasn't the day. More likely it was the night. The first night I spent in Saul's home, that Chanukah week of 1971.

It was the only place I'd ever been where Jews were quieter than other people and spoke in lovely tones that owed little, or so it seemed to my ear, to Yiddish. Saul's mother was small and slender, while his father was of moderate size, and his sister, Miriam, resembled Saul, who was tall and pleasant-looking without being handsome. Miriam was two years younger than Saul and in her final year at some junior college not far from Atlanta. She was skinny, cute and intensely lively, which made it all the more peculiar to watch her playing the helpless Southern Belle when anyone was watching. She might start to expound on some situation at school or in the neighborhood, compare it to a historical incident (I remember something about the Garden Club, which was gentile, and the War of the Roses) and upon being asked by her brother what she knew about the War of the Roses, or whatever, retreat into giggles and confusion. At one point, she began to fix the cord on my bedside light, which was not working, though it had a new bulb, but then realized, as Saul entered the room, that she simply wasn't equipped to deal with it.

This game was more difficult for me to take than the meal-time rituals Saul had been worried about or not having butter on the table when we were eating meat. (I didn't care much for butter, and from the time I was quite young I had refused milk with meat, finding the combination unpleasant.) Nor did I mind going to *shul* once or twice, although I found it boring as soon as I had looked around and listened for a while, and there was no question of my being willing to attend frequently. The fact that women had to sit upstairs and away from the men made it seem like my childhood.

We had wine with dinner at home and spent the evening drinking with some of Saul's high school friends. I drank too much and fell asleep in Mr. Berman's car, which we had borrowed, passing out quickly for the second time when I went up to my room. Saul had informed me that we would have separate rooms and ordered me not to make sexually suggestive remarks, an order as insulting as it was ludicrous. That night, he came creeping into my room, awakened me to make love with a fine passion, then fell into a sound sleep, leaving me with what he later explained was a drinker's insomnia that might well have overtaken me anyway. I lay awake for most of the night, cursing him for having disturbed my sleep but unable to rouse myself enough to want to read the book I'd brought with me.

When I refer to having developed a sense of irony that night, it has to do with the fact that Saul's lovemaking then, later when he awakened me again just as I was finally growing drowsy, and indeed during our entire stay under his parents' roof, was more frequent and spectacular than it had been since our first year or two together. I have never believed that the wine and grass we indulged in more often during those early times were the whole explanation. I had the clear sense, when Saul's mother began to ask in her genteel way questions about my background, that vibrations from our room had caused her to consider me a serious threat, or at least a long-term one, something more and worse than the *goyisheh* slut who had briefly diverted Saul from his destiny.

If I could not alleviate her fears, I could and did try to convince her that being a lousy Jew was not precisely the same as being a lousy person. In temple, I sat quietly attentive—in my own mind, a cultural anthropologist, in theirs, someone willing to learn what

145

she should have known all along. I helped with the dishes when there were more than the housekeeper could easily handle; studied in my room when Saul's old girlfriend "dropped by"; and exclaimed upon the beauty of the homes and gardens when we were taken out for drives. My working toward a law degree was treated as something that would make it possible for me, if I snared Saul, to understand what he was talking about when he came home to dinner. In short, the nature of the life I would lead if I married him and moved to Atlanta was laid out for me on that first visit.

On the trip back to New York, Saul was sweet and extremely loving, even apologetic over his earlier assumption that I would be out of place in his home. He said he had underestimated my flexibility, and that if I hadn't yet felt any real warmth from his family, the visit had gone far better than he could have hoped. He was ebullient, more in love with me than ever. It was difficult for him to assent to his father's request that he not marry me until he had finished law school.

Louisa remained in Los Angeles, and during my school years I saw her only when I went home. She had reached an agreement with the *Honey* people under which she no longer worked for the magazine but lived in the Santa Monica house and served as its caretaker (as well as something resolutely *not* called a den mother). In their spare time and in apparent harmony, she, Alice and Dagmar labored toward the inception of *FRemale*. At various points during those years Alice met a series of men with whom she lived briefly before returning to Louisa and *FRemale*. At some point I felt that her ease in finding men had become a source of irritation to my half sister. On the other hand, the housing setup Louisa had arranged for herself and Alice made the economic difference that enabled her to avoid full-time work for long enough to write *Scarsdale*, the title of which is a rather obvious pun that apparently eluded many of its readers.

Scarsdale is the strong if somewhat turgid story of a young woman named Helen who is a badly scarred victim of the 1942 Coconut Grove fire in which her twin sister was burned to death. Returning home to Scarsdale from extensive plastic surgery, which has left her better-looking than she was before and much more attractive to men (the surgery is described in an exhaustive and often unnecessary detail that apparently fascinated Louisa), Helen has an affair with her boss that is the only aspect of her new life she enjoys, but that leads to perpetual guilt because he's married. She breaks with him when an emergency forces her to call his house, his wife picks up the phone, and Helen hears the pain and suspicion in the other woman's voice.

The balance of the novel deals with her attempts to convince herself that she is real, that is to say, that she is a person with a life in spite of the fact that she has become unrecognizable to almost everyone who has known her during most of it.

The exception is her older brother, Louis, who had always favored her over her twin sister, showing an affection she's been unable to enjoy since the sister's death. Louis doesn't know she's had surgery when he shows up at her office in Manhattan, yet he recognizes her instantly with her new face. He is in San Francisco on business when, in the last chapter, Helen shoots herself far enough from the heart so that it will take her some hours to die. She has sensed that in the time of pain before she loses consciousness she will have the satisfaction of feeling her own existence. Louis calls while this is happening. She tells him she's feeling better than she has in ages, except that she is very tired.

It was in reading this book, which I still thought of as Louisa's first novel, that I first experienced what many already knew—that fiction can be enjoyed in inverse relation to one's proximity to the author. We may tend to place great value on the work of friends and relatives, but losing ourselves in their fabrications is another matter. Often, in reading *Scarsdale*, I marveled that someone in some way so familiar was telling a story so foreign to me. But just as often I was discomfited by a name (I've come to believe Louisa deliberately used names for her male characters that were close to her own), a glimmer of recognition, a bright light on an identifiable quirk or occupation (Helen is an accountant, her brother, a lawyer) or, most distracting of all, by some incident I was certain had happened to me rather than to Louisa, except that it had been given a form that made it not quite identifiable by me.

When we received an invitation to attend the publication party for *Scarsdale* at the publisher's offices, Saul said he had too much studying to do but I should go. I hesitated. He'd always tended to avoid Louisa's company, but I felt that she liked him and would be hurt by his absence.

"I know you're not crazy about her," I began.

"This has nothing to do with like or dislike," he said.

"Are you telling me that even if you were crazy about Louisa you wouldn't go to her first book party?" I demanded.

"I'm telling you," he announced loftily, "that you have no reason to assume that I'm *not* crazy about her."

"Only the way you look and act when she's around," I challenged. "And from the fact that you never exactly *want* to see her."

But I realized as I spoke that it was futile, that in fact it went against some rule in his *Good Jewish Boy's Book of Behavior* to admit to not caring for his girlfriend's sister. We had been in Los Angeles when Liane and Sonny, now eleven and fourteen, were carrying on in their particularly Los Angeles and uniquely objectionable way about various matters, and while I, or Louisa and I, united as we seldom were in point of view, sat appalled by my father's inability to control them, Saul had smiled benignly and asked questions about their favorite rock stars.

So I went alone to the party, having made up an elaborate and, I thought, particularly convincing excuse for Saul about a paper he had to turn in. But Louisa, who often talked to Saul when I was there as though the room were empty except for the two of them, appeared not even to notice. There were too many other things on her mind.

She was looking terrific. The last time I'd seen her, a year or so earlier, she'd gained a lot of weight, wore jeans all the time and wasn't bothering with makeup. Now she'd lost at least as much weight as she'd previously gained, was carefully made up, and wore her straightened, reddish blond hair to her shoulders. It was the week before Christmas, and she was wearing one of her jazzier outfits—red velvet pants and a green satin blouse with enormous full sleeves. Her shoes were satin pumps with very high heels, although the young rocker she called Merlin, who was apparently her current lover, would barely have been her height barefoot. It took me a while to realize that something other than weight and makeup was involved in her change of appearance. But I couldn't figure out what it was, and I found myself, as I talked to the few people there I knew (my father was on the Coast and unable to attend, but various of his associates had come, along with friends, editors, agents and so on), watching Louisa to figure out what was different.

As usual, she caught on and began to watch me watching her. "You're seeing it," she said at a point when her little friend had left her side for the first time in the interest of refilling their drinks. "Aren't you."

I smiled. "But I'm not sure what I'm seeing."

"Take a guess," she said. "But if Merlin comes back, change the conversation. He thinks I was always a raving beauty."

"Is it your eyes?" I asked uneasily.

"Of course it's my eyes," she announced with a big smile. "Eye, anyway. I finally had it fixed."

"Fixed?" I'd known it looked a little odd but I hadn't known there was anything actually wrong with it.

"Straightened. They can't make me use it anymore the way they—anyway, they tightened the muscle so I don't look cockeyed."

Thinking of *Scarsdale* and plastic surgery, I asked with a grin if she was sure that was all she'd had done.

"You bet your ass," she said self-righteously. "If you knew what it took to get me *that* far under the surgeon's knife. I mean, I should have had it done fifteen years ago."

When we finally married and moved to Atlanta, Saul was not unsympathetic to my attempts to find a job there, though he acknowledged in a manner both sweet and rueful that not only did these employers not know what I could do, they probably didn't want to learn. We weren't in the North anymore, he reminded me. We were in the South, where Jews were Jews and women were women. It might be just as well for me to acknowledge that fact and begin having babies.

Until this time I had not conversed with myself on the matter of having babies, and I was unfamiliar with my reluctance to do just that. Nor was there much reason to face it now. What I had to face was that having children—if you were determined not to do to your children what had been done to you, as opposed to *for* you, and who in the mental middle class does not have that determination?—was a long-term proposition that would commit me to spending the rest of my life in the company of a bunch of people who, for all my efforts to make a place for myself among them, felt like strangers. Furthermore, even the company of the person who had brought me to Atlanta, about whom I'd once cared a great deal, had become routine, uninteresting.

Saul's mind, the mind that had not simply grasped the minutiae of every tort but had appeared to remain, if not radical, then at least intent upon finding ways the law might be used to obtain equality for black people, had turned back into a nice Southern mind that thought it was just as well for black people not to have their expectations raised too high while important matters like corporate gains and rich people's wills were resolved. (That's unfair although it's not untrue. What is more true is that, like many Jews who were philosophically antiracist and in practice less malignant and/or neglectful than gentiles, Saul felt like a betrayed lover when the blacks, having expected more of the Jews, turned on us harder in their disappointment.)

In Atlanta I not only failed to find a woman friend whose

149

understanding would make the limitations of my husband's company seem less important, but the men we knew, while they could be flirted with at parties, were unable to take seriously any contribution I made to a conversation about work or the social and political issues facing us all. Any discussion of politics that I entered turned into a series of questions and/or jokes about the fairly new phrase "Women's Liberation." And sex with Saul, though still lovely, was no longer powerful enough to take my mind off such matters when I was trying to talk to him, or keep it off them the next day while his mother was trying to teach me how to make pot roast.

The next time I saw Louisa, Saul and I were living in Atlanta. She had come south to do what she always called research, although she seemed to absorb what she'd learned in such a way that none of it showed in her books. She was working on *Folly Beach*, which was published in 1975 to no more attention by the reviewers or the bookstores than had been given *Scarsdale*.

The story of a group of Southerners who live and talk like expatriates but have remained remarkably close to their homes in Charleston and Savannah, *Folly Beach* was inspired, according to Louisa, by her discovery that Thoreau's mother lived a short distance from his own home on Walden Pond. Whatever else is true, the real place called Folly Beach is in South Carolina, and Louisa was aware of having chosen a state bordering on the one where I lived.

She has a lot of fun with Southern Womanhood, setting it in opposition to what is natural as well as to the rhetoric of the movement. One of the women on her Folly Island is a medievalist with seven languages who bakes and sells whole-grain bread because commuting from the island to the university feels unnatural to her.

Louisa did visit us in Atlanta on her way to South Carolina, perhaps to confirm what she was already planning to write. She managed, though she had never done such a thing before, to leave the part of the manuscript dealing with the medievalist and her bread-baking out on the coffee table where I would see it. When I asked if she'd wanted me to see it for the obvious reasons, she shrugged and said she was surely "willing."

Saul and I were living in a small but very pretty clapboard home owned by one of his uncles, to whom we paid a nominal rent. It was autumn. Louisa had called from the Atlanta airport, where she'd already rented the car in which she would drive up the coast after her visit with us. She was interested in beaches and islands, although she wasn't yet certain whether she'd end up in North Carolina or Florida. I suspect she already knew the island name that appealed to her and didn't want to say it, flattering me so much as to think I might understand the meaning *Folly Beach* held for her.

I told her nothing would please me more, and in fact, I welcomed her visit as I did all changes from routine. But when I told Saul that Louisa was in the area and dropping in, he asked in a nearly menacing tone what I meant by "dropping in."

I said she was driving up the coast for research and it hadn't occurred to me it would be a problem since he'd always claimed she didn't bother him.

"Well," he said in a special way he had of turning a drawl into a menace, "Ah was laaahhhing."

"I wish I'd known," I lied back. "There's no way for me to reach her now."

He stormed out of the house.

When she finally arrived, he was civil but just barely. I'm not sure Louisa noticed. I think she liked him and, for all her caricatures of Southern courtliness, found him charming. At the very least she wanted *him* to like *her*, and she was careful not to ask in his presence the local-customs questions with which she deluged me when we were alone, acting as though I were a South Seas islander and she were Margaret Mead. She wanted to know what my obligations were—my "Southern lady" obligations as well as my Jewish ones—and how I handled them. She was interested in hearing any bitching and moaning I cared to do about Saul and/ or his family.

I cared to do a great deal. If I was not yet thoroughly disenchanted, the paths to disenchantment were clear, and I was often bored out of my mind.

Saul remained his usual gentlemanly self during Louisa's visit except that he turned on the television news every night during dinner and for the balance of each night of her three-day visit left on the TV no matter what else he was doing—working, reading or briefly pretending to join our conversation. On Saturday morning he locked himself in the bedroom after breakfast because he had "urgent" work to do.

The heroine of *Folly Island* is Ellen Pelmeny, a powerful Southern lady who wants to control everyone in sight but is adept at concealing her strength through a variety of mannerisms and maneuvers. The book's hero is her husband, Alan, a charmingly earnest young college professor driven to near-madness by Ellen, who, unwilling to acknowledge her own aggression, pushes him to stretch beyond his own.

In January of 1975 I decided that the gap between what I wanted of life and what life seemed routinely to be delivering was wider than I had reason to tolerate at such an early point in my adventure. I left Atlanta for New York, and Saul, five minutes after our divorce became final, married Rachel Schwartz, the rabbi's daughter he had left behind when he embarked upon the Northern adventure that included me. Rachel happily bore Saul a proper family. Every December at Chanukah time I receive a photograph of Saul and Rachel and their one-two-three children, as well as a note from Rachel detailing Saul's achievements during the previous year, the children's progress and any purchase of a larger home made since the previous card.

BOOK
3

MY FATHER HAD offered me his apartment in the Gainesborough Studios before I left for Barnard, when I'd been horrified
at the thought of not living in the dorm. He offered it again as I
was getting set to leave Atlanta, and I accepted with gratitude,
assuming it would allow me to find my own place in a leisurely
fashion. Within days I was too attached to it ever to want to leave.

The studio was one huge two-story room with a balcony-
bedroom and a tiny kitchen, the whole decorated in that California
White-Sofas-cum-Mexican-Pottery-and-Indian-Serapes style I had
come to appreciate while living in Atlanta. From the huge living
room—literally, the room where I lived when I was home and
awake—I could see all of Central Park and have a sense of the

weather and the changing seasons that was unique to such a view. I believe the studio had been the playground for some of my father's more casual affairs.

I had, with his considerable help, become the first female lawyer at Simon & Koenig, the New York law firm affiliated with Egremont's West Coast lawyers, Dalton, Gansbarg and Doyle. (If your brain reels at the notion that virtually everything I or any of us did was connected to my father in some way, then you can probably imagine how I felt about these connections. On the other hand, their doing a favor for an important client seems to have made it more tolerable to Simon & Koenig to engage in what would pass for Affirmative Action.)

I worked in the firm's entertainment division and became versed in contract issues at a time when the paper contracts were being written on seemed to be the only matter not included in the greening of America. If the clothing style (later often called lifestyle) of lawyers at leisure had loosened up considerably, love, even as it became the key word of the entertainment industry, hadn't had the slightest effect on the way its contracts were drawn. If anything, everyone was quicker to anticipate the possibility of betrayal and more intent upon tightening each contract's every word.

I drifted into an affair with one of my bosses, Byron Koenig, whose divorce was being negotiated. Byron was more than reasonably charming, if your tastes ran to the pre-Liberation male (he could restring a tennis racket but not make a cup of coffee), and more than reasonably intelligent. He was thirty-six years old, had been married for twelve years and was the father of two children who were in his wife's custody and refusing to spend time with him because they were angry with him for leaving. Byron found this particularly galling because he'd moved out at his wife's insistence.

The difficulties had begun with her reading a book about men's getting closer to their children and taking increased responsibility in the home, enabling their wives to go back to school and/or prepare for a career. She felt that Byron should spend two or three afternoons a week, from three to six, say, with the children. When he'd pointed out that he already loved his kids and a sitter could be employed if their mother wanted to go to school, she'd responded that the quality of time was different. The book said so. When he'd pointed out that, book or no book, few law practices would give a man that kind of time off, she'd grown furious and said he didn't really *want* her to go back to school. Now she was in school full time on his alimony payments, and he was supporting her and two children who barely spoke to him, *plus*, he'd just discovered, some young guy who'd come to make bookshelves and moved in with them. This last was the touch that had convinced Byron that he was ready—eager—for another wife, most particularly one with a job and a good income. He said he understood that since I had no children I would want them, and he would certainly be willing, even eager, at some point. He just couldn't think about it until this other stuff was settled.

I was scared.

I'd been too young when I realized that being in love with Saul had limited my choices to understand that the time passes when one is in love's helpless thrall. That even if sex, if life in general, remains good, one's brain gains a little distance from the proceedings. Now I knew. But I knew, too, that I was unwilling to find myself once again and so soon in that helpless position. I was twenty-six years old. When, if not now, would I have my own sixties, the free-and-easy single years I'd missed by being with Saul? When, if not now, would I find out which branch of a law practice held the most interest for me and whether I was adept at it?

I was good at contracts, but nothing about them suggested they would hold my interest for a lifetime. I'd been full of sound suggestions with regard to Byron's various divorce cases. At one point he'd made a joke about angering my father, a major client, by taking me away from contracts. Dagmar and Louisa, separately and together, had been urging me to take on Simon & Koenig's work for *FRemale*, which was about to commence publication. The male junior doing the job so far Just Didn't Get It and was, besides, a potential embarrassment to the magazine. Byron was pushing me to accede; I couldn't tell how much of my willingness and/or reluctance had to do with the magazine, and how much was concern about my relation to Byron. Finally, there was a nagging sense of something missing as a result of my not having been involved since Saul's and my SDS days with any matters even touching on politics.

It was as I'd begun trying to figure out how I might separate my outside life from Byron's without leaving his firm that fate intervened in such a way that I couldn't even accuse her of fingering me but could say, rather, that she had pointed at once in two different directions. And that the pointer she'd used had been given her by my father.

155

In setting up my original interview with Simon & Koenig, my father had made an alternative suggestion—that I return to Los Angeles and work in the legal division of Egremont. I'd not been indifferent to the siren call of family at a time when expectations of the world beyond family had been disappointed. But aside from New York's greater appeal as a city, I was leery of that very longing to return to the carefree state of being Daddy's Girl. What if I lost the small amount of ambition that being thwarted by Saul had given me? *Then* what would I do with my days?

Furthermore, even if I'd wanted to live in Los Angeles, I would have been made anxious by the notion of seeing much more than I now did of my family (half family?). Sonny, who in the absence of Estella had always been a pain in the ass, was an impossible seventeen-year-old who did a lot of dope and was screwing around in such a way that the rest of the world, if not Estella, had to be aware of what she was doing. Liane, at fourteen, was ravishingly beautiful but also incredibly dumb and utterly self-absorbed, adored by my father and desired by every other sighted male with whom she had contact. She already had the kind of composure that comes with this adoration, although it was difficult to say for sure that she would have maintained it if she hadn't been stoned all the time.

As I thought about Sonny and Liane, I realized that it was some time since my father had mentioned them or their mother. He hadn't spoken of Louisa, either, but that wasn't unusual. There had been little contact between them that I knew of, and what they did have was unsatisfactory to him, although he made no bones about thinking she was talented. Lynn had become involved in the Watts project, but I couldn't recall that I'd heard anything of *her* doings lately either.

Once or twice my father, when I'd flown up from Atlanta to meet him in New York, had begun discussing his problems with the girls, but this was the time when I was absorbed in the matter of whether and when I was going to leave Saul, and I hadn't really paid attention. Now he called from the Coast to renew his offer, saying that with the experience I'd gained, and judging by what Byron had told him about my work, I would enter his legal division at a much higher level than I might have earlier.

I told him I was pleased and flattered, but that it could be complicated—scary, even—to be working under someone who was not only the head of a studio and a very powerful person, but who happened to be my father.

There was a lengthy silence, and then, in a voice smaller and shakier than any I had ever heard issue from him, he delivered a monologue on the order of the following.

"Powerful person. Jesus Christ. [sigh] It's amazing, really. Here I am, an old man . . . sixty years old next month, in case you haven't noticed . . . sixty years old, can barely get it up to go to the office every morning, and here's this terrific, smart, strong young woman, apple of my eye, claiming I scare her. Jesus Christ. Doctor's telling me I've got high this and low that, I'd better toe this line he's drawn down the middle of my life . . . through my gut, I should say . . . a little fun on either side of it, but nothing right there . . . eat celery and drink seltzer and don't work too hard or have any fun, maybe I'll live another few years . . . and here's my favorite daughter telling me she's scared of me, I'm so powerful, if I sneeze I'll blow 'er away. Where were you when the Women's Movement got started, kiddo? Where are you *now*? Where'm *I*? *What* am I, so powerful I'm gonna die alone because the whole world's afraid to come near me?"

"Oh, Daddy . . ." I didn't know whether to laugh or cry but felt inclined to do both. My instinct told me he was in perfect health, but the doctor had ordered a weight loss. On the other hand, I didn't want to hurt his feelings by appearing unconcerned. I assured him that even if he was fine, I'd been planning to take a couple of days off to come home for his birthday. Then I asked, perhaps because we'd had phone conversations but I hadn't seen her in almost as long as I hadn't seen the "little girls," whether Louisa would also be around.

Something in the tone of his affirmative response caused me to inquire as to what was happening with my older sister.

He said, "You wouldn't believe me if I told you."

I said, after a moment of hesitation, "Try me."

"Okay." he said. "You asked for it, you got it. Your sister Louisa has very recently given birth to a girl baby she has named Penelope." His sense of timing as good as any comedian's, he waited.

"She's not married, is she?" I finally asked.

"My dear, you're being very fifties." He said something in Yiddish, startling not only because of its length, which suggested he was fluent in the language, but because it was the first time I'd ever heard him use it. When I didn't ask what it meant, he added, "Louisa is living in New York. She is not living with the father of Penelope. As a matter of fact, Louisa gave me the distinct impression that she was not certain who the father *was* and didn't care."

"I don't understand," I said as my mind groped around for questions whose answers might help.

"That," my father said, "is because you are sane."

I'd not seen Louisa since her visit to Atlanta the year before, though we'd spoken on the phone since then. I knew she hadn't made as much money on her fiction as she'd hoped, and was still working on *FRemale*. I knew she'd spent a little time in Mexico and returned to Los Angeles. She hadn't told me she was living in New York. If she'd seen my father in the preceding couple of years, neither had mentioned it to me. Alice was acting as the business manager of *FRemale* while living in the first home of *Honey*, a setup the ironies of which neither escaped nor amused Louisa. There had been difficulties between the two, but they had come back together and were working friends again. In my last phone conversation with Louisa she had urged me to take over Simon & Koenig's work for *FRemale* and referred to having less time than she'd once had to spend on the magazine without mentioning a reason.

"Have you seen the baby?" I asked my father.

"I only learned last week of Penelope's existence," my father said, "and have been advised that I will have the honor of viewing the child when she and her mother come to California, which will happen to be at the time of my birthday."

Unable to find an appropriate or humorous comment, I laughed, made some kissing noises and said I thought I'd better not ask any more questions, but I would definitely be there and would let him know when I was arriving. I assumed as I hung up that I would call Louisa or at the very least think about her a great deal, but in fact I was too busy trying to figure out my life to think about her at all until she left a message with my secretary suggesting that we book the same flight to Los Angeles. If my secretary would do the booking, all the better; it was to be charged to my father.

My three years in the South, not to speak of months in an office that claimed to think I was wonderful but to be unable to find a second competent female lawyer in the metropolitan New York area, had given me the visceral sense I'd once lacked of having a stake in feminism. But I had problems with *FRemale* as the embodiment of the feminist position. I had difficulties with its view of the male-female realities, with the humorlessness that went hand in hand with its militant posture, with its failure to acknowledge complexity, contradiction and paradox. When I'd asked Dagmar why the magazine couldn't be as appealing as its founder, she'd informed me in utter seriousness that it was like Cuba right after the overthrow of Batista, when there was not yet the security that would allow for divisiveness or humor. When I'd asked of what the overthrow of the male sex might consist, and where we would be when that goal was accomplished, Louisa had told me we didn't exactly want to *overthrow* men, we just wanted to make them behave. When I said that was cute, but what did it mean, Louisa, ever able to cover her verbal tracks when she couldn't explain them, told me we wouldn't know until it worked. When I asked whether she thought Violet was purely and simply my father's victim, she replied that nothing in Hollywood was pure and simple, but basically she'd go for the idea. Later, she admitted that if she hadn't exactly been lying, she'd known she was stretching the truth. Which brings me to an update on the tantalizing tale (later, movie and best-selling biography) of Violet Vann.

In 1970 Violet married Jesse James Tantrash, an executive of the conglomerate that had gained control of Starr-Flexner. Violet was forty-seven years old and didn't appear to be much saner than she'd been in the period after Tony's death. But she'd had her second face-lift, and the lifts were still working, and Tantrash, who was sixty-six, appeared to adore her as much as Tony ever had.

He proceeded to use his considerable power at the studio to force the people who'd forced out my father to make *Margarita*, the extraordinary Violet Vann epic that showed signs from day one of bankrupting the studio. Tantrash was hell-bent on ignoring these signs. In public he claimed the film was making money. At board meetings he said movies were like breakfast cereals, if you told the public what was good for it, sooner or later it would listen and swallow.

When the extent to which movies were different from breakfast cereals became apparent, Jesse got out of the movie business and in the same fell swoop out of Violet's life. He returned to Texas, as he now claimed he'd always intended to do when he retired, and married a widow from the widow collection he'd left behind when he came to Hollywood.

This was when Violet made the first of those halfhearted suicide attempts—she swallowed a bunch of aspirin when there were plenty of more powerful pills in the house—that turned into media food and brought to her side (from behind her back, where she'd once been) Dagmar Saperstein, who was spending most of her time and energy on *FRemale*. Dagmar had a lot of ideas about Violet as a symbol of what feminism could do for all the women in the world who hadn't even known it was there. She brought Violet and also Lynn, though I didn't know that yet, to a women's group in Santa Monica that Violet now attended regularly. Through the women's group Violet found a companion, a terrific young woman to live with her and instruct her in real life.

I had taken all this with a mineful of salt and had not been calling Violet more often. When I did phone, it was usually during a midday lull in the office routine, and she sounded more sleepy than anything else, if only, I sometimes was fair enough to remind myself, because it was still early in Los Angeles.

Now I picked up the phone and dialed the number Violet had taken with her from my father's house to our house to Tony's house to Tantrash's and finally to the apartment that Tantrash had settled on her when he went to Texas. She did not—unusual for her—answer until the third ring.

"Hello?"

There was that quivery voice I would rather have been able to forget.

"Hi, Violet," I said. "It's me. Nellie."

I couldn't blame her if she was cool; certainly I had neglected her during her recent difficulties. On the other hand, aside from having been born, nothing I'd ever done or not done had seemed to affect her much.

"Hello, Nellie," she said. "How are you?"

An interesting question I couldn't remember her having asked me before. Maybe it was manners that Dagmar had been teaching her.

I said I was all right and coming to Los Angeles, then reminded myself I didn't have to tell her that since she didn't really know there was anyplace else. After which I asked me why I was feeling bitchier than usual and quickly answered my own question: I always felt bitchy about Violet, but usually I rehearsed before talking to her so I didn't have to know it. I said I hoped we could get together, for dinner or whatever. I'd be there only the following Thursday through Monday.

"Well, certainly, dear," Violet said. "What would be a good time for you?"

There was definitely something going on. This was a different Violet, but I didn't believe that people got to be different. I'd already had my first phone calls from Saul Berman telling me what a good thing it was that I'd left him, how he'd been through a period of growth and change (G & C, as I'd begun to call them) and was entering a new era with the woman he'd really loved all along. He sounded about as different to me as I must have sounded to him when I told him there was a call on my other wire (I didn't have another wire).

As I searched frantically now for some simple answer to this simple question posed by someone who was suddenly trying to make me believe she was my mother, or at any rate a reasonable adult, Violet added the clincher.

"Perhaps we should invite Lynn to come along. She and I have been getting to know each other, and it's been lovely for both of us."

I told her this was a terrific idea and I'd call when I got to my father's house. Then I hung up and stared at the phone for some time, as though I might in so doing penetrate the secret of the fresh Violet it had delivered to me.

By the time I left for Los Angeles, I'd virtually made up my mind to do the work for *FRemale.*

Louisa's new apartment was at Sixty-third Street and Central Park West, not very far from my own on Central Park South, but since I was going to the airport directly from my office, we agreed to meet at the Kennedy flight desk. She was there when I arrived, sitting in one of the little plastic seats. I didn't see her at first because she was approximately twice the size she'd been when I last saw her, and her hair was brown. She wore a red plaid cape that made her look as though she were about to give birth to a bagpipe regiment, and held what had to be her baby, which was wrapped in a bright red blankety sort of garment.

"Hi," I said. "Dad told me about your baby."

She smiled proudly, holding it up and tenderly pulling away the part of the blanket covering its face, a tiny, pinkish, bald infant object, fast asleep through all that was happening around it.

I cooed in what seemed to be appropriate fashion, then, at a loss for the next thing to say, asked, "How did you keep her such a secret?"

She shrugged. "It was easy, really. I just didn't see the people who would tell each other. You were in Atlanta when I got pregnant, and I stayed at the beach when I went back to L.A. I didn't feel like answering a lot of questions."

161

I didn't ask who asked a lot of questions (Louisa was the only one I could think of) because she became busy as Penelope stirred and cried. She walked around with the baby, finally taking it to the ladies' room on some mission I did not attempt to determine. Returning, Louisa asked if I didn't want to get something to eat in case the plane was late.

We went to the coffee shop, where I had coffee and she had milk, a club sandwich and a Danish, taking off her cape for long enough to confirm my impression that she had put on a huge amount of weight. Half an hour or so later, we were dashing for the plane, which was very much on time. As soon as we were settled in our seats, Louisa opened her cape, pulled up her maternity-style smock, and began to nurse Penelope.

She was silent until the plane was aloft and the engines had quieted but then began one of her monologues by telling me Sam had insisted on their traveling first class, she supposed I was accustomed to it. Without waiting for a response, she informed me of how she'd found it within herself, on the baby's account, and when she was unable to secure a decent advance for her third novel without telling her publisher, who hadn't made money on the first two, what it would be about, to ask my father ("your father") for help.

In her name he had rented a two-bedroom apartment in this new building on Sixty-third Street. Louisa and Penelope would occupy one bedroom; *FRemale*'s East Coast office, the other. She and her daughter would split the living room horizontally, with Penelope having the two feet closest to the floor. Louisa made it a point to tell me why she did not need to feel grateful for my father's generosity: He was paying cash, and she was fairly certain it was money that had never seen the tax collector's light. Her own name was on the lease, and nothing in her own returns would ever cause the IRS to investigate her. When I pointed out that Sam could have found another use for the money involved, Louisa became briefly if mildly irritated, saying I would go to any lengths to defend him.

Of course, we were both right. What strikes me now, though, is that while the fictional father she was at that time creating, that is to say, Joe Stalbin, may be difficult and manipulative, he never touches anything so unsavory as gambling, much less engages in the various criminal activities connected to gambling in many people's minds, not excluding my own.

She spoke of Dagmar's and her own desire that I take on the vetting of the *FRemale* manuscripts. There was no way "the male"

162

in my office who'd been doing it until now could get "the feel" for what was acceptable and legal. When I told her I was interested in doing the vetting if I could fit it in with my other obligations, she immediately switched to the matter of when I would grant myself the extraordinary pleasure of having a child.

I was speechless. While I was more contented when I had a boyfriend I liked than when I was looking for same, which was why I had yet to shake free of Byron Koenig, and while I enjoyed talking to the articulate children of some of my friends and colleagues, I lacked utterly the desire to mesh these affections. Nor did I feel the need to examine this failure of desire.

Taking my silence for assent, Louisa promised that until such time as I had my own, I would be free to visit and enjoy Penelope. I thanked her.

I suppose the trip was most noteworthy for providing me with those answers that would be so helpful to Louisa when her lawyer evoked them from me years later at the trial.

I don't remember precisely how the subject of Alice arose. I knew that in the years since she and Louisa had met, there'd been good times and bad, and that Alice had come and gone—usually with a man—but had always been allowed to return to the fold, if only because no one else with her combination of skills was available at the same price. I may have asked Louisa whether manuscripts were sent to her or out to Alice (the magazine was printed in California) after being vetted by Simon & Koenig.

"Alice has nothing to do with the content of the magazine," Louisa said with sudden vehemence.

I was silent. She laughed. "You're right if you think the very idea pisses me off."

"Hasn't she been good at what she's doing while she's there?" I asked carefully. "Or is it just that she's not supposed to be editorial?"

"Damn right, she's not editorial. She's barely literate in English, for Christ's sake."

I said nothing.

"I wouldn't care," Louisa said, "except she's gotten delusions of grandeur. I mean, a bookkeeper doesn't *need* English, but she's been trying to decide what gets published in the magazine, and that's another story altogether."

"I don't understand," I said craftily. "Is it a general sort of thing? She wants to pass on everything you publish? Or is it something specific that bothers her?"

Louisa grinned, looked down at the baby, who was sleeping at her breast and would be feeding or sleeping there for the balance of the trip, not to say the visit.

"You can be my lawyer," she said, "if I ever have to go to court."

Words I remember with a poignant clarity, since she didn't want me anywhere in the vicinity when she finally did go to court.

I waited.

"I think she's afraid I'm going to stumble on the truth about her life. I'm pretty sure everything she's told me is a lie. Her stories don't even match from one round to the next. She might have worked in some bar in Venice, but what she was doing there, her relationship to that guy, and so on, is something else. I don't even think they came from where she says they came from. She says she's from Iowa, but her accent isn't Iowa. I mean, an Iowa accent isn't that different from places like Chicago and the Plains states, but it doesn't sound like New England, which is the way she sounds to me. One of my best friends at college was from Boston, and if she's not from around Maine, or New Hampshire, maybe . . . She tries to fix up her speech, and it changes from year to year, but when she's drunk, it's still pure New England."

"And so? I mean, how does that affect what goes on at the magazine?" I wasn't about to ask at what point in time Louisa had become aware of the discrepancy.

"So, it was when I was talking about doing a piece on the Maine coast, a seaport town, maybe, a pretty little village called Fenscot, where I went one summer with my mother before, you know, when it was just the two of us, that was when Alice got all upset. Tried to talk me out of the whole idea."

"Couldn't it be just that she didn't think it was interesting?"

"Could be. Except she got pretty hot under the collar. At first she just said she didn't think it would be interesting to our readers. I said I decided what *I* was interested in and got them to be interested *later*. She got very sarcastic. Started in with some nasty line about who I was that I thought I could make any junk in the world interesting. Get our readers involved in some depressed seaport in Maine. I said it seemed to me if the men were depressed because there was no work, the women were likely to be twice as depressed because they couldn't just go out, at least the mothers of young children couldn't just go out and do something about it. Get drunk. Sit around the general store. Whatever. That was when she really blew her stack. Where did I get off talking about mental depression as though it were the same as financial. I was using my imagination where it didn't belong. What did I know about how people reacted to poverty and deprivation. And so on. I mean, it wouldn't have been so striking if she'd ever shown any interest in what I was writing about. Even in the last round, when we had fights, it wasn't about stuff like that. So, you could say maybe she's feeling her oats. New setup. She's on a *salary* this time. Hot shit. But that wasn't the whole story, because she kept bugging me. If it wasn't about how much money I was going to spend, it was about whether I was going to do this in my last stages of pregnancy or wait until I had a tiny baby to drag around with me, and the magazine couldn't be responsible. . . .

"Sometimes she was worried about the magazine, sometimes she was worried about me, but she was always worried. When I asked why, she said it was because I'd never done anything but cities before, I hadn't talked about small towns. But that doesn't make any sense. Aside from the question of whether she's supposed to be sticking her nose into editorial matters, I mean, even if you acknowledge that the staff was small and the lines of authority weren't drawn very clearly, all you have to do is read our manifesto. Womanfesto, as we called it, although I have problems with all those name changes, they always sound like little kids in grownup clothes. Anyway, we're supposed to be reaching out to women in small towns and large, all across America. If we haven't done a small town before, that's all the *more* reason to be doing it now."

I said it sounded utterly reasonable and asked if Louisa was still planning to do the piece. She said she would rent a car after the mud season, unless she could do it when my father was in town with an extra car, which would, of course, substantially reduce the cost of the trip.

I'm not sure precisely how the matter of the car of my father turned into the matter of the father of Louisa's child. I think at some point the baby grew cranky and I commented lightly on the times Louisa might be sorry the child's father wasn't around.

She whipped around. It was the only bad moment of the trip.

"Never!" she said. "Don't even say it as a joke. He wasn't even someone I thought of that way!"

I must have looked puzzled. (I didn't understand what she meant by *that way*.)

"He was just this big piece of meat," she said. "This sexy Australian. A bartender I met at the hotel in New York where he

165

was working. It was a classic marriage, or at least screw, his beauty and my brains. He had this absolutely beautiful body, and I got a kick out of his accent. More like cockney than anything else, but different. He was very . . . He was an animal, but a very sexy one." She giggled. "A surfer-animal." Another giggle. "He was talking about hitching to California if he couldn't raise the fare to get back to Australia. To this little town on the bay where he lived before he came to the States. A surfer's town. I'm not sure why he left. I have a feeling he was in some kind of trouble." She laughed. "I seem to have the feeling everyone who leaves any place is in trouble." She shrugged. "Makes sense. If you weren't in trouble, why would you bother to leave?"

One of my father's responses to current problems in daily life had been to hire a chauffeur who didn't speak English. Pierre, a small, wiry, extraordinarily handsome black man from Chad, had been in the country less than a month but knew large portions of the map of Los Angeles by heart in addition to having the words for "air-conditioning," "unlock the bar," and "hand me the phone." He was learning English at an extremely rapid rate but was concealing the fact from my father (and thus from most of his passengers). When he picked us up at the airport, Pierre gave me a note from Peggy, introducing him and explaining that he would drive Louisa to Santa Monica, then bring me to Beverly Hills. Louisa had already told me she wanted a day of relaxation, time for herself and the baby to "unwind and get used to being here," before "having to cope with Sam."

At my father's house, Pierre took my briefcase and overnight bag and waited with me at the door, although I told him there was no need. He tipped his hat and smiled but didn't move; I was able to ascertain later that he was following instructions. As was the girl who opened the door, a very young and quite beautiful Eurasian who wore cut-off blue jeans and a halter.

She said, "Hi."

I said, "Hi," took my stuff from Pierre and tried to enter the house.

"Pardon me," she said, blocking my path. "Whom shall I say is calling?"

"My name is Nell Berman," I said coldly. "I'm Mr. Pearlstein's daughter and I'm not calling anyone."

"Mr. Pearlstein?" she asked without embarrassment. "You mean Sam?"

I nodded.

"Would you mind remaining outside for a moment?" she asked. "I'd like to talk to you before you come in."

I said that I damned well *would* mind and asked if Lynn was around, thinking that if my identity was in question—and how like my father to think of sending a car but not bothering to tell anyone at the house that I was coming—then I could confirm it through her.

"No," the girl said, "I'm sorry. Not available."

I stared at her, trying to figure out some means, violent if necessary, of gaining entry to my father's home, which I'd also at times thought of as my own. She appeared to read my thoughts and told me she was a Black Belt. I told her that whatever color her belt was, her face was going to be red when my father came home. She said Mr. Pearlstein had told her to err on the too-careful side, and whatever feelings she damaged he would take care of later on.

As I stood on the pavement wanting to ask if this would be done financially, surgically or by some as yet unknown method, a woman I would not have recognized if I'd seen her elsewhere came floating down the stairs. She had long, unkempt brown hair that was blond at the bottom and must once have been properly bleached. She wore white shorts and an utterly transparent Indian blouse under which her breasts bobbed in a manner that was disconcerting even at a distance. It was only when she reached the bottom of the long, curving staircase that I became certain, though her face showed as serious signs of destruction as the rest of her, that she was Lynn.

"Lynn!" I called, and then, when she paused, "it's me, Nellie." As though it were I who had undergone a transformation and had to be identified.

Lynn waved one hand in the air without smiling and almost as though she were summoning the words required to greet me.

"How y'all doin', Nellie? What a pleasant surprise!"

It seemed to me that not only the *y'all* but the accent and style of delivery were Southern. This was almost as confusing as the way she looked and made me want to remind her that *I* was the one who'd recently left the South (where I'd never developed an accent). Then I thought of the film Lynn had been putting together the last time I was in Los Angeles. It was about a black revolutionary group called GAT and featured an ex-Panther from Alabama with a Stanford Law degree who enjoyed telling white folks the GAT initials stood for Goodbye to All That. She'd picked up a little accent by then, though it was on-again, off-again. She had not seemed her usual calm and controlled self, but I had chalked up the difference to anxiety over the making of her first feature film. Certainly the change then had not prepared me for what I was seeing now.

The watchgirl's eyes moved back and forth between us, but the rest of her was motionless.

"Will you please tell this . . ." I looked for a word that would insult the girl without causing her to kill me, "this watchdog here who I am so I can come into the house and put down my goddamned luggage?"

Lynn sighed. "I don't know if she'll believe me." Her voice was small, thin, very shaky. "Delilah [sic], this is Sam's older daughter, not one of the . . . There are pictures of her on the wall in the den with the little girls. Take a look if you don't believe me."

Now I knew something was radically wrong. If Lynn had been less crisp the last time I was in Los Angeles two years earlier, I'd never had the sense that a different and somewhat pathetic creature was inhabiting her body. Now this creature was captive in her home to a beast only my liberal tendencies prevented me from describing in appalling racist slang.

But Delilah had decided, however reluctantly, to allow me to enter. She stepped to one side of the door, just far enough so that if I pulled a knife or a gun, she could still jump me.

"Thank you," I said as I passed. "Now, do I need security clearance to go to my bedroom?" When she hesitated, I started to describe the room, but she said that wouldn't be necessary; she didn't know what it looked like.

"Be grateful for small blessings," I muttered as I continued through the huge open foyer toward the curving staircase at the back.

At least the house itself appeared unchanged. The marble-topped bow-fronted chest in the hallway, the antique chairs, the chandelier, the Southwestern-style living room beyond, none reflected what appeared to be radical changes within the household. I walked slowly up the stairs. Lynn followed in an odd way that evoked, as I glanced back at her, a particularly obedient child trailing its mother. When I opened the door to my bedroom, she hesitated but then came in after me.

The room was stuffy; no one had thought to air it out. Security had made other amenities less important. I left the door open, set down my suitcase, opened the windows, beckoned to Lynn to sit down if she wished and looked around me.

It had the air of an abandoned stage set. Nothing had been changed since my high school days, when I had requested that a stereo system and a soft chair be added.

"Estella will be so happy you're here," Lynn said, sitting at the edge of one bed, smiling sadly, licking her lips in a gesture I would later learn was characteristic of people on tranquilizers. "Oh. No. I forgot. Estella isn't here anymore."

"How come?" I asked, closing the door and sitting in one of the chairs. It crossed my mind that Estella had moved on to yet another house and family of my father's, which I would find out about in the future.

Lynn shrugged. "Oh, you know. She couldn't keep up with"— a vague gesture with her hand—"with, you know, the times."

"Which times?" I asked, thinking maybe it was a euphemism for Delilah. "Where is she? Do you know?"

"Oh . . . somewhere out there . . . I think she went back to Mexico, actually. Sonny writes to her, but she doesn't answer."

I felt paralyzed. One thing to walk away from the karate champion at the door, another not to wonder about Estella or the once-brisk executive lady who now looked as though she hoped someone passing through would pick her up and find a use for her.

I smiled at Lynn as I cast around for a good way to ask about her own life.

"How's GAT doing these days?" I finally tried.

A vaguely troubled expression came over her face, the kind of expression people on pills get when normally they would have cried. Her right hand made circles off into space.

"Oh, you know," she said. "The film didn't work out."

"I *didn't* know."

There was no change in Lynn's expression.

"Well, first of all, George, you know, was hired away for that series. We couldn't pay him the kind of money network people could, of course . . . and we couldn't ask him to give it up . . . and then Byllye was arrested because when we sent out releases on his doing the movie . . . you know, for financing . . . someone recognized his picture from the post office, he was wanted in three states . . . so that left only Cosmo, and Cosmo and your father had a . . . I guess it was a power struggle. I don't know. At first he, your father, didn't seem to be . . . I mean, he was urging me to get involved with them, but then he got concerned that I was too involved . . . and as soon as his interest dried up . . . the money dried up, too. Cosmo was very intelligent, you know. He could win an argument with your father." Her recitation trailed off, taking whatever little of her was in the room with it.

I stood and began to unpack my bag. Lynn watched me without any particular interest but made no motion to leave. I opened the closet and saw a dress and a pair of jeans I'd forgotten when Saul and I were there two years earlier. I hung up the two dresses and the slacks I'd brought, put the rest of my stuff in the bureau drawers and turned to face Lynn.

"How're the girls?" I asked.

"Girls?" she echoed vaguely. "Oh, we're . . . girls . . ."

"Sonny and Liane?"

"Oh, yes," she said, nodding. "Sonny and Liane. They're a little better."

"Better?"

"Mmm. Sometimes I can't even tell if they're here. They've got their own entrances. I mean, Sonny has her own entrance, upstairs in the back, and he turned the cabana into an apartment for Liane. He was going to do the reverse, but Sonny said . . . Sonny was being so difficult, it was as though she was trying to get into trouble to drive us crazy, just for attention. Sonny was hardly in school her last year, and they weren't going to give her the diploma but finally they decided they might as well, except meanwhile, you know, Liane got kicked out sophomore year with the dope. For a while she had her own apartment in Hollywood, Sonny didn't want one, but even Liane's didn't work. Your father said the leash was just too long. So now she's here, they're both here, but they come in at the back. . . . We don't have to see her . . . them . . . or their friends . . . unless someone wants to check on them."

Without questions from me, Lynn had nothing more to say, but she didn't make a move to leave. I stretched out on the other bed, the one I'd always slept in, hands underneath my head, thinking I might convey the impression of wanting to take a nap.

Nothing happened.

I looked out the window next to my bed. Sprawled on the grass around the pool, as naked as though the thermometer had gone up into the eighties or nineties, were my half sister Liane and a few young people who were unfamiliar to me.

I took a deep breath. "So what else is happening at the studio these days?"

Lynn reached under the spread to take a pillow from the bed

she was sitting on and clutched it to herself as though it were a baby someone was about to snatch away.

"I don't go to the studio anymore."

"You don't?"

She looked down at the pillow, shook her head.

"Should I ask why, or would you rather I didn't?"

"I just . . ." The voice wavered. "I just . . . couldn't . . . cut the mustard."

I think I'd heard the phrase before, but it didn't really matter; the meaning could be divined from the delivery. I waited for some explanation or elaboration but none was forthcoming.

"That's hard for me to believe," I said. "You always seemed . . . You seem very competent to me."

She shook her head again.

"No," she said carefully—the shamed schoolgirl, remembering, too late, the text of the play—"I mean, yes. That is to say, I was very good at following someone else's orders, but it turned out I couldn't issue my own."

"I'm sorry," I said, sitting up when she lapsed into silence, realizing for the first time that her Southern accent had disappeared.

"As your father says, 'Dem's de breaks.' " She stood, a slightly disheveled zombie, and, licking her lips, said that she could tell I was tired and should be allowed to rest. I did not remember her ever noticing before that day that there was something I needed or didn't need, and I felt sad that it should have taken her departure from sanity, or normalcy, or whatever, to accomplish this. I thought of Violet and wondered if *her* entry into the human race had also been accompanied by some sort of severe deterioration. Or maybe it was just something in the air.

Lynn raised her hand in a sort of halfhearted beginning to a Gimme Five, turned and drifted out of the room. I went back to the window and looked down. The kids at the pool were now attired in white terry robes. There were sandwiches and drinks in front of them. I stretched out on the bed, thinking I'd relax for a while, then call Violet to set up a date. I would have to see for myself what Women's Liberation had done for the woman my birth certificate listed as Mother.

But I'd forgotten that I was three hours wearier than I'd have been if I'd awakened on the West Coast. Within minutes, I'd fallen into a sound sleep from which I was aroused by my father, who was pounding on the door and asking, as though there were no one else in the house, what the hell had happened to his favorite daughter.

"I fell asleep," I called sleepily. "Come on in. It's not locked."

The door opened.

A man walked in.

Suddenly I was wide-awake. He was my father, but he wasn't.

It would be difficult to exaggerate the confusion I felt at first, or the dismay I would continue to feel. When I was seventeen and hadn't seen him in a while I'd been startled by a change, not the least of which was his lost weight. Within days I'd grown accustomed to his appearance and ceased to notice the differences. Now I paid no attention to his weight, which had often gone up and down in the years since I'd remade his acquaintance, nor even to the fact of his wearing white jeans with his shirt, the sort of thing he'd once called "Miami britches." What was important now was that I was looking not at the familiar, beloved round and wrinkled visage that encouraged people to relax until they noticed the small, incredibly sharp eyes examining them, but at some plastic surgeon's fictional version of that face. I had no opinion at all of this face, but it didn't belong to my father, and I wanted it to go away.

"SO?"

He held out his arms and waited for me to get up and run into them, but I couldn't do it. I could only try to fool him into believing that I was still half asleep.

He didn't buy it. I'd never been too asleep (or too awake) to run into his arms.

"I know," he said. "I look too young and handsome. You're discomfited. Afraid the wrong feelings will be aroused."

"Oh, God," I said. "Don't do that." I burst into tears and buried my head in the pillow. It crossed my mind for the first time ever that this particular pillow had always been too firm and plump for me and I should have brought my old one from home, from Violet's home, when I moved.

He came to the bed, sat down at the edge, patted my shoulder.

"What's'a matta, Sunshine? Anything I can do something about? If it's not, tell me and I'll leave you alone."

"I don't want you to leave me alone. But you look . . . you look too different. You scared me."

"Yeah . . . well . . . you're the only one. Before I did it . . . The rest of the world doesn't love me like you do, and the way I looked *then* was what was scaring everyone."

I stopped crying. Turned over.

"I know that's not true." But he'd made me determined to try to stand it.

"Sure it is. You think everyone loves the real thing the way you do? Out here the real thing is exactly what no one can stand."

I smiled.

"Hey!" he said. "A smile from my girl! Finally!"

He leaned over and gave me a smoochy kiss on the forehead. I kissed his cheek.

"Listen," he said, "I understand it's harder for you than for me because all I have to do is stay away from the mirror. But you'll get used to it. I swear it. Or at least the doctor swears it."

I nodded, although I didn't believe the doctor for a minute.

"I saw Lynn," I said after a while. "Not to speak of your watch-dog. What's the watchdog about?"

"It's about a lot of things," he said grimly. He stood up, looked out of the window. "Mostly it's about the fact that I work in the movies, not in the Police Department, and I can't spend all my time controlling the comings and goings and happenings here."

"Tell me about Lynn first," I said.

He shrugged. "What about her? She was fucking one of the studs in her movie, and she couldn't handle it. She fell apart. She's better now than she was."

I don't know what I'd expected, but it hadn't been that. I was silent. The self-righteousness in his voice might have belonged to a man who'd been married to one woman for thirty years and been unquestioningly faithful to her during that time.

"Anything else you want to know, kid?" He turned around with the ironic smile that I remembered from the old days except that it had been on my real father's face then. It was still difficult for me to breathe when I looked at the person in the room with me, who didn't look so much like that man as like some Borscht Belt comic who'd spruced himself up for a part in a movie.

"Is she all right now?" I asked, as much because I needed to say something as because I wanted to know what he thought.

He shrugged.

"You saw her. You think she's all right?"

I looked at the floor, shook my head.

"Okay. Next question."

I began crying again. "Don't do that, Daddy. I can't help it if I . . . I have to get used to things."

"Yeah . . . well . . . there's been a lot to get used to, all right. Why don't you move back home and help me get used to it?"

173

Now I was more upset than I'd been before; he might have been the only person in the world whom I envisioned as having no needs he couldn't easily fill.

"What's gotten into Liane?" I asked inanely. "I mean, Sonny's always been difficult but . . ."

"But, but, but . . . What do you *think's* gotten into them? The time's gotten into them. And the place. Not to speak of a lot of dope . . . and a certain number of . . . Oh, what the hell. What difference does it make. You just go on with your life."

I waited, but he remained at the window, his shoulders hunched, looking down at the garden.

"Lynn didn't seem to notice Liane was here," I began cautiously.

A short, bitter laugh. "Lynn doesn't notice *Lynn's* here. Funny, huh?"

"None of it is funny."

It turned back to me once again, this scary new version of my precious father, searching my face as though to judge, once and for all, whether I was one of the motley crew who could take satisfaction of sorts in his difficulties. The judgment must have been satisfactory because he allowed himself to relax into the easy chair at the window.

"So, what are you doing for Simon & Koenig these days?"

I shrugged. "Lots of things. I might do the *FRemale* stuff. Dagmar would like me to take it on."

"That could be done from Los Angeles, if you were inclined."

"But it would be difficult."

"Nothing's so difficult, once you make up your mind to do it."

I smiled.

"Have you seen your mother?"

"Not yet."

"I hear Dagmar's effected a serious conversion."

I grinned in spite of myself. He was grinning too. Our first true complicity.

"You hear?" I asked. "You mean you haven't gone to see for yourself?"

"Any time I need a good laugh, I know where to get it. I don't have to go to your mother."

I felt called upon to defend the possibilities.

"We're not being fair," I said. "Something could've happened."

"Mmmm. Like what."

174

"Like . . . uh . . . she could've decided that as she gets older, she'd better find a way to take care of herself. Have something to do with her days."

"You flatter her if you think she knows she's getting older. Don't believe she believes it for a minute." He got a funny faraway look in his eyes and for a moment seemed to be lost in thought. Then he wrenched himself back to me, to us, to the room. "And as far as something to do goes, *do* is a verb that is unknown to your mother. Forget it. Whatever Dagmar or anyone else *thinks* is going on, the first time a dick with money walks into the room, she's going to forget liberation and go back to bed."

I was silent. Even if everything he said was in line with my own assumptions, there was a pessimism—worse than a pessimism, a *venom*—that made me reluctant to go along. To be doubtful was one thing, to stand on the sidelines virtually rooting for defeat something else.

"So," my father said, "is it your intention to spend the rest of your California time here in this room, or would you like to come downstairs and join the family? Maybe have a drink? Do you still drink? Tell me you haven't gone off drink and onto drugs like the rest of my children."

I smiled. "I came out with Louisa and the baby," I said. "We had a nice time. I guess you know she wanted to rest at the cottage. She said she'd be here for your birthday." I waited for questions but there were none. "Let me just wash my face and put on something else, and I'll come down and have a drink with you."

"I'll letcha." He smiled, bussed my cheek and left. A few minutes later I washed and went down to his den in a plaid shirt I'd brought with me on this trip and the jeans I'd left behind two years before.

Both ends of the huge room were one-way glass. The front looked toward the winding drive, the back to the lanai, as well as the terrace, pool and gardens. The room turned into a studio when the screen installed over the front window was lowered. One of the side walls was covered with books and scripts. The other held a huge TV screen as well as all the other imaginable kinds of equipment. My father sat at his huge leather-topped mahogany desk in the swivel chair that had always seemed like a throne.

"You're the only one," my father said, "I know'll still be yourself the next time I see you. Still be the same lovable kid."

I argued with myself over whether it was incumbent upon

me to clarify the matter of my no longer being a kid, decided to save it.

He was sitting at his desk, drinking a martini on the rocks, a tray with a pitcherful of icy martini, a small jar of cocktail onions, and bowls of big green olives and peanuts in front of him. In one corner of the brown leather sofa, with a large sewing basket next to her, a thimble on one finger, needle and thread in hand and some sort of garment on her lap, was a middle-aged, unglamorous woman I'd never seen before and whom it was almost possible not to notice.

I said, "Hello," and she said she was pleased to meet me. When my father appeared to be ignoring both of us in favor of the martini mix, she told me she was Clara. When my father displayed no inclination to clarify Clara, she informed me that she was his personal secretary. I was puzzled, not to say startled; she didn't fit the mold of any of my father's assistants-secretaries-wives-lays, being slender but not willowy, bosomy but somehow not voluptuous, regular-featured but not at all pretty.

My father poured another martini into the extra glass on the tray and held it out to me. Since he knew I never drank martinis, I had to assume this was a rite of passage, or at least of camaraderie. I took it from him, sipping it dutifully as he nibbled peanuts. It tasted awful, but I tried not to make a face. I realized for the first time that he was facing a TV set that was on. A newsman's face filled the screen, although no sound issued from his lips.

"So, what's happening?" I asked.

"War in Indo-China," he said, still looking at the screen. "Famine in Africa, Floods in the Southeast, Forest Fires in the West, Drought in the Southwest, Hippie–Drug Shit all over the place."

"Okay, okay," I laughed. "It's bad enough. Please don't turn on the sound."

Clara smiled at me with a pathetic eagerness that made me feel obliged to talk to her.

"How long have you been here, Clara?" I asked, trying to find a polite form for the question, or rather one of the questions, that had arisen in my mind.

She began to reply but he cut her off, asking if for Christ's sake he was going to have to listen to a lot of garbage when I hardly ever came to L.A. and it was almost his birthday. Then, as I remained silent, trying to figure out how to mollify him without further offending Clara, she stood up, saying she thought she'd best check on how things were going in the kitchen. She carefully folded the fabric she'd been working on, put away the rest of the equipment in her sewing basket and set both at the end of Sam's big desk. He did not object, which surprised me. In fact, he didn't appear to have heard her speak or to notice that she was leaving.

"Well," I said when she was safely gone, "did you break the mold before you hired her?"

He grinned but not with pure pleasure as I would have expected.

"Casting put out a call," he said after a while. "One super-competent but terribly ordinary-looking broad for a houseful of stars."

"But why?" I pressed. "What did you need her for?"

He stood abruptly, put down his martini so hastily that it sloshed over onto the desk.

"For nothing," he said. "I didn't need her here, I just wanted her. Someone I could yell at and not read about in the papers the next morning because she marched on the Pentagon or sold dope in her fucking high school or made a movie or went to the loony bin. *Fashtayst?*"

I knew the word for *understand*, but it was the second time in my life I'd heard him use Yiddish.

I nodded.

"Good," he said. "Then we can get on to other business. Or should I say pleasure. Is there anything in particular you'd like to do during your all-too-brief stay with us, Miz Berman?"

I shrugged. "I can't tell. There seems to have been a lot going on, and I know it's my own fault I haven't heard about it, I know you tried to tell me, but I wasn't . . . Anyway, I imagine I'll see them, see Sonny and Liane, I mean, at some point."

"Indeed you shall. Unless they're even less predictable than usual. It appears they intend to do me the great honor of attending my birthday party."

He sipped at his martini but then suddenly put down the glass, stood up and announced that there was no real reason I had to wait until tomorrow for the great pleasure of seeing my half sisters, we could pay a little visit now, at least to Liane. Ms. Sonya did not grant him the privilege of walking up the back stairs to her door.

We walked across the lawn to the poolhouse, a small version of the big, clay-colored stucco mansion. He knocked at the door. After an extraordinarily long time, during which he did not speak or look at me but I could feel him grow more tense by the second, it opened.

The girl who opened it wore a skimpy flesh-colored bikini and looked like the even more beautiful older sister of Liane. Her cheek-bones had grown more prominent, her cheeks had sunk in further, her forehead was higher, and the large gray eyes were extraordinarily limpid even under the half-closed lids that suggested she was heavily stoned. She glanced at me, trying to decide where she knew me from.

"Hi, Liane," I said. "It's Nellie. Long time no see."

"Hey . . . Nellie . . . right," she drawled. "Hey. Long see no time." One of those grassy little giggles issued from the vicinity of her mouth. She opened the door further, stepped back and, without looking at my father, at *our* father, said in what appeared to be a consciously seductive-provocative manner, "Come on in. You can bring your friend."

I looked at him. He was staring at her with an intensity that made him oblivious to me, if not to everything else. I squirm even now as I remember the acute discomfort I felt at that moment. It was as though I'd stumbled on an intercom wire between two rooms whose occupants weren't even supposed to know each other.

"Actually," I said, "I'm going back to the big house. I feel as though I haven't eaten in a day and a half." And I turned and walked rapidly across the lawn before anyone could stop me.

Nobody tried. I slipped through the back door into the big white-tile-floored kitchen I remembered so well. A couple I didn't know was preparing a meal. Ms. Karate Chop was eating at the small round table in one corner. I ignored her, introduced myself to them and moved toward the refrigerator. Except that against the wall where there had once stood just a huge stainless steel, glass-doored restaurant model, there now stood two refrigerators—the old one, on which the glass doors had been redone so they were opaque, and a smaller white home model. I opened the smaller one first. Bottles of seltzer along with rows of cut-up celery, carrot sticks, jícama and other diet staples met my eyes. On the next shelf were cold chicken, prepared tuna fish and so forth, and on the bottom were cans of Tab. In the big refrigerator were cheeses, cold cuts and other snacks, tempting but forbidden to anyone on a diet, including cookies and cake, potato chips and Fritos and other foods normally kept in cupboards, as well as Coke and ginger ale, and so on.

I took a bag of Fritos and a can of Coke and wandered back through the house to the study, sitting at my father's desk to await him, just as I had when I was very young and he would come along and, lifting me up, say that I was too small for the chair but just right for his lap. I ate some Fritos, drank some Coke and then, growing restive, pulled Clara's big wicker sewing basket toward me. I'd never seen a sewing basket so large outside of Saul's mother's workroom in Charleston.

Casually I flipped open the lid and picked up the blouse Clara had been sewing, which had a threaded needle in its collar. I noted the remaining contents of the top tray: two packets of needles, large and small scissors, spools of thread in every imaginable color. I don't think it was an imp that prevented me from stopping there, nor do I believe I had the vaguest inkling of what I would find. If I'd had a pen and paper, I would have been doodling. Instead, I picked up the tray to look in the much deeper section underneath and found a medical storehouse: a stethoscope, a thermometer, a package of syringes, vials of aspirin and prescription pills, a bag of cotton balls, a box of gauze swabs, another box of tiny blue needles and a couple of cylindrical containers with some sort of color-key charts printed on them.

She's a nurse.

My heart beating as rapidly as that of any unpracticed sneak thief, I replaced the tray, closed the basket and picked up my Coke as though the very fact of holding it would answer an accusation of prying. I became aware that my left hand, which had been inside the Fritos bag during the entire episode, was still in the bag and stuck full of bits and pieces it had, without direction from me, clutched at until they crumbled.

Where was everybody, anyway?

Lynn had disappeared as thoroughly as though she had stage directions telling her to be off when my father was on. I should go find my father, drag him back and make him talk to me, but Liane made me too uncomfortable. She looked at him as though he were a casting director she'd have to sleep with to get the job. Anyway, I didn't know how I would behave with him so soon after learning his secret. Except that I hadn't learned his secret, only that it existed.

Stop it.

And everything else, too. Stop thinking about things so much. Just take it as it comes.

But why does he have a nurse? And a first aid kit?

My father was the least hypochondriacal of people, it didn't make . . . Suddenly I thought of his phone complaint about his health, the first time I could ever remember his bringing up any aspect of his own condition, including his weight. Maybe he was really sick. Maybe he was—

Stop it.

179

Carefully I withdrew my Frito-encrusted hand from the bag and began to chew off the crumbs.

If I wanted to know how my father was or whether (!) he had been ill, the thing to do was to ask him. If I wanted to know about Clara's function in his life, I had to ask him that, too, although her being a nurse was the only thing that made any kind of sense. I had to ask him when we were alone. If she was with us, he would choose to be outrageous.

I wandered back outside. My father and Liane were still deep in conversation by the poolhouse. I turned to walk to the front of the big house and noticed the flight of wooden stairs my father had said was not to be breached, the separate stairs to Sonny's quarters. I went over and walked slowly up them, thinking that if he really didn't want me to talk to Sonny he'd interrupt his conversation for long enough to call me back. When he failed to call me, I reminded myself that not being able to bear Liane didn't mean I would suddenly find Sonny more tolerable. On the other hand, Sonny was now close to eighteen. Maybe she'd grown up a little but just couldn't handle my father.

The screen door was closed, but the wooden one was open. I couldn't see who was inside, so I called Sonny's name. After some time had passed, she came to the screen door. She was naked. I was upset but resisted the temptation to look down toward the poolhouse to see if my father was looking up. She did not speak or open the door.

"Hi," I said. "I just wanted to say hello." When she didn't respond or move to open the door, I added, "I can talk to you later if it's not a good time."

I moved toward the stairs.

"It's okay," she said. Her voice was flat. "You can come in."

I hesitated. Below, my father and Liane were walking around the pool; they might have been in bed, for all the freedom I felt to walk down to the lawn within close distance of them. I turned and went back to the door, walked in and nearly walked out again. On the large mattress that lay directly on the wooden floor, a naked male and female were, or appeared to be, sleeping.

I turned to Sonny, looking for some sign that she was enjoying my discomfort, and it would thus be all right for me to walk out. I saw no such sign. What I saw was a quarrel between villain and victim, between disdain and despair.

Sonny had never reached Liane's height but had a lush little body that probably would have become too fat if she hadn't been on dope so much of the time. She had the true redhead's almost true white, lightly freckled skin. If she was less beautiful than Liane, there was nothing wrong with her looks except to the extent that they had already been affected by the person who owned them.

The wall behind her had been drawn on, scrawled on and covered with posters of the Rolling Stones, the Who and other groups not yet familiar to me. On a long table at one side of the room were stereo equipment and a staggering number of tapes and records. Seeing me eye them, Sonny walked over to the table and put on a record of the new hard rock variety I hadn't learned to tolerate. As it blared into the room, she closed the wooden door leading outside with a wry smile and said something I couldn't hear because of the music.

The hell with this, said a voice in my brain that I could hear perfectly well.

I moved toward the door. I'm not sure what made me turn and call to her over the music that I was sorry about Estella. Whether she heard my words or read my lips, her expression altered drastically. Tears came to her eyes. Without looking at the record player, she reached back and pulled the record arm off the record, scratching it brutally as she did so. The bodies on the bed stirred, but Sonny didn't appear to notice. "How'd you find out?" she asked.

I was puzzled.

"You mean that she's gone?"

"Oh. I thought . . ." She reached down for a joint, one of several whole ones lying in a bowl on the floor next to the bed. Lighting it, she inhaled deeply and appeared in so doing to have gained the courage to complete her sentence. ". . . you knew what happened."

I shook my head.

"Well," she said, bitterness vying with pain in her expression, "if you want to know, just ask your sister Louisa."

My sister. My father. I seemed to have more relatives than anyone. Unwilling to push but wanting to know, I waited.

"Louisa?" I echoed, when nothing was forthcoming.

But Sonny had gone back into herself, and finally I made some inane comment about discussing it all later and left.

My father, looking as agitated as I felt, was coming across the lawn from the beach house. With a nod to tell me he knew where I'd been, he put an arm around me and said it had been a mistake to leave the house. We should go back to square one and get drunk. We returned to his study, where he settled on one of the leather couches, fresh martini in hand, and I observed Clara coming across the great hall of a foyer to the study.

"Whatever happened to Peg Cafferty?" I asked.

"Very little has ever happened to Peg Cafferty," he said. "If you mean, *where* is she, she's still doing nine to nine at the studio."

"She must be getting pretty old."

"We're all getting old," he grumbled. "That's what I was trying to tell you on the phone."

"Well," I said, "after all, you tell me you're getting old, but making your face look so young, it's confusing."

He gave me a dirty look, and I found myself cursing my attempts to juggle all the balls that were bouncing around this once orderly household. I should try to talk about Sonny because it was she who was on my mind. Or about Liane, except that it would be difficult to control the hostility I was feeling toward her.

"My daughter doesn't like Dr. Scully's work," he said to Clara as she entered the study.

"Oh, dear, is that so?" Clara asked in a truly concerned fashion. "And have you told her what it cost you?"

I was about to ask, in a perfectly serious manner and as much for my father's entertainment as for anything else, precisely what it had cost, when Clara noticed the glass he'd refilled upon our return to the den and registered dismay.

"Remember that expression," my father said to me. "It's the ultimate *shiksa* expression. As you can see, they don't have to be blond and beautiful to do it."

There it was again. Not the cruelty, which had always been present to be evoked by women like Clara, but the Yiddish. As used by my father, with his Brooklyn–New Jersey speech, it seemed at once harsher and more fitting than it had ever sounded in the soft Southern tones of Saul's family.

Clara's eyes filled with tears, but she held her ground. She stared at his glass, pointed out in a quavery voice that he was having a third before dinner.

"Oh, Christ," my father said to the ceiling, "take it away. I'm not going to enjoy it anyhow, with an ass braying in my ears."

Her tears remained, but Clara smiled through them, promptly taking the glass and the pitcher to another room where he wouldn't have to see them and be reminded.

"Do I have to ask why you're not drinking? Or why you're not supposed to be?"

He shrugged. "Only if you wanna know."

"I don't," I said. "I don't want there to be anything wrong with you."

He smiled, raised his empty hand in an imaginary toast. "You got it, kid."

But I couldn't quite let it go. "She's a nurse, isn't she? Clara? It's too good. You must have named her."

He nodded, grinned. "You got it. Clara Barton."

"Do you really need her here? Or is it just like having, you know, a bodyguard. Help is cheap, so you have her."

He shrugged. "I dunno. She keeps me from eating too much. And drinking. *Tries* to keep me. Sometimes she succeeds, which is worth her salary by itself. She checks my blood pressure. Gives me shots. I don't like to stick the needle into myself. Funny, huh?"

"Shots for what?" I asked without wanting to know.

He paused, sort of stared through me, grinned.

"For diabetes. You'll get a kick out of this one. If I'd never had the face work, I'd never have known. Or not now, anyway. But when they did the tests on me, my blood sugar—oh, shit, I'm talking their jargon. Forget it. Listen, my father was diabetic, and I thought I got away with it, but I didn't. It's nothing. You don't die from it. It doesn't count as a sickness."

I grinned. One thing to believe he had an illness that was an inconvenience of the body, another to acknowledge the possibility of a day when illness might take him from me.

"So what's happening that counts?" I asked, coming around the desk to kiss the top of his head. This was when I first saw, on his desk, the book with its fuzzily provocative cover photo: *A Servant's Diary* by Elena Martinez.

"Vas iss das?" I asked, showing off my own Atlanta Yiddish.

He shrugged, poured himself a Perrier from the bottles on the tray.

"Just took an option on it. Don't know if it'll ever get made. It's five or six years old, no one's even tried."

"Oh?"

I flipped through it, stopped at the passage I've already cited, then closed the book, my cheeks warm.

"What's the plot?"

"There's no plot to speak of. Just a lot of fuckin' and suckin'."

I flinched. It still made me uncomfortable for him to use that language when he was talking to me, particularly after my reading.

"Well," he said, "maybe that's not fair. A coupla things happen, they're just not . . . Why don't you read it and tell me what you think?"

He said I'd have time to read that evening because he had a business dinner he couldn't change. I said, with a lightness I did not feel, that I hoped he would manage to be home the next night, Saturday, for his birthday. He didn't bother to reply.

I called Violet, and we agreed to have dinner at seven. I asked if she wanted me to pick her up, and she said I didn't have to pick her up, she had learned to drive. If I'd been open to astonishment, I would have been overwhelmed, but my reactions were on hold. When I walked into La Boya promptly at seven, assuming I'd have at least half an hour or more before Violet made her entrance to drink, think, and/or read the book, which I'd brought with me, I was astonished to find her waiting at the table.

Her blacker-than-ever hair was swept back and into a neat bun. Her makeup was light, which was unremarkable. She wore a red jersey dress, also unremarkable in itself, except that I'd never seen her in red or any bright color when she wasn't playing a role. She held out a hand and greeted me with what appeared to be warmth.

I said hello and sat down.

"How nice," Violet said, "that you could come out for your father's birthday."

I suspect that no matter how accurately I've portrayed the vapidity and ennui that had characterized her during the years I'd been aware of her as a person, it will be impossible for the reader to accept the extent of the change. That she appeared pleased to see me was remarkable; that she remembered my father's birthday was astonishing; that she stood to peck my cheek was beyond belief. I could not remember having been kissed by her in my lifetime although my father once told me that in the first placid months of my life I had often been set down beside her in the big bed and she would kiss and fondle me.

Violet expressed regrets that Lynn, whom I'd not seen again in the house but whom she'd invited to join us, would not be able to do so. She spoke of the women's group they attended as though she were not someone who for most of her life had barely acknowledged that other women existed outside of bad dreams. She was pleasant if not lively, coherent if not fascinating. She said she had always been closer to men than to women and had never dreamed what a comfort women could be. Her friendship with Lynn was a perfect example. She was more at ease with this woman she'd hated for years than she had ever been with the man she'd been jealous over.

The only person she was fonder of than she was of Lynn was Dagmar, her best friend in the world and the person without whom she could not have broken out of the rut that had been her life. She and Dagmar were making a film about that life, which Dagmar felt had a great deal to teach all women. Perhaps I knew already about the film and about the cover story being prepared for *FRemale* in conjunction with its opening. The FRemale Foundation would get all profits beyond the investors' return on their money.

I smiled, trying to conceal my discomfort with the notion of being a character in some film of Violet's life. Would I be a hateful kid she couldn't manage or a bland standee on the sidelines as the movie actress rehearsed her roles? I wondered, I think for the first time in my adult life, if there had been a malign cast to the infantile self-absorption I'd taken for granted. I brushed that one off with a comment to myself about paranoia, but everything that was going on couldn't be brushed off so easily.

If there was no way Violet was the entirely different human she appeared to be, *something* had happened. It was one thing to say a person's behavior might alter for the better (remember this was the first I'd seen of those Women's Movement conversions that would become familiar to us all); another to believe that the fragile loon who had in some negative fashion dominated the life of my home had turned into a sane and productive human being.

Then there was the matter of Dagmar. If I'd always been a little leery of the beautiful woman who acted as if she wanted to be my best friend when she was actually my father's, and who would deny there was a conflict of interest in these positions, it was mind-boggling to reflect on Dagmar and Violet's working together on a film that covered Dagmar's being Violet's husband's mistress.

I'd registered Violet's drinking wine instead of Scotch and ordering lasagna instead of fish broiled without butter. Only now, as she stood to go to the ladies' room, did I realize that in her new life she'd gained enough weight to resemble a normal nonfilm female. If she looked even more beautiful than she once had, it was not only because she'd become more human, but because her bones had a little flesh on them. (*Her* face-lifts still didn't bother me.)

As we left the restaurant, I promised to be in touch, if not before I left Los Angeles, then soon after I flew home.

· · ·

I took *A Servant's Diary* to bed with me.

I was unsettled and exhausted and assumed I'd begin at the beginning and read for a few minutes, then fall asleep. But a combination of curiosity, arousal and discomfort kept me awake until the end (one hundred and seventy-four pages in a larger than average typeface), reading a book that never moves out of its primitive, sensual-domestic world into an adult one where feelings would be disguised and their intensity diminished or lost.

My father had told me the author's name was a fake but I would enjoy the book more if I didn't speculate on her identity until I'd finished. As I read, I tried to understand why he'd bothered to make the suggestion. I neither recognized the characters nor assumed for a moment that they had models in real life. They were dream people, untroubled by the past and unconcerned with the future, absorbed only in filling the primordial present's needs. The only negative in their lives was the sporadic sadism of S.S., for which he always apologized by increasing the women's "doses" of pleasure afterward. While one slept, another performed some pleasant act upon him or her. When they rested, it was in remembrance and anticipation.

It must have been two or three in the morning when I finished the book and turned off my light, astounded by the extent of my absorption in the antics of people who would drive me mad if I had to talk to them for ten minutes at a cocktail party. I was certain I was far too wound up to sleep. I was wrong, but not entirely; I fell into a nightmare from which I quickly awakened.

I dreamed about S.S., a heavyset man somewhat younger than my father, with a red swastika tattooed on his arm. There were a lot of people in the room with him whom I couldn't identify, but then suddenly they were gone, and S.S. was holding a needle, and the swastika on his arm was bleeding. I started looking around for the author, the only one who would be able to help him, and grew frantic as I not only failed to locate her but was unable to find any of the people who'd been there earlier.

I awakened upset but without that sense of disorientation one usually feels the first night away from home. I knew where I was. Too, the mind that dreamed had been willing to do what the waking mind had not; I understood that *A Servant's Diary* had to have been written by someone who knew our family. Louisa was the only writer, though I found it difficult to believe she could have produced this piece of pornography. Then I remembered Sonny's ask-

186

ing whether I knew what Louisa had done. I fell asleep trying to remember incidents that might have fueled Louisa's imagination to the point where it produced *A Servant's Diary.*

"So, what'd you think?" my father asked when I came down to breakfast the next morning in the blue-and-white muumuu he'd brought me from Hawaii years earlier.

"I think Happy Birthday," I said, kissing his cheek. "Do you want your present now, or tonight when the company's here?"

"Tonight," he said. "But there isn't going to be a lot of company. Maybe a couple of extra people."

Clara sat with her sewing and her sewing basket at the round glass-topped table in the lanai. On the sideboard (my father didn't like to have servants hover while he ate) were pots of regular and decaffeinated coffee (both imported from New York in the bean, the latter still difficult to find in California) as well as electrically heated baskets of bread and rolls, toasted and untoasted, and pitchers of juice and milk. Absent from the sideboard were the Danish pastries, the small pitcher of heavy cream he had always used in his morning coffee no matter what kind of diet he was on, the lumps of sugar that had to be in a certain crystal bowl that had a history he'd kept promising to tell me, and the large chunk of imported Danish butter, which had been replaced by an ordinary, presumably resistible stick of the American kind.

I said good morning to Clara, who seemed pathetically grateful for the two words, took some juice and settled at the table with coffee and a buttered bagel.

"Okay," my father finally said. "Let's have it."

"I guess," I replied hesitantly, "I don't understand why you've bought it for the movies."

"That's an easy one," he said. "Your sister needed some money and it was the cheapest way to give it to her."

"I'm a little overwhelmed," I told him after a long time. "When did it come out, 1970? She never gave a hint. It's amazing, really."

"Ain't it, though," my father said, and proceeded to tell me the story.

The book had received scant attention when it was published. Louisa, who'd not previously shown signs of being tight-lipped, had mentioned it to no one. On the contrary, she had enthusiastically promoted the lie that *Scarsdale,* two years later, was her first published work.

In 1975 one of Sonny's school chums had been in Acapulco

with her family and picked up a copy of the *Diary* left by someone in a hotel dining room. She'd brought it back to Los Angeles and shown it to all her friends. Sonny had fallen in love with the book to a point where she'd refused to relinquish her friend's copy until she'd ordered, and received, ten more. She proclaimed it a great work of art. (It was, my father said, the first book she'd read since Nancy Drew.) She never dreamed of any relation between herself and the author; she simply made that assumption of shared feeling that is one of the pleasures of fiction—unless, of course, it registers as the displeasure of being identified. She gave a few of the extra copies to friends and bought more. Her own primary copy was almost worn out.

What Sonny had not figured on was that Estella, whose English was excellent and who by this time read as well as she spoke, would be intrigued by the title and the author's Spanish name, would leaf through the book and, being smarter than Sonny, would make the connection between the Sam Pearlsteins and the Xs, the director couple in the book. Estella didn't know who'd made up these filthy lies, but she was certain which couple and maid they were supposed to be about.

The only reason she'd told Sam why she was leaving was that he'd walked into the house as she was walking out with her suitcase. One of her brothers, who had a cab, was parked at the curb.

It was a Saturday. My father had tried without luck to convince her to wait until he could get the information to prove she was wrong, that only coincidence, and not even very close coincidence, was involved. Estella was unwilling to wait, but by a few hours later, my father had read the book and knew it wasn't going to matter. Louisa, when he'd asked her, had been casual in acknowledging the accuracy of his deductions. (It was some time later that it occurred to my father to use the book as a way of giving Louisa money she needed and, at the same time, make sure no one else could film it in the current, more permissive, Hollywood environment.)

My father had not been terribly concerned about Estella's leaving, he told me. Sonny was almost eighteen years old, past the age when he should be overpaying a nursemaid. If Estella still cleaned the girl's room, that was because Sonny wouldn't allow anyone else in it. Without Estella there, Sonny could make the choice of letting in the other help or doing it herself, a prospect he found amusing.

When Sonny asked where Estella was and was told Estella had

returned to Mexico, she'd at first assumed the maid was on family business. It was a couple of weeks before she asked again and, upon receiving the specific answer that Estella had quit and would not return, had become a raving lunatic, walking around the house banging her fists into walls and throwing things. It was only after considerable time had passed with the craziness showing no sign of abatement that my father had ordered her out of the house.

At this point Sonny had gotten into her car and driven down to Estella's town in Mexico. It was a gauge of the importance of her mission that she had checked carefully to make sure that for the first time in years there was no dope of any kind in her car. She had returned a week later in a condition that might be described as anything but drug-free. Since that time she had never mentioned Estella.

"Did you ever try to talk with her about it?" I asked.

My father shrugged. "I did something better than that. I invited Shimmy Kagan out here to have dinner with us. Remember Shimmy?"

I smiled. "What kind of question is that? How could I forget him?"

Shimmy had been my father's lawyer on matters like employment contracts for as far back as I could remember.

"He's moved out here, you know, since Vivian died. He's practicing here. Hasn't found a woman he likes yet. These guys who are married for a hundred years are all finished when the wife dies. Anyway, I asked him to the birthday dinner. I've got a guy coming to do a luau. I figured with Shimmy here, and maybe one of his kids, grandkids, whatever—the daughter and her family moved out here, that's why he finally came, after years of me and everyone else trying to get him out to the Coast—and your sister and her baby, who knows, maybe the rebels without a cause'll behave themselves for a couple of hours."

Shimmy Kagan was as magical to me as snow—and could also be found, while I was growing up, only in New York. A man whose force of personality was as great as my father's, he'd lived happily with his family in a New York suburb because he agreed with his wife that Los Angeles was no place to raise children. Now, my father said, New York clients who wanted to see him had to come here. Remembering the rare occasions when my professional path had crossed his, I assumed many were willing to do this.

A little older than my father and considerably shorter than

either of us, Shimmy was bald, except for a bare fringe of gray hair, and ugly in the classic little-Jewish-guy-with-big-nose manner. The first characteristic that distinguished him from the movie tycoons I'd known, not excluding my father, was his cultivated speech. The other was some standard I think I sensed all along, but verified only later, which not only prevented him from working on nasty little divorce cases but made him refuse to represent my father on legal matters connected to his gambling interests. Of course, he'd told my father, the Constitution stated that he and the gangsters he was dealing with were entitled to legal representation, but he didn't want to be It.

In those lovely childhood days when my father was still occasionally bringing me to New York, the Kagan home in New Rochelle was the only place where I didn't mind being left for an "overnight" when my father was otherwise engaged. Shimmy took me into the family in a warm and casual way, asking me the riddle-jokes I adored and questioning me about the business so he could marvel at my command of production values and figures. His daughter, Grace, called me Cousin Nellie.

Now I found myself wishing I hadn't lost touch with both of them.

"Did it work?" I asked. "Did he get anywhere with Sonny?"

"Nah," my father said. "He told her all the right stuff, how fiction is such a pleasure for everyone except the people who think they're being written about, and he could understand how she felt, but he felt Louisa had tried to change things, disguise them, if it had to be a movie producer and a Spanish maid, at least she kept it a secret which movie producer's daughter she was, and she could make some money, and so on, without hurting anybody . . . I mean, Louisa's a big enough pain in the ass . . . this is me, talking, not Shimmy . . . without getting her for the stuff she tried to do right."

"How will the party be with all of them here?" I asked. "I mean, even forgetting about Shimmy, what about Sonny and Louisa?"

"What *about* Sonny and Louisa?" he asked. "It's my birthday and they'd *both* fucking well better behave."

If you were seeking an argument for the virtues of fiction, you might have found it at my father's real-life birthday party. He was depressed, two of his four daughters were disengaged and/or disagreeable, the casual pleasantries were provided by Shimmy Kagan (Grace was tied up and couldn't come), and the only small sense of excitement was provided by Louisa (with her baby), who might have been testing it out to see if it would work in a novel. This is the truth that lent a humorous note to the lawsuit—at times when one could gain the distance to hear it. If there were all sorts of gruesome possibilities in the air on the night of my father's luau, they were unexplored until Louisa sent Joe Stalbin's people to Palm Springs for his birthday.

The lanai, where the party was held so my father wouldn't have to admit Sonny and Liane's friends to the house proper if either girl should choose to bring them, is a huge glassed-in room about twenty feet wide and running the width of the house. The floors are terra-cotta tile, the seats a series of rattan armchairs and settees with upholstered pillows. Against the house wall are the tiled bar, sink and shelves holding various implements as well as glasses and Mexican pottery.

It was raining. Clara was posted in the front hallway of the house, having been told not to come around to the lanai until Sam called her. Delilah did guard duty on the walk between the house and Liane's quarters, from which she could also see the comings and goings from Sonny's apartment. The cook and his boyfriend-assistant scurried between the grill on the terrace and various supplies they needed from the kitchen. My father insisted on preparing the cocktails; he said if he couldn't drink the way he wanted to, he could at least "keep handling the stuff." He had informed both girls that they could bring their friends if they really wanted to, but that he'd be delighted if they didn't. Liane's came. Three boys and one other girl. When I try to picture them I remember Louisa's description of the younger daughter's friends in *Joe Stalbin's Daughters*—blond, pretty, cooled out—the most noticeable one being a young male who sat next to Liane without uttering one word during the entire party and who, from the top of his platinum hair down to the soles of his handcrafted sandals, might have been posing for Louisa's portrait of the Stalbin daughter's boyfriend.

They all slouched on either side of Liane on the long rattan settee, drinking without cease because my father had told Liane—he wouldn't talk to her pals—that if they did dope in the big house, he wouldn't wait for the cops to come, he'd kill them himself. The boys briefly eyed Dagmar when she walked in, but when they saw her in conversation with my father, they lost interest.

I knew that Dagmar had various speaking engagements across the country on behalf of *FRemale*, and I'd wondered whether, in

191

the time since I'd last seen her, she had altered herself in some way to conform to *FRemale*'s vision of the correctly nonseductive woman. But it was clear from the moment she stepped down into the lanai that she had not. Here was no drab militarist, devoid of energy, taste or physical beauty and blaming men for her deficiencies. Here was Dagmar Saperstein, who was awfully nice and terribly smart and who, with even less makeup than she'd worn in the old days, was even more beautiful than she'd been then (Louisa told me later that she'd taken a South American "cut-and-sew vacation" with my father), who wore high-heeled sling-back, patent leather pumps with a formfitting white jersey dress and big silver hoop earrings, and whose long black hair fell to her shoulders, straight and silky, as though the gods of feminism and femininity had had a conference and in rare agreement decided that here was a face that called for framing. (Louisa also told me at some point that she'd had "a sort of a yen to do a job" on Dagmar, maybe as the older sister in *Joe Stalbin*, but that she'd been unable to "find a soul" and had given up on the idea.)

Dagmar greeted me warmly, kissed my cheek and announced her intention to persuade me before the evening was over to take on *FRemale*'s legal work. My father told her to cut out recruiting on his time, and Dagmar said, "Whoops, forgot! Where's Lynn, anyway?" When my father said Lynn hadn't yet felt moved to come down, Dagmar went upstairs to get her.

Sonny came in—alone. She wore a monkish sort of white robe. Around her neck was a Mexican silver chain at the end of which dangled half of a large silver locket in which was set, behind glass, a picture of Estella. She moved majestically toward the bar, poured a glass of orange juice and brought it to sit next to me without exactly acknowledging that I was there. My father stood in back of us; she never looked at him.

A moment later, Dagmar and Lynn appeared, each with an arm around the other in a manner suggestive of solidarity among women.

"Brought to you," my father, standing behind my seat, muttered loudly enough so they could have heard him if they chose, "through the magic of bullshit vision. The first rule of the seventies is that all women are friends—as long as you're not fucking any of them. Violet would've been happy to join 'em, but there's a limit to what a man should have to endure on his birthday." He said something in Yiddish. It occurred to me that the last few times I'd seen him in New York, Dagmar hadn't been with him.

I had a beer. My father was drinking Tab. Perhaps Clara Barton's not being there made it easier for him to do what he was supposed to do. Sonny and Liane ignored one another so thoroughly as to suggest they were strangers to each other as well as to the rest of us.

Lynn followed Dagmar to the bar, where Dagmar requested something tall and sweet and pink for both of them. When my father had made their drinks, they repaired to a settee, from which Dagmar announced that she couldn't wait to see Louisa.

Sonny leaped to her feet and shouted, "Is *she* coming?"

My father said that he certainly hoped so, everyone in his family was welcome on his birthday.

"Murderers included?" Sonny shouted.

"Have her calmed down by the time I come back," my father said to no one in particular, "or she goes." He walked out of the lanai, leaving everyone in silence.

"Are you angry with Louisa," I asked in the ensuing silence, "because of the book?"

"Sure because of the book," Sonny said. "I mean, I couldn't stand her *before* the book, but *now* . . . Every time I think of what she did to Estella I want to kill her!"

I argued with myself for a moment, waited for Dagmar, for *someone*, to say something. Then, very cautiously, I observed that I understood how she felt, but I didn't think Louisa had intended to hurt anyone.

"Of course she did," Sonny said. "She *always* intends to hurt someone."

"She tried to do it so no one would know," I pointed out.

"Bullshit," Sonny said loudly. "She knew we'd find out sooner or later."

I glanced at Dagmar, who was watching Sonny with concern.

"You know," Dagmar finally said in a voice at once hesitant and tender, "I'd love to have a chance to talk to you sometime about that book, Sonya. To me, it's a really beautiful story about true love between women. Even if it were about the woman you think it's about, that wouldn't be anything to be ashamed of. I'd *glory* in it if it were about me. The man is quite incidental to the whole story, and the women are *wonderful*."

Sonny said, "You're a cunt and you're full of shit."

As everyone sane in the room tried to figure out where we were going from there—Liane hadn't noticed anything but her boyfriends were grinning at what was turning into a better party than

193

they'd hoped for—my father appeared at the glass doors with Louisa, who wore a floor-length orange muumuu and carried Penelope on one shoulder. My father's eyes were on the baby, who appeared to be fast asleep. He looked very happy.

Sonny froze as the three came into the lanai. My father hadn't mentioned Louisa's baby to either girl. At the time, I thought I understood why. Now I can't think of a good reason.

Dagmar flew to Louisa with words that I remember as "Oh, my God, she's-adorable-what-are-you-doing-about-child-care?"

Louisa laughed. "I'm caring for her, that's what I'm doing!"

My father gave her the first utterly approving look I had ever seen him bestow upon Louisa.

"This is Penelope," she said, turning the baby around so that, still sleeping, she sat with her back propped against Louisa's still large stomach.

"Happy birthday," Louisa said to my father, smiling proudly.

I wondered if this conscious cuteness would take the edge off his pleasure. Instead, his smile softened into a huge, nearly foolish grin of a sort that was foreign to me. He held out his arms for Penelope. Louisa hesitated, for a moment seemed about to quiz him on his qualifications, decided against doing so and transferred Penelope to his arms. He took her as though he had been cradling babies for a living, put her over his shoulder, kissed the top of her head and sat down in one of the rattan chairs, a contented man.

I was profoundly shaken, though I could not for the world have said why. I can admit to myself only now that this was the first time I was ever jealous of Louisa.

The chef and his assistant brought out some hors d'oeuvres. I finished my beer and watched myself with surprise as I poured a shot of whiskey into the same glass, then added another beer. Those among the living (Liane and her friends appeared to be doing everything in their sleep) commented upon the hors d'oeuvres and other important matters.

Sonny left the lanai after the following exchange with my father, during which Louisa's eyes remained downcast, her manner reminiscent of one of *The Mikado*'s three little maids.

SONNY: (*raising her glass*) Death to writers!

FATHER: Cut it out. It's my birthday.

SONNY: What do *you* care? You're not a writer.

FATHER: If you're so goddamned smart, how come you can't get a job?

The baby awakened and Louisa asked if anyone minded her

nursing on the lanai. My father announced that anyone who minded could leave. Louisa said she'd had a drink to insure our having a peaceful dinner. Being unfamiliar with the realities of nursing, most particularly with the soporific effects of a bit of liquor in a mother's milk, I felt more confused than ever. It was as I finished my beer and whiskey and Louisa was delivering a monologue about feeding the baby that my father's beeper went off. He shifted Penelope ever so slightly so he could reach it.

"Who?" he asked. "I don't know any Alice Donaldson. Yes, Dagmar and Louisa are here."

Louisa, stony-faced, demanded, "What's *she* doing here?"

"Uh, oh," Dagmar said, "you mean you didn't ask her? There must be an emergency. Just tell her to come in, Sam, okay? I'll explain."

He did so, and Dagmar told him that Alice was the woman Louisa had "sort of adopted" who was just now doing virtually the whole business side of *FRemale*. As she was explaining, Louisa, who seemed to be choking with the effort to keep herself from speaking, took the baby, settled into an armchair, pulled down the broad neck of her muumuu enough to open her nursing brassiere and gave the baby her breast.

There appeared at the terrace door a woman I'd not have recognized if I hadn't known she was Alice Donaldson. Her hair was ash blond, she was heavily made up, and she wore a slinky black dress of some crepy material that set off her curves.

"There you are, love," she said to Louisa. "I could barely make out your message on the tape, I think it's broken. You did tell me to meet you here, didn't you?"

Louisa, with Penelope sucking at her breast, had become as calm as the baby, but she wasn't about to pretend to believe Alice's story.

"Sam," said Dagmar into the awkward silence, "I want you to meet our wonderful Business Manager, Alice Donaldson."

Whether my father was being his usual ornery self or had noticed Louisa's reaction to the announcement and was proving that her new power over him was less than complete, I cannot guess. But he turned into a gentleman of the old school. He stood, bowed and said he had heard a great deal about Alice so it was a particular pleasure to have her with us on this day.

Alice tittered in a manner that was nearly intolerable even to the disengaged. Except my father, of course, who was not only accustomed to having young women throw their souls at his feet but thrived on creating the impression that they wouldn't get trampled on there when he decided to walk.

Alice, her manner an incredible combination of smarm and seduction, said she'd been working terribly hard and looking forward to the day when she would meet him, and Happy Birthday. She handed him a very small box. Our presents for him were piled on a table at the end of the room. My father did not add it to the pile but held it, a signal to the rest of us that the farce would not last long, as he asked if she would like a drink. Louisa wondered aloud if it was an engagement ring, but no one seemed to hear her. Alice told him just about any drink would do. He handed her something, took some soda for himself and raised his glass to her, saying, "Down with answering machines!" Then he turned to Louisa. "Down with everything but babies. Right, Penelope? Penny? Penelope? Nelope Pelope? What are we going to call you?"

As he spoke he opened Alice's present, an eighteen-carat gold tie clip that read "SPecial," thanked her while clipping it to the neck of his T-shirt and, without taking a breath, launched into a speech about the meaning of names, and how the name a baby adored when she was this age might become a terrible burden to her by the time she was in school.

Alice, clearly in a state of confusion about what had caused him to ignore her after such a promising beginning, was reminded of work she had to do at the Honeycomb and left. By the time her American Express bill arrived with the charge from Saks, she had disappeared from all our lives. To the best of my knowledge, no one of us, Louisa and AmEx included, ever heard from a person with that name again.

Conversation was desultory until Shimmy arrived with a California year-round-type tennis tan but otherwise looking just as he had in the days when I'd run into him around the courthouse. Our paths hadn't crossed at all since his move to the West Coast, and aside from the simple pleasure of catching up with someone remembered fondly, I found his very presence raised substantially the level of conversation in the lanai. Having briefly admired Penelope, he spoke with Dagmar about *FRemale*, and with Lynn about a piece on being an independent woman filmmaker she was supposedly writing for the magazine. Then he turned to Louisa to ask whether she was able to write yet or if the baby was occupying all her time and energy.

"Both," Louisa said with a grin. "She occupies my feelings all the time, but my brain only about ninety percent, so I have a little time for work."

"Is it politic to ask if you're thinking about another book?"

"Always."

"And of course it's a novel."

Another grin. "Always."

"I thought *Scarsdale* was an excellent piece of work," Shimmy said, causing Louisa's expression to move from guarded-friendly to your-wish-is-my-command-friendly.

"You don't mean to tell me you actually *read* it!" she exclaimed.

"I read it," Shimmy said, "and found it not only compelling but utterly truthful in terms of my experience with a couple of women who'd had plastic surgery. If they didn't develop some ailment that had nothing to do with the surgery itself, they went around worrying about it all the time, wondering who could tell they'd had it done, and what they *really* looked like behind the face in the mirror, and so on."

Louisa nodded happily and embarked upon one of her monologues, this time about men's not reading women's novels, the whys and wherefores, and her particular delight in talking to Shimmy.

Then suddenly she asked him, "Have you read the *Twenty Letters*, by any chance? Svetlana Stalin? *Twenty Letters to a Friend*?"

"I bought it ages ago," Shimmy said, "when it was published. I'm not sure why I didn't read it at the time. Perhaps family events. I remember unpacking it after I moved, but I seem to have forgotten about it, although I can picture it on the shelf." He paused, watched Louisa shaking her head. "Do I gather I've committed a sin of omission?"

She nodded earnestly. "It's extraordinary. *Fascinating.* She adored old Joe. She's very bright. The book's dedicated to her mother, who committed suicide, of course, but she not only didn't give much of a shit for her mother, she was much too crazy about old Joe ever to come to terms with who he was. She keeps complaining about the terrible influence Beria had on him. Beria was more cunning, more perfidious, more everything evil. Her father had soft spots, weaknesses, but Beria had none. She's not sure how much Beria even *told* Stalin about the atrocities he was committing."

As she spoke, Louisa's normal casual-powerful manner grew more intense, her shoulders hunched toward Shimmy, and she reached with rapid, rhythmic motions for the bowl of nuts on the end table near her. She put nuts in her mouth, then reached back for more without pausing to chew or swallow. She seemed oblivious not only to adults other than Shimmy in the room but to her baby. The change in her, or perhaps I should say the intensification of her normal traits, was remarkable to me. I would say now this was because I'd never seen her writing or heard her discuss her work.

Which was, indeed, what she was doing. In fact, we were being given a window on the book that was to become her first success and give rise to the heavily publicized lawsuit.

"Stalin's mother had a lot of children, in fact, but Joe was the only one who lived . . . She was a redhead, Svetlana. There's a scene where he's showing Churchill around their Moscow apartment and little Svetlana comes out and he pats her on the head and says to Churchill, 'This is my daughter. She's a redhead.' They were Georgian, you know. From the part of Russia called Georgia. As a matter of fact, the epigraph I'm using . . . my main character was born and raised in Atlanta, Georgia. The epigraph is a line from Svetlana's letters. She's talking about Georgia, where Joe was born and raised, and she says, 'We are barbarians of a type you'll find nowhere else on earth.' "

Shimmy glanced at me, then looked away. He knew I'd been married to an Atlantan and, with his greater sophistication in such matters, assumed her words would make me uneasy. He flattered me, thinking I would understand that Louisa's writing about a redheaded Georgian dictator's family had to end up in discomfort for one or more relatives of the dictatorial film producer named Sam Pearlstein.

But I listened, mesmerized and admiring.

Louisa appeared to have committed to memory lengthy passages from Svetlana's letters. The rest of us might as well not have been in the room as she recited one for Shimmy in which Svetlana said she well understood those Russians who'd fled to France, then needed to come home again, or who refused to live abroad after returning from prison or labor camp. In a day full of little awkwardnesses and major personality clashes, and with no interest in anything but Shimmy Kagan and Svetlana Stalin, Louisa succeeded in diverting us all, as, a couple of years later, fueled by that same intensity, she would divert millions of readers.

If my subsequent work for *FRemale* and my participation in Louisa's trial led me to a keener understanding of libel issues, I cannot claim that it has enabled me to follow the twisted path my sister's brain took to reach Georgia, a state where I had put in some time but to which she had no other connection, and the state that gave her Joe Stalbin his birthplace, his accent and the Southern charm that beguiled his Hollywood adversaries for long enough so that he might prevail.

Byron Koenig had had a long weekend alone to think about me, us, and the matter of my not wanting to marry him and have children. On my first night back from Los Angeles, he informed me that he understood my feelings perfectly and wanted me to understand his. If I did not want our relationship "to progress further," he would have to feel free to date other women in the hope of finding one who wanted what he did from life.

A week later he began dating a junior in the law firm just down the hall from Simon & Koenig, a lovely-looking thirty-three-year-old who was dying to get married and have children. A week after that, he advised me they were serious and were going to "stop seeing other people." I told him I understood perfectly, then went home and cried myself to sleep for a few nights in a row. After which I had two dates with a man I didn't like. After which I decided that I wouldn't make it as any kind of a feminist if I couldn't stay home for two consecutive Saturday nights, or enjoy having dinner with Louisa and her baby or some other woman friend, or go to a movie with the couple who were my best friends in New York, a lawyer who worked in my office and his wife, who lived on the Upper West Side only a few blocks from Louisa.

BOOK

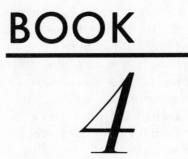

4

"Women who grasp the male point of view more than momentarily are not feminists."

Ti-Grace Atkinson

THE LEGACY OF my trip to Los Angeles was a determination not only to do *FRemale*'s legal business but to take both the magazine and feminism more seriously than I had before. I was, of course, late in this determination. The seminal events of the Women's Movement had occurred during the time I was in school, in love and in Atlanta. From the vantage points of school and love, those events had felt remote if not irrelevant; in Atlanta, they gained importance in my mind in proportion to my inability to make use of them in everyday life. With my return to New York it had become clear that the movement had effected real changes in the way some Americans lived, but there was no way as yet to calculate the effect of those changes. Not the important ones, anyway.

Coming from a Southern town where courtly manners were still very much the male mode, I was shocked almost to tears the first time a man pushed me aside to get a cab I'd hailed. Coming from circumstances in which I hadn't had to fight to go to a good school or, once I left the South, to get a job, I didn't have the visceral reaction some women did to male tactics spawned by anger at the new competition. Even now, as I allowed myself to identify more fully than I had before with the movement's reasonable aims, I felt obliged to hold aside some portion of my brain that would allow me later to say I'd never thought it was a solution to *all* the problems of the world, just to some of the more obvious ones. But for the first time, I was certain of what to answer when asked whether I was a feminist. And I was pleased to be able to tell women I met that I was the lawyer for *FRemale*.

It was supposed to be the first time in history that the way you'd been in the past didn't matter, didn't tell people who you really were. History, after all, had been made by and for men. What counted now, in the tense Feminist Present, was where you'd been standing five minutes after the call to the barricades. To hesitate even briefly to call oneself a feminist was an unforgivable, not to say a crucially revealing act. What it revealed was that words, distinctions, the play of light, were more important than liberation. (The notion that political-rhetorical enslavement was as real as, if less painful than, the other kinds remained foreign, or at least superfluous.)

Because I had gone to law school before the rush hour, I was presumed to have been standing early on the barricades. The notion that I had been standing there looking for my father did not, happily, enter anyone's mind.

Twice a week, at the end of my workday, I would walk from my office on Fifty-seventh Street between Fifth and Sixth up to Louisa's apartment at Sixty-third Street and Central Park West. I had a key. Our understanding was that I would ring, wait two minutes, then let myself in, remaining in the kitchen or the living room—office if Louisa and Penelope weren't around. As time went on and the baby began to turn into a person, I found myself looking forward to seeing her as well as Louisa. Often I'd pick up dinner for the three of us at a Chinese restaurant near my office. Penelope, from the time she had six teeth, adored Chinese food.

Louisa and Penelope each had one of the apartment's two good-sized bedrooms. Louisa's, with pink walls, patchwork quilts and ornate dark wood, marble-topped night tables and dresser, was a study in Victorian femininity. The baby's room had blue walls and ceiling with a huge yellow sun and white clouds painted on it by her mother.

The living room, headquarters of *FRemale*, looked very much like the office of a small-town newspaper, with white walls, two ancient rolltop desks, dark wood filing cabinets and chairs and two Smith Corona manual typewriters, as well as a 1953 IBM machine that seemed incongruously modern in its surroundings. The only wall adornment, aside from various deadline and printing charts, was a six-inch high, four-foot long, black-and-white sign that read: THE PERSONAL IS POLITICAL. When I asked Louisa if she thought this was always true, she shrugged and said it had been a present from a black-lesbian-separatist group she hadn't wanted to offend. When I asked about the aims of such a group, she responded, rather tersely, "A country without men." When I asked about the perpetuation of such a group, she waved her free arm in the air and said something about sperm banks. When I threw caution to the winds and asked if she thought that was funny, she became concerned about what the baby was up to in the other room, saying on her way out, "Who'm I to think it's funny?" Then, having left the office, she poked her head back in and said, "I can't laugh if they're black. It's been too rough for them."

Of course, the list of things one couldn't laugh at was longer and less reasonable than that. On the other hand, liability rather than amusement was what I was supposed to be seeking. The search was simple in that *FRemale*, with its modest circulation and lack of material assets, was not presumed to be a prime target for a lawsuit. We published no humor recognizable as such and very little fiction. Stories that served a cause and were readable by adults seldom came in, and though decent fiction could get by Louisa, Dagmar was suspicious from the first line of any story that didn't address a specific item on the feminist agenda.

Still it was essential to vet everything *FRemale* published. There had already been a lawsuit threat by an oil-rich woman in Dallas who'd given an interview about her great love for another woman and shortly thereafter decided to run for public office, insisting therefore that we kill the piece. (We did, after considerable discussion about whether she might bring such a suit in spite of what the publicity would do to her career.)

If Louisa was later blamed for some of the crazier stuff that appeared in the magazine, blame was appropriate only in that she grew less vigilant than an editor needs to be, more prone to let things go by without an argument with Dagmar. I'd noticed earlier that while verbal hyperbole was her preferred mode, she hated to commit to print anything she wasn't certain was true. But she grew careless as she became absorbed in the writing of her novel and the raising of her adored baby. There was, after all, only so much time to each day.

I can remember only a few highlights of my reading during the year and a half I did *FRemale*'s work. Of these, my favorite was a review by one Trish Remsen of an assortment of pamphlets published by various feminist presses and designed to rid children of their sexist hang-ups. Most particularly I recall *Peter Learns to Crochet*, the touching tale of a little boy whose desperate desire to learn to crochet is finally assuaged by his grade school teacher, Mr. Eliot, who crochets his own book bags; and *My Friend Clio*, the touching tale of a young girl and her clitoris. (The latter was distinguished by illustrations designed to suggest that only sexism prevented people from seeing how small was the discrepancy in size between the exterior sexual organs of the male and female.)

Of the early pieces Louisa churned out for the magazine under a variety of names, I remember best something called *Las Vegas: Pampering the Gamblers* that began, "I might have stayed longer at the gaming table if it hadn't been for the smell of urine," and went on to detail the days and nights of those compulsive gamblers who became so absorbed in the games as to wet their pants rather than briefly leave the tables. It described the heavy preponderance of middle-aged to elderly working-class women, somehow suggesting these women had no choice but to be there, a position that turned the men owning the casinos into something even worse than they were. I would have been interested in discussing this with Louisa, if only because I was curious to know whether she was aware of our father's involvement in Lake Tahoe or the nature of his business in Atlantic City, but a good moment for such a conversation did not arise. I think that during this time Louisa did not wish to have her amity with my father or her "coincidence" with the movement challenged. She was thoroughly absorbed in Penelope and Joe Stalbin and without her normal desire to observe, explain or argue about the condition of the rest of the world.

The following summer she took Penelope on a drive up through Massachusetts and Maine. Her "Letter from Fenscott"—the piece Alice had fought her doing—is one of the loveliest ever to run in the magazine. Whatever she says about her preference for fiction, she captures perfectly the sense of a tiny, cold, depressed seaport that comes to life in the summer but hates the summer people, the tourist princes and princesses, who are responsible. She shows the difficult life of the young rural wife who works hard all day, then at night stays home with her children while her husband retreats to the general store to drink whiskey and swap tales with his buddies. She makes a strong case for life in such towns being easier for the men. This, of course, she had to do in line with *FRemale*'s unwritten contract with its readers to prove that life is substantially more unfair to women. But the cloth was there; she didn't have to weave it.

Louisa's faithfulness to Fenscott distinguished her piece from much of the "nonfiction" that ran in *FRemale*, most particularly from the cover story, later a film, purporting to document the life of Violet Vann. Called *Sunflower*, the movie opened in New York just before Christmas the following year at a benefit for *FRemale* arranged by Dagmar and followed by a party she hosted at my father's Sherry Netherland apartment.

My father, having screened the movie, refused even to have his name on the invitation, saying whoever his pals were he would not traffic in "drekudrama." He wouldn't be clear on whether he would attend the party until he and Louisa agreed on a plan for Penelope, who during the screening would stay at his apartment with Grandpa, at which point he became enthusiastic. After the screening, mother and daughter would remain at the party while Penelope was agreeable and/or asleep.

My father was spending more time on the East Coast than he had in years. He was serving as consultant to something called the Commission to Rebuild Atlantic City, set up as it became increasingly clear that gambling there would become legal. It had been someone's idea that movie people would lend glamour to the Atlantic City scene. On this occasion, my father had arranged his trip back to New York in such a way as to reach the apartment before Louisa dropped off Penelope, so that aside from the help, only Louisa and I would know he was in the back, and he'd come out to the party when and if he pleased.

Neither Lynn nor her daughters would be attending the preview for reasons I am tempted to pass over, though something tells me I can't. The following mini-saga was related by a proud Violet, who assumed her credentials as a functioning feminist could never again be questioned. Fasten your seat belt, as Louisa is fond of saying, for one of our bumpier rides.

Violet had determined to effect a reconciliation between Lynn and Sonny. She had followed—quite intuitively, it appears—that cardinal rule of movements and relatives: one loves an enemy's enemy. First she had convinced mother and daughter that it was in Sam's best interests for them to be estranged from each other and in their own best interests to become friends. When Lynn expressed concern that this would be some sort of final blow to her marriage because Sam, who was now spending most of his time in New York anyway, would leave her if she and Sonny, whom he couldn't stand, grew close, Violet assured Lynn that nothing she did would either keep Sam home or send him away. He danced to his own drummer. But if he did leave, she would be happier with her daughter and her alimony than she was with the man she didn't really "have" anymore, anyway.

Violet then had the crowning inspiration of bringing mother and child together not at a fancy restaurant like Ma Maison but in a place called New York Breakfast which was on the road between the Los Angeles Airport and Beverly Hills. New York Breakfast had been Louisa's "favorite restaurant if you have to eat in Los Angeles," and she had written a piece about its "Jewish pancakes and Spanish sausage" for *FRemale*. Violet did not, of course, mention Louisa's piece to Sonny. And as it turned out, it was Louisa's body rather than Sam's that mother and daughter climbed over to become friends.

Lynn had found it difficult even to be civil to Louisa since the publication of *Scarsdale*. She was convinced that Louisa had somehow met one of her old friends and learned that as the teen-aged daughter of affluent parents, she, Lynn, had opted for plastic surgery she was certain had drastically improved her looks, although some people claimed not to be able to find a difference. She had never told Sam—or anyone in her new life—but it was quite clear to her that Louisa had found out from *someone*, and that the differences between her own story and Louisa's heroine's were artificial ones created by Louisa's need to cover her tracks.

At their lunch, Lynn, who had told her women's group this story of Louisa's describing her plastic surgery in *Scarsdale*, repeated it to Sonny, saying she had no intention of going to New York for the preview if only because Louisa would be there.

Sonny, already more sympathetic to her mother than she'd ever been, told Lynn she'd needed a mother's support upon finding out about the *Diary*. Lynn explained that she'd been on drugs and pretty much out of real life at the time in ways Sonny had been too preoccupied to notice. She hadn't even understood about the

Diary until much later, by which time Sonny was walking out of the room if she, Lynn, tried to talk to her.

Sonny began to cry; Lynn cried with her; and finally, utterly moved by what she had wrought, Violet joined them in one of New York Breakfast's most tearful-wonderful lunches ever.

Sonny and Lynn were now in Mexico. Violet hadn't heard from them as yet, but they'd planned to go first to Estella's town, where Lynn would tell Estella that Sonny had known nothing about the book's connection with their family and was as upset by it now as Estella had been. They were both convinced that Estella would believe Lynn, particularly when she saw them together, mother and daughter. Sam was just beginning to drop hints about divorce and was encouraging Lynn to initiate proceedings. She had an apartment in Santa Monica that she called her studio. In the meantime, Lynn's allowance would enable her and Sonny to live in Mexico (or anyplace) for as long as they liked.

Lynn's other daughter, the almost-fifteen-year-old, ravishingly beautiful Liane, was living on a commune in New Mexico with (at least) two men who were madly in love with her and who were said to cater to her every whim. The first of these was a fellow from Beverly Hills who had been a couple of years ahead of her in school, gone to the same birthday parties as she had, dropped out of school around the time she had been discharged, and accompanied her to their crowd's favorite discotheques. Liane was pregnant, and there were people who assumed it was this young fellow's baby she was carrying. The other man, sixty-three years old, was even more in love with Liane and had been utterly faithful since the year before, when he'd been "seeing" her sister, Sonny, then sixteen. At a party given by the girls when their father was out of town, this old geezer had caught a glimpse of the then thirteen-year-old Liane and understood that he had met his fate. He'd left his (current) family to live with Liane in a New Mexico commune where he performed his chores and did his various hallucinogenic drugs, and would, it seemed, continue to do both until Liane decided she was finished with him or death did them part. His name, which was not spoken aloud in the vicinity of my father, was Hugo Bernkastel.

My brain thought it was funny, but my stomach turned over and my heart stood still as I waited to see if Violet would remember my interest in Hugo as a teen-ager. She was forgetful, or discreet, leaving me to wonder how it was possible for the name to have any effect on me after so many years.

The premiere of *Sunflower,* labeled a work of nonfiction, the portrayal of a real woman who'd once been a movie star, was held in a small movie house on Third Avenue. The audience was your nearly classical preview hodgepodge of critics, money people, distributors, hangers-on and special-interest pushers, as well as Violet's two best friends (not counting Lynn) from their consciousness-raising group in Los Angeles; editors of various New York papers and magazines; and a group of very young and earnest girls/women with some interest in *FRemale* or the movement which was not always made specific, women with first names like Barclay, Bronwyn, Boyce, Royce and Page. (Lest anyone think I'm making those up, allow me to point out that there was, on the masthead of *FRemale* a year later, a young woman who called herself Royce Rolls and whose real name, I was told, was Royce Westley.) Then, of course, there were reporters from all the news services and newspapers in New York and Los Angeles.

The film takes the form of an interview during which Dagmar (who hadn't wanted to be in it, but whose glamorous presence had made it possible to get financing) asks Violet questions about her life. Clips from Violet's movies are used to combat visual tedium as well as to illustrate the film's main point, that had it not been for Hollywood's deep and pervasive misogyny, which allows women to be nothing more than decorative objects, Violet Vann could have evolved into a great actress.

The movie opens with a scene from *The Private Life of Mata Hari.* A young army officer and his beautiful Indonesian-looking Dutch bride are riding horseback on a mountain road in Java. Huge sunflowers—unfortunately the film was in black-and-white—border the side of the road, and at one point, the officer dismounts, using his saber to cut one of the flowers, which he presents to his wife, Margarethe MacLeod born Margarethe Zelle, who will later become known to the world as Mata Hari. Violet's voice, at once timid, breathless and sexy, explains that *kempang mata hari* is the name of those sunflowers, and that while there are other definitions and explanations of how Margarethe settled on a pseudonym, she herself is fond of this one.

As the older Violet speaks, the camera focuses on the dreamy, extraordinarily beautiful face of the young Violet, who modestly accepts the flower from the dashing young officer and sets it behind her ear. (It's almost as large as her head.) Briefly the camera follows as the officer remounts and the horses begin to move again.

Violet Vann's voice is heard. "I have always loved sunflowers, which I never saw until I came to this country. I was born in Amsterdam to a Dutch father and a Spanish mother who was a flamenco dancer."

The scene shifts to Violet's living room in Beverly Hills, photographed in full color, a modest and pleasant place around which are scattered vases full of sunflowers. Violet, looking lovely in a deep-green-and-white print dress and with a white streak through her dark hair, continues to speak.

"My father, a member of the Resistance, was killed during the Second World War when he tried to save my mother from a German soldier who was raping her. I was rescued by his comrades, then brought to America by a friend of his who adopted me. I was fortunate that this friend, who was in the movie business, thought I had potential as an actress.

"Or perhaps I was not fortunate, after all. For it seems to me now I might have been better off had my talent been allowed to develop slowly, had I been given lessons and been forced to take auditions, like most young people who want to act."

And so on. Much of it sounded legitimate, or might have if you'd never known Violet. She discusses her love of animals and says that at one point she'd thought she might become a veterinarian. Now she realizes that she could not let herself imagine becoming a doctor.

Once, when Violet and my father and I were still together in the big house, our neighbors did major construction work and we had an infestation of rats. Someone suggested we get a couple of cats, and Violet had a fit at the thought of "little furry things" running around the house. (She meant not the problem rats but the solution cats.)

There were more serious difficulties. If Violet's mother had been a dancer of any sort, much less a dancer who was raped by a German soldier, I'd never heard of it before, though I had a vague memory of Violet's having been featured in a film in which she was part of a family of flamenco dancers, one of whom met with violence. I'd never heard a word about her mother from Violet, although my own father had told me Violet's father was a prosperous businessman before the war, her mother a beautiful housewife. Nor does Violet mention her adopting mother at any point, though it was actually Sylvia Starr, not her husband, Abe, who found and decided to bring home the young Violet. How young is yet another issue fudged in this "documentary," which manages to leave the impression that Violet was a babe in arms when she arrived in the States. She was sixteen.

My father had approved a reference to his infidelities but not to his business difficulties. The filmmakers did not mind in the least being prohibited from showing the prototypical male chauvinist pig as the victim of a takeover plot.

The portrait of Violet's second marriage to a man beneath her station was brief and off-camera; Tony was dismissed as someone Violet had allowed to divert her because she lacked the confidence to attend to re-igniting her career. Tantrash was someone she'd looked to for help with that career, once she decided to give it another try. But it was only Violet's New Life as an Independent Woman, a FRemale you might have called her, that held any promise of fulfillment. The younger Violets, of course, were all in medical school.

My concern for the invasion of my own privacy had proved unwarranted. When Violet talked about the need to move to a new home after Sam's desertion, she said, "My baby and I moved across town." It was the first and last time I was mentioned. Or *someone* was mentioned. I was, as I've said earlier, fourteen at the time.

But most of the audience at the benefit was not impeded in its pleasure by any knowledge of Violet's life. The applause was generous, and afterward people milled around her, unable to contain their enthusiasm for this lovely, intelligent symbol of woman's missed opportunity. A psychotherapist from Great Neck who was writing a book about how the Women's Movement should work hand in hand with psychotherapists like himself asked for Violet's phone number so he could call her when the manuscript was ready to see if she wanted to read it. Violet's escort, a builder who'd come to give her an estimate when she decided to have some work done on her kitchen and was now a suitor, gave the man his card and said messages could be left at his office.

"So, what'd you think?" Louisa asked as she and I slipped away from the crowd around Violet and Dagmar and walked toward the Sherry Netherland.

I laughed. "It's a nice story. It's hard for me to believe anyone thought it was true."

"Maybe there should be a disclaimer," Louisa said. "Any resemblance to persons living or—hey! I like that! Or you could have a sort of filmed postscript, some people who know her coming out of the theater asking each other who the movie was about."

I grew uneasy. Louisa and I had drawn closer during this time, or so I thought, and I'd allowed myself greater latitude in conversations with her. I lacked the sense I'd eventually acquire that anything I said might be converted to fuel the engine of Louisa's anger. She'd had a lot of questions about growing up in Hollywood and I'd told her anecdotes about our lives, some of which would show up in *Joe Stalbin's Daughters*. My fondness for Penelope and her apparent affection for me had helped to make her mother warmer. It was a joke Louisa and I could share that Penny, who was normally delighted to see me, paid no attention to me or anyone else when her grandfather was around.

I learned sometime later that in each of the Maine towns Louisa visited with Penelope, she had shown people a snapshot she'd taken of Alice Donaldson at a party. In Winscotta, the man behind the counter in the general store took a close look and said if that wasn't Agnes Tearle, who'd disappeared one day and left a husband and five kids behind, then he wasn't the owner of the store they were standing in.

In other words, rather than using reality in ways that would some day upset the people who'd lived it, Louisa seemed always to be seeking out a reality that would justify the views of people she already held. In real life this negative case she was making usually seemed to be about my father. Yet readers of *Joe Stalbin* come away with the notion that Stalbin, for all his aggressiveness, is a decent, loving human being. The character they hate is Veronica, the beautiful, extraordinarily self-centered younger daughter, whom, as I read the book, I could not separate from Liane.

Having said which I should admit to having felt often as I read the novel that some event being described might well have happened. It was just that it hadn't. Someone other than Louisa had been doing the script for our lives.

"I hope," Louisa said as we walked to the Sherry Netherland, "Penelope didn't give her grandpa too hard a time." She stopped to eye herself in a store mirror. On her own special one-Chinese-meal-a-day diet, she'd lost much of the weight she had gained during pregnancy and retained while nursing the baby. If she was not able to fit into the old skintight skirts or jeans, she was wearing high heels and bright loose-fitting dresses.

"She can't," I said. "He loves it all."

Louisa laughed. "He calls himself her baby-sitter. He does the best peekaboo. He says he's going to be a clown for her second birthday party. Do you realize she's almost two years old?"

"Mmm," I said. Then, after a while, I asked a question that had been on my mind, "Has he been okay? His health, I mean? Have you had any . . . ?"

"Any what?"

"I don't know. I couldn't tell if he was staying in New York so much because of the Atlantic City business, or the stuff with his health."

"Nah," Louisa said. "He's staying in New York because of our girl Penelope. He's got a doctor here. But he just . . . I mean, it's a pain in the ass . . . or wherever he does the shots. And he can't drink the way he used to. Or eat. But you don't die from it unless you do what you're not supposed to do and you get complications. Heart. Stroke. All that stuff."

All that stuff that more often than not, he *did* do. I had so many questions, but it was difficult for me to anticipate which had answers I was willing to hear. Finally I asked—for exactly the wrong reasons, that is to say, because I thought her answer wouldn't bother me too much—"How did he get it?"

"Well," she said, "eating and drinking the way he did, of course. But he still wouldn't have gotten this kind, the kind where you need shots, if it didn't run in the family."

"Family? What family?"

I knew the words were a mistake as soon as they were out, and even before Louisa began laughing at me. But I should admit to not understanding the precise nature of the mistake. Embedded so deeply in the assumptions of my life that I'd never actually questioned it was the notion that my father had made several families but grown up independent of one of his own. I had never met any member of his original family.

"You're not kidding, are you," Louisa finally said.

I stopped walking, stared at her. She tried to keep me moving as we spoke, reminding me that Penny was waiting for her, but it was no use. With each new thing she said, I stopped again.

"You know he had a mother and father."

I nodded. "Of course." In some sense it was a lie. "But he never talked about them. He left when he was pretty young."

She smiled. "He might have left *them*, but he didn't leave their genes."

Genes. I felt like an idiot. I'd done as well in biology as Louisa had, I was sure, but aside from my red hair, I'd never really thought about what I learned as though it had anything to do with my life. I think this was the first time it occurred to me that my very thought processes had been affected by the prevailing atmosphere of Beverly Hills.

"How do you know about them?" I asked, then, feeling even dumber than I had before, I tried to fix it. "I mean, about his family. Not about genes."

"I got curious this year," Louisa said. "While I was writing. I checked out a little bit. One way or another. He answers questions if I ask while he's playing with the baby. You know how he is."

I knew, all right. And mostly I hadn't minded. But now her obvious pleasure in my naiveté was making me even uneasier than I would have been.

"There's something I haven't told you," Louisa said when I remained silent. "I mean, it's not a secret, but . . . Anyway, I've finished my book. I've given the manuscript to my agent. She's very excited about it. Thinks it's commercial, for a change."

"That's very nice," I said. "Congratulations."

"I'm not so sure Sam's going to love it," she continued. "Or anyone else. But that's something I'll deal with if it comes. *When* it comes. I mean, I wasn't going to tell anyone this, but I know you're good about secrets. I've taken my own name back. For both of us, I mean. I'm obviously not going to have a different name from my daughter, and there's no way in the world I can stand to keep using that idiot's name on everything I publish, not to say everyone I give birth to."

I was more confused than I'd been before, if that was possible. I had to stand still while I figured out what she was talking about. The name she was planning to get rid of was . . . her married name, Abrahms. The name she was going to take back was . . . Oh, my God!

"Pearlstein?"

She nodded.

"You mean," I asked, quite incredulous, "you're going to call yourself Louisa Pearlstein?"

"You make it sound as though I didn't come by it honestly," she said. "It *is* my name, you know. Or it was. And the baby'll be Penelope Pearlstein. Cute, huh? I figure there'll be a transition point with the books. I mean, a little confusion. But it's not as though everything I did was published under my own name. In fact, I've had about five names, by now. Time to settle down."

With your father's name?

Again, unspoken. I'd watched with considerable amusement the name game as it was played out at *FRemale* and its feminist

213

environs. Given that I had another name only because I'd married, women who kept their maiden names took what seemed to me an oddly skewed pride in that fact—as though the names they'd kept did not "belong" to their fathers. Now here was Louisa taking Pearlstein as though it were her proper name when in fact she had adopted her stepfather's name from the time of her mother's marriage until she herself married!

Fortunately, we'd reached the Sherry Netherland, and I didn't have to respond. In front of the hotel, people who'd been at the preview were getting out of cabs and moving toward the entrance. A few photographers were waiting, and flashbulbs began to pop. Louisa allowed as how she was happy Penelope was already upstairs and wouldn't have to deal with flashbulbs.

I asked if she knew whether Clara had come along on this trip, and Louisa laughed, saying that Sam never let her come with him anymore. Which was just as well, because Penelope couldn't stand Clara. And by the way, if he was Penelope's grandpa, she supposed she herself would have to start calling him Dad.

I said, because I had no idea of how to handle the rest of it, that I was really glad to hear she'd finished the book. I asked what its title was. She said, with a look of amused expectation, "*Joe Stalbin's Daughters.*"

I smiled and nodded, remembering her fascination with Svetlana, catching the alteration in the last name. I think she had expected me to catch much more. I asked if Svetlana hadn't been an only child, and Louisa acknowledged that she had. But she was so much aware of her own mission, it seemed so obvious to her that her dictator would *have* to be a Hollywood producer, that she failed to realize I hadn't the foggiest notion of what she was doing.

I told her I looked forward to reading it, and she said I'd be doing her a favor if I did. But then she went to some lengths, as *Joe Stalbin* was sold for her first large advance and prepublication excitement grew, to make sure I would not see the manuscript or galleys, which her publisher's lawyer reviewed. For a long time, I failed to understand that Louisa didn't want me to read the book. It is an irony I suspect has significance for many libel suits that the people she thought of herself as doing a job on in *Joe Stalbin's Daughters* were more closely related to her than the people who sued her.

At the Sherry Netherland we gave our coats to the housekeeper, and I followed Louisa through the long hallway to the room next to the master bedroom, where she knocked once, then opened the

214

door. I had not recently seen the room, which for years had been used for guests. Now it was a baby girl's bedroom with floral wallpaper, a white-enameled crib and chest, a sofa covered in a print identical to the one on the wallpaper except that the flowers were much larger, and a bathinet with various mobiles hanging above it from the ceiling.

My father was asleep on the sofa bed. Lying on his chest, her feet against the back cushions, also fast asleep, or so it seemed at first, was Penny in red Doctor Dentons with an open picture book face down across her chest.

"Do you believe what you're seeing?" Louisa asked, at which Penny wiggled around, opened her eyes, saw her mother and burst into tears. Louisa went toward the baby, arms outstretched; Penny climbed over her grandfather and into them.

"Do you believe these two?" Louisa repeated happily.

I fixed—I feel silly admitting that I still tripped across jealous feelings now and then, but truthfulness seems to compel that I do so—what I hoped was a benign expression on my face.

My father stirred, said something in his sleep. He changed his position so he was lying half to one side, the top arm across his chest, the hand clenching the arm that was more or less under him.

"I think it's the arm where he does the shot most of the time," Louisa whispered. "He's sort of covering it and saying fuck you at the same time."

I stared at her. Fuck you was about as close to anything to what I wanted to tell *her* at that moment.

"How can you say that?" I asked. "How can you—"

She shrugged. "I can say anything. 'Specially if I whisper."

Penny was still crying, and Louisa moved away from me with her, toward the bathroom. "Come on, pussycat. Let's see if you're interested in the toilet."

"Not irristed in toilet," Penny howled. She had begun speaking when she wasn't much more than a year old, but within months, like the kid in the joke who never speaks until he says, "Please pass the salt," she had gone directly to sentences. With an expression of mock despair thoroughly undercut by pride, Louisa vanished into the bathroom.

My father, awakening, rubbed his eyes and asked where the baby had gone. I told him Louisa had taken her to the bathroom, and the other guests had begun to arrive. When he seemed indifferent, I asked how things had gone in Atlantic City.

He grimaced. "A bunch of sheep in wolves' clothing."

"When did you get so clever?" Louisa asked, coming back from the bathroom with Penny, who was now ambulatory. "Or did I just not notice in the old days?"

It was the sort of crack that had always irritated him if it hadn't actually caused him to banish her from the house. But Louisa had a margin of error now. His love for her daughter was unconditional, and he would do nothing to endanger his ability to see the child. A moment later, Louisa said she had a feeling there was someone outside she needed to talk to and she'd be back in a few minutes.

Penny seemed barely to notice her leaving but walked over to the night table, where with some difficulty she succeeded in getting the phone off the hook. She proceeded to have a phone conversation with the adoring grandfather who was watching her every move.

"Are you in 'fornia, Ganpa?" is the part I remember. He said he was in New York.

"No," she said, "Ganpa in 'fornia. Come to New York. Come to Nelope in New York."

He said he had a better idea. The two of them would go to 'fornia and get rid of her mother, who wasn't really such a bad person, just a "royal pain in the ass."

As Penelope repeated "pain in the ass" with considerable precision, I rolled my eyes and with a wave toward the loving couple left the room.

There was a considerable crowd by this time, not only in the bar that had been set up at the far end of the living room, but in the living room, dining room and large entrance hall. Byron Koenig was there with the woman he still introduced to people as his bride. So was my other boss, Alan Simon, who seldom appeared at parties, or at anything else for that matter, but was inclined to have a tuna-fish sandwich in his office for lunch and a lamb chop at home for dinner. With Alan Simon were two people I didn't know who were probably the reason he'd deigned to attend.

He beckoned me over to meet them.

They were Vaughn and Franya Cameron, whose names were familiar to me from our list of clients but whom I'd not met. Actually Franya was divorcing Vaughn, and it was *his* business the firm handled. A handsome, wealthy and affable man of about forty-five who had published a couple of respectfully reviewed novels, he was dressed country-squire style in a tweed jacket, muted-plaid shirt and a brown ascot with a maroon paisley print at the neck.

Franya Cameron was something else. As tall as her husband,

she was the sort of skinny-lively Jewish girl that pale gentile boys enjoyed more than skinny-lively Jewish boys did. Attractive without being pretty, bright without being academic, talented without being an artist, Franya was all out there—you didn't have to wait for the divorce proceedings to see who she was.

When Alan mentioned my being counsel for *FRemale* she launched into a monologue about the most important article she'd ever read in a magazine, "Take Charge of Your Own Orgasm," by one Brooke Schwartz, saying that until she'd read it she hadn't known what to expect from men. Brooke Schwartz had taught her they did what you needed or they didn't come back.

Fortunately, as I was trying to decide if I was correct in remembering that Louisa had written the piece, Dagmar and Violet entered the apartment to a growing round of applause.

Louisa took back the name Abrahms for herself and Penelope shortly before the galleys of *Joe Stalbin* were printed. Her explanation had to do with her daughter's being confused about who her father was—that is to say, she thought he was Sam. The whole transaction would have been less peculiar had this not seemed to be precisely what Penny's mother had desired when she took back the first of her maiden names for both of them.

During those months I'd become aware of tension in Louisa's household involving Penelope and her grandpa. Most particularly, of the fact that the child, who was almost three, called him Papa as often as she called him Grandpa and wanted to be with him all the time.

At first, it was when Louisa and I were in conference that Penny would ask if she could call Grandpa. ("Mommy, can I call Papa collect?" was the specific line; at one point Louisa began referring to him as Papa Collect.) Or the child would be looking at one of her picture books, and if we had ignored her for a while, or Louisa had asked her to get ready for bed, Penny would hold up a book and say that some character was just like her grandpa. Grandfather Bear in the *Little Bear* books was made for the role. Penny had all the *Little Bear* books because I had found them while looking for a present for her and instantly fallen in love with them. It was Louisa's expressed opinion that buying them was the worst thing I had ever done. She only wished the books had never been published so no one could ever have bought them—"and don't tell me I should be ashamed of myself!"

My father's glee in Penelope's longing for him was held in check

217

by his sense that if he wasn't careful, Louisa would take her away from him. I assumed, when he began spending more time in Los Angeles than he had in the previous year, that he was trying to reduce the occasions for friction between them.

Louisa and I were spending less time together as well, although it had not occurred to me that she was dodging occasions when I might ask about the book. If, when I did see her, she complained a lot about the person who had metamorphosed back to *my* father, she didn't, as far as I knew, have complaints about anything *I* had done. Nor was I inclined to dwell on the matter. There was no professional reason for me to vet the manuscript if she had confidence in the publisher's lawyer. The only work of hers I'd ever seen prior to publication were the pieces for *FRemale.*

Anyway, I was much too busy to think about it, if only because she had severed her connection to the magazine, but I had yet to do the same. I think she'd been wanting to take this step for a while but hadn't known how to do it nicely. Her way of handling the dilemma was to begin writing pieces Dagmar would refuse to publish.

The first of these was called "Fallacy in Wonderland, or Through the Speculum" and constituted her first serious, you might say, attempt to bring humor to the magazine. In it she made fun of women who had become just as absorbed in gynecological issues as her own generation had been in boys and clothes. When Dagmar delivered a gentle rebuke involving the rural housewife Dagmar liked to believe was *FRemale*'s subscriber, Louisa told her it was time to drop that crap—as far as she knew their audience was a hundred and seventeen urban dykes.

In her next article, "Abuse Me Androgynous," she observed that in her experience, women who got tired of being abused by their male mates and switched to females generally picked women who ended up abusing them in ways quite similar to those of their men. This was when Dagmar told her there was no alteration she could make that would turn her piece into something suitable for *FRemale*, and Louisa said she supposed she wasn't really suitable anymore, either.

At first it was easier to understand Louisa's leaving than Dagmar's ready acceptance of the resignation of the key editor from a financially beleaguered magazine. But a few weeks later we learned that *FRemale* would be sold to the Duffy-Mintz Corporation, which published a number of magazines going to the appliance and beauty-parlor trades. Duffy-Mintz was eager to reach a general audience interested in old-fashioned womanly things like washing machines, hair dryers and the new microwave ovens.

The first Duffy-Mintz issue had a cover photo of Dagmar in a bikini and a good twenty pages of ads for diet foods and exercycles. It was an immediate success. All women had been waiting for was a magazine that would show them how to have a good job, good sex, good babies, good food, get along with the help, sleep eight hours a night and look like Dagmar Saperstein.

I had hoped for a fast and graceful exit from *FRemale*'s work, but Duffy-Mintz kept Simon & Koenig on a moderate retainer for the first year of its ownership. Few trade magazines spend any time treading on or near the libel border, their problem, if it can be called that, tending to the reverse. In a weekly conference I discussed each manuscript purchased with two of the company's lawyers, who had even more limited libel experience than I, both having been concerned with matters like product liability.

I was still handling various Egremont contractual issues that required frequent trips to the Coast. What was nice about this was the opportunity for frequent visits with my father. What was less nice was that I'd grown restive in my work. Contract matters were reasonably interesting but didn't seem *important*. It was incumbent upon me as a studio lawyer to get what I could for Egremont in the way of money, rights, etcetera. But I seldom had any sense of accomplishment when a job was finished. Nor were the actors, directors and producers who were the primary parties of the second part the kind of classical victims who might have tempted me to jump to their defense.

When my father wasn't complaining about his diet, he was talking about his battles at Egremont. The studio had begun to make movies no one older than eleven could tolerate, on the theory that eleven-year-olds were who was going to the movies these days. The latest surveys, my father had said during my previous visit, left him without a leg to stand on. The phrase brought a grim smile to his lips and some awful joke about how with one thing and another, maybe he wouldn't have *either* leg to stand on, since the doctor had informed him that diabetics were in danger of infections leading to gangrene and amputation. When I told him I couldn't stand to hear him speaking such nonsense, he said that he should be allowed to make jokes, even morbid ones, if he felt like it. He sounded like a little boy.

He had fired and rehired Clara twice since that time. She looked awful, too. She had moved from tremulousness to an awful certainty that the worst had already happened to her—and would continue to happen. Her lips were pursed, her eyes downcast, and she was even skinnier than she'd once been. Her clothes hung on her gaunt frame like a maid's old uniform in a pawnshop window.

There was a new little bimbo wandering around the house, sleeping with my father, doing errands, arguing with Clara when he wasn't listening. I can't even remember her name; she was gone by the next time I came. Physically, she was a young Dagmar; when I asked him what had happened to the real Dagmar, he said the new *FRemale* was paying her big bucks to be its touring representative. Dagmar, he added sourly, was the only person in the world who could get away with posing naked for a magazine in order to illustrate why women shouldn't pose naked for magazines.

He said that if he lost the power battle at the studio, he might close the house in Beverly Hills and move to New York. I grew uneasy because he made it sound as though it were his life, not just a house, that he was thinking of closing down. It wasn't as though he needed the money. I'd been around the people at Simon & Koenig who handled his Atlantic City business enough to know that he was making a fortune each year from just the casino, aside from his real estate and business interests. Furthermore, Egremont was having a good year in which he was sharing financially, even if he was in the midst of what he was fond of calling "the troubles."

"The only difference between Hollywood and Atlantic City," he said the one time I questioned him on why he, a nongambler, remained involved in the latter, "is that in Hollywood no one's ever found a way to load the dice." He went on to develop the distinctions; I recall his saying that for a long time the stars had been the way to load the dice, but with the breakdown of the star system, even that way of ensuring viewers had vanished.

I had made this particular trip at his request. He'd told me he had "a whole bunch of stuff" to discuss. Only after we'd spent a couple of hours reviewing contracts did he bring up the bound galleys of *Joe Stalbin's Daughters*, which the publisher's attorneys had insisted upon sending him. He hadn't looked at them yet. There was enough buzz in the trade so that he knew the book was about some shithead producer and his loony wife and two crazy daughters.

I'd heard some gossip about the novel by this time, too, but I had managed not to think about it, if only because I didn't care much about Sonny or Liane, whom I assumed Louisa had worked over in the book. My father, who clearly made the same assump-

220

tion, said there was no way in the world he was going to cause trouble for the mother of his granddaughter, no matter what kind of job she'd done on them all, but he didn't look forward to "having to wipe up someone else's crap for the next five or ten years."

He'd had a duplicate of the galleys made for me. He said he wasn't sure he had the attention span to read the whole mess, but I, as his lawyer in the matter, had no choice. I promised that if he would read one chapter before dinner, I would do the same. As it turned out, each of us read considerably more. By the time we met over dinner, he was in a marvelous mood. His mood was not only better but more understandable to me than my own.

If Louisa is adept at satirizing Americans who live vicariously through Hollywood and its stars, her portrait of Joe Stalbin is suffused with the romance that has made Hollywood America's Buckingham Palace, those stars our kings and queens. And if Joe Stalbin is ruthless in his struggles and overpowering in his personality, he is creative as a filmmaker and prophetic in terms of audience taste. Neither of which Sam Pearlstein ever was. The ways in which Joe Stalbin is villainous are ways untroubling to my father, who would have adored fighting the battles Louisa portrayed him in, especially if he could have won every time, as Joe Stalbin did.

Joe Stalbin was born in Atlanta, though his family moved to Detroit when he was young. Having worked his way up through Inroads, an auto manufacturer, he becomes president before turning forty, then is hired to bring order out of the chaos of Tripod, a movie company taken over by a conglomerate that also has an interest in Inroads. Abandoning his family, which includes a young son and daughter, Larry and Diana, he goes to Hollywood, sets Tripod on a profitable path, divorces his wife and marries a starlet with whom he has one daughter, Veronica.

Larry and Diana grow up having no contact with their father but come to Los Angeles as adults because they want to know him. They take an apartment in a part of Beverly Hills familiar to this reader because it is around the corner from the house where Violet and I lived after my father left us. ("Around the corner," Louisa said when I mentioned the coincidence, "is one of my favorite places.")

On their first night in Los Angeles a friend invites them to Flagellan, an S–M-ish disco Louisa swears she invented that apparently passes for authentic with the cognoscenti. ("Don't you understand," she asked the reporter who questioned her ability to invent walls decorated with flattened-out Crisco cans and a ceiling with a latticework made of riding whips woven through with artificial roses, "that everyone's imagination is below the same belt?" Without arguing over the basic truth of her statement, I want to mention that she'd once told me of seeing a can of Crisco in the bedroom of a homosexual friend.)

Larry is smitten with the most beautiful girl in the group, who has big dark eyes and wavy blond hair that falls over one eye. She wears no makeup but has that dope-calm aura that passed for purity in the sixties. She is, in other words, nearly a double for Liane. They return to her home where they swim together naked in the huge backyard pool, then go to bed in the "doll's house" her daddy has built for her so he won't have to be perpetually cognizant of her sexual activities. (The swimming scene did not strike me as I read. I'd seen many naked people in many pools, and Jack Campbell did not cross my mind.) In the morning Larry awakens to hear her identify herself by her real name, Veronica, rather than the one she'd used at the discotheque, and realizes he has gone to bed with his half sister. Haltingly he tells Veronica what has happened. She is unconcerned. "Everyone's sisters and brothers," she says. (It's among the book's lovelier conceits that nothing in real life can affect Veronica so strongly as what happens in a movie.)

When Larry and Diana finally introduce themselves to their father, he has just had an argument with Veronica about her rocker boyfriend, Greg, which ended with her running out of the house to her car, where Greg was waiting. Joe is even more delighted than he would otherwise have been to meet his first two children. He invites them to accompany him to his home in Palm Springs.

If Joe Stalbin's name and his need to control all he touches evoke Sam Pearlstein and Josef Stalin, his Palm Springs palace is more reminiscent, as I've said, of the one created by Teddy Marx. On ten square miles of desert land Joe has caused an artificial lake to be made. In its center is a Stalbin-made island occupied by a white castle and a series of extraordinary gardens. Visitors shuttle to and fro on a spectacular barge. The island itself is run as though it were the movie industry. The various castle wings are decorated to allow their use as movie sets, which paves the way for the island's deduction from Stalbin's and Tripod's taxes. The head gardener is a woman, as is every other permanent employee, including Joe's bodyguards.

Joe gets along better with Diana than with Larry, as he gets along better with most females than with most males. Seven years older than Veronica, Diana is described as being quite attractive enough to get through real life, if not life in the movie colony. A freckle-faced redhead, she had a weight problem until she started doing a lot of dope. Now she is pale, slender and subdued, a person of many talents with which Joe remains unacquainted because she has no need to show them off.

(I assumed at the time that Diana was a portrait of Sonny even kinder than it was imaginative.)

To celebrate Joe's seventieth birthday there is an island party beginning with a speech by Stalbin, who thanks everyone for "this wonderful surprise," which he has prepared down to the last detail. Having introduced his newfound son and daughter, he discusses the place of the other guests in his life in a way that makes it obvious there is confusion in his mind between that life and the life not of a hated dictator but of the much loved king of a monarchy in its prime.

(This was one of the portions I thought would particularly rile my father, who seems to have absorbed it without difficulty.)

Veronica and Greg appear in costume-disguise so wild that at first neither is recognized. Veronica wears a wig of shiny blue-black hair, huge sunglasses, scarlet lipstick, an ultra-short purple dress and huge lavender loop earrings. Greg is in the androgynous-rock mode with a lush mane of platinum hair matched by a gold lamé jumpsuit "cut at the crotch to lend his penis and scrotum the appeal once held by Lana Turner's sweaters." They are running from the police. In the name of the Revolution, they and three friends have trashed a Rodeo Drive boutique called Jung Man's Fancy. (The boutique specializes in importing from Eastern Europe pre-cut-and-basted men's suits that would normally sell for about four hundred dollars. They take customers' measurements, allow them to choose fabric and do whatever alterations are necessary for a precise fit, then sell the suits for about four thousand dollars. I was present when my father told Louisa about such a store, the owners of which had approached him for financing.)

Veronica tells Larry about the boutique raid, and Larry tells their father. Joe will help only if Veronica gets rid of Greg. When she refuses, Joe has a fistfight with Greg, who knocks him unconscious. Afraid that he has killed him, Greg grabs Veronica and they jump into the moat, swimming back to the desert, where they head for Mexico in Veronica's car. Greg listens to the radio for a report of Stalbin's death, but Veronica doesn't even entertain the possibility, doubtless because it didn't happen in a movie.

Greg and Veronica's adventures on the lam were the basis for Jack Campbell's lawsuit.

They drive to Mexico, where they exchange Veronica's car for several hundred dollars and an old Volkswagen (answering perfectly to the description of Hugo's). Before driving back into the States at Laredo, Texas (Veronica has called Larry and ascertained that Joe is okay but still furious), they revert to their natural appearances. Greg, after making an unsuccessful attempt to dye his hair back to its natural black, simply has the blond stuff shaved off.

Well, not so simply. The description of the handsome, dark-haired Greg, once his hair grows in, right down to his approximate height, weight and lumberjack style of clothing, reads like a precise description of the real person named Jack Campbell. Further, Greg's "real" name is Jack Burns, the last being a Scots name, as is Campbell.

Jack Burns adopted the name Greg Pope as the lead guitarist of the rock group he formed in the tiny Ontario town where he was raised. Anyone familiar with the fire motif running through Louisa's work can understand how, looking for the name of a powerful, shall we say incendiary, male character she might come up with Burns. Unfortunately, Jack Campbell was raised in a town not two hundred miles from the town where Louisa has Jack Burns grow up, and correspondingly close to Detroit.

A little research disclosed that ice hockey is a major diversion in the rural areas around Detroit. So Louisa had Jack Burns's father flood the backyard every winter so the boys could play hockey when it froze. Jack Campbell's father was an amateur hockey player who taught his five sons to play. Jack was later recruited by the Rangers and played briefly before an injury to his knee put an end to his professional career.

The final major coincidence is that both the real and the fictional Jacks had left a wife and three children behind when they moved west.

The fictional Jack and Veronica have a series of adventures as they drive across Mexico, back into the United States at Laredo, and across southern Texas. They stop in Corpus Christi because they're nearly out of cash, and it's an oil-and-mining town where Jack figures he can get work. While having a beer in a tourist bar, they get into a conversation with the bartender, whose name is

Steve Smith, and a sometime girlfriend of his, Yvonne Allison, who is drinking at the bar. At some point Veronica disappears with Steve.

Jack is furious, but Yvonne, who is attracted to him, tells him that if he's having money problems (he's already talked about job hunting), Steve could be useful. Not only does he own the bar they're in, he's a major drug dealer and always carries a lot of cash. After a series of love scenes and machinations I need not detail here, Jack, Yvonne and Veronica work out a plan to rob Steve.

Veronica tells Steve she's always wanted to see a bayou. He takes her to one, and there she and Jack mug him and take his money, as planned. Then, in a moment of panic, they murder him. (It's Veronica's idea.) Returning to town, they don't tell Yvonne what they've done. But as the three drive north toward Detroit (Louisa does a little riff on the subject of not only can you go home again, but you have to) it becomes clear that Yvonne is suspicious because Steve never returned to the bar. Finally, at Veronica's urging, Jack kills Yvonne, too.

(There was no moment in my reading about Yvonne Allison, beginning with her last name and physical description and going on to events in which she's shown as uneducated but smart, highly manipulative and a terrible liar, when she did not remind me of Louisa's monologues about Alice Donaldson.)

Eventually Stalbin arranges to pay Jack Burns a large sum over a period of five years if he will leave Veronica forever and stay out of the United States for at least the five years. Veronica flies home to Papa, at which point Burns feels the irony of his position for the first time: He has the money now to start a group and keep it going for a while, but it's the rock personality "Greg" whom Stalbin knows who is committed to staying out of the States.

Jack goes to Montreal, but he thinks all the time about Veronica, particularly after seeing a magazine photo of her at Stalbin's island in Palm Springs. She is naked in a bubble bath that conceals all but her arms and shoulders and holding up a tiny baby at whom she is smiling rapturously. The caption says that only Veronica's father knows who the baby's father is, but Jack works out from its birthdate, which is printed, that it has to have been himself. He has no way of knowing that Veronica has never picked up the baby except to pose for photographs.

Jack flies at once to Palm Springs, becoming very friendly on

225

the plane with an older woman whose name is Lilah Allimone. (Louisa, obviously, is shameless about names.) Lilah is a divorcée who started a landscaping service called Allimone's Gardens in Palm Springs. (Jack Campbell, of course, ran Tony's landscaping business for a while.)

Eventually Mrs. Allimone invites Jack to accompany her to a party at Stalbin's castle, where he approaches Veronica, thinking she'll be pleased to see him while her father won't recognize him. But she isn't pleased or anything else. As far as Veronica is concerned, Jack has shown up on the set when the script says he has no more lines.

The balance of the novel was not of direct concern in the libel suit. After leaving the island, Jack Burns, seeking revenge on Veronica even if it means imprisonment for himself, goes to some lengths to be charged with the murders. Finally it becomes clear to him that the cops have been paid not to find him precisely because his trail would lead them to Veronica.

Veronica's half sister Diana has taken her own apartment and found a job with a movie company called Solitaire Studios, where she's been given responsibility for a film of her own conception. Larry returns to Detroit to work his own way up in the auto business, sensing that Stalbin won't make room for him in the movies. Diana's movie becomes a huge commercial success, and she decides she wants to get into pop-music feature films. She is impressed by an applicant for the job of music director, and there is a suggestion that the two will become partners in more ways than one. At some point the reader realizes that this talented young man is Greg/Jack, returning to Hollywood with yet another name.

Before I'd left Los Angeles, my father had called Louisa to say he thought her novel was terrific, and he wanted to make the film.

Aside from his pleasure in the portrait of Stalbin, he must have been relieved to discover it was truly fiction. If there were bits and pieces of people he knew, there were no large chunks of our lives set like boulders in the fictional stream.

The next time I bumped into Louisa in New York I was treated to a monologue about *our* father's being a bigger and better person than she'd once thought him. I use the phrase "bumped into" advisedly. I saw very little of her during the months between then and the book's publication, nor did she ask then or later whether I had read the galleys, or offer me the chance to do so if I hadn't. The complexity of both our lives made it easy for me not to understand that she was avoiding me. It seems to me that even if I had realized she was doing so, it would have been beyond me to imagine her reasons.

Joe Stalbin's Daughters was published in 1979 and was an instant best-seller. The media responded with great interest to what it perceived as being, if not straight autobiography, a thinly disguised account of "real" Hollywood lives. The publicity people had an easy time lining up interviews with the important TV shows as well as radio and the newspapers. Louisa made no bones about enjoying the attention and consented to a staggering number of interviews. Penelope was in nursery school by this time, and Louisa had a housekeeper, a Puerto Rican grandmother named Rosa, who was willing to sleep over when Louisa was on the road or to travel with mother and daughter to California.

Any difficulty between Louisa and my father had evaporated with his approval of the book. When she traveled to the West Coast (she was doing a screenplay of *Joe Stalbin*) she, Rosa and Penny stayed with my father, who had even more time than he'd once had for the child. He had lost his studio battles, and although the new powers at Egremont were treating him nicely, he was not working very hard. He had been allowed to keep his title, his position and his full salary, but he no longer had anything he would have called power.

At the beginning of December 1981, not quite a year after softcover publication and just before the statute of limitations would have prevented the complaint's being issued at all, Louisa, Egremont, and the hardcover and paperback publishers (who have asked that their names not be recalled to the public) were notified of Jack Campbell's intention to sue them for libel. No one in the family paid much attention because we were otherwise occupied. During Thanksgiving weekend, Sonny, who had remained in Mexico when Lynn returned to Los Angeles, had killed herself by driving her car off a mountain road less than a mile from the village where Estella lived. Estella had steadfastly refused to see her, and the towns-people had grown hostile when Sonny failed to leave.

Of all the people in what I will uneasily call our family, the one most visibly affected by Sonny's death, aside from Lynn, whose mother's sorrow was of course appropriate, was Louisa, who hadn't been able to stand Sonny from Day One. If my father was less distraught than either, it was doubtless because he was drinking heavily.

I felt sad about Sonny's life, and worse about her death, and I cried, but I remember distinctly that when my father called to tell me, I nodded *before* I cried—as though I'd been waiting only for confirmation of the method Sonny would use finally to do herself in.

Louisa wrote a eulogy that was more moving if you didn't know how she'd felt about Sonny.

She described the difficulty of growing up in Hollywood and said that Sonny, a lovely young girl, had been destroyed by having a younger sister who was a great beauty in a place where normal good looks didn't even register on the scale.

She went on to apologize to Sonny for *A Servant's Diary*. (It was her first public acknowledgment of being the author.) She said that in writing the book she hadn't thought of exposing anything except her own feelings. She'd thought it fascinating, quite wonderful, that in a constantly changing household, Sonny had found an anchor for her life. The sexual part of the *Diary* had not been planned but had come naturally in the writing, though she was unimaginatively heterosexual and presumed Sonny to have been the same.

(True or not, the line had the air of a disclaimer. I had the feeling she was correcting, in her own mind if not others', some sense of herself as a female who didn't like males.)

Actually, Louisa said, she had never known Sonny very well, and now she never would. Why should Sonny have wanted to know her, "this wise-ass broad from the Bronx who shows up claiming to be related? Everyone wanted to be related to her because of her powerful father."

It's always *she*, not *they*, in the eulogy, later published as an article, which at no point mentions me. Liane is referred to only the one time I've mentioned, and not by name.

Sonny's body was virtually cremated in the accident; its remains were buried in a hastily purchased plot near Estella's town at a funeral attended by Lynn and my father, who asked Louisa and me not to come. Nobody contacted Estella to find out if she knew. Everyone thought she should be left alone. Lynn moved back in with my father upon their return. At first, they were both drinking all the time. When the notice of Campbell's lawsuit finally impressed itself on him, it had a mobilizing effect. He stopped daytime drinking so he could focus on the lawsuit (which he actually did for a brief period). He told Lynn she had to stop, too, or leave. When she was unable even to cut down, he made her stay at her "studio."

The first mention I heard of the complaint was on Saturday after their return from Mexico, following a lunch which for my father and Louisa had consisted mostly of martinis, for Lynn orange juice with a "tiny bit of vodka because of the pills."

"You know this guy Campbell?" my father asked out of the blue.

"Never laid eyes on the bastard," Louisa said.

"Campbell?" I repeated.

"Name's Jack Campbell," my father mumbled, not even looking up from his glass. "Suing us. Egremont, Louisa. Libel."

"Libel!"

He appeared to have forgotten the matter. But the name had registered, and I, of course, could not let it drop. When I tried to question him, he said we'd have to talk about it, but not now. This, of course, seemed perfectly reasonable.

Louisa, although she acknowledged the person who was suing "must be" the Jack Campbell I'd known, said she was in no condition to discuss the case. When my father and Lynn had left us and I told her there was no way for me to forget about it, she said the papers were in the study if I wanted to read them, but there was nothing to the case, although she couldn't even *think* about it yet. Besides, she had to drive Penny and Rosa someplace.

Along with surprise I felt guilt and confusion. I recalled all too clearly telling Louisa I thought I'd seen Campbell in the I-land pool. And if I remembered her questioning me about the people at Tony's will reading. But I was sure I'd told her nothing beyond their names and perhaps where they'd come from. It was incredibly farfetched to think she might have gone and found out about the lives attached to those names!

To this day Louisa denies having known anything about the life of Jack Campbell as she wrote her book. And I think I believe her. But until I read the complaint I couldn't even imagine what he might have done that he *thought* Louisa had written about. Campbell, if I seldom thought of him, still had a lovely home somewhere in my brain. I was startled to find him being moved to a new and less desirable place. However screwed up a family we were, we were still a sort of a family, and if he was Louisa's and my father's antagonist, then he would have to become mine.

As soon as Louisa had left with Penny and Rosa, I found the papers and brought them up to my room, where I read them several times but had to put them away and go back to them before I could absorb what I was reading.

The complaint sets out the major elements of the case for libel.

Those elements were breathtaking: Jack Campbell, who'd done some gardening work but made his living as a bartender, had been tried for and acquitted of the murder of Tom Page, the owner of the bar in Juneau, Alaska, where he worked. Page's body had been found in a swamp outside of Juneau, where they all lived. Campbell had also been suspected of murdering his then girlfriend, Yvette Lacombe, who'd worked in the bar and had been thought to be having an affair with Page. Lacombe's body had never been found, so he had never been tried for her murder.

Having been found not guilty of the murder with which he *had* been charged, Campbell held himself portrayed in a false and defamatory manner in the story, written by a person with whom he shared certain acquaintances, of a man named Jack Burns who murders a bar owner and a woman named Yvonne who works in the bar.

At first my brain was so thoroughly muddled by this new view of Jack Campbell as someone even *suspected* of a murder that I couldn't begin to consider the libel issues. Surely the Campbell I knew hadn't murdered anybody. But just as surely Louisa wouldn't have known if he had, or if he'd been suspected of same. On the other hand . . .

Never laid eyes on the bastard, I wrote at the top of a piece of scrap paper in my room. Her choice of denials was interesting. That Louisa had never laid eyes on the bastard did not mean, at least to my lawyer's ears, that she knew nothing about him. I proceeded to list my own points of contact with Campbell as well as anything I could remember about him or his family. It wasn't much, but of course I have learned a great deal since.

What follows is an outline of Campbell's life as pieced together from information we obtained after receiving the complaint or brought out during "discovery," or later at the trial itself. For those readers who are unfamiliar with it, let me say that discovery is designed to elicit information from both sides for their own use as well as to help a judge to determine whether the case is strong enough to go to trial.

Jack Campbell grew up one of five extremely poor boys whose mother had died giving birth to the last of them, in a small town called Leamington on the shores of Lake Erie in the province of Ontario, Canada. Leamington is a reasonable drive from Detroit, and nearby Pelee Point is visited frequently during the long cold winters by hockey-playing Detroiters. More than one Leamington boy has been known to say he is from Detroit, his excuse being that Americans don't know what Ontario is.

Following his brief hockey career, Campbell had a six-year marriage that produced three children. He worked at the local gas station, pumping gas and repairing cars, which he loved, but had difficulty supporting his family. He left his family and went to Detroit, where he worked briefly on the General Motors assembly line. But he couldn't tolerate the regimentation, and when his wife remarried someone who could support the children, he drifted west across Canada, ending up in Juneau at Tom Page's.

He and Tom were good friends by the time in 1958 when Patsy and Theresa Coletti took a vacation trip to Juneau. While having a drink at Tom Page's, they got into a conversation with Jack. He and Theresa married after a short courtship. Later Patsy married Leonard, who had proposed to her more than once. Some years after that, when Tom Page sold out to buy a bar in Anchorage, Jack and Theresa and their two children went with him.

Campbell's leg had recovered its strength, if not its flexibility, and he found a replacement for ice hockey in the Iditarod, the annual long-distance dogsled race between Anchorage and Nome. He had been teased by the other men because he loved any sport you could name, yet couldn't bear to watch any of them on television. Now the dogsledding gave him an outlet for his enormous energy. It also consumed a great deal of money in the purchase, care, feeding and training of the animals.

By the time Tony died in 1965, the Campbells were in debt, and Jack was arguing with Tom Page, who'd reneged on promises of partnership and percentages. Theresa's inheritance would pay off the debts but would not allow them to buy their own business. Patsy, who'd never gotten along with Jack for five minutes at a time, wanted her sister back in California and was willing to let Jack control the landscaping business as long as the books remained open to her and her husband. But aside from Campbell's violent dislike of his wife's sister, he couldn't imagine living in a warm place or giving up the Iditarod.

It was the end of December, and the height of the preparation period for the race. They agreed that Theresa would stay and help her sister sort and distribute their father's goods, while Jack returned to Anchorage. Then there was a phone call from the friend who was taking care of the Campbell children, one of whom was running a high temperature and crying for his mother. Knowing that with a sick child he wouldn't be able to work with the dogs anyway, Campbell agreed to Theresa's flying home while he remained to do the physical labor involved in dispersing Tony's goods.

At a bar in Los Angeles, Jack met a man who took him to Teddy Marx's I-land. There he met and fell in love with Yvette Lacombe, who had arrived some months earlier and quickly become Teddy Marx's number one girl. When it became apparent that Marx's promises to marry her were a routine he went through with each of his current favorites and would not change for her, Yvette consented to leave with Jack.

Yvette Lacombe had been born in a small town in New Hampshire, which she left at fifteen with Albert (Al) Willard, a traveling salesman who brought her to New York and talked about the day when he'd have enough money to get them both to the I-land, where she would become Honeybuns of the Month and then, with Al as her agent, a movie star. She remained with Willard when he got her a job with a relatively reasonable dial-a-hooker service. But when, during a slow period, he insisted on her working near the docks in the West Forties, she was beaten up by one of her customers and found, half-dead, by the police. When she regained consciousness she told them her real name and consented to their contacting her parents, who brought her home. Willard followed her back but was arrested and sentenced to a year in jail for an old robbery. Yvette grew restless.

She was eighteen-going-on-thirty when she took her savings from a local bank, caught a plane for Los Angeles and hitched to Santa Monica. The young man who was filling in for Louisa promptly forwarded her to the I-land.

Campbell's affair with Yvette flourished in the months before Theresa and the children moved to Los Angeles. But once the family was together, he had to cover his activities with a lot of lies about time and money. Finally Theresa guessed the truth. With her sister's encouragement, she told Jack to stay home at night or leave.

He took Yvette back to Anchorage, where he got his old job with Tom Page and a big, well-heated furnished room over the bar. But there was trouble from the beginning. Yvette attracted the attention of every man who had eyes, not excluding Tom Page. She was bored and restless, a source of perpetual anguish to Jack, who tried without success to interest her in the Iditarod. During their first year, when he couldn't bear to leave her, he let the couple who'd been tending the dogs in his absence continue to care for them. But during the second year, Iditarod excitement returned.

Yvette promised to take his place at the bar while he worked with the dogs. Page, supposedly because the Iditarod involvement was good for business, agreed with the plan. It wasn't until the race was over that Campbell realized Tom and Yvette were having an affair. He confronted Tom, and a loud argument between them was heard by everyone in the bar. Then Yvette disappeared.

When Jack asked if Page knew where Yvette was, they had an even more savage row but were urged not to fight indoors. They stopped, but later that week, Tom disappeared. There were jokes about his having forgotten his business and gone after Yvette. Then in late spring, when a swamp well out of town thawed, the remains of Tom's body were found. Questions and rumors about Yvette's body's turning up circulated. It didn't. Campbell was eventually tried for and acquitted of Tom's murder.

He had called Theresa before the trial began and vowed that if she would come back with the children, he would never again look at another woman. They had reunited. But Theresa had displayed considerable ability at running the landscaping business, and they couldn't think about the Iditarod without a second income. Reluctantly they all settled upon an arrangement under which Theresa commuted between Los Angeles and Anchorage, where she spent weekends.

It worked for years longer than anyone could have expected, but finally Theresa grew tired of the commute. Patsy, with her children growing up, tried to persuade her sister to remain so they could run the business together. Theresa refused. On the other hand, money would be an even bigger problem without her Los Angeles earnings. Jack, now too old to run the Iditarod, kept the equipment for their son, and he was drinking heavily, although Theresa didn't mention this to her sister.

Patsy, thinking the refusal to move must be based on the permanent hostilities between herself and Campbell, decided to try to make friends. By way of a first step she flew to Anchorage for a visit, something she'd never done.

The year was 1981. The paperback of *Joe Stalbin's Daughters* was in the airport bookstore. Like most of the world, Patsy had been unaware of the novelist named Louisa Abrahms. But the previous year on the *Today* show she'd seen a writer with a vaguely familiar face and red hair that reminded her of someone. She hadn't known who until the interviewer asked the writer what it had been like to grow up with a movie-producer father. Louisa replied that she hadn't actually grown up with a producer but had met Sam Pearlstein as an adult. (Louisa altered their degree of closeness according to where she was and the point she needed to make.)

Suddenly Patsy understood who Louisa was. Now, when she saw the book in the airport, she bought a copy to read on the plane.

At first she enjoyed the story, which, like most people, she read as an exposé of my father and the movie business. She took a certain pleasure in the portrayal of Pearlstein's vapid and suicidal Hollywood wives, either of whom could have been Violet, and the two sisters, the older of whom, for once, was the more sympathetic. But she began to dislike the book with the entrance of Mrs. Allimone, finding it a classic (Jewish) writer's trick that the most vulgar creature in the whole book should be an Italian with a ridiculous name. She put it aside and did not pick it up again until well into her Anchorage visit.

During the daytime Theresa showed her sister around the town. In the evenings they sat at home, talking, reading and watching television. Theresa did not invite friends to meet her sister because she was extremely nervous about the possibility of Patsy's learning things she'd managed to conceal. Paramount among these, of course, was the fact of Jack's having been tried for a murder. But there were other things she'd never mentioned, like the fact that he'd left a wife and children back in Leamington.

One evening Patsy brought out her copy of *Joe Stalbin's Daughters* and reminded Theresa of who Louisa Abrahms was. By the time she came to the part where Jack Burns murders the bar owner, she was in a teasing mood and asked Jack, who'd come home from the bar, if Louisa knew something she didn't know. Campbell, who didn't even know who Louisa was, said he sure hoped so and stomped out of the house. (This was brought out by Louisa's lawyer during discovery, not without difficulty.) Patsy sat frozen in her seat, wishing she'd never come. And Theresa picked up the book.

At the trial Patsy recalled watching her sister thumb through the pages, her face registering increasing horror. But it wasn't until she reached the point where Jack Burns murders Steve that she broke down and told her sister the whole story. Patsy immediately urged her to sue. Theresa was uncertain.

Jack at first refused to read the book, much less to think about suing the author. When he was finally persuaded, it was probably because of their continuing financial difficulties. He came to believe that since Louisa had used him to get rich, it was only fair for him to get something from her.

During the pretrial hearings and the time when Louisa's lawyer, Ronald Chow, was preparing the motion for summary judgment (that is to say, the motion that the case be decided without going to trial either because there is no real case or because the plaintiff's case is so strong that no defense is possible), I was heavily involved in Egremont's maneuvers to purchase a small Canadian production company. I flew to Los Angeles from Montreal to be deposed and flew back the next morning. I could not become absorbed in the issues. This was both a pain and a relief—a pain because the issues were fascinating, a relief in that for all the time and distance between us, I could not imagine myself actively opposing Jack Campbell.

Louisa was in California most of the time, and we had little contact. I expected a phone call during which she would broach the matter of my seeing Campbell in the pool that day, but she never called about our visit to the I-land or anything else connected to the trial. It crossed my mind that she'd forgotten the whole episode, but I found this difficult to believe. I dismissed as unfair to Louisa the thought that she might remember it perfectly well and try, partly by keeping me out of the way, to conceal from my father and Chow the little she'd actually known of Campbell through me.

When Chow's motion for summary judgment was denied and the defense had to be prepared, the purchase of the Canadian company had been negotiated. At my father's request I took a leave from Simon & Koenig and flew to California to be a sort of working observer of the case.

Louisa and Company were at the house when I arrived. Not only had my father failed to mention I was coming, he hadn't told her of his desire that I be involved. Ronald Chow was due to have Sunday brunch with us; it was at Saturday breakfast that my father told her. She reacted as though she'd been informed she would only be playing the lead on Mondays and Wednesdays.

"Are you kidding?" she asked him without looking at me, her voice full of the hostility it once had held automatically when she spoke to him. "What on earth for?"

Penelope was on his knee, looking at a picture book. My father bounced the child gently for a moment before responding.

"As a sort of a bridge," he finally responded, "from the legal to the familial."

"I don't need any bridge to Ronald Chow," she said. "He and I do just fine."

I was uncomfortable and left the lanai, but my father, of course, prevailed, and I was asked to be present at the brunch.

I had begun to believe that Louisa had never mentioned our visit to the I-land. It was my intention to raise the matter with her before mentioning it to Chow or my father. But she didn't have dinner with us, she was not in sight for the remainder of the evening and she seemed to be making it a point to stay clear of me the next morning as well. My father and I spent the evening with Penelope until Rosa put the child to bed, when he and I took a walk along Sunset Boulevard.

"Does Louisa know you want me to be here for the whole trial?" I asked, to initiate the conversation.

"Louisa knows what she wants to know," my father said.

I smiled. There was the old complicity I'd feared lost in the peacefulness between the two of them.

I said, feeling a little evil, "You seem to be having a much easier time with her than you used to."

"That's because I've decided to," he said. "I don't mean that I faked liking the book—at least it's much better than I expected in terms of the job she did on me. Some of it I really enjoyed. So I'm being careful with her, not picking up on the shit. And she's not doing as much of it, for one reason or another. She's all caught up in the trial, she's got an enemy out there, she doesn't need me to fight." He laughed. "I guess now she's fighting *you*."

"Thanks a lot."

He gave me a hug. "You can take it, kid. You're younger and healthier than I am. "

"You promised not to say things like that," I reminded him.

"Okay," he said jauntily. "So where are we. You're younger than I am—you can handle younger, right?" When I failed to respond, he said, "Don't be mad or I won't tell you the secret. Your sister's got a crush on Chow, I swear it, that's why she doesn't want you around. She wants him to herself, is all."

Did she. Was it really sexual jealousy we were talking about, or was it her fear of what I might say on the stand? What passed through my sister's feverish brain at times like this, anyway? I'd been prepared to be asked during the discovery if I could remember being with Louisa and Jack Campbell at the same time. I was, after all, the only and/or the original link between them. The lawyers hadn't thought of asking me if I'd ever visited the I-land, and so I hadn't had to talk about it. Could Louisa possibly assume I would perjure myself if I were asked directly whether I'd been there and, if so, what I'd seen? She hadn't been at the discovery when I was, but I'd been half-prepared to hear from her after she'd read the transcript. Then I would explain that I couldn't perjure myself if the right questions were asked.

My father said once that when Louisa discussed some familiar incident or argument he could recognize the words or deeds, but they'd become part of a story that was foreign to him. I have had the same experience, and I am curious to know whether this trick of altering reality is unique to the storyteller or whether we are all of us constantly filling in between reality's dots to make a story no one else sees in quite the same way.

I was still a naive reader of Louisa's as well as other people's fiction, taking at face value the storyteller's claim to not being mired in the truth. The process by which some real or imagined germ raids a writer's brain and ends up, after an incubation period of days or decades, spilling onto the printed page, a unique and full-blown disease, is almost as foreign to me now as it was then, although I'm now certain it exists.

If, in reading Louisa's earlier novels, I'd sometimes flashed on a person or event familiar to me, I'd been able to push connections and resemblances out of my mind to concentrate on the tale being told. If the portrait of the producer's older daughter was of someone Louisa wanted to see as herself, the portrait of the younger seemed cruel only in its accuracy. I did not find Liane caricatured in the portrayal of a girl incapable of absorption in anything further from herself than her clothes. Nor did I have the sense that Louisa had stretched reality far to find a situation in which "Veronica" would assist in a murder.

I had been witness before Sonny's death to Louisa's sardonic disapproval of the Hollywood kids who were our two younger half sisters and had assumed some understanding between us that Liane and Sonny were a breed apart. By the time our first conference with Ronald Chow was over it was clear that she did not share my assumption. It was also clear that she had never mentioned to my father or to any of the lawyers our visit to Marx's I-land.

Ronald was forty-five years old, handsome, well-spoken and heavily experienced in film and publishing law. He looked younger than his age and dressed in such high style as to distinguish himself from most of the California lawyers without consideration of his being Chinese. He was single and escorted around town a series of extremely attractive blond Jewish and Italian women whom he dropped, our sources told us, if he discovered they wanted to be in the movies. He had an excellent sense of humor that he was adept, said those same sources, at concealing from juries unless he was using it to charm them.

For our Sunday brunch he wore beige linen slacks and a brown-striped beige sport shirt, open at the neck in such a way that you wanted to tuck a silk ascot into it, or so Louisa announced as she breezed onto the lanai well after the rest of us. Penny was slung on her hip as though she were auditioning for the part of the Hot 'n Cool Earth Mama, despite the fact that she wore the black jeans and black T-shirt in which she looked skinniest. My father was with us during the early part of the conference, but when Penny grew restless he drifted away with her, saying they should let the grownups talk.

I had promised him I'd just sit there no matter what Louisa said, act as his ears, an informed co-conspirator. If she really bugged me, I could complain to him afterward. Oh, yes, and in the meantime, if she pulled any crap, I was to comfort myself by re-membering that she was hot for Chow, with whom she'd never get to first base. It doesn't seem to have crossed his mind that *I* might like Chow and not get to first base. Anyway, it worked for a while.

Louisa was riding high—or showing off, as we used to call it—flirting with Chow, dropping her composed one-liners while com-plaining about libel's rocky terrain. Chow always smiled in cool appreciation but never laughed aloud or displayed personal inter-est in their author. In fact, he got down to business rather quickly, advising me he'd taken the precaution, before the hearings, of hav-ing a search made for newspaper coverage of the trial in the United States. He had found absolutely nothing.

Chow asked Louisa to detail for him how she'd decided upon various characters' names, beginning with Jack Burns and Yvonne.

"Yvonne. Okay. Yvonne started out as an alias Veronica chose for herself. She's named after a movie star to begin with, remem-ber. Veronica Lake. With the blond hair over one eye, and so on. And remember how, when Larry meets her, she's using another name? Well, that used to be Yvonne. For Yvonne de Carlo. That's when she's wearing her dark-haired wig. But my editor thought it was too complicated, all those names, so I just took out her alias altogether. Then, when I was looking for a name for the woman they meet . . . Yvonne was just sort of lying around in my type-writer, you know? Unused . . . Jack Burns you're going to like even more. Jack was from *I'm All Right, Jack* with Peter Sellers. When I was married, if one of us didn't look so hot, the other would say, 'I'm all right, Jack.' It's always the first man's name that comes into my head when I'm looking for one. Burns is even better. I was look-ing at a map for someplace near Detroit for Jack to come from. I liked the idea that he was from the same general territory as Joe Stal-bin. And there on the map is a town called Burnt River. Too perfect! I had him come from Burnt River, but then I began having trouble with Jack's last name. I need to have names that feel just right. Don't ask me why. Sometimes it's easy, and sometimes it's a royal pain. Anyway, I saw an ad for a movie with George Burns and I thought, Hey, that's perfect. Burns. Jack Burns. Except I couldn't have Jack Burns from Burnt River, right? So Burnt River had to go."

"What about the fact that Burns, like Campbell, is a Scots name?" Chow asked. "Did that ever enter your mind?"

"Just about as often as it enters my mind," Louisa replied, "that lox is Scotch salmon."

Chow and his assistants independently had made lists of the coincidences, as we would insist they were, and the distinctions between the Campbells' lives and those of Louisa's characters. The fact of the brother, Larry, for example, was important in under-mining the coincidence of the two Stalbin, two Coletti sisters. As might be the existence, in effect, of two Pearlstein sisters.

Louisa laughed.

He said, "Well, you know what I mean."

"No," Louisa said with a smile that must have been meant to be flirtatious but conveyed only strain. "Tell me."

"Well," Chow began carefully, "I suppose the first thing I'd have to say is, I know there were four of you, but I never knew the one who died, or the one on the commune for that matter, so in my mind there are two sisters. And then of course those two were full sisters, not half sisters like the two of you. And they grew up together here."

"They were here," Louisa said, "but I'm not sure they were any more together than Nell and I were."

Chow waited.

"I know I sound like a wiseass," said Louisa, who hardly ever didn't, "but I'm trying to make a point."

"Which is?"

"Which is that forgetting about the two youngest Pearlstein girls . . . no, let's not forget about them. In a sense they were quite typical. That is to say, the Women's Movement made a big thing about how all women are sisters. But no one ever really dealt for a minute with the question of what it *means* to be someone's sister. I mean, if most girls purely and simply *love* their sisters, *I* don't know about it."

We were eating bagels and lox with our coffee. Ronald, on his second half bagel, had slowed down some, but now he stopped eating altogether and sat back in his chair. I have to confess to being so absorbed in the I-land issue and so frustrated at Louisa's having dodged conversation with me that I still wasn't tuned in on her wavelength.

She smiled at Ronald. A casual observer would have said she'd forgotten my presence.

"I can see you're beginning to get it."

He smiled back, fiddled with his teaspoon. "But what is it I'm beginning to get?"

"That all sisters are half sisters."

"And so?"

She shrugged. "And so . . . well, let's just say that when I was growing up in the Bronx, I was an only child. Then my father left us and had another daughter. I didn't see him again until I was grown up, but I knew who he was, and it turned out I could find him in the movie magazines. So now I had a father. And I had a baby sister. Half sister. Sister, half sister, what difference did it make what anyone called her? The fucking little brat had *my father*, and I hated her!"

Silence. Chow wasn't looking at me anymore either.

"In other words," he said, sipping at his coffee, "she was a brat because she had your father."

"Right," Louisa said. "Later, as I got to know her, I might find plenty of other reasons."

Chow smiled uncomfortably since he understood what had not quite filtered through to my brain. *She was a brat because she had your father* had registered as being about me, but it was a me who was a baby in a movie magazine.

"So," Ronald said slowly, "if I understand you correctly, you're saying that the sisters are as much about you and Nell as they are about Sonny and Liane, or anyone. Aside from the matter of Jack Campbell, there's no reason to read them as having anything to do with the Coletti sisters."

"You've got it," Louisa said. "Now you've really got it."

By this time her words were sinking in even if my surface remained calm.

I remembered how my brain had balked, without knowing why, at various points in *Joe Stalbin's Daughters*. In the scene that first came to mind the older daughter, Diana, concerned about the lack of sisterly love between herself and Veronica and seeing her sister adrift in an unreal world, takes Veronica rowing around Stalbin's island as she offers her a job on a current project. Worse than uninterested, Veronica is hostile. She has no desire to work and doesn't give a damn what her half sister's doing.

I thought of the day Louisa and I had met and of our ride after the funeral, when she'd driven all over Los Angeles instead of to the cemetery, talking incessantly, alternately confiding and hostile, willing and resentful, eager to be my friend but acting more like, or so it now seemed reasonable to believe, my enemy. And I, in a muddle of mourning rippled here and there by curiosity about something she'd said, had sat next to her in silence, responding to an occasional question with some answer she'd never have chosen to hear.

The sisters row around the island twice without Veronica's even pretending to want briefly to take the oars. When the drawbridge is lowered for Stalbin's entourage and their rowboat can't pass, Veronica leaps onto the bridge from the boat's prow without thanking her sister or offering to wait with her in the boat.

I was dazed but fighting it. I ordered myself to do something resembling a smile.

"You once said I was a good kid. I remember—"

"Ah, yes," Louisa said. "You remember. Well, I remember, too. But the part of me that occasionally thinks you're a good kid isn't the part that writes novels."

Chow feigned concentration on the matter of finishing his bagel.

Although I did have to say what I finally said, I think I wouldn't have said it in the way I did—perhaps I'd even have tried once more to find her alone—if I hadn't been hurt and eager to hurt her back.

"Speaking of things we'd say in court . . ." My manner was exaggeratedly casual as I turned to Chow. "There's something I assumed would come up during Louisa's conversations with you, if not during discovery, but I don't think it has. I wasn't asked during my deposition in such a way that I had to tell them . . . But it's clear to me it has to be mentioned . . ."

I suppose important testimony often comes in a tentative man-

241

ner, the witness not certain (s)he should even be bothering anyone with it. My guilty conscience about the way I was saying what had to be said kept me from looking at Louisa. I could feel her stiffening in anticipation—probably she knew precisely of what. Chow waited attentively.

"Some weeks after we'd met, Louisa took me to the I-land. She was working for Marx, and she wanted to show it to me. My father doesn't know about this, I didn't mention it originally because . . ." Because Louisa had asked me not to. ". . . because we figured he might not like it. I wasn't out of high school yet. Anyway, Louisa was with Marx or someplace, and I wandered around on my own for a while." My voice held steady but not without effort. "I went out through the garden where the pool is. There were a man and a woman in the pool, making love on the steps, and I thought the man was Jack Campbell."

"Mm," Chow said after a lengthy pause. "And did you tell your sister about this?"

I nodded. "I told her about seeing the man I thought might be Campbell. I wasn't at all sure. And I didn't say anything about his being with a woman. But I remember, I thought even at the time, she'd understood what was going on without my telling her. She never asked me any questions about it, and we never discussed it again. But I've been trying to find a way to talk about it for the past couple of days."

Chow turned to Louisa, calmly.

"You have the same recollection of this incident?"

Louisa laughed. "I sure do. Obviously I hoped she didn't have it." She was still refusing to look at me.

"What about time? Does either of you remember?"

"It was a few weeks after the funeral," I said. "That was one of the reasons I knew I had to tell you. Once I read the transcripts and saw the dates when he was at the I-land, I thought for the first time it must really have been Campbell."

Chow spent a few minutes looking through papers from the transcript while Louisa and I nibbled, drank more coffee and looked at anything we could find to look at. Finally he put aside the papers and looked at Louisa.

"Is there anything else I should know that you haven't told me yet?"

"I can't think of anything," she said. "I hope you don't think I've been lying and concealing a lot of things because it isn't true. I just . . . I couldn't see why it should ever come up when she wasn't even sure it was Campbell."

"You never know what's going to come up at a trial," Chow told her.

"Especially," I said, "if they think of looking in the visitors' book. Both of us signed in that night."

Jack Reilly's explanation of the lawsuit in *Variety*, for all its slangy cuteness (the piece was called "Our Vines Have Sour Grapes"), is as good an introduction as any to the subject of libel.

"Libel," says Mr. Webster's bible, is "any printed or pictorial statement that damages a person by defaming his character or exposing him to ridicule." To defame is to attack someone's good reputation. A couple of queries conjured by my own bitty brain: How do you defame someone who has no fame to begin with? How do you mess up the existence of someone who doesn't exist?

To win, Jack Campbell has to prove that the portrait of Jack Burns is "of and concerning Jack Campbell." That is to say, that Abrahms drew a word picture of him, then fingered it for a murder she doubted he'd committed. Once he's done that, proving the picture's defamatory should be easy. Abrahms, after all, has fingered him, if "him" is Campbell, for a murder he's been found not guilty of committing. Oh, yes, and there's one other little matter. Even if the judge finds there was a defamatory portrait of Campbell, the jury won't award the big bucks he's going for unless it's decided the author drew that portrait with what the law calls "actual malice."

Just for starters, folks, you might want to consider this one. I hear it's a common defense in libel-in-fiction cases that anyone who knew the real guy well enough to link him to the fictional guy also knew he wasn't the same person. In other words, your friends know you best, and they're not the ones who want to slice you up. On the other hand, if they don't use you, who-what-whom do they use?

Think about it. Especially if some of your best friends are novelists.

The trial was to be held in the Los Angeles County Superior Courthouse in Santa Monica, down the block from the Civic Auditorium and a couple of blocks from the beach. My father took Louisa and Penelope to "visit the courthouse" the Sunday before it began because Penelope wanted to go to the trial itself and he wanted to make up for some of what she'd be missing. It was October, the weather was hot and sunny, and a few bathing beauties of both sexes sunned themselves on the courthouse steps, causing Louisa to suggest we do a film called *Beach Blanket Trial*.

On Sunday evening Chow met with the three of us. My father had been deposed in discovery and Chow anticipated our both being called to testify. I had already told my father the story of being taken by Louisa to the I-land. I had thought it might upset him. Instead, he'd laughed and said it might make the trial more interesting. Now, when Chow had left and Louisa was elsewhere, I asked him if Veronica had reminded him of me. He said it was Diana who'd done that, which was why it hadn't been possible for Veronica to be Stalbin's favorite. I asked how this was possible when Diana was creative and we both knew I didn't have a creative bone in my body.

He'd laughed again. "Those guys always have to think there's a big gap between us. The creative geniuses and the slobs with no imagination. That's why they call it fiction, sweetheart. It has to leave room for the lies they tell themselves about making it all up."

Chow began by reminding us that while the judge decided questions of law, like whether or not a statement was defamatory, the jury would decide factual matters, like whether readers who knew Jack Campbell would recognize him as Jack Burns and if so, whether he was entitled to damages and how large they should be. Since the portrayal of someone as a murderer was on the face of it defamatory, our best hope was that the judge would dismiss the case before it got to the jury on the ground that the jury could not reasonably reach the conclusion that the novel was about Campbell.

It would be a particularly good idea, for reasons connected to the above, Chow suggested, to tell him about any connections between the families or individuals that hadn't been mentioned until now.

After a brief pause he continued with basic advice particularly intended for Louisa, though it was theoretically offered to us all. We were not to provide information that wasn't requested; not to be clever at the expense of the opposing attorney or his client, since it would make the jury feel sorry for them; not, in general, to overestimate the jury's sophistication or intelligence or underestimate how far it might go to right life for whomever it perceived as an underdog. His final words had to do with Louisa's wit and wisdom. Whatever her interest in libel issues, he said, she must remind herself that we had not been put in this courtroom to solve any of them. Our objective was to win the case so that she and all the defendants could get on with their lives and their work.

Occasionally during the following days it was given to me to wonder whether Louisa had heard and ignored him or if she'd decided that whether Ronald knew it or not, he was going to be captivated by her wit.

On the first morning of the trial we all came downstairs, my father, Louisa, and I, wearing navy blue; as the least important person in the proceedings, I changed into a green print silk dress (I don't like suits and have always resisted the tendency of women lawyers to wear nothing else in court) before we set out for Santa Monica. The difficulties of getting past the crowd of reporters, photographers and nonprofessional voyeurs were such that I thought little of what was ahead until we were settled in the courtroom, my father and I in the first row, behind us Peggy Cafferty and Clara. Louisa went to sit with Chow and the lawyers for Egremont and the publishers in the well, which my father persisted in calling the bullshit pen.

Jack Campbell's lawyer was Bernard Delfino, a partner of Tony's old attorney, Charles Silver. Delfino was a trial lawyer who had little experience with libel, but the Campbells had utter faith in Silver and by extension his associates, and they hadn't liked any of the other lawyers he'd urged them to interview. Tall, slender and elegant (Louisa said that if *she* had done the casting he would have been a *defense* attorney), Delfino, during the pretrial proceedings, had been courtly but humorless. One young associate without distinguishing features sat with Delfino in the well.

Jack and Theresa Campbell came in only a moment before the judge, Benedict Cobo, a fifth-generation Californian of Spanish ancestry who was said to be unpredictable in his judgments. It was only because I was wondering where they were that I recognized the pleasant, sturdy-looking man with a handsome, heavily lined face, gray hair and what could have been the blue suit he'd worn to Tony's funeral, and the chubby, gray-haired woman in a black dress. The Campbells were followed by Patsy, whose hair was a ghastly dyed black and whose mouth had taken the time since I'd last seen her to set in a ridge that looked as though it would have to be cracked by force. None of them glanced right or left as the women settled into the bench across the aisle from ours and Campbell went up front to sit next to Delfino.

For the first time I allowed myself to dwell on the irony of being in opposition to a man I'd known for an hour and a half during which he had been extremely kind to me. That is to say, of having evidence that would help his case but that family loyalty would prevent me from offering unless it were legally drawn from me.

Although the fact would seem strange to me later, Jack Campbell had never crossed my mind the first time I read *Joe Stalbin's Daughters*. In fact, the man Jack Burns had evoked was the attractive but terribly moody Canadian lawyer with whom I was then negotiating on behalf of Egremont. I remember thinking at one point that this man's mood changes altered his appearance as radically as Jack Burns's changes in hair color and clothing altered his. I'd felt some relief at not seeing Campbell during the depositions, but it had been minor. Only upon reading the transcripts and realizing that he was indeed the man I'd seen in the I-land pool had I begun to feel a profound unease.

I had reminded myself of the number of years (eighteen) since we'd taken our walk together and how unlikely it was that he would remember me. It was even less likely it had ever occurred to him that I was the intruder he'd sensed at the pool. So there was a better than even chance that I would never be questioned.

Only now did I admit to myself that while I could never betray Louisa and my father by volunteering the information, I would feel like a traitor to the truth if it were not evoked from me.

Judge Cobo moved to the bench, and I forced my brain to focus on the proceedings.

In his opening statement Delfino told the members of the jury he would show them how Louisa Abrahms's malicious lies had ruined the life of a decent man. For all his "human frailties," Jack Campbell was a loving husband and father and a very hard worker who had been accused of a murder he hadn't committed, then had been duly acquitted. He had managed to get his life back on track when he was derailed, humiliated, rejected by family members and friends, almost literally *unhinged* to find himself portrayed as having committed both that murder and another one.

Delfino listed the similarities between Jack Campbell's life and the story of the fictional Jack Burns. They had identical first names, Scots last names, and identical jobs. They had been born and raised in small ("almost bordering") Ontario towns where they played ice hockey. Both had been married, had three children, been divorced. He proceeded to the murder details, including the swamps where the bodies of the real and fictional bar owners had been found, the murder charges, and Campbell's having been investigated and cleared of the disappearance of a young woman named Yvette while the fictional Jack murders a girlfriend-accomplice who calls herself Yvonne.

"Ladies and gentlemen," he concluded, "Louisa Abrahms knew that Jack Campbell did not commit the murder of which, for her own selfish and sensational reasons, she decided to portray him as guilty. This is what the law calls 'actual malice'—publishing something that one knows is a lie. Then again, you don't sell millions of books writing the simple truth about a man like Jack Campbell, who, after making the one tragic mistake of falling in love with another woman after years of a good marriage, only wanted to work hard and remake his home with the wife and children he loved. That man and his wife and children have suffered greatly since the publication of *Joe Stalbin's Daughters*. He—they— are entitled to compensation from an author who has actually substantially damaged their lives, who has made a fortune on a portrait of Campbell without the least concern for whether it was true or, worse, as we believe, that she already knew was a lie."

It had been agreed that Chow would represent all the defendants, unless problems arose among the lawyers, that is to say, if their clients' interests diverged. His opening statement was brief but strong. He said it was one of the pleasures of fiction for the reader to feel the author knew and understood him even when this could not possibly have been the case. Good novelists were always getting letters from people asking how they'd learned about the letter writer's life. Louisa had neither known nor known of Jack Campbell; he expected to prove this to the jury's satisfaction.

"When they take creative-writing classes, young people are always being urged to write about what they have experienced, but in fact, even as they age, writers of fiction are often quite limited in their experience. Many of the best storytellers stay home and sit in a room where they experience little but imagine a great deal. Surely their imaginations tend to be more extreme than those of the average person who isn't a storyteller. And of the seven basic plots it has been claimed a writer can imagine, surely the most extreme, the most dramatic and the ones most likely to engage the writer as well as the reader involve murder.

"What we will show you is how Louisa Abrahms, sitting at her desk and letting her mind ramble, lit upon a common name and an act somewhat more common than we would like it to be, that is, the act of murder, as a way of telling the story she wanted to tell, which was a story about Hollywood and the rest of this country, about illusion and reality. Louisa Abrahms and all of us can say now that we wish she'd happened to light upon names other than Jack, which she thought of because she'd loved the title of a Peter Sellers movie, *I'm All Right, Jack,* and Burns, which appealed to her for reasons we will explain in detail and which she didn't even think of as a Scots name, and Yvonne, after Yvonne de Carlo, and Veronica after Veronica Lake, not to speak of a birthplace a greater distance from Detroit, which was important in her mind because of the car industry's real importance to America, as opposed to the fantasy importance of Hollywood.

"If she had, it would not have occurred to Mr. Campbell to bring this lawsuit. And Mrs. Abrahms would have been spared the agony of defending herself against false accusations in court. But she did not know when she was writing her story that Jack Burns was a name to avoid in writing about murder, because she did not know a man named Jack Campbell who had been tried and acquitted of one."

Ronald ended on a point he'd been conflicted about using because it could become a liability for our side but which he'd decided Delfino, who hadn't brought it up during discovery, must be saving for the trial.

"We have all at one time or another read a novel beginning with a disclaimer, something like, 'Any resemblance to actual persons living or dead is purely coincidental.' Writers do this out of the concern that people will recognize themselves or their actions and for one reason or another not like the portrait that's been drawn. But the statement is ridiculous on the face of it. Any character who bears no resemblance to an actual person living or dead is not a character we're interested in reading about. Still, caution would have dictated that Louisa Abrahms put such a disclaimer at the beginning of *Joe Stalbin's Daughters* if it had ever for a moment occurred to her that her wildly imaginative plot would seem to anyone like a violation of his real life. This wasn't her first novel, and she'd never had such a problem before. She assumed that if she wrote as she always had, keeping clear of the real life of anyone she knew, directly or indirectly, she would be treading on safe ground as she told her story.

"This has not turned out to be the case. Real life has turned out to be even stranger than fiction."

Delfino called Jack Campbell as his first witness. Clearly Campbell had not been reassured by whatever pretrial rehearsals he'd had.

He looked unwaveringly at Delfino, but his voice was tight and shaky and his hands clutched at, then released, then clutched again at the rim of the witness stand. My heart went out to him as Delfino led him through the details of his life that paralleled Burns's while trying to show he was a much better person than some of those details might lead one to believe. (Example: "And when did your first wife begin to live with your friend?" Answer: "Three days after I went to Detroit.")

All the following quotations are taken unaltered (though not uncut) from the transcripts and where possible are given in the sequence in which they arose during the trial. Parenthetical comments are mine.

DELFINO: Mr. Campbell, please describe how you happened to go to the I-land and meet Yvonne—uh—Yvette Lacombe.

CHOW: Objection, Your Honor. Mr. Delfino's confusion of the names is very suggestive and confusing as well.

JUDGE: Kindly make an attempt to keep the names straight, Counselor.

DELFINO: Sorry, Your Honor. Uh . . . Mr. Campbell, please tell us how you happened to go to the I-land and meet, uh, the woman you fell in love with.

CAMPBELL: I was having a drink at a bar in L.A. S. Cat. A guy started talking to me.

DELFINO: When was this?

CAMPBELL: January 1966.

DELFINO: Why were you in Los Angeles?

CAMPBELL: My wife's father died. We came down for the funeral. I stayed to help clean up his house.

DELFINO: Will you tell us how you came to be in the bar called S. Cat?

CAMPBELL: My wife went back to Anchorage for the kids. I was packing and cleaning up in the day. Afterward I felt like a drink, so I went to this bar.

DELFINO: And then what happened?

CAMPBELL: This guy started talking to me. I bought him a drink. He saw me looking at this girl. He said if I wanted to see some good-looking . . . whatever . . . girls, I oughta go to the I-land. I laughed. I heard of it, but I knew you didn't just go there. He said I shouldn't laugh, he worked for the accountants for the magazine. For *Honey*. He was an accountant, did *Honey*'s books. He could get me there I didn't believe him, but he kept pushing, and finally I figured, what the . . . I might as well. He drove me down to the dock where the boat was. I left my car in the lot. The guy at the dock knew him and he told the guy my name. Not my name. The name I told him. Bob Wright.

DELFINO: Why did you use a different name?

CAMPBELL: (*shrugs*) I was married.

DELFINO: So you went to the I-land as Bob Wright. Will you please describe your meeting with Yvette Lacombe.

CAMPBELL: She was at the pool, and I was at the pool.

DELFINO: And you noticed her because . . .

CAMPBELL: (*after lengthy pause*) Because she was beautiful.

DELFINO: More beautiful than the other girls?

CAMPBELL: Most of 'em weren't beautiful. They were blond, they weren't awful, some were good-looking, but they weren't . . . You got used to them real fast. She looked like a movie star. Big blue eyes, real blond hair, the whole thing.

DELFINO: Please describe your meeting.

CAMPBELL: (*It was clear that for all the preparation, it was a struggle for him to remain in the chair and answer the questions.*) She was just lying there on one of these long chairs, looking up at the stars, whatever. I went over, sat down on the stones, told her my name. (*Physical signs of agitation increased as he spoke; he glanced in the direction of his wife, who nodded reassuringly, then looked down at his lap.*) She was a good talker. Very sexy, like they're supposed to be, mostly they're not, but she also . . . She could talk.

DELFINO: Yes?

CAMPBELL: She could tell you what she wanted. They all wanted to be movie stars, but she had some reasons. Not just to have a bunch of guys after her. They were always after her. She was sick of it. She wanted a house of her own like the one where she grew up. In New Hampshire. Not like that one. It was poor and dingy. But the same kind of house, only perfect. Modern furniture. She knew the colors. Not blue. She wanted an ermine coat, even if she lived in L.A., just for when she went someplace cold. She didn't want blue clothes, either. She was sick of hearing about her blue eyes. She said if she never saw another blue eye or blue sky as long as she lived it'd be okay with her. She didn't mind the fog or the smog. (*His voice wavered on the last lines.*)

DELFINO: Please continue.

CAMPBELL: I, uh, I was nervous. I asked if she wanted to take a swim. She said how come I didn't ask if she wanted to go up to bed. I said I didn't even know her yet, and besides, maybe I wanted to be different. She said, okay, let's swim. She got up. She was wearing a bikini, top and bottom. I found out later, she was the only one who could get away with it, Marx'd still look at her. I went to the girl that had the suits and got one. She liked that. We were talking and swimming. She said she liked talking to me. She felt like I was listening, not just thinking about, you know . . . Anyhow, we ended up . . . we just kept talking but then . . . She made the first move. Like, we might as well get it over with, it's gonna happen anyway. When I had to go back, I wanted to take her with me. I didn't wanna go.

DELFINO: Why was that?

CAMPBELL: (*Looked down, was silent.*)

DELFINO: Was it because you were in love? (*A titter swept across the courtroom.*)

CAMPBELL: (*Nodded without looking up.*)

DELFINO: (*Having asked for and gotten a Yes for the record*) What happened next?

CAMPBELL: I went back the next day. Couldn't find her. That was when I found out she was Marx's girl. He was crazy about her. He was crazy about a lotta girls, only it never lasted. She didn't know that yet. She spent the whole time with him in his room. He told her he was gonna make her a star, marry her, the whole works. She was just beginning to figure maybe she'd been taken. Just beginning to talk to the other girls. They stay away at first when he goes for someone new. They figure it's good for a few weeks, maybe months. He went through the same thing with all the ones he liked when they first came. Usually they didn't look as good as her, and they didn't last as long.

DELFINO: When did you next see Miss Lacombe?

CAMPBELL: Three days. I kept going back till I found her.

DELFINO: Please tell us what happened then.

CAMPBELL: She said she was thinking about me. I told her I wanted to take her off the I-land. She said, where. I said maybe Anchorage. She said no way, Alaska was worse'n New Hampshire. She wasn't really ready to give up on him yet anyway. On Marx. I said what if I stayed in L.A. for a while. She liked that.

DELFINO: Please continue.

CAMPBELL: At first I'd meet her a little ways from the dock, take her back . . . to the house . . . But then I didn't have the house. I rented a room. We decided, I told Theresa, I told my wife I'd try the gardening business, and if it worked out okay, they'd all come down to L.A. I knew there was no way I was just leaving. Theresa said if I liked it, she'd move down with the kids when the school year was finished.

DELFINO: Yes?

CAMPBELL: So . . . she did . . . They moved down in June. But then she . . . Theresa could tell something was going on. Her sister, she got the idea from her sister, maybe I was . . . She said if I had a girlfriend, I should give her up or move out. I . . . couldn't give her up.

DELFINO: We know how pain—

CHOW: Objection, Your Honor.

DELFINO: Sorry, Your Honor. I get . . . Please continue, Mr. Campbell.

CAMPBELL: I moved out. Winter was coming. I mean, not in L.A. In Anchorage. Yvette was getting disgusted. . . . She still wanted to marry Marx for the money and all, but she was pretty sure by now it wasn't gonna happen. Meantime, Tom, my old boss, didn't like any of the guys who replaced me. I got the word through my pals, I could have the same money as before plus this big room over the bar, and ten percent of the profits after a year, if it was working, if we were getting along. Yvette still didn't know if she could take it up there, but she said she'd give it a try.

DELFINO: Is that when you moved back to Anchorage?

CAMPBELL: Mmm.

DELFINO: And then?

CAMPBELL: (*His testimony from this point on was punctuated by even lengthier pauses, visibly greater discomfort.*) It was no good. She knocked them out. They weren't even used to the girls you could see at the I-land, much less . . . They were all bowled over, they couldn't take their eyes off her . . . They couldn't get good-looking women up there; if they came, they didn't stay. The guys wouldn't leave her alone. Tom wasn't the only one, he was just . . . the worst.

DELFINO: What did you do about it?

CAMPBELL: With most of 'em, I just had to keep an eye on 'em, let 'em know I was there. With Tom there was nothing to do. He was my boss. I had no money to leave with. I tried holding out for the percentage. But when I came back one time, I was in Nome and I came back and I could tell, him and Yvette . . . We had a fight.

DELFINO: A bad fight?

CAMPBELL: Nah. Just the usual stuff that goes on. They made us stop so we wouldn't wreck anything.

DELFINO: And then what happened?

CAMPBELL: What happened? She disappeared.

DELFINO: I mean, how did the argument end?

CAMPBELL: He walked out. Said he'd fire me if I wasn't just doing my job when he got back.

DELFINO: And so?

CAMPBELL: So I did it.

DELFINO: Did you try to find out what happened to her?

CAMPBELL: Sure.

DELFINO: And?

CAMPBELL: Nobody knew. They didn't know who she went with, where she went, if she went alone or with someone. When things got a little quieter, I tried to find out if he knew, if Tom knew, where she was, but he swore he didn't. Then he took off. We all figured he knew where she was, and he went after her. I ran the place, took my money out of the cash receipts, figured when he came back I'd quit. Then it got warmer, and the swamp thawed and they found him.

Delfino led Campbell through a description of the police process during which he became the primary of several suspects, all men with whom Page had quarreled at one time or another, two of whom owed him money. Tom Page's sister, who lived in Fairbanks, testified to long-distance phone conversations in which her brother spoke of his difficulties with Campbell and said he was going to fire him as soon as he found a solid replacement. Tom had never mentioned Yvette.

Campbell had been charged with the murder after an Anchorage couple claimed to have been driving out of town on the road that went past the swamp where Page's body had been found and to have seen the two men in Campbell's Jeep in front of them, clearly having an argument. He was acquitted, in part, because Campbell's mechanic testified to having had the Jeep in his shop all that week. Page had the same model Jeep, but his was green and Campbell's was black. Both observers were sure it was the black one, but it had been dark. Another man was certain he'd seen Jack and Tom walking together and talking just outside town the following day.

Once or twice I glanced at my father to see if I could tell what he was thinking, but I couldn't. Nor could I read the notes he made occasionally in the little notebook he carried. The impression of Campbell conveyed to me by the substance and manner of his testimony was of a straight and decent man bewildered by what

253

had befallen him, most recently a book suggesting he was a murderer, acquittal or no, but determined to hold to a reasonable course, not to beg for sympathy, to return to his family with honor. My heart went out to him—a trip I kept to myself.

In his cross-examination, Chow asked Campbell if he remembered meeting Louisa at the funeral or any other time. Campbell said he'd met too many people that day, he couldn't answer the question. He could say for sure he'd never had a conversation or anything like that. He was asked if he could recall meeting me. He said he didn't remember me from the funeral, but he did remember the walk after the will reading. He was asked if he had confided in me any details of his life. He said he didn't remember—an answer in which he must have been rehearsed. Chow asked the next question as though it were part of a casual progression.

CHOW: You said earlier about your fight, argument, whatever, with Tom Page, that it was, let's see, you said, "Just the usual stuff that goes on." Please tell us what that "usual stuff" is.

CAMPBELL: (*shrugs irritably*) Guys drink, they get madder easier'n they do sober. There're fights.

CHOW: Have you ever been in a fight like that?

CAMPBELL: (*after a long time, another shrug*) Sure.

CHOW: When?

CAMPBELL: Long time ago. I don't remember.

CHOW: Have you ever been in jail? Aside from the Tom Page matter?

CAMPBELL: (*after a longer time, a bigger struggle*) Once.

CHOW: (*ironic*) Can you remember where?

CAMPBELL: Detroit.

CHOW: During your first marriage?

CAMPBELL: Mm.

CHOW: Can you tell us why?

Campbell proceeded to describe, in a strangled voice, a fistfight in a Detroit bar. The fight wasn't about money, but the guy had lost his wallet and claimed Campbell had taken it. Meanwhile, the cops had been called and Campbell landed in jail for the night. I couldn't see Delfino's face at any point during the recitation, though I could see his fist clenching and unclenching on the table. When I glanced discreetly in Theresa's direction I found her expression too painful to allow me to keep looking. I would say this testimony, unlike that about Yvette, came as a complete surprise

254

to her. (And to me. Until that time I'd never briefly considered the possibility that Jack Campbell could turn violent.) When Campbell had finished, Chow asked whether, if the fight hadn't begun with money, it had perhaps begun with a woman. As Delfino objected, Campbell acknowledged that it had. Chow asked if the other man had been flirting with a woman he liked, and Campbell said, "Something like that." Chow thanked him and allowed him to step down.

The danger in showing Campbell as violent was that it increased the possibility of his being identified with the violent Jack Burns. Chow took the risk on the assumption that it would pay if Louisa should be found to have defamed Campbell. That is to say, in setting an award for the defamation the jury would be less likely to award a large sum if he already had a reputation for violence.

Campbell had been awkward when Delfino tried to get him to describe his reactions to *Joe Stalbin's Daughters*, and Delfino had cut short that part of his testimony. When court reconvened, Delfino called one of Campbell's Anchorage pals to the stand. This man testified that when he read the book he'd identified Burns with Campbell and assumed the author had information about his friend's guilt that he didn't have. In his cross-examination, Chow tried to find out when the man had read it, that is to say, whether Campbell had given him the book when he was intending to sue. The man said that he really couldn't remember exactly when, but he was pretty sure it was long before Campbell ever saw it. He was certain Campbell had never mentioned it to him until recently. Testimony from several of the plaintiff's friends and the owner of a bar who had been considering employing Campbell until he heard "the dirt stirred up by the book" went along similar lines. The friends testified to his having been a gentle and loving friend and father whom they never associated with any kind of violence.

Next Delfino called me. We'd thought it had been established during discovery—though the judge who'd decided the case should go to trial hadn't agreed—that Louisa hadn't been within a thousand miles of Alaska or the Alaskan media or anyone who knew of Jack's life during the years when she was writing the book. Now I was asked a series of questions aimed at finding out if perhaps I had been there or somehow known of the Campbell trial and reported it to Louisa. With this out of the way, Delfino moved on to my early meeting with the Campbells, when Tony was still alive, and then to the funeral and the reading of Tony's will.

DELFINO: So within weeks of the reading of Mr. Coletti's will you had a phone conversation with Ms. Abrahms during which she inquired about how, uh, in your words, things had gone at the lawyer's office.

NELL: Something like that.

DELFINO: And what did you tell her?

NELL: I think I said they hadn't gone too badly.

DELFINO: And then?

NELL: I think she asked me who else was there.

DELFINO: What did you say?

NELL: I said, Tony's daughters and their husbands and my mother and my father's assistant, Dagmar Saperstein.

DELFINO: And then?

NELL: Then I remember she made some jokes about the names, about how even living in Los Angeles, neither of Tony's daughters had managed to marry a Jew.

DELFINO: So you remember having told her the men's names.

NELL: I don't exactly remember, but I remember her response so I must have.

DELFINO: And then?

NELL: Then she asked some question on the order of "What are they like?" and I said they weren't interesting, because I didn't want to talk about them.

DELFINO: Why not?

NELL: It made me uneasy.

DELFINO: Why is that?

NELL: I'm not sure. Maybe it was that she didn't have a reason in real life, in her own life, to be interested.

DELFINO: Please explain what you mean.

NELL: Well, for example, she was at Tony's funeral because she was curious about me, but that curiosity seemed legitimate. I was, I am, her half sister. She wanted to know about me. But Tony was *my* stepfather, not hers.

DELFINO: What about describing the way Mr. Campbell looked at the will reading?

NELL: Never. I didn't even tell her we went for a walk.

How many descriptions of someone can there actually be? How many different eye and hair colors are there? How many heights and builds? Furthermore, if it becomes a libel-wary storyteller's convention that anyone with black hair has to be turned into a blond, might not some black-haired litigant of the future argue that everyone knew he was the villain because the novelist had turned him into a blond? Unfortunately for the novelist Louisa Abrahms, the next questions led to what would be, for Delfino, considerably richer ground.

DELFINO: Did you ever see Jack Campbell again after that day at Charles Silver's office?

NELL: I'm not sure.

DELFINO: Oh? (*With a flourish he pulled out the discovery transcript and read from it the portion where, asked that question, I had responded, "Not that I know of."*) Is that correct?

NELL: Yes.

DELFINO: Has something happened to change your memory?

NELL: Yes.

DELFINO: And will you be so kind as to share this event with us?

NELL: I read the discovery transcript and saw he was . . . someplace I thought I might have seen him.

DELFINO: Where was that?

NELL: On the I-land.

DELFINO: (*markedly excited by this important piece of news*) You and your sister saw Jack Campbell on the I-land?

NELL: No, Louisa wasn't with me when I saw the man.

DELFINO: When was this?

NELL: A few weeks after Tony's funeral. Some time in January 1966. I'm not sure of the day.

DELFINO: Am I correct in believing you did not mention this in your previous testimony?

NELL: I was never asked if I'd been there. And I was never sure the man was Jack Campbell or that Campbell had been on the I-land.

DELFINO: Perhaps we'd better begin at the beginning. Tell us the circumstances under which you went to the I-land.

NELL: Louisa was working for Marx. In Santa Monica. She took me just for fun.

DELFINO: And what happened while you were there?

NELL: She went to talk to Marx, and I wandered outside on my own. I went to the pool. It was nighttime, and it was dark, but there were some dim pink lights on around the pool area. There were two people in the pool. On the far side. One of them looked to me, I just saw him for a couple of seconds, but I thought he was Jack Campbell.

DELFINO: And the other?

NELL: I didn't see her. I just saw her hair. Blond. Long and blond.

DELFINO: Did you speak to Mr. Campbell?

NELL: No.

DELFINO: Not even a hello?

NELL: No.

DELFINO: Was there a reason for this unfriendliness toward a man you've described as having been kind to you?

NELL: Yes.

DELFINO: (*sardonic*) Will you be so kind as to share this reason with us?

NELL: He was making love to the woman.

DELFINO: In the pool?

NELL: On the pool steps.

DELFINO: (*not sardonic anymore*) What did you do?

NELL: I ran back into the house.

DELFINO: Did you tell your sister what you'd seen?

NELL: No. Not precisely.

DELFINO: What precisely did you say?

NELL: I don't remember the exact words, but I think I said I'd seen someone who looked like one of Tony's sons-in-law.

DELFINO: Continue, please.

NELL: That was it.

DELFINO: Well, then, when did you tell her he was with a woman?

NELL: I didn't.

DELFINO: Come, now, Mrs. Berman, you can't bring us this far along in the truth and then go back to—

NELL: I'm not going back to anything. I didn't tell her because it seemed like a bad idea. He was married, and all the men on the I-land were supposed to be there for the women. For sex. As a matter of fact, what I remember is that Louisa sort of assumed there'd been a woman with him without my saying so. She never asked me another question about it. She didn't seem to be holding back. She just seemed to forget about it. When I read the book, I never connected Campbell with Jack Burns.

DELFINO: Please confine yourself to answering questions that have been asked.

Although it had been expected that Teddy Marx would attempt to avoid testifying at the trial, he turned out to be a willing and

258

sympathetic witness, called by Delfino to verify that Jack and Yvette had been seen together at the I-land, perhaps by Louisa. People were startled by Marx's size—he was about five feet five inches tall and very slender—by the pallor resulting from a life lived entirely indoors, and by an aura of respectability, even timorousness, lent him not only by the gray flannel suit that seemed like a relic of the fifties but by his genuine anguish over what had happened to Yvette.

Delfino treated Marx in a manner clearly intended to separate his disapproval of the dastardly goings-on at the I-land from his approval of the kindly tycoon who had readily consented to testify.

DELFINO: Can you tell us, please, when you became aware of Miss Lacombe's presence on your I-land?

MARX: (*So softly that he was asked to raise his voice, which he did, but it soon reverted to its original volume*) It's easy, actually, because I think that the first moment I saw her, I fell in love with her. (*He paused. When he resumed there was a quiver in his voice. It was clear then and during several points in his testimony that it was an effort for him to keep from crying.*) I was wandering around the grounds, feeling restless. We'd put the magazine to bed . . . uh . . . so to speak . . . that's a term that means we'd finished for the month . . . uh, it's a monthly . . . uh, so to speak . . . uh, I was approaching the pool when I saw the most extraordinarily lovely creature lying on her side, at the rim, in a sheer, diaphanous, you might say, white robe, trailing one hand lightly in the water. She barely seemed aware that anyone was around her, and she wasn't conscious of herself at all in a vain way. Yvette worried only about how to please others. I fell in love with her at that moment. She would have had to do something extraordinary to turn me off. Away. But she never did. From that first night together, we were in love.

(*A pause. When Delfino spoke again his tone was particularly gentle.*)

DELFINO: Can you tell us what the date was?

MARX: It was the twenty-eighth, because that's when we put *Honey* to bed. Uh . . . wrap it up for the month.

DELFINO: The twenty-eighth of . . . ?

MARX: September.

DELFINO: In the year . . . ?

MARX: I'm sorry. I can never keep years straight. I don't even know what year it is now. Just the month.

259

DELFINO: Does 1965 sound right to you?

MARX: Yes, of course, 1965 sounds fine.

DELFINO: So on that night of September 28, 1965, you and Miss Lacombe became lovers.

MARX: Yes.

DELFINO: Would you try to give us an idea, please, of the amount of time you spent with her in the company of others? That is to say, how much did you walk around the grounds and sit in or move through the public rooms? Places where you might have been seen by—

CHOW: Objection, Your Honor. He's leading the witness.

JUDGE: Kindly refrain from leading the witness.

DELFINO: Sorry, Your Honor. Uh, Mr. Marx, can you recall being in the presence of Miss Lacombe at any time when Ms. Abrahms was also with you?

MARX: In the first three months? We were barely out of my room, but I wouldn't have noticed, anyway. I don't . . . I didn't see anyone but Yvette. And anyone who saw me saw her. I don't mean just when they brought us meals, or whatever. There was the spread, you know, when we shot her . . . photographed her . . . for Honeybuns of the Month. I don't think Yvette noticed other people, either, but you'd have to ask . . .

DELFINO: Ask?

MARX: No. Nothing. (*His voice quivered and he could barely get out the words.*) I was going to say "Ask Yvette." I forgot, for a moment . . .

DELFINO: I'm so sorry. Are you saying, then, that you cannot recall being in the presence of Ms. Abrahms and Miss Lacombe at the same time.

MARX: Mostly Louisa reported to Sal. Sal was overseeing the staff people, and he and Louisa got along pretty well. If there was something I had to make a decision about, Louisa talked to Sal.

DELFINO: Can you tell us if you were aware of Miss Lacombe's history before she came to the I-land?

MARX: Sure. She told me the whole story. Running away from home with that rotten, exploitative son-of-a—with Willard. (*His voice cracked on the name.*) How he abused her. Beat her . . . I couldn't . . . I was happy I could give her a new life. I found her right at the beginning. Almost as soon as she arrived. She reached the I-land and went to sleep for thirty-six hours. I think it had a sort of cleansing effect on her. It was as though her life for the past few years had fallen away and she was like a young girl again.

DELFINO: (*confused*) How old did you say she was?

MARX: (*misunderstanding*) She was eighteen already, but she was like a young girl. She could have been fifteen. For the first time I thought seriously about marrying again.

(*Delfino did not ask whether Marx could recall discussing the possibility of marrying her with anyone other than Yvette. This was saved for Chow's cross-examination, when Marx confessed he had not. He said time had taught him the wisdom of waiting for some time to pass before he "plunged" into marriage. Chow then happily allowed him to digress into an extraordinary little speech about how people always thought you had to put an end to pleasure by getting married, but there was no automatic reason a life should not be lived in the service of anything but pleasure. There was a sadness to him then and throughout that belied his words.*)

DELFINO: Can you tell us what happened next?

MARX: Well, I'll try . . . not easy . . . very painful . . . She got a little, whatever you want to call it, possessive. She decided I was paying too much attention to some other girls. So I . . . (*he looked down, shook his head*) . . . This is very painful. You see, I only want to give pleasure. To myself. To others. As soon as I worry that I'm giving pain, something happens. I get . . . I have to find someone else to make happy. (*He stopped speaking, appeared lost in thought.*)

DELFINO: (*clearing his throat*) Are you saying you became involved with another girl at that point?

MARX: Not involved. My heart belonged to Yvette. I told her that. She was the one who could have been a star. I mean, not just a star in my own heaven. A movie star! But one of the other girls needed some attention from me. Some feeling that she was loved. That was when Yvette felt she had to . . . Not that I minded this business with this Jack, uh, this Alaska fellow. Or at least, I wouldn't have minded if I'd thought for a minute she was having a good time. But I didn't get the feeling she was having a good time . . . (*his voice broke*) . . . even before he dragged her off to—

DELFINO: Let's hold it for a moment, shall we, Mr. Marx? We understand how you feel, but Ms. Lacombe did not go to Anchorage against her will.

Delfino led Marx around the I-land, so to speak, trying to evoke some previously undisclosed memory of seeing Yvette with the Alaska fellow at a time when Louisa was present. He began with Louisa's first trip out there and led Marx through the occasional

261

day when Louisa did come for business reasons. But no matter how circuitous his path, he was always blocked by an ingenuous Marx, assuring him that he had barely seen Louisa, that most of their business had been done by her with one of their associates and on the phone.

Marx's testimony could be enjoyed, more by women than men, for the light it cast on him. (Even my father confessed later to having been given pause by the suggestion that a girl of eighteen was a little old for him.) But if one was looking for pleasure in the words themselves, the best testimony came from Louisa, who was in her element on the subject of fiction. Delfino let her ramble on, perhaps because he thought she'd reveal something she hadn't meant to, perhaps because he hoped she would make a bad impression on the jury. But if her words often suggested the cocky *artiste*, her manner was extremely polite, never conveying impatience or disdain.

In her testimony Louisa never referred to me as anything other than "my sister."

DELFINO: Ms. Abrahms, will you please tell us where you were when Tom Page and Yvette Lacombe were murdered outside of Anchorage?

LOUISA: You mean they found her body? I thought they only found his.

DELFINO: Allow me to rephrase the question. Can you recall when you first heard about any murder in or near Anchorage?

LOUISA: When I read the complaint to find out who was suing me.

DELFINO: Do you remember where you were when you read the news stories about the Campbell trial?

LOUISA: I remember that I never read the news stories.

DELFINO: Are you saying you remember everything you haven't read in addition to what you have read?

LOUISA: Not only am I not saying that, but it isn't true. What *is* true is that I remember just about anything that's grist for my mill. I forget details of foreign policy, the workings of the U.N., the stock market and so on, even when I read the stuff. Although there are exceptions. For example, I don't absorb stock-market fluctuations, but I remember some of the swindlers, like Lowell Birrell and the guy with the Mazola Oil. Because they spun my wheels.

DELFINO: So you would've remembered this murder story if it had spun your wheels.

LOUISA: It *would have* spun my wheels if I'd read about it. That's how I know I didn't.

DELFINO: Where were you living between the fall of 1978 and the spring of 1979?

LOUISA: I was doing some stuff in New York for *FRemale*, but aside from that I was mostly in Los Angeles.

DELFINO: Did you do any traveling other than the trips between the two cities?

LOUISA: Not really. Oh, I visited my sister Nell and her husband once.

DELFINO: In which city was that?

LOUISA: Atlanta. Atlanta, Georgia. As a matter of fact . . .

DELFINO: Yes?

LOUISA: I don't know if it's relevant. If you'll think it's relevant.

DELFINO: Try us.

LOUISA: Well, it's about the first time it occurred to me to use Alaska. I'd made some notes about Atlanta, which is an interesting city because it's very Southern and very J—Well, anyway, I thought it was interesting when I was visiting Nellie. (*The nickname, a first*) I'd scrawled some notes on a yellow pad, and when I went to read them, my handwriting's sort of rotten, I mean, sometimes it's illegible even to me, and anyway, at first I thought I was seeing "Alaska."

DELFINO: (*after a long pause*) Are you seriously proposing—

LOUISA: (*offended but demure*) I'm not proposing anything, Mr. Delfino. I'm telling you something I just remembered, which is the first time it occurred to me to use Alaska.

DELFINO: (*another long pause*) Leaving aside the plausibility of such a decision, will you please tell us what you did after you decided to use Alaska?

LOUISA: What I did? I used it.

DELFINO: When did you do your research?

LOUISA: Mostly after I'd written it.

DELFINO: And what form did that research take?

LOUISA: Oh, I went to a bookstore and got a couple of guidebooks, AAA, Mobil, stuff like that. One of them was where I found out about the Iditarod.

DELFINO: And did you find a reference to the Campbell trial in anything you read?

LOUISA: If *you* didn't find anything when *you* tried, Mr. Delfino, then why would—

DELFINO: Objection, Your Honor. Would you ask the witness to simply answer the questions?

Unable to make a dent in Louisa's denials of having seen Jack Campbell on the I-land or anywhere else, or having read news from Alaska, Delfino made a concentrated effort to get her to acknowledge that she'd become curious about Campbell after I told her of seeing him in the pool. Louisa said that with the trial coming up, I had reminded her of the incident, and she'd had to laugh because it sounded familiar yet she'd never thought of it once while writing the book. Delfino turned his attention to the other "parallel" characters in the book. He began with the matter of Campbell's being married to one of two sisters from Los Angeles.

DELFINO: Can you explain why you told your sister, your half sister, Mrs. Berman, that the book would be about Stalin's daughter (*I had testified to our original conversation about the book*)—singular, that is, and leaving aside the question of why you said Stalin, not Stalbin—and why you instead had two daughters in the book?

LOUISA: God knows, it wasn't because I wanted him to have two. He just insisted on doing it in spite of me.

DELFINO: What does that mean?

LOUISA: Just what I said. You see, when you write journalism, you announce to the world that you're only telling the truth, and once you say that, you're obliged to come as close to it as you can. But when you write fiction, you sort of announce that you're *not* telling the truth, and then you can let the characters take over. Because it *didn't* happen.

DELFINO: *What* didn't happen?

LOUISA: The event you're describing.

DELFINO: Then how can you describe it?

LOUISA: Well, that's just the point. Half the time you don't exactly *know* how you can describe what you're describing. It's a combination of what you've heard and what you haven't heard but you thought you might hear, and—

DELFINO: What does *that* mean?

LOUISA: I'm really not sure I can explain, at least not to someone who's so hostile to—

DELFINO: Your Honor, will you please instruct the witness not to express her opinion of the proceedings to the jury?

JUDGE: You are so instructed.

LOUISA: I'm sorry, Your Honor. It's not very easy to separate opinion from the rest of it in this matter. What I was trying to say was that half the time you don't exactly *know* what you're up to.

You meet someone, he looks a certain way to you, and you make up a story about him in your mind.

DELFINO: Are you saying that you met Jack Campbell and he looked a certain way to you and you made up a story about him?

LOUISA: No! I'm not saying that! I've already told you I never met Jack Campbell at the funeral or the I-land or anywhere else. If I had, I would have *changed* him. It's easier to make up a story about someone if you *don't* know him. You have less of a rein on your imagination.

DELFINO: Aren't you having it both ways? Aren't you—

CHOW: Objection, Your Honor.

JUDGE: To?

CHOW: Mr. Delfino is accusing the witness of duplicity when he's asked her to explain an extremely complicated process that can occur in a variety of ways. She's trying to show that she herself is often uncertain which process she went through in writing a particular piece.

JUDGE: Sustained.

DELFINO: All right, then. So sometimes you'd rather . . . you say you'd rather not meet a person so you don't have a rein on your imagination. Is that correct?

LOUISA: Mm. But then the next thing you're going to ask—

DELFINO: Perhaps you could confine yourself to answering truthfully what I *have* asked.

LOUISA: Sorry. (*little laugh*) You see, it's all the same sort of thing. I make it up, and once in a while it turns out—

DELFINO: Fine. Why don't you go ahead, Ms. Abrahms, and tell me what you think I was going to say.

LOUISA: I thought you were going to ask if I wasn't basically denying responsibility for what comes out of my own typewriter.

JUDGE: Is that correct?

DELFINO: (*after a long pause*) It's close enough.

JUDGE: And do you still wish to have Miss Abrahms answer the question?

DELFINO: Why not.

LOUISA: Well, it's a very tricky one, of course, and being sued for libel makes it that much trickier. I mean, what *is* that responsibility, when you come right down to it. But before anyone gets mad again, let me say, in a way, yes, I deny responsibility for a lot of what comes out. I mean, I don't deny responsibility for hurting the feelings of some people. For being willing to do that rather than change what I need to say. I wanted to have a button made

265

once: "Novelist: Associate with Me At Your Own Risk." As a way of telling people that whether I liked them or not wasn't going to change the way my mind works, which is to turn events into stories, people into characters. Anyway, if I write something I know is libelous, then I'm obliged—if only to myself—to fix it so I won't be held responsible under the law. But as far as what comes out in the first place, as far as what my fingers do when you put a typewriter under them, it's more like a Ouija Board than (*giggled*) . . . hey, Ouija Broad. I like that. (*She became serious when no one else laughed.*) I mean, it's true. A lot of the time I have no idea when I sit down at the typewriter which keys my fingers are going to hit. The same thing happens when I sit down to describe an event. Which is why I know that's not what I should be doing.

DELFINO: Yet you feel comfortable with the notion of giving testimony under oath?

LOUISA: That's not funny. In real life I am truthful to a fault.

Delfino failed to appreciate the distinction that was crucial to Louisa and tried repeatedly to trap her in the space between real life and fiction.

DELFINO: In your book, a man called Larry swims naked in a pool with a beautiful blonde whose name he does not yet know. When you were writing this scene, had you forgotten that you saw Jack Campbell making love to Miss Lacombe in—

CHOW: Objection. She never saw either of them. Mrs. Berman did. And Mrs. Berman didn't see the woman's face, just some hair.

DELFINO: Sorry. You said you were *inspired,* I believe was your word, by other people you knew. Can you elaborate on that for us, please?

LOUISA: How can I? I mean, I know they can't sue me over what I say in court, but people have a way of getting into the machinery, I mean, into my brain, and then coming back over and over again with different names, in maybe slightly different forms. There's a mother type who's always in bed in all three of the books I've published. If she was inspired by someone, and I tell you that here, maybe she'll sue me three books from now.

DELFINO: Your Honor, can Miss . . . pardon me, Ms. Abrahms . . . (*Delfino consistently called the other women Miss or Mrs. and Louisa Ms. as though to establish the notion that she was of another race of impossibly aggressive liberated women*) be instructed to describe these people in specific terms, with the court allowing for some concealment, uh, that is, for some dis-guise of their true identities? Names and so on? (*Louisa is so in-structed.*)

DELFINO: Please begin with the person who inspired Yvonne Allison, the woman who is involved in the theft and is herself murdered.

LOUISA: (*sigh*) I don't know if it'll work. But I'll give it a try.

DELFINO: (*sardonic*) Thank you.

LOUISA: (*after a pause*) I was doing a series for *FRemale* on the nature of women's lives in various parts of the United States. I ran into this woman in Corpus Christi, Texas. I tried putting her in Charleston when I decided to use her, but it didn't work, it's just a different kind of place. She had to be in an oil town. A man's town. And with a mixed population. She was working as a waitress in this bar . . . Donna Reeda's . . . where I had dinner one night. We struck up a conversation. She spoke to me first, actually, because she hadn't seen me before, and she knew I wasn't a regular, but she could tell I wasn't a hooker, either. She got very friendly when she heard I was from New York and a writer. She was wearing a wedding ring, but she told me she wasn't exactly living with her husband anymore. In fact, she wanted to go to New York, a town where he'd never think of looking for her. She needed to find a job, settle down. She talked as if she were a real victim, he beat her up and so on. I think she actually used the line "I'm a battered wife." She must've read it someplace. Anyway, I sort of liked her at first. She aroused some sort of protective, an older-sister kind of feeling in me, even though . . . she was kind of tough-looking. She had that look some men like, bleached blond, lots of makeup, and so on, but if you analyzed her features, there was nothing great about them, and she had a sort of set to her jaw. Unless memory deceives me, even though I was sympathetic at first, she always made me nervous.

DELFINO: Unless memory deceives you?

LOUISA: (*a little laugh*) Well, maybe I should say, unless it de-ceives *you*. And it isn't supposed to be memory, exactly, anyway. Right? You said I should disguise it.

DELFINO: (*after a pause*) We'll come back to that in a minute. For now, let's just go on with your meeting this woman and how you came to write about her.

LOUISA: Mmm. How I came to write about her. Well, as I said, Joe Stalbin was insisting on having another kid. So I had to find one for him. I decided . . . The first daughter, the one who was there first, was sort of a younger-sister type. I liked her. So I wanted a difficult one to not like. I'd never written about sisters. I was interested in the question of siblings, of whether your place in the family, in birth order, that is, affects your personality, even your whole life, in some way. This waitress from Donna Reeda's popped into my mind. The one I'd felt sort of older-sisterly toward. Later on, when I could see she was much more complicated, not just little-sisterly, I'd wanted to do a piece about her for the magazine, for *FRemale*, but it hadn't worked out, partly because everyone was afraid she was just the type to sue us out of existence. Anyway, the magazine wasn't really interested in a woman who claimed her husband beat her, but once you knew her, it was easier to picture *her* beating up a third party *with* him. I mean, *FRemale* wants its battered woman *battered*. So, if I was going to write about her, and she wasn't going to be a total victim, it was going to have to be in fiction. My brain started working on it, but I had trouble finding a situation where it felt right for her to meet Jack and Veronica. I had to get them to some remote place where Veronica's famous father wasn't known so she couldn't use his name to get what she wanted, the way she always could in Hollywood, but also a place where there aren't a lot of real people. I mean, they come there for Oil with a capital O, or whatever, but everyone's from someplace else. It's not hard to get a job just because no one knows you. Not that *she's* going to be the one who looks for a job. Her father's not talking to her, won't give her a cent, and they need money, but it would never occur to her to look for a job—little girls in Beverly Hills do not grow up planning to work in the Five and Dime if they ever have to—it'll be Jack who gets the job. But Jack doesn't have the feel of the town, yet, so they had to meet people who'd help them find their way around. Into legal stuff, or illegal. A bar or restaurant is the first place they'd go to when they hit a town, aside from a motel, and they don't have enough money left for motels. At first I had Veronica be the one to meet Yvonne and start plotting how to get some money, but it didn't work. I found out she couldn't even conceive of a crime.

DELFINO: You found out?

LOUISA: That's the Ouija Broad stuff I was talking about.

DELFINO: (*heavily sarcastic*) So your Ouija Board told you Yve—Veronica—couldn't have conceived of the crime.

LOUISA: Mmm.

DELFINO: And what did it tell you about the murder in the swamp?

LOUISA: Nothing. I had to make up that part myself.

DELFINO: (*still sarcastic*) Oh. You had to make up that part by yourself.

LOUISA: I mean, it didn't just come. I had a pretty bad time with it, as a matter of fact, until I realized I was putting too much of it on Jack and Veronica, who hardly knew the town. So I made up the bar owner who had a lot of money, and Yvonne knew a lot about him and his dope trade, and so on. And that was when I started developing *Jack's* background. Until then he was just this sexy rocker Veronica hung out with. But he needed a past. A real life. He had to come out of a life where the physical, including physical fights, isn't such a big deal, isn't so separate from everyday events as it is in middle-class life in a city. You know? A rural life. You have an argument with someone, you fight it out in the back-yard. Unless it's flooded for ice hockey, which I figured is what they might do up there for the boys to play. Anyway, Veronica could just sort of go along with the two of them, with Jack and Yvonne, never planning, just ready to do anything because it doesn't matter, because none of it's real. . . . I'm interested in the extent to which Hollywood has affected the way we live. Even if we're not a producer's daughter. I mean, even if we don't live right there practically inside the movies.

DELFINO: (*He had been making notes.*) All right, now. Let's try to . . . Will you please tell us when you were in Corpus Christi?

LOUISA: Never. Can't think of a reason to go.

DELFINO: (*after a pause*) So, what you are saying is that choosing Corpus Christi just now . . . No, you used it in the book, too.

LOUISA: Tricky, huh?

DELFINO: Was the original use of Corpus Christi part of the disguise?

LOUISA: Yes. Just like Alaska.

DELFINO: Have you ever at any time in your life been in any part of Alaska?

LOUISA: No way. Too cold.

DELFINO: What about the name of the bar where she worked? Is, uh, Donna Reeda's a bar you'd actually heard of?

LOUISA: If it had been, I wouldn't have used it. When I needed a name, my brain went to a movie star's, just the way it does when I'm at home. Veronica Lake, Yvonne de Carlo, Donna Reed.

DELFINO: (*embarrassed at not having made the Donna Reed connection*) What about the bar where this woman actually worked?

LOUISA: Which woman?

DELFINO: The waitress.

LOUISA: I never became friendly with any waitress. The woman I was thinking of wasn't a waitress. You told me I could—You see, the problem we're having here is the same as you have when you're writing fiction. How much change is *too* much, and how much is not enough. Sometimes you change things the most by changing them just a little.

DELFINO: How about Canada? Have you ever been in Canada?

LOUISA: I went to Toronto for a few days to give a writing seminar. Right after *Joe Stalbin* was published.

DELFINO: (*after extensive questions about Canadian broadcasts she might have heard or publications she might have read failed to evoke any evidence that Louisa might have known of the trial*) Would you say the portrait of Joe Stalbin is based in any way on someone you know?

LOUISA: Everyone.

DELFINO: What does that mean?

LOUISA: It means the characters are full of bits and pieces of lots of people. My father's a film producer. I met other producers when I moved out here. There are parts of *me* in the film producer. The business of liking to control the story. And there's a guy . . . Where I grew up in the Bronx there was this guy who came around with a truck selling fruits and vegetables, calling out what he had, telling the housewives to come and get it, giving away cherries to the little girls he liked and yelling at others if they even tried to touch something to see if it was ripe. He was an important person to me when I was growing up. He's in Joe Stalbin, too. This guy who gives the prettiest little girl at the studio the plum role and doesn't have the time of day for the rest.

DELFINO: Ms. Abrahms, you said you were doing a series on women's lives for, uh, *FRemale,* and you were considering writing about this woman in your series. Leaving aside your novel, did the woman appear as herself in anything you wrote?

LOUISA: No. She wasn't interesting enough.

DELFINO: So, someone has to lead an interesting life before you want to write about him or her?

LOUISA: Well, yes and no. At least there's a reverse side to it. I mean, I was once offered a lot of money, when I needed money, to write a biography of a woman who had an absolutely fascinating life. She was a spy, had extraordinary love affairs, that sort of thing.

I wrote an outline but then I had to give it up because she hadn't left me anything to do. I mean, if I had stumbled upon Watergate, I'd have walked away from it. The whole story was there already. It didn't *need* me.

Delfino went on to another subject, asking whether there was any particular reason Louisa had given the owner of the landscaping business an Italian name.

LOUISA: Absolutely. In the suburb where I used to live and have a little vegetable garden, there were a lot of spectacular gardens, and at some point I realized they were all owned, not just owned but *cared for* by Italians. I still associate . . . I remember the time I asked an old man who was out tending to his tomatoes what he did to make them so wonderful, and he just shrugged, but then later I drove by and I saw him talking to them, and I said to myself, now all I need is to find out the words! Then when all that business about talking to your houseplants came out, I—
DELFINO: Thank you, Ms. Abrahms, I think that will be enough.

If I had to guess, I would say it was a miscalculation that caused Delfino to put my father on the stand. Aside from the vain wish that a previously unknown connection between him and Jack Campbell would be divulged, Delfino might have hoped the jury would be offended by his studio head's arrogance. And surely they would have been, had it been displayed by anyone other than a man who still, in their and the world's eyes, ran a large studio. (My father did nothing to alter the impression that he was in control at Tripod.)

DELFINO: Mr. Pearlstein, will you kindly explain the sequence of events that led to your buying movie rights to *Joe Stalbin's Daughters*.
SAM: I read it, I decided to buy it. I picked up the phone and told someone to buy it.
DELFINO: (*pause*) Those of us in the real world can only envy—
CHOW: Objection, Your Honor.
DELFINO: Sorry. I . . . Uh . . . Would you say, uh, that your decision was in any way related to the author's being your daughter?
SAM: Sure.
DELFINO: Can you tell us how?
SAM: The main consideration is, if you give money to one of

your kids, and the movie doesn't get made, it's not like giving it to a stranger. One of your kids doesn't need money from you for a few months.

DELFINO: Are you always this honest with everyone?

SAM: No. I lie sometimes when I'm not under oath.

DELFINO: (*having waited for the laughter in the courtroom to subside*) What were the other considerations in your buying the rights to the book?

SAM: Being able to control the damage.

DELFINO: Please explain.

SAM: My daughter did a job on a studio head in a book that was read by a couple of million people. Ten, twenty times that number, more, can see a movie if it gets made. If my studio owns it, I can control the damage. If I care enough to bother.

DELFINO: And did you care enough to bother with *Joe Stalbin's Daughters?*

SAM: Nah. I cared enough, but there was nothing in it that disturbed me. I mean, they picked a guy to play the chief who's even better-looking than I am.

DELFINO: Was it your understanding that the portrait of the studio head was the only one in the book based on a real person?

SAM: It's my understanding that if one of my kids writes a book about a studio head there's no way everyone's not going to think it's me.

DELFINO: And what are your thoughts along those lines about the daughters of Joe Stalbin?

SAM: As a matter of fact, I have the same thoughts about the daughters. What people don't know about you . . . about me, any-way . . . maybe about anyone, they make up. The less they know, as Louisa said, the easier it is for them to make it up.

DELFINO: Many people would say it was easier if there was some basis in fact for the imagination to work with.

SAM: (*shrugs*) Many people say many things.

DELFINO: Well, if I understand you correctly, Mr. Pearlstein, what you are saying is that in your own mind, the producer's daughters in Ms. Abrahms's book are not based on your own daughters.

SAM: I'm saying I was able to put matters like that out of my mind and read the story.

DELFINO: But if you brought it back to your mind, whom would they remind you of?

SAM: I see elements of all my daughters and of hundreds of other females I've known in each of the ladies in the book.

DELFINO: Was there anyone else who had to be put out of your mind as you read?

CHOW: Objection, Your Honor. This is a fishing expedition.

JUDGE: Fishing per se is not against the law, Mr. Chow.

DELFINO: Allow me to reword the question. Was there anyone from your years with Mr. Marx and *Honey* magazine whom you had to put out of your mind while reading about Yvonne?

SAM: Nah. Most of those girls, being forgettable is one of their virtues.

DELFINO: If you think about her now, does Yvonne remind you of anyone?

SAM: No.

DELFINO: How about Jack Burns? Was there anyone who had to be put out of your mind when you read about him?

SAM: I wish there was. My daughters' boyfriends were never smart enough to get into my mind in the first place.

CHOW: Mrs. Berman, you flew from New York to Los Angeles with Mrs. Abrahms in February of 1976?

NELL: Yes.

CHOW: Please tell us about your conversation during that flight.

NELL: Well, we talked about organizing work for the magazine. For *FRemale*. The complexities of having offices on two coasts. That sort of thing.

CHOW: Anything else?

NELL: Yes. We talked some about a woman both of us knew. Louisa didn't trust this woman. Felt she was a liar. Wasn't really from the place where she claimed to have grown up. She felt that this woman might have committed some criminal act she was hiding. And maybe was using a false name. That sort of thing.

CHOW: Can you tell us whether this woman is a member of any of the families involved in this trial, or whether she has been referred to during the trial in even the most tangential, casual manner?

NELL: She is not a member of any of the families, and she has not been referred to here at all. By name or otherwise. But when Louisa was talking about this woman she met . . . I kept remembering how, the first time I read the book, and I came upon Yvonne, this woman in Corpus Christi, it crossed my mind that it was she. This woman we both knew.

CHOW: Did you have any other conversations with Mrs. Abrahms during the plane trip that you feel might have bearing on these proceedings?

NELL: Yes.

CHOW: Tell us about them, please.

NELL: Well, I don't remember precisely how it came up, but I recall her mentioning a man she'd met, I think in New York. An Australian. He was a surfer, but I don't remember much else about him. I guess she said he was . . . a little wild. She thought maybe he'd been in some kind of trouble. That was the other time . . . When I was reading the book, I kept remembering that fellow and thinking she put him together with the woman . . . the woman she thought might have been in trouble . . . and then she, Louisa, made him *Canadian* instead of *Australian*. Whatever. I remember I kept thinking when I was reading the book that Burns's being Canadian was a *disguise.*

Chow asked Louisa to explain to the jury how she had decided to get Jack Burns into the landscaping business in Palm Springs.

LOUISA: I remember I wanted him to become friendly with an older woman who could help him. Not with money. He has more money from Stalbin than he knows what to do with at the moment. But he needs some emotional support. Maybe she'd go for him, but his brain's all wrapped up in Veronica. She's the reason he's in Palm Springs. Only it's the kind of place, when he gets there, well, ten minutes after he gets there, he knows it could drive him out of his skull in a short time. A lot of desert with air-conditioning. He figures he might as well work while he's deciding what to do next. He doesn't even know if he's wanted by the police. If *they're* wanted. For the Corpus Christi caper. But here's this nice woman who likes him, and she knows a lot of people, has access to the fancy homes. It had to be catering, or landscaping, or something like that, and Stalbin wouldn't use caterers, he'd have his own chefs. Jack looks in her address book and finds numbers for Stalbin's home, but nobody ever answers except the servants. I guess that was the main thing about gardening . . . landscaping . . . Nothing worked as well for getting into rich people's houses.

The trial had been going on for more than a week. I had what I'd thought of as a cold, but when I took my temperature, it was 102. I told my father that even if Delfino was doing his summation, perhaps I should stay home for the day. He said this would be a serious error unless I was terribly ill. It was the first clue I had that there was something up his sleeve; suddenly I remembered

274

that he'd had three phone calls so early in the morning that I'd barely been awake.

"Nothing, really," was his reply when I asked what was happening, but he grinned in such a way as to insure my not believing him.

It is possible, even now, to read Ronald's summation and assume he hadn't been told. In any event, 98.6 or 102, there was no way in the world I was going to stay home that day.

Delfino's summation would have upset me more if I hadn't assumed a surprise was coming. He carefully reviewed the many aspects of *Joe Stalbin's Daughters* that he said were simply too close to the Campbells' lives to be coincidence, "artistic or otherwise." He proceeded to offer the jury members what he called "a reasonable suggestion." If they found it difficult to figure out the intricacies of the Campbells' lives, or those parts of the Campbells' lives that were "a storyteller's fodder, not to say her meal ticket, whether or not she needs a meal," they should not, in reaching a verdict, "underestimate your own common sense."

I remember noticing with concern that a couple of them were nodding in a righteous fashion as they listened to this dangerous appeal to deal sensibly with an issue in which common sense had a limited place. I looked at my father to see if he shared my concern. He was turned, as he had been periodically that morning and as he would continue to be during Chow's summation, toward the back of the courtroom.

CHOW: Ladies and gentlemen of the jury, this is an extraordinary case you have been asked to judge. It would have been extraordinary, in my view, even if Yvette Lacombe's body had been found and identifying marks had led people to the certainty that she'd been murdered by Jack Campbell. Because there would still be nothing in the history of Louisa Abrahms, nothing Campbell's attorney or anyone else has been able to find that suggests Mrs. Abrahms ever knew anything about Tom Page, or Yvette Lacombe, or Jack Campbell except his name, which she heard once or twice eighteen years ago, along with her sister's comment that she might have seen him in the poor light of the swimming pool at the I-land.

If the plaintiff's attorney has been able to demonstrate some remarkable coincidences between the real lives of Jack Campbell and Yvette Lacombe and the fictional lives of Mrs. Abrahms's made-up characters, please bear in mind that those lives are closer to the average piece of fiction than to the life of your ordinary American or Canadian who is born, goes to school, has a career, gets married, perhaps has the excitement of a divorce. Most people live undramatic lives and die undramatic deaths.

Chow had just reminded the jury of his opening statement, and I was just thinking of how feeble he sounded on the matter of the pool, when a functional-looking man in a dark suit appeared in the aisle next to my father and handed him a note. He read it and went through motions of being astonished. Then, slowly, still looking at the note, he stood, leaned over the railing that separated us from the front of the courtroom, and called to Chow. Chow turned and my father handed him the note.

Chow excused himself, read it and requested a conference with the judge, which was granted. A short while later the judge announced that due to an unusual circumstance, the defense would be permitted to bring in another witness who had just been located. Delfino objected, but he was overruled. Chow asked Mrs. Vivienne Mills to come forward.

I turned, as did everyone in the courtroom.

The woman who came down the aisle was tall, slender and pretty in the manner of a faded Valley housewife. She wore a sedate pale coral dress with navy trim and shoes and handbag that matched the trim of the dress. All had the look of having been purchased for this occasion. Her hair was curled and fell, loose but neat, to below her shoulders; her manner was shy to the point of timidity.

I glanced toward the plaintiff's table in the front of the courtroom. Jack Campbell, who had turned in his seat to see who was coming, had that uncanny whiteness-under-ruddiness of the outdoor man who has just seen a ghost. As I watched, tears began to stream from his eyes although his expression did not change. I looked at Theresa, in a seat across the aisle from me; she, too, was crying. Patsy Biancardi, looking upset and angry, seemed to be trying without success to get her sister's attention.

Louisa's face as she, too, turned to see, was a study in watchful waiting. (She told me later she'd thought she was recognizing "Vivienne Mills" from old photographs, but it seemed "too corny" to be true.)

The witness, her eyes down, was sworn in. Her voice as she answered Chow's first questions was so shaky it might have belonged to a cartoon mouse confronting its first cat.

Vivienne Mills was married to Bob Mills, a plumber. They had four children, two boys and two girls, ranging in age from one to eight. They lived in the town of Newhall, in the Valley. Her voice grew even smaller and tighter, if that was possible, when Chow asked if she'd ever had another name. She said that she had. Until she'd married Mills and legally changed her first name as well as her last, she had been Yvette Lacombe.

Needless to say, pandemonium struck the courtroom. Reporters ran to the back to alert their photographers and made deals with each other about who'd run to the phones and who'd cover. Spectators living vicariously turned to talk with neighbors they hadn't previously acknowledged. Jury members struggled to maintain composure and with it the myth of objectivity. Jack Campbell sat separate, immobile, stony-faced. Unmoved, or so it would seem if you hadn't seen him crying. Patsy's arm was around Theresa, whose face was buried in a scarf. Louisa, grinning widely, was talking to my father.

When order was restored Yvette was asked a series of questions intended to establish that she was the person she claimed to be. (Aside from any other proof, she'd brought her birth certificate.) This done, Chow set out to determine whether her memory of the events described by Campbell was the same as his and, if not, where it differed. Yvette's differed primarily in that she remembered him as having been much nastier and becoming much more violent during their last big fight.

One day in 1976 the newly divorced Bob Mills had left his plumbing business in the hands of his assistant and gone to surprise an old Army buddy in Anchorage who'd talked about the Iditarod. Mills had been drinking at Tom Page's when Yvette, after the big fight with Campbell, ran down the back stairs and out of the building—without a coat on. Mills had seen her earlier and been taken with her beauty. Now he ran after her to help. A week later, they were back in the Valley and married.

DELFINO: Mrs. Mills, you say you knew nothing of Jack Campbell's murder trial in Anchorage?

YVETTE: I never heard anything about Jack or Anchorage from the day I left.

DELFINO: You saw nothing in any newspaper?

YVETTE: We don't get papers.

DELFINO: How about television?

YVETTE: (*hesitates, glances toward spectator section, then looks back at her hands*) I don't watch the news on TV. The kids are watching their shows.

DELFINO: Including the ones late at night? The eleven o'clock news?

YVETTE: I'm asleep at eleven. Ten.

DELFINO: Is there someone else in your family, your husband, for example, who might have known of this trial?

YVETTE: (*sounding rehearsed*) If he did, he didn't tell me.

DELFINO: All right, then. You've said that two men came knocking at your door yesterday. No. Last Friday.

YVETTE: Yes.

DELFINO: What did they say to you?

YVETTE: They said they were looking for Yvette Lacombe and was I her.

DELFINO: And you said?

YVETTE: Nothing. They said they were detectives, could they come in, and they showed me their cards, that they really were. Detectives. The kids were inside . . . watching TV . . . Anyhow, I came out on the steps. They told me about the trial, and part of it was about a guy who killed this guy and his girlfriend. Jack . . . (*She stopped speaking but never glanced at Jack then or at any point during her testimony.*)

DELFINO: And then?

YVETTE: They asked me to come here to show I was alive.

DELFINO: And you said?

YVETTE: (*Another hesitation. I thought she looked at my father, then toward the back of the room.*) At first I said no.

DELFINO: Why was that?

YVETTE: I didn't want to . . . the children . . .

DELFINO: You felt it would hurt the children?

YVETTE: My husband did.

DELFINO: So your husband knew about the trial.

YVETTE: He came home when the detectives were still there.

DELFINO: And he did not want you to testify because of the children?

YVETTE: Yes. They don't know nothing about . . . everything.

DELFINO: Can you tell us what made you decide to testify?

YVETTE: (*a long pause this time*) They said . . .

DELFINO: Who said?

YVETTE: The detectives. Mr. Pearlstein's detectives.

DELFINO: Continue, please.

YVETTE: They said I could make some money.

DELFINO: Oh? They said they would give you money?

YVETTE: No. I mean, they said my expenses if I came, if the whole family came, but the real money . . . They said everyone was writing about the trial, I could sell my story to one of those. . . . Somebody'd buy it, if I testified.

DELFINO: Did they promise they would buy your story if no one else did?

YVETTE: No. They got on the phone and called the papers for me.

DELFINO: Did they warn you about anything that would happen if you didn't testify?

YVETTE: No. They were real gentlemen. Like businessmen, not like detectives.

DELFINO: And have you reached any publishing agreement with any newspaper or magazine?

YVETTE: Sure. Otherwise I wouldn't've come.

If she'd begun as a somewhat intimidated Valley housewife, Yvette Lacombe became herself as her testimony progressed. And that self was a person who felt life hadn't given her what it once promised, but there was no reason not to give it another chance. I don't think she understood how much of her beauty had—almost literally— faded. This wasn't a trial but an audition. By the time she was asked about people she knew who might have talked about her and Campbell to Louisa, she was quite flirtatious and said people used to talk about her a lot, but she had no idea of who said what to whom. Asked if she'd ever met Sam Pearlstein, she replied with a siren's smile, "No, but I sure did want to."

She was utterly comfortable with money as the motive for coming to court to tell the truth. Her husband was convinced the notoriety would be bad for the children; she was convinced that not being able to pay the dentist's bills was worse. (Perhaps she was not yet in touch with the desire, realized only after she had the *Enquirer* money as well as a large sum for television rights to a miniseries based on her life, to leave her children with their father and move south on the freeway to seek Hollywood stardom.)

When the cross-examination was finished, Yvette stood, smoothed her hair and her dress and stepped down from the stand, then glanced over toward Jack Campbell for the first time. As she did so, she tripped over the stand's edge and did a flying fall, managing to land more gracefully than one would have anticipated, that is to say, slightly to her side, with knees (and dress) up, rather than flat out on her belly.

I glanced at Campbell; he hadn't moved during her testimony and didn't move now. Chow helped Yvette to her feet. She was anxious-giggly but clearly felt the fall had done her no harm. Maybe, Louisa said later, she was thinking of *Bringing up Baby* with all its adorable accidents and pratfalls. Or even more likely, of Monroe's skirts flying up in *The Seven-Year Itch*.

Chow moved that a weak case had been made so much weaker by Yvette's appearance, which had destroyed the primary coincidence leading to the lawsuit, that the case should be dismissed without going to the jury. The judge turned down the motion, saying that the double murder had been only one of several striking "quote coincidences unquote."

Chow resumed the summary he'd begun before Lacombe's appearance by hashing over some of the less savory aspects of Campbell's life and reminding the jury indirectly to consider the possibility that Campbell had committed the murder of which he'd been found innocent. Then he went on to the matter of what it meant to tell stories.

CHOW: Ladies and gentlemen, often during this trial I have found myself thinking of various novelists and journalists I've represented in libel proceedings. The two kinds of writers seem to me so different as to be barely members of the same species. Journalists, even those who are fine writers, seem to live in and for their investigations and discoveries. Their primary reward comes in ferreting out some fascinating, previously unknown fact of criminal life, some crucial, carefully hidden ingredient in the government stew.

Novelists are quite another matter—and Louisa Abrahms is a novelist down to the very bone. Louisa once said in the most matter-of-fact fashion that eating, sleeping and writing stories are the three things she needs to live. And when she talks about writing stories, she means the stories that come to her in her dreams, or as she sits at her desk, or as she watches the actions of various people and thinks of how much more interesting they would be if she were making them up.

It is an irony that has become clear during this trial that beyond having heard his name once all those years ago, then having heard her half sister say she'd seen someone who looked like him in the near darkness of a pool, Louisa Abrahms did not know Jack Campbell or have the desire to know him, even when, many years later, she began to write a novel about a handsome, powerful dark-haired man who worked in bars and other places dominated by men and was capable of murder. I dare not think of how many men there are across this country who would fit that same description.

. . . In fact, ladies and gentlemen, on any busy sidewalk in the business center of any city on any day of the week there are probably dozens of people who fit perfectly the descriptions of the characters in each of Louisa Abrahms's books as well as in other authors' books you've read and loved.

We need to read wonderful stories as much as authors need to tell them. We need authors' flights of fancy because we want to soar with them out of everyday life and into realms the imagination makes interesting. We will not have places to go with our writers if their flights are grounded because the weather in the courts has grown dangerous.

Chow wound up with a brief discussion of the jury's options, the only reasonable one, of course, being full acquittal. (In a conference with my father before Delfino came forward, Chow had had great difficulty providing an explanation my father found satisfactory for the fact that Yvette's appearance hadn't simply ended the proceedings as my father had envisioned it would.) Then Delfino summed up Campbell's case.

DELFINO: Judge Cobo reminded us earlier that one striking coincidence did not this lawsuit make. It has never occurred to my client to sue any of the hundreds of authors who each year turn out books in which a man and a woman are murdered. Jack Campbell, a private man who hated the very thought of going to court, felt that in the case of Louisa Abrahms, he had no choice. Ms. Abrahms, whose life had touched his at what we now know was more than one point, wrote a book about a man who looked like him, whose life resembled his at many points, and who unlike him was a murderer. Friends and acquaintances who'd known he was innocent read the book, which showed him as a murderer and feared, for the first time, that they'd been mistaken, that he had actually killed someone. You have heard testimony that he lost at least one good job as a result.

My brain has had trouble believing some of the statements my ears have heard uttered in this court. First, we have Ms. Abrahms's words. If I read them in a transcript, I would have wondered if the court stenographer was a little tipsy when she was recording them. (*He waited until the tittering in the courtroom subsided.*) Someone's from Alaska because the author misread her own handwriting when she wrote Atlanta? The same guy's raised near Detroit because she wants to write about cars and capitalism? Sometimes it's difficult to tell whether the author wants us to believe what she's saying or is just doing research to find out how much she can put over on people so she can write about a courtroom of fools.

I urge you not to let the verbal dust that has been thrown up here keep you from seeing the truth. Louisa Abrahms has libeled Jack Campbell, hurt him beyond the possibility of full repair. Think of what it means to have the most serious of all charges leveled at you; dismissed; then years later raised all over again—and in a way described perfectly by the term "actual malice."

I ask that you use your common sense in judging the effect of Louisa Abrahms's malicious charges on Jack Campbell, and your humanity in making restitution for the terrible harm that has been done to him and his wife and their children. Ms. Abrahms can live a comfortable life with money earned from a book that might as well have been written with their blood. With or without money in his pocket, Jack Campbell will have to live for the rest of his life with a portrait of him as a murderer and a thief. When a friend turns away, when he loses a job he'd thought he'd secured, he will never again be sure whether it's something he's done or a book of lies someone has written. Money can ease but never erase the harm that has been done him.

The judge instructed the jury that to call someone a murderer was on the face of it defamatory. Their work was to decide whether the someone who had been pictured in Louisa's book was Jack Campbell, whether the portrait had been done with actual malice and, if so, whether Jack Campbell was entitled to damages.

I am not giving myself undue credit when I say I was fairly certain of the verdict long before the jury returned. There was a small homely woman of perhaps sixty whom I'd watched sporadically throughout the trial; if you hadn't known what she was looking at, you would have sworn she was glued to her favorite soap opera on TV. If she had shown no particular interest in Louisa, she had giggled girlishly when my father made jokes, pursed her lips when Marx was on the stand, clapped her hands a couple of times when Yvette Lacombe announced her name and shook her head disapprovingly when Judge Cobo refused Chow's motion to dismiss. Whatever Judge Cobo thought, she was just as certain as my father had been that there was no case left. What was perhaps most important was that I hadn't seen anyone else on the jury looking irritated with her as she clapped, made her little noises and, once or twice, nudged the man and woman sitting to her left and right.

It took the members of the jury less than three hours to arrive at the conclusion that Louisa had never known Jack Campbell and could not have been writing about him. Several of them were looking at my father and working hard at not smiling as the verdict was announced.

The courtroom erupted. Spectators were silenced by the court officers just long enough for the judge to thank the jurors and dismiss them. As he left the bench and the doors were opened, I found myself looking at the back of Jack Campbell's head. He hadn't moved. Theresa was making her way to his side through the reporters shouting brilliant questions like, "How do you feel about losing this suit?" I couldn't see Patsy. Within seconds I couldn't see anyone else, either, because we were surrounded.

In the hallway outside the courtroom, when we succeeded in making our way there, it was worse. People, flashbulbs, microphones and TV cameras conspired to bury us at rock-concert volume. With the best will in the world, we couldn't have answered the questions we were being asked or struck the poses we were being asked to strike. I'd moved toward my father but now I couldn't see him. When I got through the crowd closest to me, the smaller of the two and composed mostly of women, I found Louisa at the center.

"Do you feel good about the verdict?" one of the women was asking her, perhaps because if you'd had to guess from her demeanor, you would have assumed she'd lost.

Louisa shrugged. "Of course. Why wouldn't I?"

"Because," the woman offered, her navy-suited body rigid, her lips pursed, "everyone's acting as though it's just *his* victory."

Louisa laughed and launched into her Hollywood-as-Buckingham Palace number. "It's not about men–women, it's about how important producers are, compared to writers. Aside from who makes more money, there are just too many writers for any-body to care about us." She paused for effect. "On the other hand, if you think there'd be a bigger crowd around me if I were a male novelist, you're right. But then it'd be harder to breathe."

She was in her element now, her own patter making up for the attention she wasn't getting. A young woman asked her why men didn't like women who accomplished things.

"Actually," Louisa said, "they're only that way until they start paying alimony."

Another asked how she was able to cope with the pressure of being an author, a mother and so on. (Delfino had managed to insinuate the matter of her unwed motherhood into the trial, at which point Louisa, her voice breaking, had managed to suggest without saying so that it had been not her idea, but the man's, not to be around when the babies were crying.) After a moment, Louisa replied that whenever life seemed too difficult, she paid a visit to the Statue of Limitations. She glanced at me and winked, then turned to the woman and asked, so seriously as to confuse a number of her listeners, "Haven't you ever seen the Statue of Limitations? She stands in the harbor off Santa Monica with an usher's flashlight in her hand. The inscription at her base reads, 'Give me your tired, your humble, your unliberated, and I'll give 'em a nickel to forget it at the movies.' "

The woman stared at Louisa, trying to decide whether there could conceivably be such a statue. In the meantime, Louisa's mood had improved even more.

"So what are we going to do to celebrate, kid?" she shouted, grinning at me as though I were her best friend in the world. "Is it still morning? Am I allowed to have a drink?"

The triumph in court had dissipated her hostility for the time being. When I didn't respond, she fielded a few more questions, then whispered in my ear that no matter what she did, I should follow her.

"All right!" my father's voice boomed suddenly through the crowd. "That's enough! Back off! Everyone back off!"

The circle around him and Clara, who clutched at her bag and the embroidered satchel that was her traveling version of the sewing basket, opened somewhat. In the relative quiet that followed, an attractive young woman from the *San Francisco Chronicle*, who made it a point to tell him her name as she tossed her long, dark hair around like the models in the shampoo com-mercials, asked in a manner at once cool and flirtatious whether my father didn't think this trial had been the stuff movies were made of.

"I'll have to think about it," he said. "If you leave me your phone number, I'll call and let you know."

Someone else asked how long it had taken the detectives to find Yvette Lacombe, who was already on her way out with the cameramen and photographers.

"About a week," my father said.

"Do you mean," she asked, "you only started trying a week ago?"

"You got it," he said.

"How come?" she asked.

"Because," my father said, "until I heard the guy talk, it never occurred to me that he didn't kill her."

"Could you please explain?" someone called.

My father shrugged. "He was just someone who wouldn't kill a woman."

When the first person asked if he thought Campbell had killed a man, my father said, "I have no idea. All I know is, a lot more men would kill another man than'd kill a woman."

In the seconds of silence following this pronouncement, Clara suggested it would be "a good idea to go home and have a little rest after all this ex—"

"Home!" my father boomed. "Rest! Are you mad, girl-whoops-woman? Have you no sense of the appropriate? How come Saint Magilla Gorilla never taught you anything but to write neat?" Then, as Clara bit her lip to keep from crying, he called out, "Where the hell is my oldest daughter and co-accused?" He spied Louisa, slightly in back of me. "Come here, daughter, so we can figure out where to have our celebration!"

In spite of herself, Louisa was pleased. She moved around me so she was next to him. He put his arm around her, and those few flashbulbs that hadn't followed Yvette Lacombe out of the court-room began popping again.

"So where do we celebrate when we get rid of these monkeys?" he asked.

"Wherever you like," Louisa said, "as long as I can get a stiff drink."

"Ah! A chip off the old block!" He looked around. "Let's get out of here. Where's my fucking nanny?"

Clara had melted into the crowd moving out of the courthouse. Slowly we followed. In the back right corner of the courtroom Jack

Campbell remained in the relative privacy of the loser, his arm around Theresa as he talked to Delfino. When reporters came close enough to talk to them, Campbell raised his hand in a stop-where-you-are gesture they obeyed.

A few minutes later, we, as well as reporters, photographers, members of the jury, observer-hangers-on and television crews, were in the parking lot in back of the courthouse. The only crowd larger than the one following us was at the somewhat beat-up Chevrolet station wagon a few yards from the lot's edge where our driver waited with my father's car. In that car the attractive suburban family of Robert and Vivienne Mills posed for the cameras. Someone asked if Yvette by any chance had a bathing suit with her, and before Mills had gathered the wit to object, his wife pulled from her pocketbook a wispy bikini she waved for all to see.

When the press refused to let us enter our car, my father's driver and two temporary bodyguards came out of it and began not precisely to push but to radiate slowly and firmly out in ever-widening circles so that everyone else was forced to back off. In a momentary clearing, we could see Jack and Theresa Campbell making their way toward the mall called Santa Monica Place. A man ran up to them and tried to hand Campbell a card. Campbell wouldn't take it, so the man gave it to Theresa, who put it in her bag.

"CBS Two-Hour Special," my father said, looking after him.

The chauffeur opened the door for us while the two bodyguards continued to fend off the crowd. My father beckoned to Louisa, who went in first. He followed, signaling me to come in and sit on his other side, then, as Clara climbed into the jump seat and the two (huge) bodyguards squeezed into the front with the chauffeur, we edged out of the lot. As we did so, Peggy Cafferty came running toward the car. We stopped, let her in to the other jump seat and headed toward Beverly Hills. My father agreed to go home only when Louisa reminded him that Penelope was waiting for him.

BOOK
5

I HAD NEVER seen my father quite so affectionate with Louisa or, for that matter, had I seen her enjoy him so freely, couching her words in such a way as to end up with something he was willing to hear. It would have been easy to assume it was his warm treatment of her that was making her relax, but other days had begun with his being almost like this, and she'd always done something to upset him. When I search for clues to what was about to happen, that simple amity—which I explained at the time by their victory— is the only thing I find that was in some sense out of order. And when I read those words, I'm repelled by my own disgruntlement. The community of well-being formed by the verdict had left me in some suburb where I remained as the two of them tried to decide upon a location grand enough for the celebration they had in mind.

My father said home wasn't good enough since it wasn't a castle with a moat around it but "just one of your cruddy little ten-million-dollar Beverly Hills bungalows."

"I've got it," Louisa announced suddenly. "Why don't we do it at the studio?"

My father began singing, "Why don't we do it at the studio?" to the tune of "Why don't we do it in the road?"

"Like on the set of *Back Court?*" Louisa continued.

My father stopped singing. "She's a genius," he announced, sending a pang through me until he gave me a hug. "All my daughters are geniuses. It's obviously in the genes. Get it? Genes? Geniuses? Ha ha. And we know *which* genes, don't we, since they have different . . . Okay. Never mind. First of all, we call my granddaughter and tell her we're on the way." He dialed her on the car phone. Penelope, who was now five, picked up the phone because Grandpa had ordered that she be allowed to do so whenever she wished. "Is this my granddaughter, Penny—Penelope?" After a pause, he covered the receiver to announce that we wouldn't *believe* what she had responded to his query. She'd told him if he would hold on for a minute, she'd look and see. As he began speaking to her again, Louisa muttered that it was a game she and Penelope played. He did not hear her. He told the child we were on the way home and we were going to have a party. He then had a detailed conversation with her about where the party was going to be and what food should be served, after which he told her he'd have more time for her later if he said goodbye now, and he was allowed to do so.

Back Court had begun with a movie about the rigging of a game by a white coach from the Midwest which was blamed on two black players on his team. At some point the writers' knowledge of our impending lawsuit had given them the idea of playing out the court pun. In the series, which had been aired for the first time a few weeks before, two of the men from the team, one black and one white, have become lawyers trying cases and/or negotiating behind the scenes, often in a restaurant across the street from the back of the courthouse. At other times one or both join in a basketball game with local kids, playing hard as they discuss criminal and other matters touching on the neighborhood.

My father proceeded to give orders. Peggy was to call so-and-so at the studio to have the set made ready and then the publicity department because the series was still at the stage where it needed attention, so if some "cameras and mouths" got in, it wouldn't do any harm. Then there was the food and drink.

He was as high and expansive as I'd ever seen him. Clara made furtive motions indicating he should have a rest and a shot and a little food. He saw her motions and turned it all into a game, rolling his eyes and licking his lips as though he were already eating and drinking the stuff he was listing. Clara reacted as though this were the case and he hadn't had any insulin. From Forbidden Fruitjuice Peggy was to order four cases of that excellent Mondavi Bordeaux he couldn't drink anymore and a few cases of Meursault. From Rising Son, a ton of sushi for all the idiots who'd pass out from hunger before they'd eat anything that wasn't raw fish. In the midst of a lively discussion with himself about which other foods to order, he suddenly began to talk, for the first time since he'd become absorbed in the trial, about leaving Beverly Hills.

He said that as Louisa must know, since it had been one of her cute tricks in the book to reverse it, he had never cared a hell of a lot where he lived. Home was a place to be comfortable, to eat and drink and sleep and play with your kids. Now he was beginning to wonder. . . . Maybe he should sell this house. Or not sell it, but just allow Lynn and anyone else in the family who wished to use it, and he would travel. His base would be in New York, but sometimes he'd just pick up Penny and of course her mother and anyone else in the family who wanted to come and take off for Europe. *Australia.* It was ridiculous for someone like him never to have seen a kangaroo. And his grandchild should see one that wasn't, for Christ's sake, in a zoo.

Clara grew increasingly agitated, and at some point I became uneasy, too. His gestures were more expansive than usual, his face was bright red and he was perspiring heavily in spite of the air-conditioning. He returned to the matter of food.

Peggy was to call NoKoFoo and get a few dozen barbecued ducks and some stacks of their shrimp-and-scallop-and-olive thingies, oliveoygevalts, or whatever they were called. She could get some vegetables if Nursie insisted. And let's see what else.

I'm not sure whether my own instincts were functioning or Clara's anxiety was contagious, but I grew increasingly nervous, and by the time Clara began to cry, I was struggling with myself to keep from doing the same. She had exerted considerable effort to escape unnoticed, but my father chose to see.

"Are you not touched?" he interrupted his food monologue to

ask everyone. "Are you not all moved to tears by Ms. Kennelly's concern for me? Can I infer from what is happening in this car that she loves me more than my daughters do?"

Neither Louisa nor I was so foolish as to respond.

His arms came out from around us where they had been during most of the trip. His hands came to rest gently on Clara's shoulders. He exerted gentle pressure to make her turn toward us on the little seat. Her eyes remained downcast; her face was wet.

"Look at that," he said. "Look how she cares."

Louisa and I both glanced sharply at him because he'd always treated Clara so badly we couldn't believe there was no hitch to what he was saying now. What followed, bizarre as it was, seemed to be without ironic content. At no time did Clara turn to meet anyone else's eyes; her back simply grew stiffer and stiffer until it looked as though if you touched her, she would break.

"She really loves me, you know, old Clara does. I oughta marry her. Lynn would never know the difference as long as I let her hang around, too. Right, Clara sweetheart? Isn't that right? Lynn just needs her bottle now, but Clara needs Sammy to have something to do."

Clara's eyes had taken on a haunted look, at once eager and disbelieving. If he was playing the torturer, it was a different kind of torture than any to which she'd previously been subjected.

"And she's a voigin, I betcha!"

Clara didn't smile, just nodded ever so slightly.

"Where's a guy my age gonna find a genuine virgin of a legal age? Whatcha say, old Clara? Will you marry me when I get my shituation straightened out?"

Again the haunted nod.

"Okay, then. We'll do it. We'll get married and live happily ever after. Maybe we'll have some more children. Some company for Penelope. Do you want to have children, little Clara? How old are you, anyway?"

She glanced at me and at Louisa, then whispered that she was thirty-eight.

"Hmm. Still time if we act fast. All right. That takes care of the end of the week, when all the excitement from the trial's going to die down."

With Louisa and me silenced by the possibility that he was serious, he proceeded to ask Peggy if she'd told the studio we needed comfortable furniture on the set for the party; reminded us that he had to decide if he wanted to bother maintaining an apartment someplace or he'd just travel with his bride; then informed us of his top secret plan to convince his daughter Louisa to move to Los Angeles so his favorite granddaughter could attend school there. When Louisa, smiling, pointed out he'd never see Penny if she was in Los Angeles and he was traveling all the time, he told her he'd take Penny with him, and Penny's mommy, too, because they were both smarter than he was. He wouldn't leave home without 'em.

At the house, all of us got out of the car except Peggy, who would continue on to the studio. Even before Clara whispered to me that he should *really* have a rest before we went, as well as insulin and some food to cushion what he was going to drink, I was as anxious as she was. I told her I knew she was right but that didn't mean I knew how to make him do it. I suggested the two of us take a walk together sometime in the next few days to discuss his condition and whether there was anything more I could be doing. She said that in the meantime, if I could get him to take a little food, and rest . . . I remember noticing she'd grown more rather than less intense on the subject and wondered if it was because she now had reason to hope he was going to marry her.

Louisa came up behind us and said that if we couldn't get him to rest, Penny might be able to. As she spoke, the front door opened and Penny ran out, all dressed up in a blue dotted-swiss dress and patent-leather Mary Janes.

"There's my girl!" exclaimed my father. "Waiting for me just like she promised!"

I feel compelled to admit that a terrible pang went through me. I'd never heard him call anyone else "my girl."

Penny ran to him and he scooped her up, kissing her noisily. At first they sang "Happy Birthday" because they couldn't think of anything else celebratory to sing, but then Penny switched to "Happy Lawsuit," to her grandfather's transcending delight. As the two headed upstairs so he could change for the party, Louisa called to Penny that maybe while they were upstairs, she and Grandpa would like to take a little nap. My father whispered something into the child's ear, and as they reached the head of the stairs, Penny called down, "Grandpa says everyone who needs a nap should take a nap!" Then they disappeared into his bedroom, where they remained for a good fifteen or twenty minutes.

It was close to two by the time we arrived, and Egremont's miracle workers had transformed the set. The grapevine, not to mention the first news broadcasts of the better-than-fiction trial ending, had caused many people, who after a less successful conclusion would have been working too hard for a break, to stop by to congratulate us. The studio executive who'd argued hardest against buying film rights to *Joe Stalbin* (there were too many women in it, for one thing, and nobody was going to the movies to see women anymore; men were the new pinups) and had acceded to my father's wishes only when Louisa had offers from two other studios came for long enough to let everyone see from his expression that he'd wanted to do it all along. An irony attendant upon the lawsuit was that the Campbells had given the most extraordinary publicity to a movie Egremont nearly hadn't bothered to make. Television cameras were taking pictures of the known and the maybe-known. When Louisa saw them, she whispered something to my father, who once again had Penelope on his shoulders, and he announced the cameras could have five more minutes and that would be it.

The basketball court had been turned into a huge living room without walls. White sectional sofas lined its perimeter, with spaces at the corners so people could circulate. Baskets of fresh flowers had been set in the hoops at either end of the court. A fully equipped bar stood under each. Bread and cheese, bagels and lox, fruits and salads were on the banquet table at the court's center.

My father had refused to take any insulin before entering the party. Clara suggested this meant he planned to drink himself into a stupor without eating since insulin wasn't required for the digestion of alcohol. Unfortunately, he needed food to prevent passing out from the drinks. I grew irritated by her worrying because there was nothing I could do. My father, with the cameras still running, marched to the closer bar, ordered "Six ounces of Scotch, three ice cubes and two ounces of club soda" for himself and a Horse's Neck (ginger ale with a maraschino cherry) for Penny.

He was surrounded by reporters asking questions and studio people congratulating him. Nobody asked if he had arranged the spectacular timing of Yvette's arrival. They probably assumed that he had and thought it was fine. My father, Penny on his shoulders, one of their drinks in each hand, walked to a sofa where he sat down and called a waiter from Rising Son, who had just begun making his way around the set, to bring over some sushi for his granddaughter. When the waiter reached the sofa, my father, who'd eased Penelope down onto the cushions and given her the Horse's Neck, took the tray, thanked the man and told him to get another.

"That's a lot of sushi," one of the reporters remarked.

My father proceeded to deliver a proud lecture on Penny's

incredibly cosmopolitan taste in food. If they thought it interesting a five-year-old adored raw tuna, they might like to know that her favorite breakfast was a croissant that had been filled with Brie mashed with walnuts, then roasted. Penny told him what she really wanted now wasn't sushi but half a bagel with cream cheese and lox as well as plenty of capers and a little lemon juice. With a wink at those assembled around him, my father told her if she'd wait right there, he'd be back with it in a minute. When one of the reporters offered to get it for him, he said only he knew how to do it exactly the way Penelope liked it. "Except for her mother, of course," he said, though Louisa, standing nearby and surrounded by people, didn't appear to be listening.

My eyes caught Clara's, which immediately turned toward my father. She looked like a mother watching her son go into a football game when she's the only one who knows he's already had a concussion. I kept an eye on him from the sofa. On his way to the food table, he stopped off at Louisa's and various other groups to drop some line of his own or one of Louisa's he'd liked. I remember the sort of jaunty way he walked after each of these little visits. What made me uneasy was that it wasn't his usual walk but seemed, rather, like that of an actor who is shy and retiring in real life but has just been told his character is cocksure and must have a walk to match.

I finished my drink, talked with Penny as well as anyone else who came by and tried not to be aware of Clara so her nervousness wouldn't make me more miserable than I was. But I remember with painful clarity the moment when the sense of anxiety that had been growing over the previous hour or two turned to a numbing fear.

My father returned to the sofa and with a bow handed Penny her beautifully decked out bagel.

Penny said, "Come and sit down, Grandpa."

My father, looking at his empty glass, said, "In a minute, sweetheart. I just want to—"

Clara stood up. "Perhaps you'd let me give you a shot and make you a plate of food. I don't think you've had anything solid to eat except for a bite of toast at breakfast."

My father regarded her seriously. "Why don't we talk about it over a drink."

She was concerned enough to stand firm. "Because you should have something to eat before you have anything more to drink."

A long moment passed as those in attendance waited to see if he would explode at her. Instead he said, "Trouble is, there's no real food here. Just a bunch of . . . salty . . . pansy . . . shit."

His voice had grown loud enough so that people in the vicinity had turned to watch him.

He looked around the room. "We need some real food. . . . Where is she, anyway?" As his eyes came back to Clara, he stopped looking and shouted, "Esther! Where the hell're the pot roast and kasha? I don't want any of this pansy shit!"

All conversation in the area ceased. Clara came over and took his arm, her face white, her hands shaking. Louisa, having heard him call out her mother's name, joined them. Without shaking off Clara's hand, my father held out his glass to a nearby waiter and asked for a glass of Scotch with no room taken up by ice or any of that crap. As I began a sentence calculated to divert him from the idea of another drink, Louisa said she felt ill, perhaps the whole day had been a little more than she could handle. Where was Penny? She wanted to relax on one of the sofas for a while. Maybe Sam and Penny would like to join her.

"Terrific idea," my father said. "Where is she, anyway? Someone stole her from me. Aha! There she is. It was only the bagel and lox that stole her. The lox is too salty. I tasted it. Don't tell me to have the Nova. The Nova's too salty, too."

With Clara's hand still on his arm, he returned to the sofa where Penny was methodically eating her bagel. He picked her up, then sat down with her on his lap.

"Esther, sweetheart," he said to Clara, "let's get some decent food in here, uh? Not just pot roast and kasha. Maybe a noodle pudding. Some macaroons." He waited for her to scurry off, then looked down to Penelope and said, "How's my little Louielou?"

Nearly frozen with fear, I looked at Louisa. Her face was white.

"I can't tell if he knows what he's doing," she muttered under her breath.

My father looked up, caught some expression on her face.

"Feeling any better, Toots?"

"I don't know," Louisa said. "It's been quite a day."

"You don't want to go home, do you?" he asked with an anxiety that was as uncharacteristic as virtually everything else that was happening. "Because if you do, you can leave the baby with me, and we'll come along in a few minutes."

Usually he didn't bargain with her but waited for Penny to do it; today he was unwilling to let go of the child.

"Fine, fine," Louisa said. "I don't have to go anyplace. I can sit here and rest, too."

"Mm," my father said happily. "If we stay close, the vultures can't get us. Right, Louielou? Sweetheart?"

He kissed the top of Penelope's head but could not see, as we could, that the child had fallen asleep. The bagel remnants slid down his pants leg to the floor. No one bothered to pick them up.

Louisa smiled. "She's asleep. She's been up since five in the morning, after all."

My father began to sing, "It's five o'clock in the mo—orning," then corrected himself to, "It's four o'clock in the . . . no, wait a minute, was it three?" He began to sing again but caught himself. "Too loud. My baby's sleeping, aren't you, baby? Where the hell is Esther with my drink? And my kasha varnishkes?"

His voice had grown loud again and Louisa pointed to Penny to remind him. He nodded, put a finger on his lip in a childishly conspiratorial manner. In a whisper, he apologized to Penny for making so much noise. He kissed the top of her head. She squirmed in his lap and settled into a more comfortable position, her head resting on his right arm, which was bare below the sleeve of the green polo shirt he'd changed into when we went home.

"I'm gonna set out border guards," he said to Louisa, "the next time you try to leave."

"Let's not even think about it," Louisa said. "It's too far away to think about."

"Okay," he replied, "then let's think about who the hell we have to shoot to get me a drink."

A moment later Clara returned, explaining she'd been able to get the food he wanted from the restaurant-deli on Fairfax that he liked. He allowed her to give him a shot through the sleeve of his shirt, then she handed him a glass which, one could see immediately, was full of a liquid much too pale to be straight Scotch.

"Oh, for Christ's sake," he said, "did you fill it with Scotch or did you piss in it?" But he took the glass and began to sip at it, looking down at Penny sleeping in his arms as he did so. "Ah, Passion Flower," he said, smoothing back her hair with the last two fingers of the hand that held his drink. "If only my grandfather Moishe could see you."

Louisa, sitting next to him, laughed nervously.

"You laugh!" my father exclaimed. "But Moishe was an extraordinary man. Without him none of us would be here today."

We were silent. I could barely breathe.

"He had a terrific operation in Rovno, Moishe did. Rovno was a railroad center. In Byelorussia. I must've mentioned it." He looked at each of us in turn. "No? All right, then, it's time for me to tell you."

Silence. Louisa and I exchanged apprehensive glances and looked away because we didn't know precisely what our apprehension was about.

"He was a poultry dealer. Chicken, ducks, geese. He sold them in town, then he sewed the money he got for them into his clothes and went to other towns and bought manufactured goods you couldn't get in Rovno. When he got home, he bartered the manufactured stuff for more poultry. And crops. Because that's what the farmers had, they never had cash. The poultry he got, he slaughtered and dressed and sold to the townspeople for more cash."

Slowly, other conversation around the room had ceased. People were gathered around us, listening.

"He was a rich man by the time the Czar's henchmen came to get his two oldest sons, Schmuel and Max, for the army. He used the money . . . After all, the Jews weren't allowed to buy land and they didn't know from booze, what was he going to spend it on . . . ? He used it to buy them railroad tickets across Europe. The ships going to America all left from Hamburg. . . . Steamship tickets to the new country . . . Esther, you told them to make the kasha varnishkes with chicken fat, not butter? This is a meat meal, remember. M-e-a-t me in Saint Louis, Louis. Anyhow, when they got off the boat in Manhattan maybe a year later . . . remember, everything took *time* in those days. You needed *time*. None of this close your eyes and you're eating at the Gritti Palace. Anyhow . . . they had eight languages between 'em, but not a word of English. They finally found some Jews down on the East Side who had Yiddish. One of them had a fur-dressing plant on Avenue A, and Schmuel went to work for him because that's what he'd been doing in the old country. Fur dressing. When Schmuel got married, he took over the place. Wily son-of-a-bitch, my uncle Schmuel. By the time I was old enough to know what was happening, he owned the plant. Not that my father would have wanted it. It's a disgusting business. The smell of the raw skins . . . And the treatment was worse than the cure. The cure was no cure. The filth was unbelievable. They were constantly putting sawdust on the floor because it was wet. But the sawdust picked up the smell of the chemicals they treated the furs with. I don't know how they could stand it. Yes I do. You stand what you have to stand. No more, no less. At one point they

296

cut through the floors and made their own elevator. I swear to God. It was a crude pulley job, but it worked. Four floors' worth. It didn't look the way it would look if we made it with our fucking overpaid help, but it worked. Until the Depression. Once the Depression came, nothing worked. They had to come live with us and the chickens.

"My father hated the city. He wasn't as aggressive as Schmuel. Never went for the city life, except maybe for Saturday night. He just wanted to be back in the country. He got a job with a cap maker. Slept on the cutting table until he could afford a room and a wife. Worked hard, saved his money, and the first minute he could do it, got us to Vineland. Just the name turned him on. His English was fine by this time. Not that he thought of wine. Wine was something you had at a seder. He never even touched schnapps. Schmuel had a taste for schnapps, but my father loved *grapes*. And grapevines. He kept hearing about Vineland. This place across the river where Jews were buying land. Furthermore, you want to know if he was bored when he finally got there? Never. Not for a minute. Vineland was Paradise if you were raised on a shtetl and came to the— Esther! Where the hell are my kasha varnishkes? I'm not gonna marry you if I don't get my kasha varnishkes!"

There was tittering from the audience. Nobody moved, including Clara.

"So they got their farm in Vineland. Always something going on in the Jewish community in Vineland. But from the first time I went to New York and Esther . . . Esther sneaked me into a cabaret. She was sixteen, I was fourteen." He handed Clara his empty glass. "Get me another one, will you?" She didn't move. He didn't appear to notice. He was stroking Penny's hair. "I bet Esther never told you she was two years older than me." He winked at Louisa. "Never mind. As long as she told you she was my cousin." She stared at him with a momentary hostility that made me certain she hadn't known. He said, "Don't look so upset. Just a fourth cousin. Nothing serious in the incest department. Especially if you look at what goes on these days. In those days it passed for hot stuff. I mean, marrying your sister wasn't as serious as marrying a Murphy, but still . . . Rosemary Murphy. Was that her name? Jesus, you kids don't even know from *Abie's Irish Rose*. A seminal work of our time."

A waiter wheeled over a cart full of covered dishes that might or might not have been the foods he'd requested. He waved away the waiter, too intent upon *Abie's Irish Rose* to interrupt himself.

Clara prepared a dish of food which he ignored when she tried to present it to him.

"Rosie Murphyberg. Or whatever. Abie had to give her a fake name when he brought her home so they'd think she was Jewish. They would've had a fit if . . . Anyway, the next thing you know . . ."

We did not learn because at this point he lapsed into what sounded like fluent Yiddish. He was apparently outlining the plot of *Abie's Irish Rose*, the ending of which I now know because as he reached it, he stood up, carefully holding Penny so he wouldn't drop her or have her taken away from him, and switched back to English.

"And then Rosemary Levy gives birth to twins!" he said.

With one hand he reached over to the plate Clara stood holding, picked up a moist piece of meat, dropped it into his mouth, and continued speaking as he chewed that piece and took another.

"Why can't you be twins, sweetheart?" he crooned to Penny, who was beginning to awaken. "Why can't I have twice as much of you?"

The room was quite silent, by now, everyone in it having gathered around us.

He popped the other piece of meat into his mouth. He was sort of waltzing around in the small area left by the crowd.

"It's true, they were boys, and if I had to choose between twenty boys and one little Penelope, I'd take the Penelope, but still . . ."

What with his dancing and his eating and his talking, Penelope was wide-awake. My father was eying a glass with liquid in it that someone had left on the food cart. He bent over to grab it, and as he did so, Penelope, afraid of falling, reached out toward her mother. As Louisa in one motion stood and held out her arms for Penelope, my father froze in his tracks, an expression of shock on his face. At the moment that Penelope was safely in her mother's arms, he crumpled to the floor.

He lived for another three months, in the hospital, in a condition I would find it unbearable to describe in any detail. For the first few days, when he lay immobile in a coma, we thought he would remain that way until he died. But on the fifth day, he opened his eyes and spoke. Although his words were at first unintelligible, they gave me hope that he would live and recover. At least that *someone* would live and recover. For the real person seemed to have been scooped out from behind the face he'd acquired a few years earlier and a small recording machine inserted in his place.

He could move his right side but not his left. He did not appear to be aware of this limitation, much less disturbed by it. As his speech grew intelligible, it became clear that he had no interest in the physical details of his condition. He was also uninterested in the business information relayed to him by those studio subordinates either concerned for his well-being or hedging their bets against his recovery. What interested him were the plots of various movies he remembered, most of them having been made in the twenties or thirties. Of the ones he evoked, the latest I can remember had been produced around the outset of World War II.

He would ask in a sort of sleepy-rhetorical fashion if whoever was in the room (no distinction between us was made and no affection displayed) remembered a particular movie. When Clara, who stayed with him most of each twenty-four hours, or Violet or Shimmy or Louisa or I said (usually) that we did not, he would recount the plot in great detail. To the extent that Louisa or Shimmy or any other visitor was able to recall these movies, the plot summaries were accurate. It was in naming the characters he went furthest afield—and in ways to give us all pause.

The male lead, whether he was the newsman of *After Office Hours* (1935) who solved a mystery with the help of a lovely socialite, or the wounded Jewish soldier of *Abie's Irish Rose* who falls in love with his Irish nurse, was called Sam. The Irish nurse and all other female leads (when there is a triangle she is the wife rather than the girlfriend) was Esther. The other woman—vamp, sexpot, thief—was invariably Renée, a name no one could make sense of until one of the few studio people older than my father asked if he mightn't be thinking of Renée Adorée, who'd been big in the movies when he and my father were young. A boy child was Lou, a girl Louisa. Two girls were Louisa and Nellie. If there was a male in direct competition with the lead, his name was Abe. (We did not know who Abe was. In going through some cartons of memorabilia in the basement after his death, we found he'd had a brother named Abe who had disavowed him after the war when he refused to return to Esther.) When he referred to the actors and actresses who played the roles, my father usually used their correct names.

"So Louisa Colleen Lapidowitz is engaged to Sam Sweeney, a good cop, but she gets a crush on this *gonif*, Abe Gold, a real no-goodnik. Her father asks her . . . [lengthy dialogue in what Shimmy and others attested to as good Yiddish]. Fortunately, Sam gets her out of that one, and they go off together on his motorcycle. A girl named Sally O'Neil played Louisa Colleen. Not bad, but not, you know, a real beauty. All the Irish girls wanted Jewish boys because we didn't drink. Or at least we didn't stop eating when we drank."

He did not have the sense then, or at any time after the stroke, as far as anyone could tell, that he was being funny.

Work was impossible. I told my bosses they could extend my leave or let me go altogether. They reserved judgment.

When I was not sitting at the edge of my father's bed in the hospital, I was sitting in a chair in his home, looking at television, often with a drunken Lynn beside me. (She couldn't bear to be alone in her apartment.) Louisa and I tended to spell each other at the hospital, partly because Penny, who kept asking for her grandpa, had decided she found me more tolerable than any of the help. If my childish jealousy of her had evaporated so that I found her not only tolerable but my sole diversion from worry, I can't say I felt the same about Louisa, who sat around thinking of ways we, or at least *she*, could have made my father behave so he wouldn't have had the stroke.

"If only you'd *told* me," she said to Clara one day in the hospital corridor. "I should've *asked*. We should've put handcuffs on him, if it was the only way to make him behave."

Any discussion about courses of action was fraught with hazards. Louisa and I disagreed about almost everything, beginning with the matter of Violet's coming to the hospital (it clearly made no difference to my father, but Louisa discussed the matter as though Violet's very presence damaged his health) and going on to the question of whether Liane, on the commune, ought to be notified. (When I finally called and told Liane her father had had a stroke, she said she had an oil he should be rubbed down with and she was sending a bottle in the mail.)

It was only through a freak of fate, or perhaps I should say through a freak of motherhood, that I and not Louisa was with him when he died. It was Louisa's usual time, but she was interviewing a woman to be Penny's sitter for as long as they remained in Los Angeles, and the woman, who had another job, could only make it at that hour.

Violet was with me (I regularly let her know when Louisa would not be around) and had just finished describing her attempts to get Dagmar to visit Sam. Dagmar was going to Japan with a Japanese tycoon whose companies included USAKE, an exporter of sake, who was wooing her, whether to become his bride or the drink's American spokeswoman was unclear. Violet was more fluttery than she'd been in a while, either with anxiety over Dagmar's imminent departure from the States or my father's condition, I couldn't tell which. I was relieved when she fluttered out of the room. I had no idea whether she was coming back.

Clara sat in a straight-backed chair in one corner, fast asleep. She had eaten very little during the weeks of my father's hospitalization and could have played a concentration-camp inmate by this time.

My father, who appeared to be asleep, also appeared to be smiling. He began to speak, at first unintelligibly. Babble turned into the speech of a child, and it became apparent he thought he was on the chicken farm in Vineland. The person he seemed to be talking to was his father. He was asking why only the hen could sit on the egg, how could his father, or whomever he was arguing with, be so sure he would break it if *he* sat on it.

His eyes opened. He began to talk, smiling, about how when everyone was asleep he was going to sneak back to the henhouse and sit on an egg in his nice soft flannel pajamas, so it wouldn't break. Then, still smiling, he closed his eyes. I don't know how many minutes had gone by before I found myself thinking of Tony, remembering how I had come into his study to find him sitting in the red leather armchair with his eyes open very wide.

It was only then it came to me that my father might be dead.

I stopped breathing. My body froze. I don't know how long it would have taken me to move, but Clara awakened, looked at me, then at him, and flew to his side. She took his pulse, rang the buzzer and made other tests and motions as I sat watching like a zombie. Finally the doctor came and after a moment said with what was clearly a premeasured dose of sympathy that he was afraid Mr. Pearlstein was gone.

Clara was crying. I held her. I did not begin to cry until they unhooked my father from the tubes and wires that had failed to keep him alive. I had assumed as I watched him in his comatose state that I could feel no worse if he were actually dead.

I knew already that I'd been wrong.

Almost from the moment I called, Louisa acted as though I'd been part of a conspiracy to keep her from being at the hospital at the important moment. When I said, "He's gone," she asked what I meant, as though I might be telling her he'd decided to walk out of the hospital. When I managed to get out, "Died," she said, "Wait a second," as though I'd made some decision she could persuade me to reverse.

I understand that I'm being unfair and that her unwillingness to believe paralleled my own. But she acted as though it had been through my choice rather than her necessity that she'd been absent. In any event, matters between us quickly grew so much worse that it's difficult as I write about that time to summon up another when each of her actions did not appear tinged with her own malignance or an assumption on her part of mine.

She arrived at the hospital not twenty minutes after my call and stormed into the room as though important decisions had been made without her. If we didn't fight in those first hours and days it was because I was more than willing to let her make all the arrangements. I didn't feel they had anything to do with him.

Shimmy told us she and I had inherited the bulk of his substantial estate, although there were provisions for Liane and each of his wives and various other people as well as a trust fund for Penelope. Perhaps the huge and equal sums that went to us guaranteed that Louisa and I would have to find other matters to fight about.

The first argument was about where the memorial service (we'd agreed not to have a funeral because of privacy problems) would be held. Grace and David Fisher, Shimmy's daughter and her husband, had offered us their lovely terrace and lawn in Westwood. Louisa hadn't liked the idea. She'd decided during our meetings that Shimmy tended to side with me and therefore could not be trusted. (She could offer, when challenged, no evidence of this favoritism.) She proposed half a dozen alternatives including the absurd one of holding the service at my father's New York apartment, although most of the people who would attend lived in Los Angeles. She gave in when Grace, seeing me in need and in mourning, managed to convince her that she and her father were fond of both of us.

We managed to keep down the size of the group to fewer than a hundred people and to keep out those members of the press who found out When and Where by locking the gate to the high fence ringing the Fishers' home and lawn. There was a guard with a list at the front door.

It was a pleasant ceremony, held in the living room because the lawn was more vulnerable to invasion. Various people whom my father had worked with or who'd been fond of him spoke briefly of their feelings. This did not include his wives other than Violet.

Violet had become spokeswoman for an anti-aging cream called Zoe. She carried a large tapestry bag on which was embroidered in one corner, "Violet Vann for Zoe," and wore a bright yellow dress she'd told me in advance she would wear because it had been my father's favorite. She stood next to the small mahogany table that had been set at one end of the long living room for the use of the speakers and said, as her eyes filled with tears, "He was the only man I ever loved." Then she sat down.

It was remarkably affecting, perhaps because I believed her. But my tears dried during the speeches of the various studio executives, and Louisa, who delivered the closest thing we had to a eulogy, did nothing to evoke more. She came to the front in the black tent dress she'd been wearing each day during the previous week, perhaps because she'd been eating all the time and had gained ten or fifteen pounds. After a somber search of the faces in the audience, she began speaking in a quiet voice that felt theatrical to me, perhaps because I didn't trust her anymore. She never referred to him as other than "My father," and did not look at me at any time during the speech.

"When I was young the weekends were special because my father was very much with me. My mother was usually tired or busy."

(Perhaps this is the moment for me to mention that I met Esther during Christmas vacation the following year, when she'd come to New York to visit Louisa and her grandchild. She is a small, pleasant and extraordinarily energetic woman.)

"My favorite of our trips was the one to the Bronx Zoo, which was just a few blocks from our home. There were rides on the zoo train during which we pretended we were in Africa, where my father had told me many of the animals once lived. There was watching the two o'clock feeding of the seals and then going off to get cotton candy, which he loved almost as much as I did. Later he would set me on his shoulders and ride me home, where we would both imitate the animals. Our favorite trick was one in which I held his hands and stood on his shoes while he clumped around the house being what he called a four-legged dadalou. When it rained, we went to the movies. If the weather was good and we still wanted to see a movie, we had to sort of fake it because my mother didn't approve."

Louisa spoke of her misery when he went off to do his patriotic duty in the war and quoted an affectionate letter from him as though it were one of hundreds, though she had once complained to me that aside from "a letter or two," he had disappeared from her life. She described how when the war ended, knowing he was in California and believing he'd soon be back, she'd begun to attend the neighborhood movie and read anything she could find about what were still called "the movies," not "the films," and about which little (other than gossip about the stars) was written in those days. Her mother, sensing the movie bug was about him, tried to discourage her interest. It was already clear that she, Louisa, wasn't going to be a movie star, and her mother couldn't envision a day when she might do something else connected to film. (A small, sharing smile. In the wake of my father's death the studio was going ahead in an even bigger way than planned after the lawsuit with the release of the movie, the title of which would be changed to *Joe's Daughters*.)

I'd managed not to cry during Louisa's monologue, but as she was winding up her particular blend of fiction and reminiscence, I glanced down at the space between Violet's chair and mine, where Violet had left her large Zoe bag. The bag was just open enough, when she went for tissues, so that I could see her doll, Mooty, huddled inside it, a piece of cut-up blanket covering the decrepit little body so it wouldn't grow too cold.

I began crying and didn't stop for days.

Or was it months.

Since I could think about little beyond my father and my life as he had both dominated and made it worth living, I decided to set down my thoughts and memories of him. Louisa's skewed eulogy must have been an additional spur for me to provide my own more accurate—I'm being sarcastic but I also mean it—memories of our lives. I think I hoped for a sort of exorcism; instead I was swamped by the feelings those memories aroused.

I began to despair of the notion that I might live a reasonable life unrelated to him. I tried to comfort myself with the thought that the money he'd left me would allow me to do *anything I felt like doing*. It was the most frightening thought I'd yet had. What was I to do? Turn into one of those ladies who shopped at Saks in the late morning and sat behind the counter of a hospital gift shop in the afternoon? Each activity had its points, but neither would engage my mind to a point where life might pass in a tolerable way.

I tried settling in to write the difficult parts of my account but found a different reason for being unable to work in each room of my apartment. The view of the Park from the living room was so beautiful as to encourage forgetfulness. Writing in the bedroom, I grew sleepy; in the kitchen, I grew hungry; and the back portion of the living room, from which I might work without being distracted by the view, was dark and unappealing.

I began walking down to the Public Library on Forty-second Street weekday mornings with a yellow legal pad and some ball-point pens. Sitting at one of the long tables in the reading room, I made notes of what came to mind and read magazines when nothing did.

Saturdays and Sundays were even more difficult. Without a job, I had no need to get done the tasks I'd always saved for the weekends. I remember thinking at one point that I should travel, if only to accumulate obligations at home. My New York pals were solicitous, careful to include me in dinner parties, even more eager than before to fix me up with the rare interesting and available man, as though I were somehow more eligible than I had been before my father died. When I was home, I listened to music all the time.

On a Saturday morning a couple of months after my father's death, I was straightening up the desk in the living room and looking down at the Park. I became aware that on the radio, the news had turned into a powerful baritone singing an aria, and I hadn't turned it off. Tony had been dead for twenty years and I hadn't played an opera in that time.

I allowed the music to continue. Sherrill Milnes was singing, although I didn't know any of the singers who'd come up since 1965 and could not have identified him at the time. The opera was *Macbeth*. I stood at the window, not exactly thinking, until an announcer's voice replaced the music. Then I began hunting in the back of my storage closet for the cartons of records Tony had left me. Only when I'd found them and with considerable effort had moved them from the back of the closet to the middle of the living room did I remember that the record player had broken a year or two earlier and I'd been playing only tapes since then.

Once it was fixed, I played every opera I owned. Of course, the sound was terrible by the standards of 1985. I began to collect tapes and, when they existed, discs for the CD player I'd bought, and to learn which of the "new" singers—Pavarotti, Milnes, Verrett, Te Kanawa and so on—I loved.

It was as though the fact of my real father's death had finally shifted the locus of pain so I could accept, once again, the solace of Tony's music.

Technically, my leave of absence had expired. I hadn't spoken with Byron Koenig since the service for my father in Los Angeles, when he'd told me in a rather weighted fashion that he was looking forward to seeing me back at the office. He'd left a few messages on my machine since then, but I'd avoided responding to them.

A little over a year after his divorce from Franya, Vaughn Cameron, the client Simon had introduced me to at the Sherry Netherland, had published a novel called *Miriam's Days of Rage*. Franya, who hadn't asked for alimony, was now suing for two million dollars for libel. There was no strong libel specialist in the firm although Dick Cullen, who'd handled contracts for Cameron and others, had done some libel work. He had prepared the motion for summary judgment, but now I was being offered a partnership if I would return and take over the case. The offer was particularly flattering because there was a new C.E.O. at Egremont, a man recruited from another studio to which I had no connection, so the partnership offer had to do not only with Cameron but with the general quality of my work. Or with the quality of the work I'd once done.

The reason I knew what Byron's calls were about was that I'd had lunch a couple of times with Vaughn Cameron, who, in his gentle way, had expressed dissatisfaction with Cullen and said he hoped I'd return and take over the case. I had promised to read his novel and the papers and try to bring my intelligence to bear on them.

I saw very little of Louisa. Penny, who'd gone to three different nursery schools, each of which her mother found unsatisfactory for a different reason, had been in a fourth school for kindergarten and was in a fifth for first grade. Between full-time school and Rosa's continued presence, Louisa felt free to spend a considerable amount of time away from home. She had taken an assignment to do a new screenplay for Egremont and appeared to be dividing her days almost evenly between New York and Los Angeles. The conversations we had were so difficult that I was relieved not to be having more. Among other things, there were estate issues she'd apparently hoped to handle, as she had the funeral, without concern for my opinions.

Even had I been willing to let her make all those decisions, Shimmy's was a calm voice reminding me that I would have to live with them for the rest of my life. Without saying a word against Louisa, he encouraged me to form my own ideas about whether I wanted to sell the gambling interests managed by Simon & Koenig, the apartment in the Sherry Netherland (my father had left me the one where I lived), the Egremont shares, and so on. Lynn had been left the house in Beverly Hills with the proviso that I was to be allowed to take from it anything I wanted that wasn't specifically hers.

So I was astonished, the first time I was in Louisa's apartment after his death, to see the little marble-topped antique chest that had been in the entrance foyer of the house since I was a child. When she saw me looking at it, Louisa informed me blithely that she'd always been "attached" to it, and Lynn had told her to take it by all means. When I said I wasn't sure that was how the system was supposed to work, Louisa said that since I'd gotten a whole gorgeous apartment and practically anything else I wanted, she hadn't thought I'd mind her having "one tiny chest." Then she took a large slug of whatever was in the glass on the kitchen counter and went about chopping vegetables.

I gaped at her. If I'd become aware of the extent of Louisa's resentment over my existence, I had failed to connect this resentment to the physical details of my father's bequests. Suddenly I remembered his saying to Lynn one day years earlier as he hugged me approvingly, "This kid never noticed that she lost her station in life, only that she lost her papa." He'd been wrong. I *had* noticed, but it wasn't what mattered. Now I was registering the importance to Louisa of the objects I'd not even thought about yet, the physical details of what my father had left and to whom.

Shimmy had come into New York on business, and Grace had accompanied him for the first time since moving West. Grace and I had been talking on the phone at least two or three times a week, and when Louisa invited the two of them for dinner, Grace told her she'd love to see me and her other two nights weren't free. Louisa consented to invite me as well. She and I would meet with Shimmy on estate matters the following morning.

Her manner now as I stood in the arch between her kitchen and dining room, watching her chop vegetables, was an extraordinary combination of hostility and bravado. Periodically she looked at me, waiting for a complaint.

"You're such an ingenue," she finally said, pushing aside the vegetables and beginning to beat something in a bowl. "Nobody can look 'Oh-dear-I'm-so-shocked' as well as you can."

"Go fuck yourself," I said. I was startled but not displeased by my own vehemence. "I don't know what I came for but it's not this."

"I'm sorry," she said instantly. "I'm really sorry. I was just so surprised to see you making such a big fuss about a little piece of furniture that it never oc—"

"Please—" I cut her off. "I don't feel like listening to a whole story. All I was saying was that the furniture was left to me, not to you."

"All right," she said after a moment. "I'm sorry. I didn't know you cared."

But it wasn't even a question, yet, of whether I cared, though it might be futile to try to convince her of that. For the first time I found my eyes roaming over the kitchen, or, more precisely, over the open shelves that lined the small dinette. On one shelf I could see the heavy, beautifully engraved one-quart Steuben glass measuring cup that had been a birthday present to my father years before. I walked into the living room, where I noticed the extraordinary burled wooden box in which he'd kept his cigars and the crystal ashtray engraved with the signatures of the studio people who'd given it to him for his fiftieth birthday. I went through the hall to Penny's bedroom. Penny was sleeping over at a friend's. I sat on her bed until the buzzer sounded and I could hear Louisa tell the man at the desk to send them up. Then I meandered back into the living room.

"There's something I maybe should mention before they come up," Louisa called to me. "Oh, never mind. Well . . . "

I told myself I had to get out of there as soon as possible, I really couldn't stand her. Which doesn't sound like a big deal except I hadn't admitted it to myself before in anything like those terms.

"I'm thinking of moving to the other apartment," she said.

"Other apartment?"

"The Sherry Netherland."

I think I felt precisely as I had the day she told me she was changing her name to Pearlstein; the presumption of a shared reality was false in the case of Louisa and me. If she'd told me earlier that she wanted to live in "a real neighborhood" where Penny would have friends close by, instead of at the edge of Lincoln Center and various other "non-neighborhoody" places, it had never occurred to me she would consider living at my father's apartment, one of the few places I could think of which was even less in a neighborhood than this one was.

"I know all the arguments against it," she said, "but there are plenty for it, too. Anyway, it's easy for you to knock it. He left you the nicest place of all."

And before I had to decide whether to ask if she was referring to the apartment where I'd been living since my return to New York seven years earlier, the doorbell rang. I knew even then that it wasn't my saner self who was considering asking her the question.

The evening was a disaster.

Louisa served good food and wine but had too much of both, and apparently the clear liquid she'd been drinking since before my arrival was gin. She talked constantly, including at times when someone else was trying to answer one of *her* questions—as though the queries were nothing more than filler for periods when she couldn't beguile us with some fascinating tale about herself. She got drunker and drunker, giving herself license to discuss not only matters of publishing (now that she didn't need them anymore, the publishers were all vying for her) but also her visits to a psychiatrist, something she'd decided she just *had* to do. It was much better than having to live with someone and get along with him and compromise all the time, you just did what you wanted, and a few times a week you went to tell this guy who didn't give a damn about anybody else in the whole world while you were there.

I don't remember the details of the story Louisa was telling when she held up her glass, which had yet to endure an empty moment, said, "Remember, King Kong was only eighteen inches tall!" and collapsed on the rug in a fit of laughter that soon turned into snores.

Grace and Shimmy dropped me off on the way back to their hotel, with Grace telling me how lucky I was not having had to grow up in the same house as Louisa, and Shimmy looking discreetly out of the window the whole time.

Sober and in Shimmy's presence at our meeting the next day, Louisa didn't say a word about holding on to the apartment in the Sherry Netherland, which we agreed to put up for sale. Major decisions involving the gambling interests had to be made, but Shimmy didn't handle that stuff and was reluctant to move even briefly onto Simon & Koenig terrain. Egremont was doing well, and there was no reason to think about its stock yet unless we wanted to. I was disappointed to realize that I/we wouldn't be able to have lunch with Shimmy. He was meeting Grace right after our discussion and grabbing a cab for the airport. He told me, at a

309

moment when Louisa was in the ladies' room, that I should feel
free to call him with questions or just to talk at any time.

Once again, for reasons not having to do with anything I could
perceive in the real world, Louisa decided to be my friend. Frequently she called to talk about Penny, or to invite me to visit, or
to ask if I knew anything about real estate. She was spending
weekdays looking at city apartments and weekends looking at
country homes. She needed to be near Penny's school but couldn't
stand the East Side, needed space and flowers but hadn't the time
to take care of them or the desire to hire a lot of help. Millionaire
or no, she wasn't going to spend more than her own income could
cover.

Actually, if there was one thing that seemed to increase her
trust in me, it was that she'd prepared an argument for our both
getting rid of our gambling interests, assuming I would resist. With
Shimmy's help I'd gained a sense of the staggering amount of
money involved, if not of operational details. My telling her that
my instinct in the matter paralleled hers took her aback but finally
pleased her. I had the distinct sense that if I had been unwilling
to divest myself of my shares, she would have held on to hers.

Early on a rainy Saturday afternoon, as I was trying to decide
whether to write, shop or force myself to read the first draft of the
motion for summary judgment in the matter of Cameron vs. Aldebaran Press and Cameron, my buzzer sounded. It was Louisa,
asking if she could drop up for a moment. She was with someone
she wanted me to meet. As I hesitated, she said she was on her
way downtown and wouldn't stay long. A minute later I opened
the door.

Louisa, looking flushed and happy, stood next to an extremely
tall and extremely thin young man with a long, mournful face, a
first-scraggly-beard-kind-of-beard, and wire-rimmed spectacles.
Both wore slickers and carried umbrellas. The thought that crossed
my mind was that Louisa was robbing the cradle.

"Nell," she said with a wide grin, "I'd like you to meet my
older child and only son, Benjamin Abrahms. Ben, this is my sister
Nellie."

I stood with my mouth open. I'm not sure she had ever mentioned Ben since our first conversation in Santa Monica.

"We can come in for a minute if you like," she said. "We're on
our way downtown for theater tickets. Not that it was easy to wrest
Ben from his sister for long enough."

I opened the door farther and stood aside as they came in. I couldn't take my eyes off Ben Abrahms but didn't know whether it was acceptable to look at him at all. I took their raincoats and umbrellas, asked if I could give them a cup of coffee or a drink, then remembered the last time I'd seen Louisa with a drink and tried to figure out whether Ben was old enough to be offered one.

Louisa laughed and said she thought coffee. As we went back to the kitchenette and I made the coffee, they sat on the nearest sofa and Louisa proceeded to tell Ben the story of our last evening together, about trying to be on good behavior for this lawyer and his daughter, both of whom were clearly partial to Nell, and about how she drank too much, talked too much and did a veritable alphabet of unpardonable acts. Clearly she needed me to know she knew how she'd been. Just as clearly, Ben didn't care. He volunteered nothing but, in response to her questions and prompting, told me he was twenty years old and would graduate from MIT the following year. He and the girl he'd been living with would stay in Boston and become engineers.

If you'd seen him and Louisa without knowing they were related, you would not have guessed. I remember thinking that perhaps Ben had been told by his father that he had to put in time with his mother to reap certain financial rewards. His very manner was an announcement that he would make no concessions beyond spending the time and being civil. He eyed Louisa from what appeared to be an extraordinary distance as she talked about the making up they had to do and how sorry she was that her father, Ben's grandfather, could not be a part of it.

At first, as we sat over coffee, Louisa seemed to be hunkering down for a visit and forgetting about theater tickets. Then, in response to a question from me, Ben said his entire family was in Brookline, where he'd been raised.

I asked about siblings.

"Two sisters and a brother," he said. "My mother stays home with them."

There was no hint of defiance; she'd been his mother all those years and he wasn't going to stop calling her that now. Louisa seemed about to say something, but instead she remembered the theater tickets. A few minutes later they had on their slickers. It was as she was searching for her bag that she came upon my notes for this book, which I'd realized were on the table near the front door only as I was opening the door to her.

I froze.

Louisa leaned over to see better, looked at me with a strained smile. The working title I had given the chapter about my developing relation with Louisa was "Actual Malice."

"What have we here? Have you gone back to work?"

I shrugged. "Sort of." But I wasn't comfortable with the lie. "I mean, not at the office. I've just been . . . setting down some memories . . . you know . . . of Dad."

"Oh-ho," she said with forced gaiety, "another writer in the family, huh?"

"Not really," I said. "I just haven't been able to think of very much else."

I had actually come to a point in the writing when I needed a better sense of the part his gambling interests had played in my father's life. Byron Koenig could be helpful on the financial issues, but they weren't the ones that most interested me. And I was reluctant to call Byron during this period that was understood to be the last part of my leave, if not the first part of my resignation.

The more I thought about it, the more convinced I became that Shimmy would be the best person to talk to. Furthermore, I missed Grace and was dying to tell her face-to-face the latest chapter in the Louisa saga. From the day of the service, Shimmy and Grace had been the only people to offer me something resembling real comfort. I thought of how at the memorial service, with all the others gone (Louisa had returned to Penelope), we'd sat around at Grace's, talking. At one point I'd told them I knew for the first time why religion had been invented and only wished I were a proper Jew so I could find some consolation in it. Shimmy, smiling, had said, "You know, Moses didn't say, 'I made you a religion,' he said, 'I made you a *people*.' If we can't offer the idea of a God, what we offer might still provide a reasonable life."

I phoned Shimmy now to ask if we could have a talk. We made a dinner date for the following Sunday night as casually as though I were already in Los Angeles. I called Grace to tell her I was coming out on Sunday. She said I must be dodging her on purpose; she and the family were going to Hawaii. I promised to try to extend my stay so I could see her when they returned.

It's difficult for me, in talking about Shimmy, to know whether to describe him as I knew him for most of my life or as I came to know him. He is the only educated man I've ever known whose force of personality is as great as my father's was. Having been skinny-muscular though small, a superb tennis player all his life, he'd finally developed a small pot, which he had the habit of patting after a good dinner. He adored and still adores it, and once gave a friend who teased him about it a speech on the pleasures of having such a possession. Aside from what I will have to call a loveliness of the soul, the characteristic that distinguishes Shimmy from a lot of other men who are something like him is his beautiful and cultivated speech, riding on a baritone that would probably, if he were a different person, have been trained for the opera.

Having called him on what I thought of as a practical matter, I was surprised and pleased to find myself looking forward simply to seeing Shimmy. I made reservations at the Beverly Hills Hotel, which was pleasant but large enough to be impersonal, and decided not to tell anyone who didn't know already of my visit. I packed the motion for summary judgment and a copy of *Miriam's Days of Rage*, which Vaughn had sent over with the motion. I would have to get a better feeling for the novel if I was going even to consider returning to Simon & Koenig to represent Vaughn in court. This was another matter to discuss with Shimmy, who'd been responsible for my father's finding Ronald Chow and who had a wonderful brain for all kinds of considerations beyond the legal.

Our first evening was even better than I'd expected, and in ways I hadn't foreseen. At six-thirty Shimmy met me in the hotel lobby. (He said he *could* do late dinners, but he had never gotten over liking early ones.) We walked around the block, then back into one of the hotel's dining rooms, where he'd made reservations. I chattered the whole time, I'm not sure about what, except I remember telling him about *Miriam's Days of Rage*.

When we'd ordered drinks, Shimmy—I think to slow down the torrent of words coming from me—took my hands between his and asked how I was doing with life in general.

I burst into tears.

"Oh, my God," I said, when the tears had diminished enough to allow speech, "I can't believe it. I'm sorry. I didn't know I . . . If I'd known this was going to happen . . . I don't know what's wrong with me." Once again, I was really crying. A waiter came over. Out of the corner of one eye I could see Shimmy motion him away.

"There's nothing wrong with you, Sweetheart," he said. (I had not been called that name since my father's death.) "Your papa was a powerful guy, and he loved you, and he left a big gap in your life, and you need to . . . talk about him. Talk about whatever is on your mind, including him."

"Oh, Shimmy," I sobbed, "thank you so much. Thank you, thank you, you're absolutely right, I just . . . " I finished my martini; he ordered another one for each of us. I said that in the months since my father's death, he had dominated my life more thoroughly than he had when he was alive, and that I'd begun writing a memoir as much to combat the situation as to take advantage of it. I told him that, leave of absence or none, I found it difficult to work alone, or at least not to have other people to talk to when I came up for air. I felt much needier than I ever had upon coming home from the office at night.

I talked my way through dinner, dessert, coffee and liqueur, holding back virtually nothing, before it occurred to me that I had failed to talk about what had brought me to Los Angeles in the first place. I felt myself blush. "I not only haven't talked about the gambling stuff, I haven't even asked about you or Grace or anything. I know she's in Hawaii. I said maybe I'd stay till she got back. I know the kids are fine. And I know she's doing a lot of work for Cedars of Lebanon."

Shimmy smiled. "Remember when the Women's Movement was convincing rich women it was evil to work for no money?"

I nodded but then grew concerned. "Well, there were real issues, even if—"

"Sure, sure," Shimmy said, "but they didn't touch Gracie. Gracie wanted to stay home and watch her children grow up."

I was too happy just then to tell him Grace had recently confided in me some sense of regret, as her youngest began reading college brochures, at not having attended law school.

"Meanwhile," I said, "I've blown my chance to ask you all the stuff I wanted to about my father."

"Well," Shimmy said, "I guess we'll do that tomorrow night. Unless you have other plans."

"Do you mean it?" I asked. "Can you really? You're not busy?"

He shrugged. "If I am, it'll have to be changed."

"Oh, Shimmy, you're being too good, I can't stand it."

I was crying again. This time he didn't try to comfort me but just sat there looking amused. When I'd calmed down, he paid the check, and we took another walk, this time along Wilshire.

I told him I was certain the decision to get rid of the business interest in the casinos had been a good one, but that now, as I wrote about my father, I felt the need to learn a little more about what went on in them. Shimmy said I was welcome to read whatever files he had—duplicates, basically, of the ones at Simon & Koenig, although he wasn't sure he had everything—and I told him I was scared of finding out more than I actually wanted to know.

"Ah, yes," he said.

"The casinos are a real problem for me," I admitted. "Tahoe more than Atlantic City, because I have a better idea of who runs Tahoe than I do of the whole Jersey scene. Maybe I've just avoided knowing too much. I know it sounds ridiculous, but I didn't want to know where the money was coming from. Even if it's legal, it's . . . it's . . . " But I couldn't finish the sentence.

"You're a real sweetheart," Shimmy said after a moment. "A sweetheart describing a serious problem as though it were some *mishegoss* of your own."

I didn't know whether to cry again or to hug him. My solution, as we neared the hotel, was to blow him a kiss and run inside, saying I'd phone him in the morning.

"I know he was involved with some pretty unsavory guys at Tahoe," I said on Monday night, as we sat in Shimmy's favorite Italian restaurant.

"Mmm," Shimmy said. His manner was more cautious than it had been the previous evening. "You know I didn't handle that part of his life."

"Yes. And I know you know plenty about it anyway."

He shrugged. "A lot of it is widely known. The building of the Henley Plaza and so on."

"I suppose what I want to know is whether the stuff that's widely known is true."

He smiled. "I suppose you could say that what's widely known is usually partly true."

I smiled back. "Why are you being cagy?"

"Because," Shimmy said, "I'm not sure what you really want to know."

"Was the Henley controlled by gangsters?"

"Yes."

"Is that why he left as soon as he could? Or did he just want to get back into the movies?"

Shimmy hesitated.

"More hesitation," I said.

"For the first time you've phrased a question in a way that makes it difficult to answer simply."

"Why?"

315

Still he hesitated.

"I'm not going to get upset," I promised, without being certain I could keep the promise.

"Well," Shimmy said, "I think you're upset already. But I think you want to know, and even if it upsets you, we'll live through it."

I felt a great surge of affection for him, and as the feeling passed through me, so did the casual observation that Shimmy wasn't as homely as I'd once thought him. If he was awfully short and not at all handsome, the intelligence and kindness in his face made him appealing in some way much more important than good features.

"I couldn't answer the question because when he came back into the movies, Antsy Lantz came back with him."

"Antsy Lantz?" I knew I'd heard the name somewhere. "Wasn't he a gangster?"

"Mmm. Albert Lantz."

Again, Shimmy waited to see if I wanted him to continue.

"Okay," I said—a statement and a question.

"We all knew each other in the Bronx," Shimmy said. "Antsy and I from the time we were very young. Your dad from the time he came to live with his aunt and uncle. Your dad was intrigued with all the tough-guy stuff, Antsy and the others. He was a country boy but a very restless one. The city was enormously exciting to him. He wanted to know how everything worked, including the gangsters Antsy hung out with from pretty early on."

I nodded.

"They saw each other occasionally when your father was in college, but then they lost touch when he got married, and so on. But after the war Antsy was out West and he saw your dad's name in the papers. I don't know exactly when. When he married your mother. Or when he went to work for Abe Starr. Whenever.

"Antsy wanted to be in the movies. He was a very handsome fellow, curly black hair, a Garfield type, as we used to say. Except there was something in his face that came out of who he was. He looked like a hood and sounded like a hood, and he couldn't really play anything else. Your father got him a couple of hood parts, but that was all he could do, and Antsy got bored. He was a very restless character—the nickname didn't come out of nothing. I don't know that he'd have been good as a matinee idol even if they'd been willing to try to turn him into one. The real matinee idols I've known have been capable of just being there, soaking up the camera's admiration the way the rest of us take in the sun or a cool drink.

316

"Anyway, Antsy took off for Tahoe. He hooked into his old pals, who were just beginning to build casinos. By the time your father was in trouble at Starr-Flexner, Antsy was able to repay the old favor. He got Sam into his group's casino with a relatively small investment. They were delighted to have a Hollywood producer in with them, actually. Hollywood was their idea of class."

Shimmy paused to gauge how I was reacting to all this, but I had passed the point of no return.

"That was all they wanted from him? The association?"

"Well . . . obviously there were other considerations. Connections. Later—"

"Later?"

"Later, when he came back, he . . . started Egremont."

"Mmm." I remembered the time when he'd been absorbed in those negotiations. But there was some restraint in Shimmy's manner suggestive of something being left out. "He started Egremont and . . . ?"

He paused. "And aside from Antsy, a lot of their money came with him."

So that was it. The gangsters had come back to Hollywood with my father.

Shimmy was eating slowly, but I had lost my appetite. I was trying to think of what I might have known about Egremont and the rest of my father's business life that I hadn't known that I knew.

"They had a substantial share in Egremont?"

"I have all the papers, but I haven't really looked at them. Your dad liked me, you know, to have the records. Unless I'm mistaken, it was in the neighborhood of fifty percent."

"Unless you're mistaken. You don't know for sure because you didn't handle that stuff for him."

Shimmy shook his head, avoided my eyes.

"How come?" I asked. "I'm sure he would have *wanted* you to do it."

Shimmy smiled sadly. "Let's just say I found it necessary . . . and possible . . . to draw the lines in different places than Sam did."

I spent most of the next three days in Shimmy's office, alternately talking with him and reading the fairly extensive files that my father had asked him to keep, even on matters he didn't handle. Bits and pieces of what I learned I had known in a general way all along but hadn't thought much about.

At the end of those three days I had a good sense of Egremont's history. A lot of it was interesting; some was funny; some anything but. One of the reasons Shimmy and I drew close over those days was that our sense of which was which was almost identical. Another was our common sense of the difficulties I might face with my half sister, whichever way I decided to go in the matter of holding on to my Egremont shares. Shimmy still felt constrained from any real conversation about Louisa by his lawyerly relation to her. But each time her name came up I felt more certain it was self-restraint rather than lack of opinion that kept him from advising me.

By the end of the second day I had stopped apologizing to him for the amount of time I was taking. By the middle of the third, I was asking him whether I had done anything specific, beyond taking too much of his time, to anger his secretary, a beautiful, black ex-actress named Livia Gibbons.

"Of course you have," Shimmy said.

"What?" I asked, startled in spite of myself.

"You have," Shimmy said, "engaged the attention of her favorite boss."

I smiled, pretending to look at the file in my lap. The three days and two evenings with him had been my best since my father's death—perhaps for some considerable time before that. We'd walked, talked, eaten, drunk and laughed, then walked and talked some more. He and the material at hand had fully absorbed me. But there was something, either in the words or in his way of saying them, that I hadn't heard before and that made me uncomfortable.

I shrugged, looked past his shoulder, laughed.

"Well, then, I guess she's just going to have to be mad."

"Looks that way," Shimmy said, which made me even more uneasy.

I asked if Grace and her family weren't due home that day. He said, Oh, yes, he'd meant to tell me. Grace had called. They were having too good a time to leave, and she requested I hang in for another couple of days. I said I wasn't sure hanging in was precisely what I was doing, but if Shimmy was willing for me to keep bothering him, I was delighted to do so. Shimmy said that not only was he willing, but he had decided to cook dinner for me.

I laughed.

He feigned injury.

I laughed again.

"You don't believe me?" he asked.

I shook my head.

"So . . . you are unwilling to take a chance on my cooking an acceptable dinner?"

"I would take *any* chance on you," I said. "And eat any dinner you cooked. Acceptable or not."

"Very well then. We shall go our separate ways for the nonce, in the hope that Miss Livia will show up for work tomorrow not looking as though a spiked heel just went into her toe. When I've finished what I have to do here, I will ring you in your room, and you will come down, and I will drive you to my home, where I will make your dinner."

"And shall I dress for the occasion?" I asked happily.

"Indeed. Jeans, and something spilled tomato sauce looks good on," Shimmy said.

He picked me up shortly after six in the red Triumph that was his only apparent concession to having moved to Southern California. His home was in Westwood because he was "more comfortable with dry academics than with all-wet Hollywood types." It was a pretty brick-and-stucco two-story house set on a street that might have been in one of the comfortable Eastern suburbs, and was furnished with the pleasant traditional furniture I remembered from New Rochelle. Photographs of him and Vivian, their children and grandchildren, lined the hallway, but there was only one photograph, of Vivian with their grandchildren, in the living room. (He could deal with *grand*children, he said, at any time of day or night.) The only alteration he'd made to the house had been to add a large Eastern-style screened porch in the back, to be entered through the kitchen.

The phone was ringing when we walked in but stopped.

I had worn jeans, as ordered. Shimmy excused himself for long enough to change into chinos and a red-and-black-checked flannel shirt that made me think of Barnard and Columbia, no doubt because that was where I'd first seen one.

"I remember Vivi's cooking," I said, as he opened wine and began taking covered dishes out of the refrigerator. He'd already informed me that he had cooked the stew early in the morning and left a note for the housekeeper to put it away when it was cool. He took a rather touching pride in his competence in the kitchen, which had come only since Vivian's death.

He looked at me. "You do?"

"She made turkey the first time we came for Christmas. Turkey with a divine chestnut stuffing. I remember meeting the kids, and then we were playing Ping-Pong in the basement. When we came upstairs for lunch Vivi served it. But it still didn't really hit me until I wanted something, a glass of milk maybe with dessert, and she said I should just go and take it, and I went into this huge kitchen, and there was no one there. At first I was puzzled. I'd been in houses like that, no help in the kitchen, but they were the other side of the tracks. You were on the right side of the tracks. Suddenly I realized Vivi was wearing an apron. She must have done the cooking. Furthermore, she looked *happy*. As if she'd been having a good time. It was a major revelation."

Shimmy, smiling, poured two glasses of red wine and sat at the kitchen table, facing me. We clinked glasses.

"To more good times," Shimmy said. "And more major revelations."

I did not take this toast to have specific meaning. Having managed not to perceive his interest in me until then, I suppose it's unsurprising that I should have continued not to understand. Anyway, Shimmy set the stew over a low flame, made a Caesar salad and continued to pour the delicious California red he called one of the compensations for having moved there. He was one of the few people I'd ever known who, in the course of becoming a wine expert, had not lost the simple pleasure of drinking. He did none of those routines that have become familiar from the people he calls the *nouveau fineschmeckern*. But he'd stood up two bottles in the morning, and he opened one in my view, then the other while I was washing up. By the time the food was ready, he'd fetched the other bottle, and by the time we'd finished the food, which was wonderful, that bottle was nearly empty, too.

I was so *happy*. There again was that word whispering itself into my ear. I was having such a *good time*. My brain became absorbed in any issue Shimmy raised, whether it was my memory with regard to some case or if I had been a guest on the day that his kids decided to do such and such, but that wasn't what I was happy about. I was happy to *be* with him, to be responding to his stories. How on earth had I ever been able to think of Shimmy as homely? Those eyes that had once seemed small now had an irrelevant size and twinkled in a luscious way when he told a funny story; the big bony nose was a lovable, comfortable nose on the wonderful face of a man who could be trusted with my life as well as my father's.

The phone was ringing. Shimmy answered and told whoever it was he'd call back in the morning. I announced, feeling I spoke nothing less than the truth, that this was the best meal I'd ever had. Shimmy suggested we bring what remained of the second bottle out to the porch. I giggled. I was about to make a joke about what he was trying to do to me, then became flustered because this was an inappropriate remark to make to Grace's father.

"What happened?" Shimmy asked.

"Nothing," I said, but I stood up too quickly and knocked over my wineglass.

"Are you sure?" he asked, picking up the glass and motioning to me not to bother trying to clean the table with my cloth napkin.

"I'm just a little drunk, I think. I know that's ridiculous, on half a bottle of wine."

"You had more than a bottle, actually."

"Oh?" I giggled again. "But who's counting?"

"*I* was," Shimmy said. "I wasn't counting yours, but I was counting mine."

"Why?"

"I was pacing myself," he said solemnly. "For a seduction."

"Oh, indeed." There was another one of those foolish giggles. "I'm sure. Well, then, by all means, let me have the last glass. I'll take it out to the porch while you pace yourself."

With the glass, I walked out to the porch, where I stood watching a cluster of birds on the feeder that hung from the biggest tree in the yard. The phone rang again, but a moment later he had joined me on the porch. We were standing side by side, looking out at the backyard, when my brain finally processed the conversation we'd had moments before, and my hand squeezed the wineglass so tightly that it broke and cut the hand even as wine dribbled down on my jeans.

I turned to him. "That wasn't funny."

"I'll say," he muttered.

He set down his own glass, pried my fingers away from the part of the glass they still held, took my wrist and led me into the kitchen. At the sink, he ran warm and then cold water over the bleeding cuts. He ordered me to stay under the cold water while he fetched Mercurochrome, cotton, tape and gauze to dress my hand. The wounds were superficial, he informed me.

"I meant it wasn't funny to say you were pacing yourself for a seduction," I said when he'd finished dressing the hand and was closing the gauze package.

"I wasn't trying to be funny," Shimmy said.

"Then what were you trying to do?" I demanded.

"I was trying," Shimmy said after a pause, "to place in your mind a thought to which it had not previously given a home."

"Shimmy!" I wailed. "You were one of my father's best friends! You were surely his best lawyer!"

"So?"

"So . . . so . . . so I don't know! But it's crazy! How old are you, anyway? Sixty-two?"

"Sixty-three, actually. In two years I get my first Social Security check. On the other hand, I can still get it up when I'm so inclined and have had enough sleep, and I—"

"Stop!"

"Why? After all, you're no spring chicken either. How old are you? Thirty-six-almost-seven? That's not so far from forty. Soon you'll be too old to have children, if you're not already."

"That's just fine with me! I have no intention of having children!"

We had begun to shout and now, as he answered me, Shimmy took my elbow and led me back into the kitchen, closing the door behind us.

"Okay," he said, "that's one reason gone. You don't have to worry about whether I'm too old to get you pregnant. Or whether I'll be around to help with the children."

I burst into tears. He looked around the kitchen, led me into the living room, where my eyes fell on the series of snapshots scattered around the room.

"Grace!" I said. "Your grandchildren! What will they say?"

"I have no idea," Shimmy replied. "Are you suggesting I be guided in my affections by what my daughter or grandchildren will say?"

"Grace is one of my best friends!" I wailed.

"Well, then," Shimmy said, "I can only hope that if we were by some chance to find ourselves together, she would be happy for both of us."

My head was reeling. I stared at him, trying to focus on his face as though in so doing I might come to understand what I wanted from him. I thought I might pass out; I think I must have reeled slightly. As I did, Shimmy came toward me, held out his arms and (standing on tiptoe, as he confessed much later) wrapped them around me and engaged me in a long, sensual kiss to which I was almost instantly responsive and in the middle of which the phone began to ring.

Shimmy seemed bent on ignoring it, but I froze and pushed

322

him away, probably because the thought that had come into my mind was that it was Grace calling. He let go of me and went to the kitchen phone rather than the one in the living room, perhaps because the thought in *his* mind was that it was one of the many women friends he'd already made in Los Angeles.

I'm not sure I can explain adequately what I did next. If I had been as drunk as it will make me sound, surely I would have been too drunk to do it.

I couldn't tell how much time was passing. How much time, that is, Shimmy was spending on the phone. My eye fell on the attaché case full of papers about the estate that I'd brought with me. It was on a chair to the left of the living room entrance along with the large handbag in which I toted around the essentials of life. As I stood waiting and weaving in the middle of the living room, my feelings altered from a willingness to consider the possibilities to a simmering indignation and finally to a powerful drunken rage that here I was finally ready to give Shimmy a chance at my sovereign person, and he wasn't even appreciative, certainly he was in no rush to give it a shot.

I grabbed my pocketbook and attaché case and left his house, walked the half mile or so into the center of Westwood, called a cab from the first phone I found and told the driver to take me to the hotel. Shimmy would worry. It would serve him right. What kind of games was he playing with me, anyway? *What would Grace say?* By the time we were within blocks of the hotel, I'd changed my mind. I told the driver to take me to the airport. My clothes and other stuff could be shipped back after me. No way I was staying in this dumb town for another minute!

The Red Eye was leaving in ten minutes and there were plenty of seats. I did not sleep on the plane. The Scotch I had toward that end seemed to undo the effects of the earlier wine instead of enhancing them, and I grew tense to the point of a sort of rigid bounciness. Magazines were useless. The in-flight movie was painless but uncompelling. The man on my left, after ignoring me for the first three hours, talked constantly and asked for my number in New York. I gave it to him although if he had told me his name, I didn't remember it by this time. It seemed just as well to be collecting males. Shimmy had pointed out I'd be forty before I knew it. I'd never felt as though birthdays aged me while they'd been celebrated with my father. Now . . . I was probably lucky anyone at all was interested in me. It couldn't last forever.

Reaching my apartment around seven on Wednesday morning, I collected my mail from the elevator man, lay down with it on the sofa and fell into a deep sleep from which I awakened at eleven o'clock. I was hungry, filthy and miserable but I was also feeling something that made other feelings unimportant: I was feeling the absence of a life.

I'd come to understand since my father's death, if not earlier, that my life was more bound up with his than was good for me. But I'd never felt any constraint in the matter of being interested in other men. I had been divorced for seven years and dated quite a few people. More than once I'd been told by some woman that I was lucky still to have men interested in me. I felt luckier when *I* was interested in *them*, since there were remarkably few who held my attention. Only since my father's death had it occurred to me to wonder if interest was enough. Wasn't it about time I fell in love again? On the other hand, I could not imagine that some man might come along and fill the enormous gap that had been left in my life.

That was what I was feeling right now: Women I knew talked about having good lives *except*, the except being the absence of a man. What I was feeling was the absence of a *woman*—me. I had a perfectly good life with things to do and people to see. What I didn't have was a person to enjoy that life!

The only time in recent months I'd felt otherwise was during my evenings with Shimmy. And this might mean I was in trouble. I could easily forgive myself for any worry or trouble I might cause Shimmy, who, if he hadn't created my difficulties, had at the very least made them too clear to me. He had presented himself as a solution, but the problem on his mind was not the one on my own.

Perhaps Shimmy had called, and I'd been too deeply asleep to hear the phone ring.

No. That was silly. Why would it even occur to him that I had left California?

Maybe I wasn't being nice. If I was feeling better about him in a while, perhaps I'd call his office and ask Livia to tell him I'd flown back.

The only things in my kitchen worth eating were a bag of Fritos and some salsa in a jar. I polished them off with a Coke as I looked through my mail, none of which interested me in the least. Then I ran water for a bath I got out of five minutes after getting in, taking a shower that was slightly more acceptable, if only because I could pace in the stall. I think I washed my hair three times. It was shoulder length at this point and took a while to dry if I didn't use the dryer. I could barely remember which city I was in, much less what the weather was like outside, but I had no intention of sitting indoors with a dryer for any length of time. I was going to take a walk, get some real breakfast and then come back to the house and look at Vaughn Cameron's . . . Uh-oh. All that stuff was still in my hotel room. . . . No big deal. When Shimmy called I'd ask him if he could have . . . Shimmy must have been trying frantically the various places in Los Angeles where he thought I might be. It would never in a million years have occurred to him . . .

I called the Beverly Hills Hotel and asked for messages. Vaughn Cameron had called, as well as another New York friend who'd guessed where I might be when I didn't pick up my phone. I hung up, then called again and asked for the hotel office, explaining that I'd been forced to leave suddenly and requesting they gather and hold my belongings until I could have them picked up.

I called Shimmy's office. Livia did not exclaim about their efforts to find me. Either he hadn't told her or . . . Or what? The possibility that he hadn't made an effort did not enter my mind. That is to say, when it tried, I closed the door. I asked Livia to tell Shimmy, when he was free, that I was in my apartment in New York. Diabolically, she asked whether I wanted him to call. "Only if he feels like it," I said, cursing myself as the words came out of my mouth. Livia said she would give him the message and hung up, leaving me in a state of rage and humiliation unbecoming to the professional woman I was supposed to be.

Maybe it was time to go back to Simon & Koenig, if only to get back my grown-up bearings.

I put on a pair of jeans and a sweatshirt, combed my wet hair and left the house without a jacket. But it was New York, and spring hadn't returned when I did. I was freezing but took a vengeful pleasure in my own discomfort—as though it represented a way of getting even with Shimmy, not to speak of everyone else in the world who wasn't taking proper care of me.

I made up my mind not to think about Shimmy.

I wanted to think about . . . What? Who I was? Who I wasn't? The words meant everything and nothing at the same time. I was a lawyer, but that was the only thing I was certain I was. Didn't other people have better I.D. than just their jobs?

As I walked down Seventh Avenue, debating whether to negotiate the crowds on Fifth, I found myself thinking I'd *like* to know what was going on at Simon & Koenig, aside from the Cameron suit. It was more than four months since I'd been in my office.

There had been times when I'd felt I would be better off forgetting the memoirs and going back to work. On the other hand, the only matter that had interested me until now was Vaughn's libel suit. I was going to have to have *someone* send me the book as well as the motion for summary judgment.

What day of the week was it, anyway? Unless my head was even more messed up than I knew, it was still Wednesday. But of course it was the end of a New York workday, or close to the end, if only for the secretaries.

Shimmy would be out to lunch.

I didn't like the fact that this had even entered my mind. Shimmy had a lot of nerve, acting as though he were someone I might fall in love with . . . or at any rate acting as though our ages were not an appropriate issue. Denying that I might . . . might . . . might what?

The sun had gone behind clouds, and I could no longer ignore the fact that I was freezing. I went into a doughnut place on Seventh Avenue and had a sandwich and three coffees, the last with a doughnut. Or was it a muffin? By the time I was heading for home, I wasn't sure anymore.

The phone was ringing as I entered the apartment. I ran to it only to be greeted by the voice of a solicitor for someone running for Congress. I hung up on her, cursing myself for having dashed to pick it up, vowing I wouldn't do the same on the next ring no matter what, a vow I did not have a chance to test because it did not ring again.

At some point I called Vaughn Cameron and left a message on his machine, saying that I was in New York but I'd left the book and papers in California. I told him that if this didn't irritate him so much that he wanted to have nothing further to do with me, perhaps he would like to have duplicates sent to my apartment, where I expected to be for at least a few days. An hour later, the elevator man brought me a package containing duplicates of everything Vaughn had given me.

I'd tried reading various papers, magazines and books that were around the house, but my mind had bounced off them like a Spaldeen from a sidewalk. Besides, it angered me that the expression, which was Shimmy's, even came into my mind. I determined to settle in with Cameron vs. Aldebaran Press and Cameron. When I'd tried talking to Shimmy about my interest in the case, he'd laughed and said that since he liked having me in California, he wasn't about to encourage me to get involved with a libel suit in

New York. Come to think of it, that was the first hint I'd had of Shimmy's whatever-you-wanted-to-call-it, his interest in me. I hadn't taken it that way, but it seemed now . . .

For the first time it occurred to me, at least occurred to me in some way that made it seem important, that I might have hurt Shimmy's feelings. I bounced up from the sofa, bolted to the phone, dialed his number and was rewarded when he picked it up himself on the first ring, as he often did when Livia was out or with him taking dictation.

"It's me, Nellie," I said. "I'm sorry."

After a moment, Shimmy said, "Okay."

I said, "I didn't mean to worry you."

Shimmy said, "You didn't."

It hadn't sounded like a question.

"I can't tell whether you're asking if I did or saying that I didn't."

"The latter."

This, of course, gave me pause. After a moment, I asked him if this was a bad time to talk. He said that it wasn't, if I would just give him a minute. The minute passed, and he returned to the phone.

I asked him if he was angry with me, and instead of dismissing the idea, he said, "Of course."

I asked whether it would make things better if I apologized, and he said, "Why don't you give it a shot and see?"

Smiling in spite of myself, I said, "I'm truly sorry that I worried you."

"No, no," Shimmy said. "You asked if I was worried and I said that I wasn't. You're not apologizing for worrying me, you're apologizing for your rudeness."

"My God!" I exploded. "I can see why you're such a bitch of a lawyer!" Then I got scared that he would become angry again and hang up. "I'm sorry. I'm sorry I called you a bitch of a lawyer, and I'm sorry that I . . . I'm sorry I was thoughtless, but I don't see why I'm apologizing if you weren't even worried."

"I wasn't worried. You're not my daughter, after all, or some little kid who can't take care of herself. Acting like one doesn't turn you back into one, or even more people would do it. You are apologizing for having behaved badly. I made you a beautiful dinner and attempted a seduction. You not only rejected me, but you did it in a rude and untoward manner and hurt my feelings."

I was on the verge of tears.

"All right," I said. "I get it. I'm sorry." My voice broke over the edge. I sat down on the rug and collapsed into a real cry. I apologized but I couldn't stop. After a while, Shimmy said that he thought it would be a good idea if I hung up and he finished what he was doing and called me in a couple of hours. I nodded as though he were there with me.

"Okay?" Shimmy asked.

I said that of course it was okay and hung up. Only as I replaced the receiver did I remember my clothes and stuff at the hotel. I picked up the phone, ordered enough food for ten people from the closest Chinese restaurant and sat down on the sofa with *Miriam's Days of Rage.*

The novel's title has a dual meaning, referring to the 1968 actions of the Chicago "radicals" but also to the rage the main female character lives with every day of her life and the hero envies. Grant Marsh is a wealthy but pallid to the point of caricature academic teaching at the University. He falls in love with Miriam's rage as much as with her beautiful, intense Jewish looks and her general creativity. She's welcomed by a radical-action group because of Grant's wealth. But the way she's treated by the group's young male radicals, most of whom are at least as interested in waging war against Jewish Mothers as against Gentile Politicians, brings her rage to full flower. What she does with this rage is to allow herself to become pregnant with a baby she doesn't want. In the book's eerily quiet denouement, she jumps from the terrace of their Lake Shore Drive apartment, her three-week-old baby in her arms. The baby dies, but she lives.

I'd finished *Miriam's Days of Rage,* eaten enough Chinese food to last me for weeks, put away the leftovers, cleaned up after myself in a way I seldom did, and written down some of my thoughts about the novel, and still Shimmy hadn't called. When I asked myself how he could do this to me, a voice came back to ask me what I meant by "this." So I stopped thinking about it at all.

It was almost six-thirty. The phone rang. I let it ring twice, not without effort, then picked it up and said hello as though no one in particular were on my mind.

It was Vaughn, wanting to make sure I'd received the stuff. I told him that I'd already skimmed the book and was about to tackle the papers. He asked me if I might by chance be free to have dinner with him, and I said I'd be delighted. He said he was down at the offices of Simon & Koenig, and if it was all right with me, he'd walk directly over to my place. I told him that would be fine and hung up. The phone rang again. I picked it up and said hello.

"Hiya, Toots," Shimmy said. "How you doin'?"

I said I was okay, although I wasn't certain it was true. I told him I'd realized only after speaking to him that I'd been so upset I'd left all my stuff at the hotel.

Shimmy laughed.

I told him I wasn't feeling interested in the gambling-movie business, that in fact the only matter I'd been able to think about at all was the Cameron libel suit.

He said I'd mentioned it but not discussed it at any length, unless he'd forgotten, and I said he knew perfectly well he never forgot anything. He said that in point of fact, age was taking its toll and this simply wasn't true anymore.

I cite this as an example of how we could no longer have a simple conversation.

"I was really sorry before," I told him after a pause. "I wasn't just saying it."

"Fine," he said. "It's over and done with."

I laughed. "At least it will be when I get my papers and clothes."

I waited for him to offer to mail them to me. Instead he asked how I proposed to do this. I laughed again and asked if he was hinting I ought to get back on a plane and pick them up.

"Well," he said, "if you're looking for an excuse to come back and finish your visit, that might be as good as any you'll find."

Thus did Shimmy Kagan advise me that if I'd come to California five days earlier innocent of the possibilities and of him as a living, breathing, sexual male, I might not do the same again.

"Well," I said, "then I guess all I have to do is figure out whether that's what I'm looking for."

He was silent.

"I'll call you later," I said. I was having so much difficulty breathing it was difficult to envision getting to an airport, much less onto a plane. "Good-bye."

I hung up and jogged around my living room for a while, trying to figure out why I'd been such an idiot as to complicate my life by planning dinner with Vaughn Cameron. The answer came rather more quickly than I would have willed it to: I had accepted Vaughn's invitation because I was terrified of how I would feel if Shimmy didn't call me again. Or if he did.

329

Oh, Jesus.

Vaughn would be there in a few minutes and all I could think about was the next plane to Los Angeles.

I dialed Simon & Koenig. The receptionist told me Mr. Cameron had left. I dialed his home number and left a message on his machine that if he by any chance picked up his messages before coming to my house, he should please call me. Then I called TWA and ascertained that the last flight would be at 10:15, an iffy proposition even if I were to succeed in heading off Vaughn. I reserved a seat on the 8:55 the next morning, washed my face and hands and was looking for a dress to put on when Vaughn knocked at the door.

"Vaughn," I said, "I'm sorry. I'm not ready. I'm slightly hysterical. I never should've accepted your invitation because I ate like a pig a couple of hours ago."

Vaughn smiled, shrugged. "I'm not hungry, either, it was just the right time to say dinner. If we need food later, we'll get some pizza."

I was reminded once again of what an utterly amiable human being he was, how much easier to get along with than someone like Shimmy. Which was not to say that Vaughn wasn't intelligent. Or talented. He was all of these. I really liked him. It was going to be a problem to get him out early enough to get some sleep before I left for the airport at seven-thirty in the morning.

I opened a bottle of white wine, and we settled into one of the sofas, raising glasses in a vaguely formal acknowledgment that we felt as though we knew each other better than we actually did. Vaughn said he had followed Louisa's libel suit as closely as he could from the papers, but the papers had been so absorbed in Yvette Lacombe and who was doing what to whom that they'd failed to deal with the interesting issues.

I relayed a bit of movie news heard on my trip, that Yvette Lacombe was about to be signed to play herself in a movie about her life with Campbell.

He winced.

"I suppose if I can't sell the rights to *Miriam's Days of Rage* it'll be just as well. Franya can sell her own story if she needs money."

I smiled.

"I guess you know I've offered her money." He sighed. "Money isn't what she wants. *Vindication* is. She claims her friends who haven't known her all along think she had a baby she threw off the roof."

I shook my head sympathetically, but I was careful to say nothing because it was my sense of Vaughn that if Franya suddenly decided to come back to him, he might take her.

I told him I would be happy to get him transcripts of the *Joe Stalbin* trial, but that I felt the issues in his case and Louisa's were quite different.

"I agree," he said. "That's one of the things I've been trying to get through to Cullen, but Cullen still thinks your sister put one over on the jury. It's not that he's stupid, but his brain just doesn't work the way . . . He has no grasp . . . One of the problems is that he, Cullen, *my own lawyer*, doesn't believe me when I tell him I've never met some friend of Franya's she's claiming I put in the book. One of the things Franya's doing . . . When she's finished finding similarities between the characters and real people, she waxes indignant over the differences! She's never had a pregnancy, an abortion or anything like it, so I thought it was safe. Her father takes a shot of whiskey perhaps twice a year. 'You made my father a drunk!' was one of the first things she said to me."

He had already emptied the last of the bottle into his glass. Now he grinned. "That reminds me . . . do you have more wine or shall I order some?"

I looked in the refrigerator and found half a bottle that had to be two weeks old. He called his liquor store, and in fifteen minutes a case with six bottles of refrigerator-cold white and six of room-temperature red had been delivered. He held up a bottle of red, asked how I felt about switching, and when I said red was fine, found the corkscrew and opened it. Once we were settled with the wine, he urged me to tell him more about the *Joe Stalbin* trial. His questions, when he interrupted me, were very much to the point.

I found myself in a pleasant and, of course, increasingly drunken mood. By the time we were on our second bottle of red, Vaughn had sent for a pizza, saying it seemed we should do so for safety's sake, a phrase that made us both laugh.

I was getting drunker and happier. I was delighted to find that the details of the book and the lawsuit, not to speak of Vaughn's life, interested me, even if I had increasing trouble keeping track of them. Or of anything else. Once or twice I reminded myself I had to call Shimmy to tell him I was flying back in the morning, but there was no sense of urgency attached to the reminder, and I forgot almost at the moment I remembered.

I had a couple of friends—one, another lawyer, the second woman ever hired by Simon & Koenig—who'd been to bed with

Vaughn Cameron and afterward sung his praises. They said he had the body of a Greek god, the stamina of a man who doesn't have to work for a living, and the desire to please of a slum kid fucking a movie star. I hadn't thought a great deal about these attributes. This was beginning to seem like a shame.

The pizza hadn't done a thing to sober me up, perhaps because I hadn't stopped drinking.

Vaughn was saying he had a series of index cards on which he'd noted, person by person, the similarities and differences between his characters and all the people they might be thought to have been based upon. I told him what a sensational idea this was and said I'd love to see the cards. He said he could get the cards right away, or *we* could, if I wished. I jumped up from the sofa, found my bag and announced my readiness with the bravado of the incapacitated. Vaughn said we could give it a shot, but he wouldn't put any money on our being able to make it. He wasn't really worried, though. There is a legacy of growing up with money I've observed only since knowing a lot of people who didn't, an assumption that even if the worst happens, something can be done about it.

He supported me to the elevator upstairs and from the elevator downstairs, where the first thing we saw (I should say *he* saw; I was walking in my sleep) was a horse-driven hansom cab, which he hailed and directed to his apartment house at Sixty-first and Park. At the house, the doorman, summoned by house phone, called someone else in a uniform who without any explanations being required, assisted Vaughn in assisting me from the cab, then accompanied us to his apartment, where Vaughn gave him the keys, and he opened the door for us, then disappeared.

Slightly more alert now, I told Vaughn that I was only accustomed to that sort of service in Los Angeles.

He said that Franya not only hadn't grown accustomed to it but had taken it as a challenge to her own capabilities.

"Oh, Christ," I said, "let's not talk about Franya right now."

"Sorry," he said, taking my hand and turning on lights as he guided me through the apartment.

We were standing in a large room with dark wood paneling that appeared to be a combination of bedroom and study. Vaughn led me to a leather love seat, where I plunked down without grace or delay.

"Welcome to what a friend of mine calls Ralph Lauren's Hunting World," said Vaughn. "Decorated by someone whose name shall not again pass my lips."

"You work here or sleep here?" I asked, half asleep but still curious.

"I do almost everything here. There are thirteen rooms in this apartment, and it would be fair to say I haven't been in five of them since . . . well, in years."

I yawned.

"Make yourself comfortable," Vaughn said. "I'll get something to drink."

"Mmm. Just what I need." I had the vague feeling there was a reason I shouldn't drink anymore, but I couldn't think of what it was.

Three walls of the room were lined, except for the fireplace in the middle of one, with bookcases of the same wood as the walls; against the fourth was a large bed with huge floral-patterned sheets and pillowcases and a tweedy throw that managed to tilt the balance back to where you could believe a heterosexual male voluntarily occupied the place. Floral rugs, until recently unacceptable to same if he was a bachelor, had been woven in the dark colors that would allow them to pass. A bearskin rug, complete with the bear's big old head, stretched in front of the love seat. A huge, beautiful mahogany-and-rosewood desk was set in front of the windows, which had louvered shutters. The green leather chair behind it was matched by a deep, soft armchair in one corner as well as a love seat in which I settled.

Vaughn returned with a tray holding yet another (it seemed like the hundredth although it might have been only the fourth or fifth) bottle of red wine, as well as glasses, a pitcher of water and a jar of macadamia nuts. More practiced in the art of seduction than circumstances required him to be, he poured wine for each of us, set the tray on an end table, then, his own glass in one hand, the jar of macadamia nuts in the other, stretched out on the bearskin and suggested that I might wish to do the same—unless I would prefer that he get the index cards for me.

"Oh, the index cards," I said, although I was having trouble keeping my eyes open, "I certainly do want to see the index cards."

Amiably, he stood, got them from his desk, brought them over and handed them to me.

I looked at the first one, giggled.

"Funny?" he asked.

"No," I said. "I forgot to bring my glasses."

"Oh? You wear glasses?" Vaughn asked.

"Only for reading," I assured him, then heard myself and giggled again. "But of course, that's what I'm trying to do. Isn't it?"

"I'm not sure," Vaughn said. He had resettled on the rug, a foot or two away and facing me. "You're being quite seductive, but I know you're drunk, and I understand that it might be . . . That is, I can't tell if you're doing it on purpose."

"The question," I said, "is whether you're willing to take advantage of it whether it's on purpose or not."

"Absolutely," he assured me. "As long as you won't be angry with me later."

"I'm never angry later," I promised, without having the vaguest idea of whether I spoke the truth.

He took from my hand the glass he had put into it, placing it, along with his own, back on the tray.

"I wish I'd known that sooner," he said, resettling on the rug but much closer, embracing me, giving me a splendid, long kiss.

He proceeded to help me undress in my drunken, half-asleep condition, led me to the bed, where he said I would be much more comfortable, and made love to my body with that combination of strength and tenderness so much sought in the making of TV commercials. When my body came and my brain traveled into oblivion, he waited quietly inside me for long enough so that I finally opened my eyes, and we repeated the process. Or, I should say, *he* repeated the process, and I was still there. It was only the third time this happened that my brain began to function just enough for me to realize something was wrong. Most particularly, that even as I was getting off with the democratic abandon of the drunk, Vaughn had not once surrendered himself to me.

I became uneasy. I'd heard about men like this—most often from friends saying they were going to put an ad in the paper to find one—but I hadn't previously encountered such a wonder. And I wasn't sure now was the right time to—

"Oh, my God!"

I tried to wriggle around from under him, but he had taken the exclamation for one of pleasure and pushed into me with greater force than before.

"No! Wait a minute!" I called out. "What time is it?"

Vaughn stopped moving. "Have I hurt you?" he asked anxiously, it being impossible for a sane person to believe I might be concerned about the time.

"No! Not at all! It's been delightful! I just . . . You're not going to believe this. What time is it?"

He looked at the clock on the table next to the bed.

"Four-twenty."

"Oh, Jesus."

I was awake, sober and aware that I was to be on a plane leaving Kennedy in four and a half hours while I, in the dark hours of the night, was at someone else's house, without my clothing, my glasses or my bag (I'd put my keys in my jeans), not to speak of my brains.

"I'm supposed to be at Kennedy in three and a half hours. I'm flying to Los Angeles."

He stopped moving and was silent. After a moment, he withdrew. I turned to face him.

"I'm sorry, Vaughn. I forgot when I got drunk."

He nodded. I couldn't read his expression well in the darkness, but it seemed that he was just waiting. Beneath the blanket, his rock-hard member was waiting for both of us.

I hesitated. "I don't have to run off this *second*," I said tentatively. "I mean . . . the plane isn't leaving in ten minutes."

He smiled, I thought sadly.

"You know I'm not kidding, don't you?" I was anxious. "I mean, it's bad enough to screw up like this . . . to let you come this far . . . " I winced as I heard my words. "But I—"

"It's all right," he said. "I'll be this way in ten minutes, too, even if we . . ."

"An hour?" I asked, more out of curiosity than consideration. He nodded.

I took his hand and stroked it in a slow and friendly fashion. Gradually the atmosphere became more relaxed.

"I have some business to clean up in Los Angeles," I said. "This isn't a fake. When we talked about dinner it never occurred to me we were going to . . . If you'll let me take the cards with me, I'll call you when I've gone over them and read the motion for summary judgment."

Vaughn nodded. "Sure. Fine. I just—I want you to understand that we're at the day of reckoning. I'm going to decide within a few days. I'm not dealing with Cullen anymore, so if you aren't taking the case, I'm going to change lawyers." He got out of bed, came over to my side, bowed and held out his hand, the gesture made somewhat more comic by the erection he seemed no longer to notice.

"I promise to call you within twenty-four hours."

I allowed myself to be helped up, gave him a big, slightly sideways, affectionate hug and scrambled into my clothes without washing or looking for a comb. Vaughn insisted on escorting me

335

home although I told him cab fare would do it. It was after five by now, and there would be cabs on the street. Only as he brought me to my apartment door and waited for me to dig my keys out of my pocket did I wonder what had happened to his erection, and when. I giggled.

"What?"

I shook my head.

"Never mind," he said sadly. "I know."

"You do not!" I exclaimed.

"Fine," he said. "I don't know."

"Tell me," I challenged.

He smiled sadly. "When you call me from Los Angeles. If you remember to ask."

I was about as awake as I'd ever been. I showered again, washed my hair again, got dressed again and packed a small bag. At the moment I had no memory of which clothes I'd left at the Beverly Hills Hotel. It had been warmer there than here and past the rainy season. I put sneakers in my bag and wondered why I was doing so when I hadn't played tennis for years and I wore sandals for walking. I was ready by six but told myself it was too early to leave.

I should make coffee and sit down with the cards Vaughn had left me in a Simon & Koenig envelope labeled Confidential.

No way. Even if I'd had milk in the house for the coffee. Even if I'd been able to phone Shimmy and thus relax because he knew my intention to come to L.A. Even if . . . No way. I put the envelope with the index cards in the large tan leather shoulder bag I'd set up to take with me. I left a note for the housekeeper saying she was right if she thought I'd been home but I'd had to leave again suddenly, could be reached at . . . I debated for a couple of minutes whether to leave Shimmy's numbers or the hotel's and finally decided the hotel's would be safer.

At the airport I waited in the first-class line, which I found remarkably long for that hour of a weekday morning, except I was suddenly uncertain it *was* a weekday, or at any rate, which weekday it was. I turned to ask the man in back of me in the line but felt too embarrassed. The man in front of me was holding a *Times* on which, I was finally able to determine, it said Thursday, but then of course there was no guarantee it was this morning's paper he was reading.

Having gotten my ticket and a paper (it was, of course, Thursday), I took myself and my satchel and bag to a coffee shop in the concourse, where I sat down without coffee, figured out in the newspaper margin that I'd arrived in New York on the Red Eye almost precisely twenty-four hours earlier, and stared at the figures as though I might find the error in my calculations that would alter them to the point of believability.

I got a cup of coffee and sat down again. If I was wide-awake, I was also floating. What I needed was not just to sit here resting my elbow on the *Times* but to read the damn thing for long enough to become convinced there was a world out there. If only I could talk to Shimmy for a minute! If he knew I was coming . . . If *I* knew that *he* knew, perhaps I would lose that weird sensation I'd had since awakening at Vaughn's; I was floating, but not in liquid.

It was simply too early to call Shimmy. Even when I'd had two more cups of coffee and flipped through the paper for a substantial length of time, trying without success to interest myself in the day's news, it wasn't eight-thirty yet, which meant it wasn't five-thirty in Los Angeles. I was fairly certain I remembered Shimmy from my childhood visits as an early riser, sitting at the kitchen table reading the newspaper when I came down before the other kids awakened, but how early that had been was another matter, and I had to board the plane. I decided not to take the chance of disturbing him.

Once on the plane, I read Cullen's motion, which was, to say the least, unimpressive, then pulled out the index cards. With them came some clippings as well as a copy of one of those small weeklies that had flourished in the seventies. Called *'Tenshun!* (as in Attention! rather than tension), its logo showed a woman wearing an army uniform and carrying a bayonet drawn up to meet the command. *'Tenshun!* contained an interview with Franya Cameron on the subject of the lawsuit she was bringing against her ex-husband. The title was "The Libel of Masochism." Ms. Cameron (the matter of her having decided to hold on to her married name, the name of the villain who'd exploited her so badly, was not raised) explained that the difficulties and expenses of a lawsuit were such that she had come close to deciding not to bring one but had become convinced that she owed it to all women. For centuries the libel that women wanted to suffer had been used as an excuse for making them suffer. *Miriam's Days of Rage,* with its portrait of a woman who cannot tolerate comfort, who gets involved in radical politics because nothing short of confrontation and imprisonment can possibly satisfy her neurotic urges, had to be shown for what

337

it was. The matter never raised in the article, though it was of paramount importance if one trusted the lawsuit papers, was of pregnancy, wanted or unwanted.

I put the article aside and took up the cards. They made wonderful reading, and I spent the time when I wasn't trying to sleep, trying to drink away my hangover with juice and seltzer, eating or wandering back and forth between the bathroom, the first-class lounge and my seat, reviewing them and checking them carefully against the copy of the novel I had brought with me.

We set down in the Los Angeles airport at eleven-thirty. I went directly to a pay phone to call Shimmy's office. All the lines were busy. I flirted with the notion of going there, thought of Miss Livia and went directly to the hotel. There, having straightened out the matter of my belongings and the abandoned room, I re-presented my credit card, signed the old and the new charge slips and checked into Room 503. Then I called Shimmy's office, reached Miss Livia and was told he was out to lunch. I held my voice steady as I asked her to tell him my room number when he returned.

Shortly after one-thirty, Shimmy called. I explained that I hadn't been able to reach him before leaving New York but had decided to take the flight anyway. He asked if he might pick me up at seven for dinner, and I said that would be all right, although I could not imagine at that moment how I would occupy myself in the interim. I suggested he call before coming over because I'd been awake most of the time since we'd last spoken, and I was likely to fall into a deep sleep. He said he would come up to my room so I need not worry about hearing the phone.

I took off my clothes, stretched out on the bed, closed my eyes and for the first time since parting from him thought of Vaughn Cameron the Person rather than the Author Being Sued. I saw him facing me in bed, erection intact, waiting for my version of the bad news.

I sat up.

Ridiculous. Worse than ridiculous, in the sovereign year of 1986, not to be able to sleep because you'd gone to bed with a perfectly nice man, the kind of man you should be looking for to marry.

It's not about going to bed with Vaughn. It's about Shimmy.

No. It was out of the question for my actions to be controlled by a sixty-three-year-old man, however wonderful, who was mad at me because I hadn't wanted to go to bed with him the first time he . . . In fact, you could make the case for its having been because of Shimmy that I went to bed with Vaughn. Indeed Vaughn was a bright, charming, handsome, talented man. Yet the more I thought about it the less doubt I had that it was Shimmy who had driven me into his arms—whether I *should* have been there, or not.

I thought of Grace. Poor Grace. I'd always envied her the steadiness of her life, never thought of what it would be like to have someone so . . . I picked up the phone and called Grace. Nobody home. They must still be in Hawaii. I hung up, picked up the phone again and called Violet; I got an answering machine. I left a message that I'd come out unexpectedly on business and had hoped to find her around.

For the first time, and I do not exaggerate, it occurred to me that it was peculiar to have grown up in a place, to have had friends there, and to have had so little to do with them, no matter what I thought of the place. The three-thousand-mile distance between us wasn't reason enough; after all, one way or another, I'd seen a lot of my father.

I was getting too introspective for my own taste. Writing about my father, if it hadn't opened a floodgate, seemed to have wrecked a small, neat dam my professional life had enabled me to maintain. The thought crossed my mind that having gone to bed with a client for the first time had contributed to my mental disarray. But I needed to think about my sexual encounter with Vaughn Cameron about as much as . . .

What I did need was to take a walk.

I got out of bed, put on jeans and a sweater, grabbed my bag and left the room and the hotel. For all the time I'd been awake, it was days since I'd done anything you could reasonably classify as exercise. Even the sex I wasn't precisely prepared to acknowledge as having happened hadn't involved much motion on my part. Perhaps with a fifteen- or twenty-minute walk behind me, I would be able to take the nap that would make me fit for Shimmy's company. For *anyone's*.

What I most feared was losing Shimmy's *friendship*. Aside from his not being an obvious person for me to be attracted to romantically, it was scary to think that if whatever he had in mind didn't work out, he would no longer be my friend and counselor. I decided this was the first matter I would discuss with him when I saw him. If I saw him. If, that was, the day ever passed.

I'd walked as far as Santa Monica Boulevard. Across the Boulevard was the section of Beverly Hills where I'd lived as a child. Behind me was the house where I'd lived with Tony. I didn't feel like going in either direction but instead walked over to Beverly and then to La Cienega. At some point I became oblivious not only to where I was but to what I was passing. I don't know precisely how long this lasted, but I remember quite distinctly the moment—I was between Washington Boulevard and Palm, a street on the alternate route from the airport, although I couldn't remember the last time I'd been in a car that took this route—when I stopped short because something had touched my brain without being identified.

I turned and looked back. On the side of the street where I was walking was the small, diner-like restaurant called New York Breakfast about which Louisa had written. I didn't know how long it had been there, but I knew I'd never noticed it before. I walked back and turned so I was leaning against the wall bordering the restaurant's windows. Across the street was a small florist's shop. Next to it was a large, open space full of trees and bushes. The sign on the storefront read COLETTI'S NURSERY.

How long had it been there and when, if ever, had Louisa seen it? I tried to remember her testimony on the matter of knowing that Jack Campbell had run Tony's landscaping business; surely she had denied any knowledge of this as of anything else about Campbell. She'd claimed to have not even been thinking of the I-land incident while she was writing the book, although when pressed, she'd admitted that she remembered taking me there. Her explanation of Jack Burns's getting into gardening in Palm Springs had been a model of common sense.

I don't know how long I stood there, arguing with myself about whether to go in, telling myself there was really no reason to do so. If there was something I wanted to know, I should ask Louisa. I turned and took the long walk back to the hotel without having any idea, as yet, whether I would manage to do this.

I showered, shampooed, and put on the terry-cloth robe left in the bathroom by the management. I felt as though I'd been showering constantly. Flying and showering. Showering and flying.

Coletti's on La Cienega.

Louisa had gotten through the trial without anyone's observing there was a Coletti's nursery near a restaurant Louisa had written about, perhaps simply because the people who wanted most to know this were the ones least likely to have read *FRemale*. If Louisa really hadn't noticed Coletti's was there, and if we could get her to testify to this fact, perhaps it would be useful to Vaughn. I'd come to believe that the issue of what the fiction writer knew and/or knew (s)he knew was very much more difficult than the same issue was for the journalist. The latter could use, if not always happily, the various standards of what could be surmised, checked, verified beyond doubt. But there wasn't a book, a witness or any objective standard to assure the storyteller finally that no germ or detail was a mirror reflection of the real world rather than the world in her brain.

It was almost six-thirty. As I stood looking at the dresses in the closet and trying to remember which one I'd given the valet when I arrived, there was a knock at the door. How convenient— I wouldn't have to remember because it was being returned. I opened the door. It was Shimmy.

"Shimmy!" I felt confused, upset, guilty. Now I would never have my nap. "Don't tell me I'm . . . Is it really seven o'clock?"

"No," Shimmy said, "it isn't. But I wound up my work, and I hoped you would forgive me for being early."

"Forgive you! Don't be ridiculous! I've just been waiting, and I took a walk and actually I have something wild to tell you. . . ." I launched into an account of my walk and seeing Coletti's. I was beginning to explain the significance of Coletti's location when I realized I was still standing at a somewhat public door in a terry-cloth robe and Shimmy was still in the hall.

"I'm so tired, I'm crazy!" I wailed. "I haven't had six hours of sleep since the last time I was here!"

Shimmy came in, closed the door, took my hand, led me to the bed and pointed to it.

"Lie down," he said. "I am going to order a drink and a snack for myself. Would you like something?"

"I don't know," I said, lying down obediently. "Maybe a martini with a lot of ice. Or some wine . . . whatever."

I didn't hear him place the order. I was thinking about Coletti's Nursery and about Vaughn Cameron's case and about the feeling I had of melting into the bed in such a way that I would never be able to separate myself from it again.

When I awakened, the room was dark because the drapes had been drawn and Shimmy was asleep on the other side of the king-sized bed, his hands clasped on his chest. His tie and jacket were draped over a chair.

I looked around the room. I'd been certain I would never be hungry again, but I'd been mistaken. Shimmy had said something about a snack. I got up. On the coffee table in front of the settee at the far side of the huge room was a tray with a corked bottle of white wine, a bucket of cubes, a couple of glasses, an untouched and probably warm martini and an empty plate. On the bathroom phone, I ordered a rare cheeseburger and a martini on the rocks with lots of onions. Then I listened at the door until room service arrived so I could open it before the knock.

I took the tray to the settee, set it down next to the first tray, and took a sip of the martini and a bite of the cheeseburger. Shimmy hadn't moved, but a voice now said, "Something smells wonderful."

"You want me to order you one?" I asked.

"Mm-mm," the voice said. "I just want a bite."

I brought over my drink and my cheeseburger, sat down on Shimmy's side of the bed and held out the cheeseburger. He took a bite without opening his eyes. I held out my martini; he took a sip, grimaced and asked where his wine was. When I returned with his glass, he opened his eyes and sat up against the headboard.

"Did you have a good nap?" I asked.

"Naps are always good," Shimmy said. "Nighttime sleep is sometimes good and sometimes bad, but you only have a nap because you want one."

I smiled. "Everything is always so clear in your mind."

"It wouldn't be," he said solemnly, "if I didn't have my nap."

He was fully awake now and watching the cheeseburger as it went back to my mouth. I offered him another bite.

"Mmm. Haven't had a cheeseburger in a long time."

If I asked why, he would say something about age or cholesterol. He had decided to shove his age down my throat before I could shove it down his. I found myself thinking about how the statistics on age were changing every year as more and more people lived to be ninety and a hundred.

"Should I order you something to eat?" I asked.

"Unless you'd prefer to go out," he said.

I shrugged. "I've been out plenty. I've had a crazy couple of days."

"Mmm. I'll say."

"No. Crazier than you know." Crazier, I hoped, than he would ever know.

I gave him the room-service menu and found his glasses in his suit jacket. He wanted a turkey club and an iced tea. I ordered them and got myself a fruit-salad plate as well. I asked how long it would take and they said they'd try for half an hour but it could be three-quarters. I said I'd appreciate their trying.

"I should comb my hair and put on a dress," I said when I'd hung up.

"Not on my account," Shimmy said. "You look fine to me."

"You mean," I asked playfully, "that you can imagine seducing someone in a Beverly Hills Hotel terry-cloth robe?"

"Indeed I can," Shimmy said solemnly. "However, I am not going to seduce you. If there is a seduction here today, *you* will be the seducer."

"Oh, my God!" I said, so solemnly that I made Shimmy laugh. "But I'm not the one who . . . I'm not sure I've ever done that. I don't know if I know *how*."

"Mm," Shimmy said. "Your problem interests me. Let me think of what I might do to help. I know! I'll move over to the center of the bed so there's room for you to stretch out beside me . . . if you're so inclined."

I laughed nervously. "You remember we ordered from room service?"

"I perceive that the locus of your concern has shifted," Shimmy said, still terribly solemn, "from the question of whether I'm too old to get it up at all to whether I might go for three-quarters of an hour at a shot."

"Oh, Shimmy! Stop making fun of me. I'm nervous enough without some guy knocking on the door and then I have to—"

"You don't actually have to do *anything*," he pointed out. "You can ignore him. Or tell him to leave the stuff at the door. I can assure you that you are unlikely to be the first woman ever to be making love in the Beverly Hills Hotel when room service arrived."

I stared at him.

I think if he had said *getting laid* instead of *making love*, I would have jumped up from the bed and run into the bathroom. But the idea of making love caused me to bend over to kiss his wonderful, big, crooked nose, and when he closed his eyes, I kissed his lids and then his mouth. He didn't move. I lay down beside him and we embraced and really kissed, as we had done once before when my lips were the same but I'd had a somewhat different brain in my head. By the time we opened my robe, I had forgotten about room service. By the time room service arrived and Shimmy called out, "Nobody home," I didn't even think it was funny. We drifted in and out of sleep and we drifted in and out of lovemaking, and we spoke very little.

Although Vaughn Cameron never entered my mind during this time, it occurred to me later that Vaughn never forgot the intention to please and somehow never fully accomplished it, whereas Shimmy simply moved to do what would please us both.

"You're really a wonderful lover," I whispered into his left ear at some point.

"Not without a nap," he whispered back into my right one.

We napped a lot. We also ate a lot (after we finally brought in the tray, we demolished every bit of food on it and ordered more) talked a lot and drank a moderate amount. It was one of the best nights of my life. When I say that Vaughn Cameron didn't enter my mind, I am being truthful only if it's understood that the libel suit tapped lightly at my brain from time to time. Ideas and issues connected to it that I looked forward to discussing with Shimmy came up but did not insist upon being dealt with and left when I showed no inclination to raise them. I remember at one point wanting to ask if he knew how much the specifics varied between, say, Los Angeles and New York, on the issue of reasonable iden- tification, and at another, if it was true, as I'd heard, that New York courts made it more difficult than others for a plaintiff to establish herself as the source of a character. (The suit was being brought in California.) Shimmy was asleep both times, and of course I did not wake him.

In the morning, when I opened my eyes, he was sitting on my side of the bed, wearing a clean shirt and a fresh tie but the same suit, his attaché case on his lap.

I smiled sleepily. "I see you travel well prepared."

"I was a Boy Scout," he said solemnly, opening the attaché case to show me the old shirt and tie, a razor and a toothbrush. He leaned over to kiss me.

"Does this mean you're going to work?" I asked disconsolately.

"I'm late," he said. "Unfortunately, I have a real meeting I can't change. I'll call you when it's over. Or you can call me."

"I don't know if I'm up to dealing with Whatsername this morning," I said.

"Sure you are," he laughed. "Just be civil."

"I'm always civil," I protested.

"She says the same thing. Anyway, I'll tell her to put you through, no matter. Okay?"

I nodded, but my hand was on his arm and I didn't want to let it go. At that moment I could not imagine how I would spend the time until I saw him again.

"I tried to call Grace yesterday," I said, "but she wasn't home."

"Mmm."

344

I opened my eyes.

"What's the matter?" I asked.

"Matter?" Shimmy said.

"You sounded funny. As though . . . Is there a reason I shouldn't call Grace?"

He paused, then said, "Only if you think there is."

"I can't think of any reason at all," I said, wondering why I felt as though I weren't telling the truth when I was. Well, I could *think* of a reason, but it seemed too foolish to talk about.

"She *is* my friend, isn't she? She *does* like me, doesn't she?"

"Yes," Shimmy said, "I'm sure she does."

"Well, *I* like *her*. I like her so much I've been calling her from New York sometimes to talk about stuff there was no one else I could talk to about."

"Okay," Shimmy said. Gently he freed my hand from his arm, kissed it, gave it back to me. "Gotta go. In case I haven't mentioned it, it's ten o'clock."

I was startled, but not so startled as to forget what we were talking about.

"Just tell me before you go," I said, "if there's some reason you think I shouldn't talk to Grace."

"Dunno, sweetheart," Shimmy said. "If talking to Grace means talking about her daddy . . . Girls, I'm talking about grown women, obviously, are funny about their daddies. Grace hasn't liked any of the women she knows I've gone out with, and I just can't tell. You have to use your own judgment."

As I tried to think of an appropriate response, a strong reproach, a way to point out that Grace and I were close friends and there was no way in the world, et cetera, he stood up, blew me another kiss and half walked, half ran out of the room.

My own judgment. My own judgment. My own judgment was that there was no reason in the world for me not to call the woman who had become my best friend just because her father had become my . . . my what? Well, he was my lover, but that wasn't a word you could imagine using when you were talking to your best friend about her father. Maybe *he* was the one who was the best friend now, and she had become . . . well, a very good friend. I *needed* good friends and I didn't want her to be . . . On the other hand, I would have to say that I didn't feel the need as strongly as I had in the weeks before . . . in the weeks before Shimmy. Shimmy had altered my needs, at least for the time being. Shimmy had really . . . I was growing sleepy again. Just as well I hadn't gotten out of bed.

When I did get up, I would call Grace and make a date, maybe for lunch, at least if Shimmy was busy and couldn't see me then.

My eyes were closing. I had the sense that there was something else I had to think about . . . figure out . . . but I couldn't remember what it was. It had something to do with New York.

I was awakened by a call from Vaughn Cameron, who said he'd waited until then because he figured I'd be catching up on my sleep. I told him he was considerate as well as correct. He asked if I'd had a chance to read the stuff. I told him I'd been reading it and giving it a great deal of thought.

There was a long pause and Vaughn asked, slowly and in what was for him a rather heavy manner, "Does that mean you want to take on the case?"

Oh, Jesus. In fact, I hadn't given the case a thought except in its substance. Certainly I wasn't willing to turn it over to Dick Cullen or some other young twerp who wouldn't notice the most interesting points in it.

"Perhaps I should ask you another question first," Vaughn said. "Did you look at the motion for summary judgment?"

"Yes," I admitted unwillingly.

"What did you think of it?"

"Oh," I said, extremely uncomfortable because there was no way in the world that it would be correct for me to tell him how badly I thought the motion had been prepared, "probably the same thing as you did."

"Well, then, you understand why I won't work with Cullen anymore."

I was silent. Correctly, he took my silence for assent.

"I mean, I *want* to work with you if I stay with the firm. But as I've told you, I'm investigating possibilities elsewhere."

I was silent.

"You understand, don't you?" he asked after a while.

"I'm afraid I do."

"It doesn't come naturally to me to deliver ultimatums. But it's not like . . . If you'll forgive me for saying so, we might have a nice time together, but we're not, you might say, uh, natural sexual partners. We probably both like to be led around by the nose a little more than either of us is willing to do."

I smiled even as my breath was taken away—by both the observation and the fact of his making it.

"But as far as this case goes," he went on, "we're a natural. And if you're not going to take it on, I've got to find someone else who'll be just as good. Or almost as good."

"To me," I said, reacting to the notion of losing this case that had finally lodged itself firmly and interestingly in my mind, "this case involves one of the more interesting issues we barely touched on at Louisa's trial, the question of how a fiction writer's supposed to write about his life if he can't use people he's known in some way. They need some cover, of course, but his right to work has to be protected."

"It's lovely to hear someone discuss it who knows that," Vaughn said. "Does this mean you're going to take it on?"

"All I have to do," I heard myself saying, "is figure out how to handle your case in New York while I'm . . . I sort of have a whole other life in California. There's no question of my *wanting* to do it, if you'll just . . . give me until Monday to figure out how."

He said Monday would be acceptable. I told him I appreciated his patience.

I took the phone off the hook, showered, put the phone back on the hook and got dressed in a blouse and skirt—just in case Shimmy should turn out to be free for lunch. He was, but he didn't have enough time to leave the office and suggested I bring in sandwiches. I asked if I should bring coffee as well, or if someone could possibly be prevailed upon to make a fresh pot. With a smile in his voice, he asked me to bring him an iced tea.

"I love you," I said, "but I want some coffee, myself. I haven't even had my breakfast coffee, yet."

It was only when I'd hung up that I heard myself saying, "I love you," and wondered what I had meant. I had very little time to think about this, however, before Byron Koenig called. Vaughn Cameron had told him he wouldn't have anything more to do with Dick Cullen. Upon being pressed, Vaughn had also told him that he and I had been talking. Byron said that while they'd tried very hard not to pressure me, I could probably understand I had to make a decision. It was intolerable for them to continue holding open a position in the firm while I was showing Vaughn Cameron I was better than the guy they had. I said I appreciated what he was telling me and was sorry to have made matters so complicated. I was going to take the weekend to figure out how to proceed. I would tell him my decision before I called Vaughn.

Livia was as frosty as though Shimmy had fired her and given me her job. I followed her to his office with my bag from the hotel coffee shop. I'd left the hotel assuming I would find a luncheonette along the way but had had to remind myself after two blocks that I wasn't in New York but in Los Angeles. This had put me back in mind of New York Breakfast, which in turn had made me think about Vaughn's case and about talking to Louisa. When, as we walked into his office, Livia advised Shimmy of a call he *had* to take, he winked at me, and I told him that I would use the conference room because I had to make a call. It was four o'clock, New York time. Penelope picked up the phone, sounding at least ten years older than she had the last time I'd spoken with her.

I said, "Hi, Penny, it's Nell."

She said, "Aunt Nell?"

"Yes."

"Where are you?"

I hesitated, then said, "I'm in California."

She said, "Can I talk to Grandpa?" at which point the phone was taken from her, and Louisa got on.

"Hi," I said. "I'm sorry. I didn't . . ." What hadn't I? "I hadn't realized that Penny didn't . . . understand. . . ."

Thank God I didn't have children.

"So now you realize. So what else can I do for you?"

She sounded so hostile that I asked if she was angry with me about something.

"Everything," she said.

I had, obviously, no response.

She laughed. "All right. I'm sorry. I meant I was writing something, and it's bringing up a lot of shit, and I'm mad at my childhood, and that includes you."

I was silent. Louisa asked if I had ever considered entering psychoanalysis, and I said that I had not, although what came to mind was to ask why *I* should enter analysis because *she* was angry. She gave me a brief speech about the benefits I might gain from such treatment. When I failed to respond, she asked, "Anyway, was this just a friendly call, ha ha, or is there something I can do for you?"

I hesitated, decided I had nothing to lose.

"Yes," I said. "There was actually a question I wanted to ask you. The other day I was over near that place you wrote about, New York Breakfast. . . ." I paused, but she did not speak. ". . . And I noticed, across the street . . . I suppose you know what I'm going to say. . . ." She definitely wasn't going to make this easy. Was it possible she didn't know? After all, I hadn't checked to find out how long Coletti's had been in that location. It hadn't occurred to me until now, but they could have moved there last week. "I saw . . . it was the weirdest coincidence that I was there . . . And I saw the sign for, you know, for Tony's nursery. For Coletti's."

Louisa said, "Mmmm."

"I couldn't help wondering," I said, "if you'd known about it from the beginning."

"What is this for?" Louisa asked after what seemed like an hour. "I mean, how come you're obsessing over the trial? Is it for the thing you're writing?"

"No," I said quickly. "Not at all." (Later she said I'd been lying, but I certainly didn't think of it as a lie at the time.) "As a matter of fact, I'm not even sure I'm writing it anymore. It's because of a libel case someone wants me to take on in New York. It's about what the writer knows he knows. Nothing to do with us or our family."

There was a long pause, then Louisa said in a somewhat mechanical voice, "I didn't know it when I wrote it. I mean, I actually thought Coletti was the name of the guy who wrote *Pinocchio*. I discovered halfway through I got even that wrong, it was Collodi. I never remembered your pal's name. Sorry. Your stepfather's name. *Pinocchio* was my favorite book when I was a kid. Somewhere along the way. . . . If I saw the sign before I wrote the book, I don't know it. And that's the truth. It's also true I *knew* before the trial, and no one raised it, and I figured I should just keep quiet about it. It was the kind of thing that could have worked for us or against us."

I was silent, trying to absorb what she was saying and figure out what else to ask so I wouldn't have to call her again. But then Shimmy appeared at the door, signaling that he'd finished his call and would be waiting in the office. I thanked Louisa and told her I hoped we could have dinner when I got back to New York. She said that by the time I got back to New York, she would very likely be in Los Angeles.

The small table in Shimmy's office had been covered with a cloth. Our sandwiches, still wrapped but on plates, were on it, as was the coffee maker, full of freshly made coffee. I turned to tease Shimmy about who'd made it, but he had closed the door and was holding out his arms for me, so I went to him and kissed him instead. A moment earlier I'd had an overwhelming desire to tell him about my conversation with Louisa, but by the time we pulled apart, I'd forgotten what it was that I wanted to say.

"I missed you," I said.

"Mm, and *I* missed *you*," Shimmy said. "In fact, I bet I missed you more because I was awake for longer."

I laughed. "That's undoubtedly true. As a matter of fact, I slept until eleven, then I had a call from New York from Vaughn Cameron, you know, the one I wanted to talk to you about, the libel case, and then from my boss, and then . . ."

As I flailed around, Shimmy, who'd unwrapped both sandwiches, said, "I gather you didn't get to call Grace."

"Mmm. I forgot. Or there just wasn't time, I guess, betw—"

"Wait a minute, wait a minute," Shimmy said, laughing but raising a hand to stop me. "No excuses required. She just called me, and when I told her you were here, she asked us to dinner tomorrow night."

"How nice!" I said. "I mean, it *is* nice, isn't it? We don't have any other plans, do we?" Only then did it occur to me that Grace had been vindicated. "You see?" I said. "And you were so worried that she was going to turn on me when she found out that we were . . ." I grinned. ". . . whatever we are."

"We don't actually know that she's found out anything at all," Shimmy said, "except that you're still in Los Angeles. I gather you do want to have dinner there tomorrow night."

"Of course I do," I assured him. "I would absolutely *love* to have dinner at Grace and David's tomorrow night."

I spent the rest of the day going over Vaughn's index cards. Aside from the matter of the pregnancy and childbirth, the invented details Franya found most objectionable had to do with Vaughn's having Miriam use her Lower East Side clothing shop as a cover for a bomb factory. Since Franya had never belonged to any group and her violence was purely verbal, Vaughn had thought he was safe. She now accused him of having cast suspicion on her among all the people she knew. He had libeled her by painting her as a terrorist. What we had to prove was that he had been painting an imaginary person. A person, though we could not say this, probably, capable of acts Franya would only *imagine.*

I noticed that I was calling the defense "We."

I had a wonderful night and then day with Shimmy.

I swam in the hotel pool and slept afterward, so I was wide-awake and happy when he came to get me. When we'd had some iced tea, made love and slept for a little while, he asked what I would like to do next.

I was startled and must have looked it, for he laughed at me.

"I dunno," I said. "I haven't thought about it."

The only thing I *had* thought about was getting his help in deciding, or perhaps it would be more honest to say, getting his approval of my decision, to take on Vaughn Cameron's suit.

"Well," Shimmy said, "here is my proposal. I propose we pack up your stuff and move it over to my house for the duration."

I was startled. It had occurred to me that I would spend the weekend there with him, but I hadn't translated this to . . .

"On the other hand," Shimmy said, all too quickly picking up my hesitation, "if there are things you want to do from the hotel that'll be more difficult from my house . . ."

"How long am I going to stay?" I asked. Then we both laughed.

"I think I have to leave that up to you," Shimmy said.

"What if it were up to you to decide?" I don't think I was just being dumb or, for that matter, flirtatious. I hadn't thought about the future, and I was looking for some sort of starting line.

"Well," Shimmy said, poker-faced, "if it were up to me to decide, you would pack up and come home with me, and we would immediately begin to look for a small apartment, preferably within a three-minute walk of my house, and we would begin having dates like a normal boy and girl and see whether something more might evolve."

"Well," I said nervously, "I'll stay at least through the weekend. Maybe Monday or Tuesday."

"Maybe Monday or Tuesday," Shimmy said, still expressionless.

"Don't look that way," I said.

"Which way is that? As though I want you to stay?"

I laughed and moaned at the same time. "I want you to want me to stay, Shimmy, but there's something in New York . . . I've tried to talk to you about it a couple of times, but you've never . . . There's a case I'm enormously interested in, and I have to decide whether I'm going back to my office."

"I know my view on the subject," Shimmy said. "I don't need to discuss it."

"Oh, God." I leaned over and kissed the top of his head. "I think you might not be as reasonable as you used to seem." I told him that even if I was going to take on the case in New York, which I would *insist* upon discussing with him at some point, that didn't mean I had to fly back on Tuesday; it only meant I had to call my office and tell them. Furthermore, if I did take the case, I would be able to spend a great deal of time in California except for the time that I was actually in court.

Within an hour I was checked out of the hotel, we were back at Shimmy's house, and he was making grilled cheese sandwiches and a green salad for dinner. We sat on the porch, drinking Tecate beer from the bottle, holding hands across the white wrought-iron table when we weren't also eating. At some point I remembered the phone conversation with Louisa and was going to tell him about it, but then I changed my mind. Louisa and that suit would lead to Vaughn and the other suit and I was unwilling to disturb the peace.

The next twenty-four hours passed in a sort of domestic contentment that can be laughed at only by people who've had more domesticity than they can enjoy. We talked, ate, made love, slept, brought Shimmy's shirts to the laundry in town (his housekeeper wanted to do them but he liked having errands) and, while in town, decided on what we would make for dinner at home on Sunday so we could shop for the ingredients while we were there. It seemed to me, when I thought about it, that even with Saul, before we were married, I had not enjoyed anything you could accurately term "domestic" bliss. We'd had a lot of fun together before the move to Atlanta, but the fun had not had very much to do with the ordinariness of life.

Shimmy and I seem to have stayed away, by common consent, from issues touching upon my return to New York. He talked about his children and about his decision to move to California when Grace and her family were moving there. He said he'd never considered retiring, but he did think about cutting back. The most interesting part of his work could actually be done from home, but he would have to be settled with a woman before he seriously considered moving his practice to the house. His grandchildren were almost equidistant between here and his office. Grace's children, that was. He'd never seen quite as much of his son's kids in Connecticut, although he adored them, too, of course.

It was only as I was putting on a dress to go to dinner that I remembered Shimmy's concern about Grace. I turned to him. He was stretched out on the bed in his socks and underwear, watching me, and I was about to ask if he was still concerned. Instead, I pulled my dress back off, set it over the chair, and got back into bed with him, the result being that we arrived at Grace's closer to eight o'clock than to the between-seven-and-seven-thirty she had suggested.

My brain resists reconstruction of the evening as though it were a tornado that, once remembered, might pick me up and buffet me around helplessly all over again.

Shelly, the daughter who was still home, opened the door. Grace came bustling out of the kitchen to kiss each of us and announce that we were late, late, late, and she just hoped the fire could be rekindled, David was outside working on it. She'd been trying to reach me at the hotel but had been told I'd checked out. I said that I had, and I was staying with Shimmy. Grace said, oh, terrific, she supposed that made a lot of sense, and dashed back to the kitchen because she smelled something burning. I followed her out to the kitchen and, once she'd moved the pot in question off the stove, told her I hoped we could have a quiet lunch together while I was there. Grace said, absolutely, there were a lot of things we really had to talk about, most particularly—she was checking the stove, stirring stuff in bowls on the counter and taking dishes and glasses from cabinets as she spoke—she wanted my advice on something it was quite new to her to be thinking about. She checked all the entrances to make sure we were alone. Had she mentioned she was thinking of going back to school or getting a job? What did I think of law school? I told her she'd mentioned it once before and I thought it was a terrific idea.

She stopped, turned around to face me.

"You're wonderful," she said. "Why can't everyone be like you. You wouldn't believe some of the reactions. . . ."

Through the back window I could see that Shimmy, holding Shelly's hand, was standing near the grill, talking to David. Shimmy always looked comfortable, wherever he was. Like Grace and David, he looked as though he had a life.

I turned from the window.

"What happened?" Grace asked.

I shook my head.

"Did anyone offer you a drink? I guess not. Everyone's in the yard. Do you want one?"

I said I'd wait.

She came over to me and gave me a hug. "God," she said, "I can't tell you how good it is to see you. I nearly died when you said you were coming for the first time in months and I wasn't going to be here. I've been wanting to talk to you about the work thing, school, law school, *everything*. But I wasn't sure—I didn't remember we'd talked about it. People have been acting as though it's some kind of sacrilege, I'm this fantasy mother, the last person in the world to abandon the family and go off on some tack of her own."

"That's just silly," I said. "Your kids are old enough. You must be getting bored at home."

She nodded. There were tears in her eyes. "You make it sound so simple. God, I'm so glad you came. How long are you going to be here anyway? How come you're here? Why don't you stay for a while? You can stay here, for that matter. We have a spare room. On the other hand, why don't you move out and stay for good? There's nothing to keep you in New York, is there? You don't have a good guy there, now, do you?"

I shook my head, deeply uneasy for the first time.

"What's the matter?" Grace asked. "Why'd you look away? What aren't you telling me?"

I laughed a small laugh. "I haven't been here for very long. I could hardly have told you everything."

She laughed a larger one. "You're right. I apologize. I didn't mean to grill you. I just . . . I mean, I've hardly talked to you, and I have this feeling . . . How come you're staying at my dad's? I mean, I know you're talking to him about your father and Egremont and all, but wouldn't the hotel be more comfortable? He hasn't had any of his bimbos around while you're there, has he?"

"Bimbos?"

"Well, technically they're not bimbos, I suppose. But you would not believe . . . my father's gone out with the most awful . . . I guess he wouldn't do it with you there, but honestly, some of the women he's been taking around look like— What's the matter?"

I don't know precisely what my expression was revealing, but it had stopped her.

"Matter?"

She nodded. "You look upset."

"Upset? I don't know if I'm upset. I guess I'm uncomfortable."

"With what? With my joking around about my father? My God, I finally find a friend who doesn't think it's funny for me to go to law school, but I'm not allowed—what is it, precisely, that I'm not allowed to do?"

"It's not a matter of being allowed. That's an awful way to talk about your father."

"I'm not talking about my father," she said, still eying me as though she were trying to figure out what strange force had grabbed hold of my brain. "I'm talking about my father's b—girl-friends!"

I nodded but found no words.

Silence.

Shelly came to the back door with a glass to say that Daddy wanted the steak and another Scotch. Grace took the glass from her, poured in some Scotch, handed her the glass and told her to come back for the steak. Shimmy called in that he'd have the same, thanks very much for asking. I went to the small hallway between the kitchen and the dining room that held a second sink and all the liquor bottles. I made myself a martini on the rocks except that I didn't see any vermouth and I wasn't about to ask for it. I made a Scotch on the rocks for Shimmy, which I brought to the door, gesturing to him to come and take it. When he arrived, I signaled to him by expression and voiceless words that he was to come in.

Shimmy, never slow to understand, came into the kitchen and took the drink with a bow. When Grace wasn't looking, I grabbed his hand and squeezed it.

David called from the yard that he'd turned over the steak. Grace called to Shelly to finish setting the table. Then, as she busied herself at the stove, she told Shimmy that I was protecting him, that I didn't seem to like the way she talked about his girlfriends. Shimmy said that wasn't so surprising, he wasn't crazy about it himself. Grace said I'd understand better if I'd met any of them, and Shimmy said it wasn't likely I'd meet any of the *them* she was talking about since I was one of them, and a serious favorite at that.

Grace dropped a pot into the sink.

Shelly came back to the kitchen for the plates and flatware.

Grace turned around. She was staring not at Shimmy, but at me.

"I'm sorry," I said, "I was tr—"

"You should be," she said.

David came in, bearing the steak, looking happy.

"It's perfect!" he announced. "Rare, medium and well done. We've got 'em all. Mark my words, this is . . . is . . ." He looked from Grace to me. "What's going on?"

"You won't believe me," Grace said, "if I tell you." David put down the steak as Shelly came into the kitchen. Grace told her to go into the dining room and sit down.

"Try me," David said.

"Well," Grace said, her manner dramatic, her voice shaking, "what's going on . . . is that my father, who will be sixty-four years old on his next birthday . . . has just informed me that he and my friend, here . . . I should say, my ex-friend, my thirty-five-or-forty-year-old ex-girlfriend . . . are . . . are . . ."

"Oh, Jesus," David said. "Look, is there any chance that we can just stay cool through dinner? Then Shelly'll go up to do her homework and we can talk."

We talked, but we accomplished nothing. Grace was as angry with me as if it were her husband I was sleeping with, as little interested in my or her father's happiness as in the well-being of unknown neighbors down the block. She said Shimmy was doing a terrible thing to his grandchildren, although Shelly, the only one there, hadn't evinced the least curiosity about my relationship to him (and, as far as I know, never did). She asked why of all the people in the world, of all the possibilities we both had—Shimmy reminded her that until now, his possibilities had been witches and/ or bimbos—we chose to "do this" to our friends and family. A woman in her thirties and . . . I was about to interrupt her to tell her that choice wasn't precisely what was involved, but at this point Shimmy, having endured a lengthy tirade, spoke. Shimmy the Articulate, as I later, when we were alone and kidding around, called him. Shimmy the Trial Lawyer.

"Look," he said, "I'm going to try to answer a couple of your questions. I'm not sure it's the smart thing to do. This isn't a labor negotiation. On the other hand, we've been a reasonably contented family, and we're going to remain a family whether Nellie joins us or not. I might be able to tolerate not seeing you for a while, but my grandchildren . . . that's something else. And so I'm going to try to answer your questions even if I don't think you have the right to ask them."

Grace began to protest, but he held up his hand.

"You have the right to *care*, but you don't have the right to *determine*. You wouldn't have it even if it were easy. But it's not. It's very difficult, once you reach a certain age, to find compatible people. I know about all the women out there, that there are far more women than men. Far more good ones, and so on. But there are questions of compatibility that aren't so much about good and bad as about the way you happen to like to live. The way you happen to think. And then, of course, there's whom you happen to be attracted to. I happen to have been strongly attracted to Nell. I liked her when she was a kid, I liked her when she was grown up, and after spending some time with her recently, discussing various matters she was interested in, I became interested in her in a new way. I then persuaded her, not without difficulty, to be interested in me.

"I would be the last person in the world to claim that this attraction has nothing to do with the past. The fact that Nell is related to my past is one of the things that makes her appealing to me, although there are plenty of other reasons—our minds work in similar ways on certain issues, and so on. In any event, here I am, at my age, having begun what some people would call a new life in California. Well, I don't happen to *want* a new life. Or, if it's new, I want some aspects of it to be an extension of the old one. Beyond the fact of having some family here.

"My old life was a *good* one. I don't particularly want to throw it away. I don't particularly want to live with someone who requires extensive background material every time I tell a simple story about the past. I *like* the fact that Nellie knows my family, that she was fond of your mother, that you and she are friends."

"Were friends," said Grace after a long pause. "And I don't know how you dare to talk about my mother. How do you think *she* would feel if she knew!"

"That's a game I'm not willing to play," Shimmy said. "Although I *will* tell you, one of the things your mother and I talked about a lot, was . . . She teased me about being faithful. Why wasn't I like those other men we heard about who were leaving their wives for young women? And I told her, and it was something she understood and we talked about a lot, I told her that it was a relief to me to come home at night to the familiar.

"Every morning I got out of the train at Grand Central and walked to my office past buildings that weren't there a few years ago, through crowds so dense it felt as though all New York's seven million inhabitants—that's not an accurate figure but it's the one I always knew—bought film for my camera from people with faces so unfamiliar I couldn't even tell which country they were from, went up to my office in an automatic elevator that was run until five years ago by a guy who used to give me the results of the ball games and the races every morning, and once in my office . . . well, if I needed, if I need now, to look up a case, I no longer climb a nice little old wooden ladder to reach a well-worn leather-bound book, or even have an assistant do it for me. Instead, he or she presses some buttons on a machine and the information comes onto a TV screen.

"It has to be emphasized that I'm one of the lucky ones. There's usually someone there who can operate the machine for me. Sanity requires me to have one of these machines, but I don't like it. In general, I don't like what's happening to the world, even if I try not to romanticize the old days. I mean, a vacuum cleaner is a loathsome animal, and women certainly look nicer and sound better with a feather duster. On the other hand . . .

"Anyway, I think I've pretty much said what I wanted to say. Obviously, it would be nice for you if I fell in love with someone you were fond of . . ." He paused for the first time, smiled winsomely and gave his summation its final flourish. "On the other hand, I thought it just so happened that that was what I was doing."

Grace was silent, if not appeased. David proposed a drink, but no one was in the mood, and we prepared to go. I wanted to grab Shimmy's hand and hold on to it. I also wanted to cry. I did neither—if only because my mind could conjure up a scene in which Grace, pointing a finger at me, said, "You see? You see? She's a baby! A little crybaby!"

We drove back to Shimmy's home in silence, his hand resting on mine across the front seat of the car. In the driveway, he took the remote-control door opener from the dashboard, pressed it, drove in the car.

"Now *that*," he said with a grin, "unlike the vacuum cleaner, is a really useful tool of civilization."

He turned off the engine and the lights, and in the silence we twisted around and hugged each other tightly.

"I don't know," I said, "how I could have been so naive."

"The price of having children," Shimmy said, "aside from anything else, is your naiveté. You sat in Psych One thinking you'd never have anything to do with that sickie Freud, and you never change your mind until your three-year-old wants you to sleep in her bed and you say you can't, you sleep with Mommy, and she says what if Mommy goes to the hospital, and the next few weeks she trails her mother around the house, asking if she's feeling okay."

I smiled. "Oh, Shimmy. You're wonderful." We were walking up the steps from the garage side door into the kitchen. "So wonderful." We were in the kitchen, and he turned to face me. "I don't know how I could've . . ."

"Could've what?" he asked with a grin.

"I don't know how I could've not loved you," I said, leaning forward to kiss the shiny top of his head.

BOOK

6

"The love of power which sleeps in the bosoms of the best of little women woke up all of a sudden and took possession of her."
—Louisa May Alcott, *Little Women*

SHIMMY LATER CITED my telling him just then that I loved him as an example of my timing. He said if he hadn't been feeling reasonably secure in my affections when Grace called the next day to say she thought it might be best if he didn't see her or the kids for a while, he might not have told her without missing a beat that she should let him know when, because at that point he'd put her back in his will. I gasped when he reported this and asked if he'd meant it. He said, with a grin, that he wasn't certain, but Grace was someone who'd always required a firm hand. And in fact she had immediately become more open to reason, at least superficially, which was all he required.

She had suggested the two of them have dinner later that week to discuss "where we're all going from here."

"Before this happened," I said, "she was talking about going to law school."

Shimmy nodded solemnly. "Excellent. I think that's an excellent place for my daughter to be going for the next few years. She has a great deal of energy and her children are growing up faster than they would if she had her way. Or I had mine, for that matter."

I grinned. "Keep the girls busy by sending them to law school once the kids aren't a full-time job, is that what you're advocating?"

"Absolutely," he said. "As long as they don't take it too seriously."

"Is that supposed to include me?" I asked.

"If you'll allow it to," he said.

"Are you trying to get into a fight about junk," I asked, "so we won't have to talk about whether I'm going to take on the Cameron case?"

"No question I'd rather talk about anything than about your taking on the Cameron case."

So I didn't even try until Sunday evening.

We'd had a wonderful, peaceful day that included a walk into Westwood, with Shimmy over and over pointing out some store he liked only to remind himself that I was a native. For dinner he barbecued chicken on the grill and made rice and a salad. We opened a bottle of red wine ("Just one bottle because I'm not seducing you anymore, I've got you in my clutches") and as we sat on the porch, full and mildly tipsy, he told me he was working on a case that would amuse me. I said I would love to hear about his case, but first we had to talk about Vaughn Cameron whether he liked it or not.

"Oh?" he asked politely.

"Vaughn has a low opinion of the guy who's taken it on."

"Vaughn does?" Shimmy asked.

"Are you being that way on purpose?" I asked.

"Indeed," Shimmy said.

"Why?" I asked.

"Because," Shimmy said, "the last thing in the world I'm in the mood to hear about is a case that requires you to be in New York."

"You know I'm perfectly willing to be the one who goes back and forth."

He nodded. "But back and forth . . . is back and forth."

"I need to have something to *do* every day, Shimmy," I said.

"Even those who hate Los Angeles don't claim there's no work out here," Shimmy replied. "Legal issues including libel are dealt with every day of the week at every studio and—"

"I'm talking about a specific case that is interesting to me because of the similarities and the differences from Louisa's. A case Simon & Koenig, which has been very good to me, is going to lose if I don't handle it."

"Aha! A new element has been added!"

I started guiltily and reminded myself not to let my guilt over the brief fling with Vaughn affect the important issues.

"It *is* a new element. Because if Cameron leaves, a lot of business goes with him. They've been patient until now but if they lose him on account of me, I go out in a bad way. And they're not wrong. Cameron's not wrong, either. The guy who's handling it is no good on libel."

"Indeed," Shimmy said. "There's not a first-rate libel person in the firm. Not to speak of most of the other firms."

"Why shouldn't I become their first-rate libel person?"

"Why shouldn't you become the first-rate libel person for someone out here?"

"Because I owe it to them to be there, at least for this case— which happens to be a fascinating case."

"I don't believe it can be that much better than—"

"That's because you haven't let me tell you about it."

He smacked his forehead, stood up, groaned.

"Why can't I just hear you say you love me again?"

"Because it's not enough, Shimmy. Maybe it is while you're first in that state. The State of Being in Love. After that, it just isn't enough. It's not something to *do*. Even if I continue to adore you, to love, honor, all of it, I have to have something to *do*. I'm not a cook or any of that stuff. There are moments lately when I've almost wished I were, but I'm not. And if I were, I'd be in trouble, at this stage of my life. If I became completely dependent on you, on doing things for you, for us, what if you weren't around? I mean, I can't be sure. You could live for a long time or you could die. You could leave me. . . ."

"Ah, yes," Shimmy said. "Men die, men leave, and so there had to be a Women's Movement."

"But there *should* have been one *anyway*. I mean, even if women could rely on men, some of us would need to be able to work."

"The issue," he said after a brief pause, "is whether you need to work three thousand miles away from me."

"On this specific case, yes."

"All right," he said after a long time. "I give up. Tell me about it."

We went into the living room, where I had Vaughn's book and my notepad as well as the index cards he had given me. Shimmy picked up the book.

"Good-looking fellow," he said, eying the back jacket.

"If you go for the type," I responded.

"Is he a good writer?"

I hesitated. "Yes and no. He's a *decent* writer, certainly. More than decent. But there's no force to his work. It's gentle. *He's* gentle, which is why I guess he was attracted to this woman . . . the ex-wife . . . the one who's suing him. She's a ball of fire." I told Shimmy some of the salient facts of the case. I was aware as I spoke of how careful I was being. I was also aware of using the truth to suggest an untruth—that there'd been nothing sexual between us.

Finally I showed Shimmy the index cards Vaughn had allowed me to bring with me.

He read them and shrugged. "So it's interesting. I never said it wasn't interesting. I said there were interesting cases out here, too."

"But I'm already involved in this one. And I feel as if I owe it to Simon & Koenig. And I don't think it'll take *that* much time in New York. I can do a lot of the stuff out here."

"Show me," Shimmy said.

"Show you what?" I asked, truly puzzled.

"Show me what you can do out here. No, better yet, come upstairs and show me," he said.

Thus was I given notice that if for now Shimmy had to accept my remaining in New York some of the time, he was not about to let me dominate his life with my libel case while I was in California. I don't know if it was that night . . . when we had made love and he had warned me that I was not to be taken in by the extraordinary circumstances, he was just this energetic sixty-three-year-old who, once he took me for granted, would need a nap before he could get it up . . . or at some later time, when he had spoken of his desire to have the sort of warm and reasonable home that he'd had with the person he called "The first Mrs. Kagan" . . . that Shimmy dropped the line the memory of which carried me through all the trips back and forth, the delays, and, finally, the libel trial of Vaughn Cameron which probably would not have come to court had the motion for summary judgment been well done.

What Shimmy said was, "Life's a bitch, and if you're lucky, she's called Lassie."

"It's too good," I said. "You've been planning it."

"Damned right," he replied. "Maybe you'd have liked me to drop it at the office when I thought of it?"

Shimmy and Grace together made the decision to abandon frequent, regular family dinners for an unspecified time. He would take out whichever of his grandchildren were around for an occasional meal, movie, whatever; occasionally he might have dinner with the family. If I was in California and free for the evening, and if I was so inclined, I would join them. There would be no routine until the tension was gone. Shimmy felt that if we didn't push matters such a time would come.

Grace made a new and close friend whose "staggering insight" helped enormously with those problems caused by her father's inept and ornery choice of a second mate. She could not understand how she had failed to appreciate Louisa until this time, couldn't believe the amount of time she'd spent dodging the "big-mouthed drunk" she remembered from our dinner in New York.

Grace told me during one of our rare dinners (if Louisa was in Los Angeles, she was always invited) how much easier it was to be sympathetic to Louisa when you understood about her awful childhood. It seemed to Grace that if you looked at all the details, "the trauma of her eye and everything," Louisa had had a much worse time than I did when Sam left. I must know that Louisa was very psychological and talked about that sort of thing a great deal. So much that Grace, who'd always been "sort of psychological" herself, had become very much interested in "family issues" and was considering studying psychology in graduate school instead of getting involved in the law. One factor pushing her in this direction was that as Louisa wrote them, she was showing Grace the chapters of her "perfectly wonderful, *incredibly moving* autobiography."

Penny and Rosa were ensconced in a Westwood house not far from Shimmy's. Louisa, who had a young boyfriend in New York, was traveling between the coasts a great deal. She had decided to send Penny to school in Westwood, so it no longer made sense to

363

maintain a three-bedroom apartment in Manhattan. On the other hand, she wasn't about to pull up her New York stakes, even after Pepé Le Moko, as she called her young friend, had "run his full course." Although she'd signed to do another screenplay, she could not imagine living full time on the West Coast.

Following a cool period, Louisa had become fair and warmer toward me, sometimes too warm for comfort. I could find no explanation for this change until the night when she told me that what she *really needed* in New York was a *studio*. Big enough for some work and play, but not a Real Second Home that had to be Cared For. And try as she might, Louisa could think of no studio in Manhattan—in the whole world—where she would rather live than the one in the Gainesborough Studios my father had given to me.

At first she'd just dropped hints, and it had been possible not to understand what she was after, although I'd registered a couple of lines about some people's bequests under the will being "more equal than others."

The first time she chose actually to pressure me was during a dinner with Grace in Los Angeles. With the help of a few drinks, she launched into a monologue on the women's group we could start when I married Shimmy, pulled up my New York stakes and moved to California. Grace got more interested than I did, deciding she had been wrong in her recent generous assessment of my half sister. She also decided that I was a correspondingly better person than she'd recently thought me, after which she applied for the fall term at the law school of the University of Southern California.

Weeks later, at a New York restaurant, after hints, promptings and "innocent" questions about whether I'd ever finally give in, marry Shimmy and "get rid of" the studio, I told Louisa I meant to hold on to it forever, whether or not I moved to California. When she asked how come, I said I was unprepared to defend my decision as a rational one. In fact, I didn't wish to discuss it anymore. Now or ever.

Louisa stood up and walked out of the restaurant without another word. Nor would she speak to me for some time. But I did, and do, get word from the front, most particularly in the form of the first chapters of her autobiography, which are being published in *Vanity Fair* as she writes them.

The book will be called *False Light*, a phrase taken from legal terminology and related to libel. The differences between the two

364

terms have not been fully delineated by the courts, but a crucial distinction is that false light need only say something untrue about a person, while libel must be hurtful as well.

Here is the lovely opening paragraph that includes the sentence I've already quoted, at the beginning of this account of my own.

The fiction writer always seems to be breaking some contract with reality her friends and relations were sure she'd signed. In fact, the only agreement she has made is with herself and has to do with creating a truth either better or worse, but in either event quite different, from the one others know. The truth is a springboard that shoots her into the choppy waters of her mind. It is my intention now to stay off that springboard. The most important adult in my life has died and with his death I need to tell the truth about events seen in a false light in my fiction.

But if *False Light* tells only the truth, some new definition of the word *truth* is called for. If it can be called nonfiction, a study of the complicated relation between nonfiction and the truth is in order.

False Light is about the great and complex love of a father for his first-born daughter that permits him to leave her mother for another woman without ever spiritually leaving the child. (If the rule applies to second daughters who are left, no space is wasted on the fact. In fact, there is the strong suggestion that her firstness endears her beyond all others.)

Aside from the (unspecified number of) beautiful letters Louisa received from her father, she kept him alive within her through her involvement in the movies. When she was at the movies, or thinking about them, she was with him. When she finally sought him out in Hollywood, it was her deep interest in the filmmaking process that united them, made him understand that she had come not in reproach but to breathe life into their connection. The author does not dwell on mundane facts like time and place, so that one can read these chapters closely without discovering that she was twenty-seven when she came West and well into her forties when her father had this perception. She does dwell at length upon her father's having used *her* name for all his girls as he lay dying, and gives the fact meanings that chip away at and destroy the person he was.

In other words, it is not only as a novelist that Louisa dwells in the emotional home where she is most comfortable.

For all *Joe Stalbin's* being labeled as fiction (a disclaimer has been printed in post-trial editions), its characters are more recognizable to me than the ones in *False Light*. The glimmer of recognition as I read about Veronica and Diana, even when I wasn't recognizing the person the author had in mind, was just that, recognition. If there are changes, exaggerations and additions cut out of whole cloth, the picture of an overwhelming father and his two daughters—the older homely, talented and unloved, the younger, pretty and intelligent but without creative spark or maternal instinct—hits that spot that is satisfied by the terribly-simple-but-utterly-true.

I've come to think there is some complicity between reader and author in an account that makes no claim to the truth. My task in picking up *Joe Stalbin's Daughters* is to *forget* that it has anything to do with reality. While my task in reading *False Light* is to remember.

It goes without saying that I would like the reader to regard my own account as an exception to this truth.

Judith Rossner is the author of seven novels including the national best-sellers *Looking for Mr. Goodbar* and *August.* She lives in New York City.